FACTION

Faction

by Karl Dahl

First Printing, 2019
Burning Twenties Edition, 2020

ISBN 9781082596452

Inquiries: karldahl@protonmail.com

For Jim

"Boys, in an ambush, always err on the side of violence."

Table of Contents

1982

"It's up here."

Sheriff Paul Shea turns his Plymouth Gran Fury off the paved rural highway onto a poorly maintained gravel road. Fifty feet from the highway the long, dry grass behind a sparse barbed wire fence with rotting posts gives way to second growth forest, mixed spruce and mossy deciduous trees bare of leaves. A blanket of decaying leaves covers the road. Sheriff Shea downshifts to maintain traction and retrieves the radio handset. "Aida, can you call the house and tell my dad I'll be there by noon? Thanks."

Drug Enforcement Agency Special Agent Matthew Vickers, a serious-looking, clean cut man in his 30s, turns in the front passenger seat to rest his hand on the Ithaca 12 gauge pump shotgun mounted vertically between the front seats. Sheriff Shea, older by ten years and slightly less kempt, speaks through his thick moustache while shooting a hard look at Vickers.

"No, we won't be needing that."

Sheriff Shea gestures to a clearing ahead, slowing the patrol car. "This is it." Shea turns the car through a wide gravel loop and brings it to a halt before the front porch of a single story home with grey cedar roof shingles, the ten-year-old blue paint sun-faded but intact. The two men step out of the car into shallow puddles of last night's rain and scan the area. An unmarked federal vehicle parks behind them, two suited FBI agents from the joint task force exiting. Soft grey sunlight filters through the cloud cover. Sheriff Shea, six feet tall and still lithe, removes his patrol hat, reaching through the open driver side window to set the hat on the dash. He adjusts his duty belt on his hips, shifting the large holstered revolver as he walks towards the home's front steps. The agents from the second car split around the house in each direction, one gesturing to Shea and Vickers, twirling his index finger. Vickers stands behind Shea in the gravel driveway, ten feet to his rear. He holds his hand to his right ear, then nods. Shea clears his throat and knocks three times on the sagging wooden door.

Muffled from inside, a male voice – "Who is it?"

Sheriff Shea projects his voice: "John, it's Paul. I was wondering if we could talk. Won't take long."

The door opens and John McDougall looks out, disheveled, long, scraggly hair, balding pate, grey skin aging him beyond his 34 years. "Aw, hell, Paul. I haven't done anything and you know it." He glances to Agent Vickers, then to the cars in the driveway, and swallows, a look of confusion and concern on his face. "Who – who is that?"

Sheriff Shea leans in a bit, speaking softly. "An Agent Vickers from the DEA would like to talk to you about your brother. His name has come up in a multi-agency investigation – as has yours. We – I, John – want them to ask their questions and be on their way. I know that you're staying out of trouble. We want them to know that, too."

McDougall hesitates, his hand fixed firmly on the door.

"Now, I know that you've been keeping out of trouble, John, and you know that I've gone to bat for your family several times, yeah?"

McDougall weakly responds, "Yeah."

Shea drops his voice just above a whisper. "So let's do this and get these feds the hell out of town, OK?"

McDougall sags and steps back, beckoning them into the house. Shea stands aside for Agent Vickers, glancing about for the others. As Vickers turns sideways to step into the house, Shea quietly whispers, "Where...?" Vickers waves his hand dismissively.

The interior is sparsely furnished but clean. Agent Vickers looms over McDougall, who perches lightly on a threadbare loveseat, gesturing to a couch. Shea and Vickers remain standing. Shea scans the small home, his eyes resting on family photos on the wall, particularly one of John McDougall wearing a suit, smiling with a woman and a young boy.

"John, how are Katie and Steven doing?" Shea asks, a smile on his face as he turns.

He watches one of the FBI agents appear on the porch through the window, then step into the room, holding a lever action rifle in latex-gloved hands. The other Agent, Eric Levin, young and eager, bangs through the screen door in the kitchen and pounds into the living room, holding up a small gym bag. "We've got it."

McDougall puts his hand over his face. "Fuck."

Agent Vickers draws a revolver from a cross-draw holster on his left hip and fires four rounds into McDougall's chest. Shea turns sharply, his right hand on the butt of his large service revolver. "What the hell -"

His words are cut short by a .30 caliber bullet entering his chest, fired by Agent Martinelli from the lever action rifle. Shea falls to the floor on his right side, shock on his face, but draws a small automatic with his left hand from his back pocket and fires three rounds towards the nearest Agent, Vickers. Martinelli kicks the pistol out of Shea's hand and jacks another round into the chamber of the rifle, aiming it at Shea. Shea looks wildly about, blood rapidly soaking into the orange shag carpet, as Vickers drops to one knee with his hand over his lower abdomen.

Vickers grunts. "Son of a bitch. Aw, he got me under the vest. God it hurts. Get me the kit." Vickers sits on the couch and looks down at Shea, now flat on his back and fading fast.

Agent Levin sprints out the door and retrieves a gunshot wound kit from the trunk of their unmarked car. Vickers stares hard into Shea's eyes as they glaze over. "Asshole."

Shea opens his mouth but only soft incoherent syllables escape. "D... D... D..." He collapses and sighs, his last.

Martinelli relaxes and rests the butt of the lever action on his hip, licking his lower lip and looking at the nickel-plated Colt 1903 automatic he kicked from Shea's hand. "Boss, it's a .32. You're lucky that he didn't draw that hand cannon. Levin will patch you up. The boys have cleared out, so I'll prepare the scene." He depresses the loading gate on the rifle to empty the magazine of its remaining cartridge, swings the lever down to clear the chamber, then scans the room for the empty cartridge. Finding it, Martinelli returns the empty to the chamber, lowers the hammer and jacks two live shells into the magazine again. Finally, he wipes down the gun, removes an envelope from his coat pocket and unpeels a transparency, which he places against the receiver of the rifle and rubs it there and on the stock several times.

Agent Levin re-enters the house with a medical response bag and ushers Agent Vickers to a strikingly modern black leather armchair, setting him in a seated position. "Boss, the revolver." Levin takes the .38 from Vickers' leather gloved hand and places it into Sheriff Shea's limp hand, moving his fingers about, then lets the gun fall to the carpet with a soft thud. He returns to Vickers, removes his jacket and unbuttons his shirt, then applies a large wad of gauze to a gunshot wound an inch below his body armor.

Martinelli pops a cigarette into his mouth and sighs. "Alright, I'll prep the rifle." He walks out the front door and heads in a straight line to the corner of an outbuilding, where he turns towards the house and drops the rifle into the mud. He walks back towards the porch, draws a Browning Hi-Power 9mm automatic from his holster, and fires two rounds into the corner of the outbuilding at chest level. He reholsters the automatic, walks to Sheriff Shea's squad car and reaches through the open window to lift the radio handset to his mouth. He clears his throat and keys the handset.

"Shots fired! Shots fired! Sheriff Shea and Agent Vickers are down! Send medics to 14835 West Liljedahl Road, south of Highway 112! Agents securing scene."

Gravel grinds and scuffs as a Clallam County Sheriff's Department cruiser slides to a halt before a large lodge-style timber home set among the trees. Nine-year-old Doug Shea, swimming in baggy woodland camouflage over his wiry frame, raises his crew-cut head from a Forest Service map on the floor of the living room and looks to his grandfather, who rises quickly from the couch. Josef Shea narrows his eyes on the cruiser as a young sheriffs' deputy steps out, straightens himself, and sighs, walking slowly to the porch with his hat in hand.

Josef turns, says softly, "Doug, stay here," and steps around two scoped bolt-action rifles leaning against the wall beside the couch. Doug, confused, springs to the window as his grandfather gently closes the door and puts his hand on the shoulder of the deputy, who begins to sob. Josef Shea glances back at Doug, a deep frown spreading across his face, beginning to tremble. Doug's eyes go wide.

1994

A jangle of keys, the click of a deadbolt, and the door swings inward. Twenty-year-old Doug Shea, fit but slightly shaggy, steps across the threshold of his tiny University District apartment and scans the room. A fourth-hand fabric sofa, shipping crates serving as a coffee table strewn with video game cartridges, a small TV atop two milk crates in the corner. The imposing stereo is not blaring dreary Cure ripoff bands; his roommate isn't home. A glance out the window reveals the pillars of the I-5 freeway and slanting rain in the soft grey mid-afternoon light.

Doug closes the door, sets his backpack on the floor, hangs his green flight jacket on a wall hook, kicks off his boots and steps into the kitchen to catalogue the mess. Bread crumbs on the cutting board, a knife encrusted with drying cheese scum, a glass with a quarter-inch of milk coagulating in the bottom, a half-eaten bowl of cereal in the sink. Doug says under his breath, "I have to get my own place." The refrigerator scene is better – the left side of the shelves, his own, are orderly and well stocked. He places vegetables and a piece of venison sausage on a plate with a paring knife and fills a glass with water before heading into his crowded ten by twelve bedroom.

He sets his food on a desk bearing a large computer monitor, printer and a desktop stereo. The room mirrors his personality – tidy, symmetrical, but busy, with framed Spanish Civil War and World War II propaganda posters on the wall. His bed is neatly made, and two stacked legal filing cabinets against one wall serve as display space for framed photos - smiling American and Asian soldiers in black and white, Doug's high school wrestling career, him as a baby with mother and father, his grandfather and grandmother in Catalonia during the war, and reprints of hundred year old family portraits. A large Randall fighting knife lies among the photographs in its weathered brown leather sheath.

Doug powers up the computer and monitor and retrieves his backpack from the hall, leaving the door open. He takes advantage of the 1.5-minute boot time for his

486-66 desktop to sort his classwork and reading material on his bed and hang his backpack on a peg in the closet, which he slides closed. He logs into Windows, opens his mail app to sync his mailbox, then opens a plain-text Lynx web browser. Doug bites into a slice of sausage and turns on the stereo, Alice In Chains' Dirt album blaring at ear-melting volume. He jumps, lowers the volume, then navigates in the browser to the Usenet group "rec.guns," querying for new threads from the past 24 hours.

Yesterday's inquiry regarding .32 ACP ballistics, historic load metrics, and reloading tips is bearing fruit – the retired Secret Service agent in San Francisco has posted a long, poetic stroll through possibly-apocryphal CIA testing protocols of compact handguns, bullet types, and currently-available flash-retarding powder analogues. Doug retrieves a binder labeled "projects" from the filing cabinet, opens to a post-it note scrawled with ".32," prints the retired agent's post, then hole-punches it and adds it to the binder. He saves the article as a .txt file in his university Unix account folder, navigates in the text browser to an electronic fax tool, and transmits it to his grandfather's office.

Doug grazes on his food while browsing additional threads, losing himself.

"SHIT." Doug jumps back and looks at the clock, opens a drawer and grabs a vibrating pager. He keys the display and reads a brief alphanumeric message. Pocketing the clip-less pager, he opens the desk's bottom drawer and lifts the false base, revealing a small, flat safe with a keypad. He jams his jangling keychain into a keyhole, punches in a combo, swings the door open, and withdraws a thick Ziploc bag densely stuffed with green plant material. Doug locks the safe, closes the drawer, and grabs a small drawsack, jams the quarter pound of marijuana into the sack, slides the looped drawstring over his right arm, then storms into the hall. He wraps himself and his package in his flight jacket, and slips quickly into his side-zip boots.

Eighteen minutes later, Doug squats under a footbridge in Ravenna Park with a knit cap crammed down on his head. Path lights blink on in the gentle drizzle as day gives way to night. Doug draws his sleeve back to check his watch. Five minutes early. Perfect.

A lone walker crosses the path down the slope from him, stopping under the bridge's shadow, the backlit dial of a watch lighting his face briefly. Gaxiola. Doug rises and silently strides down the hill, slowing and calling out softly ten feet from the path. "Hey, Gax."

James Gaxiola's curly red ponytail has survived the style wars of the early-middle nineties; in the shadows, it and his pale late adolescent face stand out from his plain black baseball cap, black denim jacket and black BDU pants. "Doug." They shake hands. "Shit, it's already getting cold. I thought we had at least another week."

Doug cocks his head. "Dude, Halloween is next Thursday."

Gaxiola sighs. "I'm still not used to it here. So, where are we gonna smoke a bowl?"

Doug points to the underside of the pedestrian bridge at the opposite end of his roost. They glance about for observers before plodding up the pebbly concrete embankment to a quiet, breezeless nook. "Here you go; it's loaded." Doug opens his left hand to reveal an aluminum screw-together pipe with a screw-on bowl lid and a white Bic lighter.

Gaxiola starts. "BOLD man, using a white lighter." With a Cheshire grin, he adds, "Hmmm, I don't know about you." He takes the pipe from Doug's hand, leaving the lighter, and draws a black Bic of his own. "My crack lighter throws a better flame." Gaxiola twists the bowl lid off, smells the nug, and lights up, holding a large draw. "Mmmm, mmm." Exhaling, with a crack in his voice: "Smooth." He blows the last bit of smoke out the side of his mouth. "Not bad, man."

Doug says, "They call it 'Dagobah Dank,' on account of growing it in a swampy ravine. I got plenty more. Long-time growers who have been upping their game recently. I'm a family friend." Gaxiola gestures with the pipe. Doug waves it away. "I have to write a paper tonight."

"Dude." Gaxiola tilts his head. "You are essentially obligated to smoke with me, or no deal. Eight hundred bucks...."

Doug grabs the lighter. "Fine. I have to really bullshit this one – I'm supposed to care about Joyce Carroll Oates, a creaky cat lady who couldn't write anything relevant if someone put a gun to her head." He sparks the lighter, taking and holding a long, deep draw.

Gaxiola nods. "Nice. OK. I was just messing with you. You look a little tense. The 7:30 Simpsons is a Halloween episode? Wanna watch it at my place?"

Doug passes the pipe back. "Thanks, but like I said, I gotta work on this paper. Maybe I can come over next week? I'm heading home tomorrow after class. Re-upping and helping my granddad with a project. They're playing Halloween episodes all the way until, uh, Halloween."

Gaxiola nods and shakes his legs out. "OK. Yeah, here you go." He draws a roll of rubber-banded bills from his hip pocket. "Eight hundee. Gonna count it?"

"Yes." Doug unrolls the cash and counts out eight $100 bills. "Thanks, man."

Gaxiola takes another drag, and on the exhale asks, "Weed?"

Doug points to the other end of the bridge. "Hanging from a drawsack right over there, just over eye level. I added a little extra. Keep the pipe. Later, man."

Doug smacks Gaxiola on the shoulder, turns and scrambles up the bank to the footpath, and heads home to do his penance.

Homeland

Doug flips the sun visor down to cut the glare as he steers his black mid-80s Ford Bronco into the setting sun. While most of Western Washington is shrouded in mist and rain, the Shea family holdings lie in the heart of Clallam County, within the rain shadow of the imposing Olympic mountain range. Due to the clear weather this evening, visibility is spectacular; across the Strait of Juan de Fuca, Victoria, Canada sparkles. At the sparsely populated far northwestern corner of the lower 48, traffic is light and nearly disappears after Doug leaves Port Angeles, westbound on Highway 101. Doug cranes his neck to peek through the windows as he passes the Clallam County Sheriff's Department headquarters.

Continuing northwest on Highway 112, third growth evergreens block the view to the Strait, the foothills crowd closer to the road, and the sky darkens rapidly. Familiar fields and stump farms to his left ease Doug's tension as he nears home. Turning south after several miles, an arrow-straight, somewhat neglected paved road crowded by evergreens leads into green rolling hills. Pulling off to a well-tended gravel road, Doug flips on his high beams and steers to a keypad at the automated gate. He rolls down the driver's side window by hand, punches a code into the keypad, then taps the steering wheel as the gate slowly swings open. Reaching under the Bronco's dashboard, he flips open a panel and presses two buttons before pulling forward. Doug eases down the road slowly, several cameras as well as more active countermeasures noting his passing. The gate trundles shut behind him as he steers through several sharp incline turns at a crawl, noting the undergrowth receding beneath the trees as winter takes hold.

Doug passes through another automated gate before he emerges into a well-tended clearing one hundred meters from the house. The large Northwest lodge style home at the northern edge of the clearing has large windows and a recent sunroom addition facing south to gather precious sunlight during the winter, the wrap-around porch shielding the family from rain under both fixed and retractable awnings. Doug sees a silhouette backlit in the living room window. He pulls his Bronco into one of the open bays of a 20' x 40' metal pole building fifty feet from the house, and notes a stack of crates labeled with Cyrillic text in his headlights.

Doug grabs his backpack from the shotgun seat floorboard and walks into the house, the roll-up garage door closing behind him.

The next morning, Doug and an aged Josef Shea - greyer, slightly more hunched, but still radiating relative strength and vitality - sip coffee at the kitchen table after breakfast, newspapers spread out in front of Josef on the table. Josef smiles. "Good coffee. You know, I miss you being here, but I'm glad you're off making something of yourself."

Doug says, "I miss you, too. This is home."

Josef asks, "What are your plans for next summer?"

Doug shrugs. "Fall quarter just started. That's like nine months from now."

Josef removes his reading glasses and sets them on the table. "Yes, but you need to plan ahead. I could talk to some old friends, arrange an internship or job. At State, at the Agency, wherever."

Doug leans back, an uncomfortable look on his face. "Grandpa, I don't know."

"Still not sure what you're doing after graduation? Your business analysis paper was good. Public or private?" Josef raises an eyebrow. "Have you thought about Vanguard?"

Doug crinkles his face. "Your old company?"

"Sure. It would depend on who is really running things there now. Charles would jump to get you in, quite enthusiastically, I'm sure. He's still in charge, on paper. I spoke with him a few weeks ago. Special project. I can set up a meeting – he still lives in the big house in Magnolia."

Doug shrugs. "Actually, that would be more my speed than D.C. I'd rather stay close by so that I can visit."

"How about this," Joseph says, standing. "I'll make some calls on Monday, and that will at least give you some options. Then you can think about it, and take it or leave it. No pressure. I think you'll get more out of it than another construction job."

"Thanks." Doug stands and begins stacking their breakfast plates. "I mean it."

Josef sets his hand on Doug's shoulder. "I understand your reluctance. These days, I can't blame you. Anyway, enough of that. Put the plates in the sink; we'll get them later. I have something to show you. Come with me."

Down the hallway, Josef leads Doug into a large den decorated more formally than the cabin theme of the rest of the house. An imposing hardwood desk, bookshelves, deep green and brown tones. Josef opens a cabinet door and withdraws a small gym bag with some effort, places it on the desk and waves his hand. "Here it is. Did you see the crates in the garage?"

Doug nods. "What is it?" He steps forward and places his hand on the bag.

Josef nods. "Open it."

Doug unzips the gym bag and peeks in. He glances to Josef, who nods again. Doug withdraws the contents, multiple padded bags of varying size that clunk or rattle as he places them individually on the desk's padded blotter, then pulls cords and unsnaps the bags to unseat the contents. Finally, he whistles softly as he holds a tiny, wicked-looking machine pistol by its wooden pistol grip. "Holy shit. A Skorpion."

Josef nods. "Yep. I saved some from the last time I was in Italy."

Doug flips the stock open, pulls the bolt back to check the chamber, and brings it to his shoulder, sighting out the window, his finger off the trigger. "How'd a bunch of Czech machine pistols end up in Italy?"

Josef says, "Red Brigades. There's a suppressor and nine magazines. Let's put it through its paces on the range after you do the dishes."

Doug folds the stock closed and sets the weapon down, then opens the rest of the packages. The vz.61 Skorpion, eight curved 20-round magazines, one short 10-round magazine, all loaded, one four-cell magazine pouch, one two-cell, a black suppressor and its carrying pouch, a shoulder holster, and a cleaning kit clutter the desk, padded storage bags in a pile behind the gym bag. Ten fifty-round boxes of Czech .32 ACP ammunition are spread out in front of two sets of earmuffs, along with two semi-transparent blue plastic boxes that Doug knows indicates handloads.

Josef waves his hand. "Forget the dishes for now. Get everything back into the bag; let's hit the range."

Doug loads the equipment into the gym bag. "So this is why you had me research reloading .32 ACP cartridges. It's not for dad's old Colt pocket pistol, huh?"

Josef nods. "This, and the Modern Welrod project. I have article excerpts printed out detailing incidents where terrorists used Skorpions in Europe and Latin America that I want you to read, then burn." They don jackets and shoes at the front door, and walk out into bright fall sunshine. As they walk slowly to the southwest, between a woodshed and a greenhouse, Josef points to the hillside. "What's the distance from the front door to the rock formation up there?"

Doug squints. "Five hundred twenty meters. Sixty meters vertical."

Josef: "From the shop door to the horizon of the driveway."

Doug: "One hundred eighteen meters, twenty meters vertical. From the second story of the house, two hundred meters to the south treeline. I noticed some new plantings on the road. What do you have there now?"

Josef flips his hand. "I had to replace some shrubs that shed too much foliage in the winter. I changed the camera units to IR, too. They're much less expensive these days."

Josef and Doug stop fifty meters beyond a 10' x 20' greenhouse at a roofed shooting stall, a weather-worn wooden deck floor beneath their feet hosting two shooting benches. One hundred meters down range, a thirty-foot cliff face forms a shooting berm, with several steel gongs planted into the ground. Josef walks out to a series of target stands thirty feet from the bench. "Doug, take off your jacket, gear up in the shoulder harness and put the magazine pouches on your belt. I'll frame the targets."

Doug opens the gym bag and lays out the equipment, dons the shoulder harness and snaps it and the magazine carriers to his belt. Josef returns and snaps the suppressor pouch under Doug's right arm, a counterweight to the machine pistol under his left.

Josef holds his hand out. "Grab me a magazine, please, and I'll take that." Doug hands him a magazine and the weapon; Josef loads the magazine but does not chamber a cartridge. He slowly demonstrates each move while explaining his technique. "As you draw, flip the stock over with your weak hand until it clicks open. Bring weak hand forward to the magazine as the stock comes into your shoulder—wrench your wrist forward so that you're pushing it into your shoulder tightly. You now have a solid mount."

He continues. "It's not a very large magazine, so keep to short bursts or single shots. Use trigger control, not the selector switch. Hand me the suppressor."

Doug draws the foot-long suppressor from its carrier with his left hand and hands it to Josef, who continues speaking. "You slide it over the barrel and turn it until it tightens into place. This bulge in the barrel is what the collet inside cinches down over. Pretty primitive can—it uses wipes. There are extra wipes in the bottom cell of the suppressor's pouch. You can hold the can with your off hand but I still think it's more stable to grip the magazine. Enough talk."

Josef reaches over the weapon with his left hand and pinches the bolt handles, punches the bolt all the way back and lets go, chambering a round. He flips the selector to full auto with his thumb and brings the weapon in tight to his shoulder. He fires of a long burst at a wooden silhouette twenty meters away. The gun makes a staccato sound muffled significantly by the suppressor.

Josef pauses. "Long burst. The rate of fire is slow enough that you can trigger singles or doubles fairly easily." He demonstrates. "Thirty-two caliber is considered obsolete for self-defense because it has much lower energy and bullet weight than modern service cartridges. Don't worry about that. Compare it to a suppressed .22. We don't use hollow points, because the thirty-two lacks the energy for hollow points to penetrate adequately. These bullets are steel jacketed, so they will penetrate, but I prefer the heavier lead handloads with the old style flat nosed bullets. The Skorpion was designed for hits, force disparity situations, not gunfights. Don't let them see or hear it – or you. Let them feel it." Josef quickly puts two-round bursts into the head area of three targets. The bolt locks open, magazine empty.

Doug comments, "It's getting louder. Is that from the wipes wearing out?"

Josef nods. "Old tech; it works well enough. Wipes. I'm working on a modernized one with baffles in the shop. It's smaller. We've got a lot of wipes, though. This one will be good for another magazine. Here, try it out."

Doug takes the weapon, drops the magazine, clears the chamber, and reloads it with a magazine from one of the belt pouches. He chambers the first round and brings the weapon up. A gentle rain begins to fall.

Doug and Josef sit before the large stone fireplace in the living room, a crackling fire drying them out as Doug scrubs the barrel of the disassembled machine pistol with a bore brush in his rubber-gloved hands. "This thing is really cool," Doug says.

Josef nods. "Glad you like it. I'm going to need you to take it back to Seattle with you. I'm going to experiment with one of the others as part of this project."

"Wait." Doug puts a hand up. "It's illegal as hell. You can get away with it here. I live in the middle of the city, in a small apartment with a roommate. It'd be a ticking time bomb."

Josef crosses his arms. "Didn't you get your off-site caches set up?"

"I guess so." Doug concentrates. "There's the garage, and the mail drop, and two in the woods."

"So quit complaining. First job of the fall. Add this to one of the caches. Pick the safest one. You'll prep it tonight using my caching supplies; I'll inspect." Josef stands. "Second – Stuart told me that you and Blake had set up a little sideline. I want that to end now. It's too risky. If you're concerned about money, like I said, let's get you a job. College life means loads of free time, so let's fill it up with something productive, and not some retail or restaurant nonsense. Or dope dealing."

Doug sheepishly grins. "OK, uh, sorry about going behind your back on that."

Josef points a finger in the air. "And Stuart's back. Blake peeled a pound off. A pound. Didn't tell his father about that."

Doug cringes. "Sorry, I didn't know that."

Josef continues. "You should think about how ne'er-do-wells have wonderful bargains for you. Are you selling it? Smoking it? Well?"

Doug hangs his head. "Sorry, pop. I've sold half of it, and cut off some – it was a little heavy – for samples. What do you want me to do?"

Josef crosses his arms. "Not do it again. Blake is making up for it with his father. Do what you like with the rest, I just want this to be the last time. I don't want you getting either a reputation or police attention. What does my guy you deliver to in Bellevue look like? A hippie? A druggie kid?"

"No," Doug answers, "He looks like a normal suburban guy."

Josef nods. "Exactly. That's why I never let you grow your hair out long, and I always keep you stocked with good clothes, and made you shave every day since age fourteen. Which I've noticed you've relaxed on, based on those nicks. Don't. People judge you. Women judge you. How do you think I survived for decades doing what I do? Fit the image of respectability, and you'll be respectable." He pauses. "Anyhow. Another bundle to Bellevue tomorrow when you go back to school, then that's it. I should have known better than to put you around dope and dope heads. I figured, make hay while the sun shines. It's going to be legal soon anyway. I'll drop it, if you do."

Doug nods. "Okay, pops."

Josef relaxes, the point made. "Item three. Let's watch your caching technique."

With the Skorpion cleaned and lubricated, Doug carries it and its accessories out to the garage in the gym bag, Josef bringing up the rear. Doug lays everything out on a table, then draws a large plastic box from a shelf and places the supplies on one of the large clear benches. From one box he selects a food saver vacuum device, which he plugs in, then dons thin rubber gloves. He places a roll of plastic vacuum bags, and a box containing desiccant bags of varying sizes, on the table. He then wipes down the machine pistol thoroughly with a rag, then goes over the magazines. Doug then lightly oils the surfaces of six of his magazines, cuts an oversized piece of the vacuum bag, seals it on one end, then adds the six magazines to it with a desiccant pack, locking down the vacuum over the other end and sucking out the air. He sets this package to the side, then oils and seals the gun in the same fashion. Next he packages the large magazine pouch, holster and suppressor pouch, then the cleaning kit and suppressor. Doug pauses and turns to his grandfather. "It seems like I should have some ready to go in case I need to employ it in a hurry. Can

I just load the magazines, or do you want me to pack boxed ammunition in the same bag as the remaining mags?"

Josef nods. "If this was a stay-behind cache, we wouldn't keep the magazines loaded. For our purposes, load a few, very lightly oil the outside surface, and put them in the same bag as the two-cell pouch, but not in the pouch. Load the ten round magazine, too. That's fifty rounds to start with. Do you like the handloads, or factory rounds?"

Doug nods. "Handloads. They hit hard, and were quieter."

Josef nods back. "OK, load those mags, then. Package the other cartridge boxes in their own bag."

Doug obeys. He then selects a two-foot section of eight-inch diameter PVC drainage pipe from a shelf with several rows of the pipe, places it on the table, then grabs two pipe plugs, one threaded, one flush. One end of the pipe is threaded, while the other is saw cut. Doug squeezes marine epoxy from a tube around the flush plug and seats it in the pipe. He then fills the pipe with his treasures, adding a desiccant bag and oxygen absorber from time to time, greases the threaded plug, and twists the unit closed. He places this into the gym bag and zips it shut before removing his gloves. "OK. I'll throw this into the panel in the cargo area. It'll fit."

Josef pats him on the shoulder. "Not bad. Practice makes perfect, I guess. Let's do steak for dinner. Load up." Doug opens the tailgate of his Bronco, lifts the floor mat of the cargo area, and massages the gym bag into a deep cargo space crammed with bags and hard cases. Josef draws a bulging envelope from an inner pocket of his jacket and drops it through the Bronco's driver side window onto the seat.

Proffer

Monday morning. Doug Shea blinks with boredom as a disheveled professor belabors some point about Margaret Mead in a tiny underground lecture hall. Doug casts his gaze about the room in search of something interesting.

At the far left end of his row of seats he spots two young women, and stares at them until they return the favor. Liz, his roommate's recently ex-girlfriend, scribbles notes while focusing on the professorial droning from the front of the hall. Cathy Ruiz – nineteen, fit, Filipina, Liz's roommate – rolls her eyes and glances right, seeing Doug. She flashes a flat grin, turns to Liz, nudges her and whispers. Liz looks over at him, slightly annoyed and uncomfortable. Doug nods up with his chin and looks back at Cathy, giving her a once-over. Unlike most of the class, she appears polished and professional, wearing a fitted suit jacket, white blouse, long skirt that only exposes her knees and calves, and black flats that appear fairly expensive for a college student. Cathy meets his eyes and bulges hers exasperatedly, but Doug maintains eye contact.

A bell rings and students erupt out of their seats, jostling about and fleeing the room. Doug strolls over to the two ladies. "Hey Cathy. Liz."

Cathy looks up from her seat as she zips her sling bag shut. "Hey, Doug. How you doin'?"

"Not bad." Doug nods towards the door. "Shall we?"

The trio walk into the hallway, moving towards the quad. Liz clears her throat finally. "So." They exit the building onto the quad, grey skies and a soft rain meeting them. Liz pulls up her hood, and Cathy deploys an umbrella. Doug just gets wet.

He finally speaks. "Liz, I promise that I'm not going to be a go-between. I told Mike that when he asked, so don't worry. That said, please don't let Mike's idiocy reflect poorly on me."

Liz smiles. "Whatever. Later." She winks at Cathy, peels off and cuts across the quad.

Cathy tilts back her umbrella and looks up at Doug. His heart flutters. "Screw Mike. Anyway, are you in a hurry?"

Doug pretends to think. "Well, we are both headed south – right? – but today, I have a bad attitude about learning. What's up?"

Cathy smiles. He can get used to this. "I'm starving, and I can't wait until one thirty to have my lunch."

Doug stops walking. "OK, where do you want to go?"

Cathy feigns deep thinking. "Well, I want some chicken, and I want some rice. Teriyaki is the closest thing."

They pivot to the west, walking slowly through the rushing throngs on their way to classes that are a challenge to reach within a ten-minute break period. Cathy leans towards Doug and sniffs his jacket theatrically. "You smell like gunpowder."

Two hours later, Doug enters his apartment. Mike is smoking weed in front of the TV, as is traditional, with Tekken paused on the screen. Alice in Chains' "Rooster" blares from the stereo. Doug stows his shoes and jacket and steps over in front of Mike.

Mike looks up, grins, and holds up a glass bong filled with smoke, some wafting lightly though the open carb. "Ey, uh, want to hit this?"

Doug waves it off. "No thanks. Dude, I have to ask you something. It's important."

Mike slumps in the couch. "Man, I'm high."

Doug sighs. "Please, please, please resolve this Liz thing in as classy a manner as possible. I just don't want to get involved."

Mike's eyes go wide. "Then don't."

Doug smiles. "Solid point. What have you been doing all day?"

"Smoking all of your grandpa's weed. Come on, hit this shit." He aims the bong mouthpiece at Doug, who shrugs, leans in and draws the stalled smoke from the chamber in one burst.

Doug looks about the room and slowly exhales the smoke through his nose. "You couldn't do that in a day. This from the sample bag?"

Mike nods, takes the bong back and replaces the stem in the carb, then tamps the marijuana in the bowl. "What's up your ass, man? Seriously."

Doug cocks his neck to the left. "Wew, that's dank. No wonder Gax wants the rest. I better lay off – work to do."

Mike shrugs. "More for me. At least get in here for Simpsons."

Doug stands. "You got it. I'm gonna go read. If you need me," and he points to his room with both hands and clicks his tongue. In his room, Doug picks several folded bundles of paper from his desk, which lay atop a manila folder labeled "Your dad" in Josef's handwriting. He spreads out the material on his bed – photos, old photocopies of newspapers and government documents, maps and Xeroxes. Doug's hand trembles as he lifts a black and white glossy photo of his father lying on his back in a pool of blood. He puts the photo down quickly and grabs another document, a hand-drawn diagram of his father's death scene on Clallam County Sheriff's Department letterhead. A dashed line from an outbuilding, through the front door to his father's body with the hand-written note: RANGE SIXTY THREE FEET. Hash marks behind the outbuilding on the hillside marked: OP - Observation Post? McDougall's body with the notation: FOUR SHOTS .38 REVOLVER. The revolver lies next to his father's body. A sketched pistol on the ground, labelled SHER. SHEA'S COLT .32, with three dashed lines into a wall, one intersecting a human silhouette: AGT VICKERS, ONE .32.

Doug picks up a notepad from his desk and begins scribbling notes as he flips through the documents. The name of the medical examiner, agents on scene, details of the layout. Ranking agents who oversaw the agents on the scene. Doug puts the notepad and pen down. He looks at the clock on his stereo — 2:15 p.m. He picks up the phone and dials. His grandfather answers. "Doug."

"Grandpa. How long have you known?"

Silence. Josef responds sharply – "Ears."

Doug looks around. A code for a potential wire-tap. "You're kidding."

Josef asks, "Can you come see me Friday?"

Doug covers his eyes with one hand. "I, uh, have this thing. How about I come out there Saturday. By noon. Ish."

"OK. Write this down. Library trip. Ready?"

Doug tears a page from the notepad and folds it in quarters, then positions his pen. "Ready."

Josef speaks in clipped, clear tones. "Three seven ten. Alpha Delta X-ray. Mark. Got it?"

"Got it. Checking." Doug opens his closet door and squats, pulling a rack of shoes out and setting them aside. He grips the carpet corner and pulls it up, then swings open a floor panel. He spins the dial on a floor safe, then swings it open. He draws out a large Smith and Wesson revolver and a bundle of cash, then a small folio. He sits on the bed and flips to page 70, revealing a one-time pad. He underlines row headers A, D and X. The three in Josef's comments tells Doug to use only every third letter in the message while decoding. Still cradling the phone headset on his shoulder, he says, "Got it."

Josef continues. "Mark. Mark. Phone, Bear, Pack, Twin, Light, Comb, Earth, Radio, Star, India, October, Bear, Comb, Xylophone. Break."

Doug writes out the string, skips to a new line, and continues to write out the sequence Josef feeds him. "Got it."

Josef sighs. "OK, I'm getting up with the chickens, so I'll talk to you Saturday. Let me know what you figure out, and what you think. OK?"

Doug nods. "OK. I'll see you then. Love ya." He hangs up and works out the letter matches to the one-time pad. He squints at the results.

LA TIMES HOPKINS OCTOBER 22 1982

"Hopkins, Hopkins." Doug searches through the document bundle, but finds no reference to a Hopkins. He stops, and turns. On his bookshelf, a framed black and white photo of five men, two of them Caucasian, three Asian, in olive drab fatigues with WWII-era weapons. One is his father, Paul Shea, as a young man. Doug flips the frame over and pulls the photo out. On the back, written in block letters, "Me, Tien, Kham, Hopkins, and Billy. Savannakhet, July 1967."

"Damn."

Doug leans against a low handrail on the worn red brick stairs of a building in the UW Quad, bundled against the increasing cold. Soggy leaves from the cherry trees clutter the lawns, paths and stairs. Liz and Cathy exit the building in co-ed standard issue university sweatshirts and jeans, stealthily approaching him from behind. Cathy sets her bag on Doug's head. He looks up, bemused. "Hey."

"You ready?" Cathy asks.

They head west towards the off-campus residential apartment zone of the southwestern U District, dodging student bicycle commuters and street kids spare changing or offering low quality marijuana. Liz stops at one, turning to Doug and Cathy inquisitively; Doug shakes his head in the negative.

In an obviously female-inhabited apartment – clean, possessing decent furniture and posters with frames – the three begin their preparations. Doug draws items out of his backpack for the girls' inspection. A wide-mouthed water bottle is rejected. Cathy notes, "Sealed, disposable plastic bottles only." A bag of fruit-flavored hard candies is proffered; Cathy says, "Add it." Liz adds four plastic water bottles to the pile, crams it into a small shoulder bag and zips the bag shut.

"Doug." Cathy snaps her fingers. "Anything pointy?" She removes a stainless steel folding knife from her waistband and places it on the table. "You can't take anything pointy in there."

Doug eyes her knife. "That's a big Spyderco for, um."

"A girl?" Cathy laughs. Doug shakes his head; all of his hardware is safely stowed in his book bag.

Liz puts her hand up. "OK, you two; it's time. Doug – weed. Do you have a plan getting it in there? We have to pre-funk too."

Doug nods. "I have two joints for later. They won't find it in a pat-down. Two lighters... just in case. One joint for now."

Cathy goes to the kitchen and places three glasses on the counter. "OK, guys. We need to drink some water. Anyone need to eat? We have to roll in ten minutes."

Liz peeks into the refrigerator. "Beer for when we get back. I have some smoothies blended up, too. Let's do the smoothies."

Doug watches as Liz pours frothing green into the glasses. "I gotta tell ya – you ladies know how to do it. With the guys, it's like, 'We'll figure it out,' then I'm spending hours taking care of them."

Cathy runs into a bedroom and returns as Liz and Doug drink their smoothies. She opens a tiny jewelry box and removes three small chalky pink tablets imprinted with a cartoon rabbit head. "Bottom's up." All three swallow the pills dutifully.

"Known provenance?" Doug asks.

Cathy shrugs. "My cousin. Knows a guy, knows the chemist. He graduated two years ago. Works at a biotech firm and cooks this up in the lab there. Supposed to be very clean."

Liz squints. "You should probably ask that before you slam drugs, young man."

Doug pulls out a joint. "Pre-funk. I sprinkled heroin in it and then dipped it in embalming fluid."

"What?" Cathy recoils.

"That's a joke." Doug sparks it up, gets the cherry going, and takes a modest hit. "Top quality organic outdoor grow from this summer, just finished curing." He leans his hip into Cathy's, handing her the joint. "If you're going to put bad things in your body, you could do worse than something grown in the wilds of the Olympic Peninsula."

Liz laughs. Cathy cracks a coy grin before taking a long drag, eyes locked with Doug.

The trio walks several blocks from a far-flung bus stop into the industrial district south of the Kingdome. Liz, veteran rave kid, leads them down an alley between warehouses and factories. Swing shift workers on cigarette breaks watch them and others skulking through the rain, all flowing in a single direction. They approach the side door of a warehouse flanked by two massive bouncers wearing black t-shirts with STAFF emblazoned in vivid white across their chests. An unkempt, unshaven mid-20s male with inch-diameter ebony plugs in each earlobe and a large stainless ring through his lower lip counts out the wad of bills Liz proffers before nodding them through. Through a dark, black-painted clapboard hallway, the thrum of an urgent bass line surrounds them and explodes into actual music as they pass through soundproof doors into a writhing mass illuminated by purple flashes of light. They lock hands, Liz-Cathy-Doug, and wind their way through the crowd towards a doorway emitting gently rotating colors and soothing tunes, caressed by angelic female vocals.

"I like this," Doug shouts to the two over the music. "Um, I'm starting to get a little, yeah."

Liz and Cathy turn to him, their eyes all pupils.

Cathy pulls Doug's ear down to her mouth. "I thought I was going to lose it about two blocks back. Did you see the rats attacking the dumpsters behind that bakery?" She shudders.

"Fuck it – let's dance!" Liz shouts, putting her hands over her head, and swaying into the crowd.

"Come on, let's go!" Cathy grabs Doug's hands and pulls him in.

Doug awkwardly attempts to follow Cathy's lead, then decides to take over and direct her. They begin flowing with one another and the music, waves of emotion, comfort, and ease washing over them, the energy of the crowd and each other becoming smoothly tangible.

Doug attempts to speak, laughs, and scoops Cathy up, throwing her into the air with a whoop, catching her and spinning her around, his left arm cradling under her thighs. Cathy erupts in laughter, her eyes bright and shining. I can do this forever, he thinks, an urgency rising warm and strong in his chest, as visual distortions and emanations surge through the crowd.

After a brief eternity, Liz and Cathy confer, then grab Doug and shout. "Drum and Bass! Let's do it!" They drag him towards a third room, as dark and as grim as the music aggressively heaping its scorn upon them. Machine noises and angry film samples assault them and they fight back, dancing with combative grace. Cathy watches Doug and begins mirroring him with Filipino short sword forms. He returns her drills barehanded, Cathy rapidly speeding up their hand slaps, until they collapse into each other, laughing with glee. Cathy grabs his collars and drags him down again. "Hey, boy, you know sinawali! Why didn't you tell me?"

Doug puts his hands on her waist. "And vice versa." They kiss, long and hard, losing themselves. Doug becomes vaguely aware of something slapping the back of his head. They break contact, staring into each other's eyes.

"HEY." They turn to Liz, who playfully has her fists jammed against her sides, elbows akimbo, comically mugging. "No fair. I don't have anybody to kiss." She shoves her lower lip out in a ridiculous pout.

Cathy pushes herself off of Doug's chest playfully. "Down, boy. Dance."

The music shifts into new avenues of aggression, and the three form a circle, Doug and Cathy dancing, punching, kicking, thrusting with virtual sticks, Liz doing her own thing.

Doug's mind drifts, file folders with names, places, clinically detached phrasing of his father's death. A pool of blood in shag carpet, brass casings marked with little tents of paper hand-labeled with a number, his father's lifeless eyes staring somewhere over Doug's shoulder in black and white.

He stops dancing, jerks his head, squinting, shaking it out. He flexes his knees and puts out a hand to steady himself.

Cathy's eyes go wide with concern; she takes his hand and wraps her other arm around his waist. "Doug, are you OK?"

Doug looks down at her upraised face. Gorgeous. "Yeah, I think I'm peaking. A little intense. I need something."

Cathy swings her tiny backpack from her back and zips it open in one fluid motion. "Water and some candy." She waves Liz over. "Doctor's orders." They all rip open their own water bottles, drink, and then pop Jolly Ranchers into their mouths.

Doug stares blankly, intensely, at nothing. Cathy grabs his chin. "Hey boy, you there?"

Doug shakes his head, coming out of a trance. "Hey. Hi."

Cathy keeps her grip on his chin. "Hi. You having fun? Where'd you go off to there?"

"Ah. I'm right here."

Cathy frowns. "Don't get all e-tarded on us. We're not leaving for another four hours. Let's sit down."

They walk to a nearby corner, sitting on the floor. To their right, in a dark, slightly quieter corner of the warehouse, a large mass of people sprawl out on the floor together. Doug blinks, seeing them bloodied, vacant eyes staring at the ceiling, like his father in a crime scene photo. Security staff stream through the room to another hallway, looking down towards him, and their faces appear as black and white photos from a dossier – agents Martinelli, Levin and Vickers. Doug rolls his feet beneath him, into a squat, tense and rigid.

Cathy grabs his arm. "Doug, what's going on? Are you doing OK?"

Doug leans back against the wall and slides down, looking Cathy in the eyes, bringing him down with her. "I'm fine. Sit a minute?" He scoops her up and sets her in his lap, wrapping his arms around her.

Cathy speaks softly into his ear. "You've never done E before, have you?"

Doug shakes his head. "That's not it. Just got stuck on something unpleasant. I'm fine."

"It's okay." Cathy slides her arm behind his back, pulling him in tighter. "Let's just hang out here a bit. Cuddle up." He rests his cheek against her long, smooth hair.

Time passes. A new clarity and warmth spreads through Doug's body. He eventually speaks. "I could get used to this."

Cathy draws her head out and locks her eyes with his. "Me, too. What do you think?"

Doug smiles. "Do I need to say it?"

"Yes, yes you do."

Doug sips still-steaming black coffee from a thermos cup in his right hand, the left on the steering wheel of his Bronco, the fog around him brightening as the sunrise peeks above the gloom to his east. After his first-ever cab ride from the rave to the girls' apartment – a bit of genius courtesy of Liz – Doug got them settled in, cooked pancakes, then left. Cathy is Catholic. Cathy Catholic. Nothing more would happen, he didn't want to come on strong and turn her off. Another girl would have taken him to bed. Not that he didn't want to. She kissed him goodbye at the door, smiling wanly as she wished him good night. Brutal.

What is that smell, he wondered, the thing with her hair. Coconut, but not over-powering. No, there's more of a citrus sharpness, just a touch. Her poise, her skill in manipulating – no, directing – him emotionally. This girl has training. As a rural kid in an area without many Catholics, Doug had only heard the worst about Catholic girls – in only the best way – but that wasn't the case with Cathy. Maybe it's a Filipino thing. Her family has high expectations, The night spins over and over and over in his head.

The three leveled out the ecstasy's speedy edge with one of Doug's joints at the rave; he left the girls the other upon departure. Doug has some experience with hallucinogenics, but MDMA is something else entirely. Like an urgent warmth within his chest, emotional frailty, splitting open his ribcage like a deer and displaying everything he had felt in recent days for the world on a stone altar. A public ritual of becoming, plus jitters. Ridiculous. The urgency and feeling still danced within him, beyond fatigue, caffeine propping him up on his four-hour drive home to the Peninsula. If they had taken acid, he'd still be a wreck, Doug knew, and he would not be driving. Still probably not a great idea, but there was no way he was going to get any sleep for some time.

Westbound, finally, Doug gazes at the Clallam County Sheriff's Department office at his right, a ritual of his. Decision: he will visit Martin Bryce, his late father's protégé, to catch up. He'll call this afternoon.

Thirty minutes later, as he eases the Bronco up to the gate of their property, Doug sees a red blinking light on the console. Visitors. Doug opens his truck's center console and keys in a passcode; a panel flips open, and he draws a nickel-plated Browning Hi Power and spare magazine from within. He tucks the magazine into his left front pocket and slides the handgun under his right leg, already cocked and locked. He pulls into the property, rolling slowly with his headlights off, looking for sign. Nobody should be here at this time of morning. At the second to last switchback before coming to the rise and into the clearing where there house lies, Doug turns the Bronco off of the road to a clear, level gravel area, then grabs the handgun and a flashlight. The dome light remains unlit as he steps out into the forest, courtesy of a police-style kill switch on his dash. He moves through the woods quickly but silently, examining the clearing around the house. A dark late-model American sedan is parked in front of the house, seemingly empty. Doug pads around to the back porch, ascending silently – there's a trick to it, thanks to clever joinery – peeking through the lit window of Josef's office. Josef sits at his desk, speaking to two men. A white, middle-aged man with the look of a bureaucrat, dressed in a rumpled suit – on an early Saturday morning – sits on the corner of the desk. The other man sticks out like a sore thumb here – black, mid- to late-twenties, military bearing and hard eyes, silently observing with his arms crossed.

Doug moves along the one floorboard fastened with deck screws to the rear door and peeks in, seeing nobody, before moving past the kitchen and living room. Nobody. In front? Nobody, unless they're in an overwatch position. Too aggressive – bad move, kid, as Josef would have said.

Screw it. Doug tries the front door, and the knob turns in his hand. He enters the house without a sound, the voices rising as he approaches.

Josef: "Fifty years, I have never heard these kinds of terms."

Man: "It's simple. We want this to go as smoothly as possible. You know what you know, and you have your friends. We don't have the juice to put you over a barrel, so don't think of it that way."

Man 2: "But there's a rub."

Man 1: "This must go smoothly. Keep in mind which direction the political winds are blowing."

Man 2: "Yugoslavia."

Man 1: "That information could leak – and interested parties may act on it."

Josef: "So. Let's say that I agree to your terms. What next?"

Man 1: "Call this number.... A short trip. A few days at most. And then I'll contact you again with permission to proceed."

Doug steps into the room with his pistol aimed at a ribcage index. "Hello, fuckers. May I help you?"

The men start, then freeze; Man 1, the white bureaucrat, splays his hands lightly to his side. Man 2, the intense black guy with a military bearing, is three feet from him. "Watch it, boy," the black guy says softly, through tight lips, eyeing Doug intensely.

Doug locks eyes with the soldier. "Whose home is this? Do you know where in the world you are?"

The bureaucrat moves softly off the desk to a full stand. "Calm down, you two. There's no need for this. Mr. Shea – let us know how you want this to go. Douglas." He points to a business card on the desk, then nods to his compatriot.

Doug backs into the hallway, keeping his gun indexed. "After you."

The soldier sneers at him, leading the two towards the front door. "I'll remember this."

The bureaucrat commands the soldier, "Shut up." He turns to Doug. "I hope we can develop a more cordial relationship, Douglas." Doug watches from the window as they make their way down the stairs. He turns the porch lights off and the soldier stumbles in a puddle, curses.

Doug flips the light back on. "Oops." The pair continue to the car, looking over their shoulders. The soldier scans the property quickly before flashing the tires with a light before unlocking the car, entering, and starting the engine.

Josef walks up beside him. "Doug, that was pointless."

Doug screws up his courage. "What was that shit all about? I'm supposed to let them threaten you?"

Josef sighs. "This is the way it works. No such thing as a favor with these people. You want something, information, let's say, it always comes at a price."

"In other words," Doug says, "you traded the information you gave me for a promise to do something dirty. At your age."

Josef puts his hand on Doug's shoulder. "This is about your daddy. Look, I wanted you to know what happened to him. I'm willing to do what it takes for you to know."

Doug watches the car roll slowly out of the clearing before moving to the hall closet to observe the surveillance monitors, tracking the car past his truck and out to the road, the gate swinging shut automatically. "Well now I know, and it doesn't mean anything, because the L.A. Times had an article about a Justice Department official named Hopkins whose car went into a ravine for no reason in 1982."

"He was a friend of your dad's."

Doug turns. "They kill him for something, and more than ten years later, send you to your death, and let me guess. If you don't go, it makes no difference, because something incredibly bad will happen to you, am I right?"

Josef pauses before responding. "It could."

"That's great." Doug gestures helplessly. "Now, on top of a vendetta against some federal agents, you expect me to watch you get played by those faggots." He pauses. "You need me to come with you."

Josef looks at him with hard eyes. "Perhaps."

Doug stomps into the living room, slams his body onto a couch, and stares out the window. "So how does this work?"

Josef sits down next to him, slowly, placing his hand on Doug's leg to steady himself. While healthy for his age, his invulnerable whipcord bearing has faded rapidly in the past two years.

"Tuesday, I go up to Victoria. To visit a friend. Pick up some prepared equipment, so there is no border complication. Wednesday and Thursday, I prepare, but have to be ready at a moment's notice. They leave Sunday, or so I'm told, so I have to act by then."

"Who are 'they?'" Doug asks.

"Two principals, another two possibles. All four is best, but the principals are critical. Albanian heroin traffickers involved with a terrorist organization."

Doug leans back, sighing. Clarity through chemicals. "I'm going to have to kill those fuckers before this is over."

Josef turns. "What are you talking about?"

Doug stands and turns, looking down at Josef. "Those motherfuckers that were just in here. They have this look... this is worse than you think. I'm going to have to kill them."

Josef waves his hand, looking exhausted. "Don't take it personally. Let me handle that."

Doug shakes his head. "They have you over a barrel. And they don't want you. They want me."

Josef points accusingly, a little shaky. "Boy, you are talking in circles. Look at me. I am going to do this. There won't be a problem."

Doug puts his hands together. "With all due respect. I'm going with you. I am not going to leave you out there by yourself. You're nearly eighty years old, for God's sake. It's simple. They already have you, they want me so they can wring their last bit of leverage out of you and your faction."

Josef waves his hand dismissively. "No, I want you to stay out of this."

Doug gives his grandfather the hardest look he's capable of mustering against him. "You just lied. You trained me my whole life for this. They have us already. I'm sure they have a nice profile on me." He laughs. "I feel like I finally have something to lose that isn't abstract, like my 'future.' What a night."

Josef stands, slowly. "Okay then. Tuesday. Do you need to call in to school to take a few days off?"

"Yeah. I'll see what I can work out. I was planning to visit Sheriff Bryce this weekend, too. Haven't seen him since graduation."

Josef smiles. "I have something for you to give him. Your dad's files. The feds never made it available to the county. He'll be good and pissed. Could help us out. Doug." He looks at his feet, then up to meet Doug's eyes. "Doug... whatever happens, I'm sorry. Your father wanted a different life for you. It's complicated, but that's why he did what he did. He wanted to protect everyone here. I don't know if that makes sense."

Doug lets out a long breath, tension melting away as the reality of his life hardens like a shell of armor within him. He feels a force drawing him forward, beyond his control. "That's where he was wrong, but I can't hold it against him. I've thought about this a lot. Avoidance, political maneuvers to create an island of tranquility for his family and neighbors... that has never worked. There's only two paths. Victory or submission. I'm going to bed. See you in a few hours." He begins ascending the stairs.

"I love you, Doug." Doug turns to see Josef standing in the living room, arms at his side, looking a hundred years old. "I'm sorry."

"Pops." Doug's love and hate wells up inside him. "I love you, too. No hard feelings. We do what we must." He walks up into the darkness to his room, to stare at the ceiling for an hour, thinking thoughts of scx and murder.

Impôt du Sang

Five nights later, Doug and Josef walk briskly along a paved trail through a suburban park, clad in earth tone outdoor clothing and knit caps, each wearing a small backpack. The moonlight illuminates their path, streetlights far off in the distance. They enter a landscape of mostly evergreens, a trail leading to a cul de sac appearing to their right.

Josef swings his backpack off his shoulder and zips it open. "It's time." The two don red lens polarized safety glasses and electronic earmuffs, adjusting the volume knobs. Foreign voices and music pop into their heads. Their eyes meet.

"This is it," Doug says. "I'll scope."

Doug swings his backpack to his chest and unzips the main compartment, resting his hand on top, casually striding into the cul de sac. Josef steps to the side behind a tree, drawing a suppressed handgun from his bag and holding it along his leg, watching and listening. Doug returns after a short loop, leaning against Josef and whispering.

"The car hasn't moved from earlier. I'll plant the charge."

Josef taps his shoulder. "You remember every step?"

Doug nods, taking Josef's satchel. They move along the edge of the trail into the cul de sac, concealed in shadow, padding flat-footed into the gravel of the first lot on the left. Josef takes up a position against a run-down carriage house, scanning the street for movement, a suppressed handgun in his right hand, an unlit flashlight in his left, indexed under his right wrist. The previous night, Doug shot the cul de sac's two street lights out with a pellet gun, and later swept up the broken glass beneath. Only two driveway lights shine nearby, leaving most of the street cast in moonlight alone.

Moving up in the shadows, Doug squats beside the carriage house, removing a small wad of plastic explosive fitted with a delay mechanism from his backpack. He carefully pushes two blasting caps into the lump of explosives and activates a switch. Looking up at his grandfather, Doug nods, and then soundlessly squat-walks to a Jeep Wagoneer parked in the gravel driveway, facing into the property.

Josef, stepping out from the corner of the carriage house, steadily transfers his aim between the doorway and box window of the small brick residence. Golden light glows behind a drawn window shade. Doug shuffles on his back beneath the Wagoneer and places the charge under the drive shaft, between the driver and passenger's seats. He slides out and hustles back to the carriage house. Doug and Josef nod at each other and split, Doug moving deeper into the lot and taking a position behind a large Douglas fir, drawing a Skorpion machine pistol from his front-mounted backpack. He extends the stock and attaches a suppressor before thumbing off the safety and bracing the suppressor against the tree with his support hand.

Josef moves back ten yards to the edge of the trail, leaning down behind the low brick perimeter fence, drawing a small two-way radio from his jacket. He keys the radio, muttering, "Call," replaces the radio in his pocket, and draws another small box with an antenna, switching on the power and resting his thumb against the switch shield.

A minute passes before three men, talking back and forth in a rough, barely European language, exit the house. Two slide into the Jeep's driver and shotgun seats quickly. The last man pauses in the doorway, shouting into the house. He is in his early 20s, swarthy with curly hair and a beard, dressed casually in a European-cut tan suede jacket, clutching a small paper bag.

Josef, still leaning behind the low brick fence, translates in his head. Confirmed for Albanian. "<Be done when we get back. We have to be ready with the rest.>"

The driver starts the engine of the Wagoneer and rolls down the passenger side window. He shouts, "<Get in the car, big shot.>"

Big Shot is halfway into the back seat when the car blows in a short, sharp flash, lifting it four feet into the air before it crumples, its back broken. Big Shot is flung casually against the side of the house. Doug moves as the car lands, both eyes open, aiming down the top of his weapon, and puts a short burst into Big Shot's head. Josef shuffles up to the shattered driver side window, firing his long, suppressed handgun into the brainpans of the two broken men in the car. He notes a small gym bag on the shotgun seat floor before turning his view to the house.

The door of the house flies open and a fourth Albanian runs out into the cold air, wearing a tank top and brandishing a handgun; Doug stitches him with short bursts until he drops, a final burst anchoring him. Doug removes his nearly empty magazine and puts it in his outer jacket pocket, then locks in a fresh one and press checks the bolt. He keeps the Skorpion pointed at the doorway with one hand while removing a tiny hand grenade from a pocket with the other. Holding the spoon down, he pulls the pin out with his strong-hand pinkie. Josef walks up with his pistol pointed at the door. "Do it."

Doug ducks into the house and throws the grenade down a hallway to the left, stepping back out of the doorway. BANG. Doug moves in, the Skorpion locked in his shoulder in a firing stance; Josef follows, pausing in the smoking main room, and scans with his pistol. Doug sprints quickly down the short hallway, checking the bathroom, bedroom and a closet before returning. "Clear," Doug notes to Josef, who then searches the room. A collapsed table on its side has spilled white powder from a mixing bowl, and assorted bags and boxes are blown open onto the floor and the room's only couch. Awful Balkan music blares out of a cheap tabletop stereo.

Josef pokes through the bags, finding his target – stuffed with rolls of Canadian and American bills. "Let's go," he says to Doug, nodding at the door. They exit the house quickly, scanning outside with their weapons, then duck back into the shadowy trail and stow their weapons in their satchels. Josef peeks at his watch, the illuminated hands jumping out against the darkness. In the cul de sac, a dog barks, and neighbors begin poking their heads out of doors and windows.

Josef puts his hand on Doug's shoulder, squeezing it. "We have to keep moving or I'm going to drop dead." Doug steps in closer, supporting Josef's sagging frame with his left arm, slowing their pace, but maintaining steady movement. Doug wonders at the ease with which he moves the iron mountain of his childhood, still healthy but shrinking, through the black. After several minutes, Josef checks his watch again. The wail of odd sirens sound in the distance, moving laterally down a main street. Josef sucks in a gulp of air, speaking. "Ignition of the charge to exfiltration, seventy seconds. Three minutes and change since we hit the trail. Doing a little better than I thought I could."

Doug tugs Josef to the right. "Over here." They move off the main trail onto a branch that crosses a small park with a soccer field, then enter the parking lot of a medical practice. Doug opens the passenger door of a ten-year-old hatchback and unzips Josef's jacket and pants, pulling them off, revealing a layer of casual clothing beneath. He eases Josef down into his seat in the darkness, having previously disabled the interior dome light, then squats and removes Josef's shoes. He bags them, pulls several layers of socks from his grandfather's feet, and slides on boat shoes. Josef slows his heavy breathing consciously, leaning back in the seat, looking up through the sunroof at the Milky Way.

Doug pauses, putting his hand on Josef's chest. "Grampa, are you okay?"

Josef breathes for several beats before speaking in a labored tone. "I'll be fine. Just finish your job." Doug shrugs, stands and removes his outer garments. He closes the passenger door, circles around back to the trunk with handfuls of clothing and pops the trunk, stuffing the clothing into a gym bag under a blanket and assorted gear. The two weapons satchels go into the gym bag, and Doug removes his own shoes and several pairs of socks before slipping on running shoes. He removes a small handgun from his pocket, pauses, then returns it to the same pocket. He zips the bag closed before covering the entire assembly with blankets. He shuts the trunk, gets into the driver's seat and starts the engine. "Here we go."

Doug flips the headlights on before pulling out onto an arterial, heading south towards downtown. Scant traffic populates the roads, save for the occasional emergency vehicle whipping past on cross streets towards the scene of their operation. Doug glances at Josef occasionally with a concerned expression, but Josef smiles, pats Doug's leg, and points forward. "Doug, I'm fine. Just keep your eye on your job."

They pull to a stop at a red light in front of a fire station. The two watch a team of men scramble onto a ladder truck, crank on the siren, and head out, lead by a supervisor's truck. Josef looks at Doug and smiles calmly. "You did good, kid. You did good. Just keep breathing and driving."

Doug's heart races, but he feels elated, rather than the expected panic. "That was fucked. They were like sitting ducks. That was some easy shit. Oh my God."

Josef pats Doug's leg again, reassuringly. "That was the easy part, boy. The hard part comes next. Never mind. If you feel sick, pull over so's you don't throw up in your lap."

Doug shakes his head. "No, I'm fine. I just want to get out of here. Driving slowly... is taking considerable effort."

Josef nods. "Just get to the garage without speeding."

Minutes later, Doug pulls the little hatchback into a blacked-out gas station next to a marina, one of the garage doors rolls up as planned. Doug pulls into the service bay and sees their contact standing by the door at his left. Doug puts the car into park, shuts off the engine and steps out, removing his gloves and holding them out to their host.

Jim McReady – slightly doughy, sandy brown hair, about sixty years old, a prototypical working class west coast Canadian of his age – closes the garage door and shakes Doug's hand enthusiastically, taking the gloves in his left hand. "Doug!" He circles the car to assist Josef. "Mr. Shea! It's great to see you."

Josef, now on his feet, pats McReady's shoulder as they shake hands, also handing over his gloves. "Good to see you, Jimmy. Are you ready for us?"

McReady nods, serious now. "I've got you covered from here." He leads them into a side office, chatting, and steps aside to reveal the bureaucrat and the soldier standing in front of a desk, the soldier holding a black SIG handgun at his side. The soldier edges to the wall, keeping his distance and waving the weapon to two chairs. "Sit down and keep your hands where we can see them." Doug and Josef comply.

The bureaucrat turns to McReady. "Get the equipment." He waits for McReady to leave the room before speaking further. "Okay, the weapon is a precautionary measure thanks to the young hothead there. Sorry, Josef. Nothing personal."

Josef shrugs. "Didn't take it that way. Would appreciate it if your man would put it away, however."

The soldier looks to the bureaucrat and back at the seated pair, shakes his head but keeps his gun pointed at the floor.

The bureaucrat sits on the desk. "With that out of the way, let's get down to business. The weapons are ready, correct?"

"Correct." Josef nods. "Everything is bagged up, no prints. Mags are unchanged. Do what you do."

McReady enters the office behind Doug and Josef, holding up the unzipped duffel bag. "Got two bags with all weapons accounted for, another with bundles of cash, and of course the clothes. Clothes go into the furnace here. The weapons will be discovered by an RCMP-DEA joint task force. A biker gang expanding from marijuana into the heroin business."

Doug puts his hand up. "Should you be saying all of this in front of us? Is this really something we need to know?"

The other men laugh. Josef turns to Doug. "Of course you need to know. You're one of us now. You've made your bones, kid."

The soldier puts away his pistol and grins, holding out his hand. "Welcome to the team, Douglas Shea."

Doug, feeling the weight of the eyes in the room on him, stands and accepts the offered hand, shaking it firmly. He flashes a smile to reduce the tension. "Thanks. And what's your name?"

"Green. Lawrence Green. I'll be keeping in touch with you. You report to your granddad, and I report to Mr. Miller," gesturing to the bureaucrat. "We'll get lunch sometime; I'll fill you in on how this works, and you can introduce me to some of them college girls." The other men laugh as Doug stares. "Come on, man, just fucking around. Your grandfather, well, seniority has its privileges. We're just trying to patch up a rough spot. Mr. Shea," he says, turning to Josef and standing almost at attention. "I apologize for the impertinent act. That was for Douglas's benefit, since he was an unknown quantity. It wasn't my idea, sir."

Josef stands quickly, looking more like his old self than Doug has seen in some time, extending his hand. They shake. "My pleasure, Mr. Green. Doug is an extremely capable young man, and a fast learner. That said, I still have veto power during his probationary period. Charles and I," he pauses to catch Mr. Miller's eyes, "have a pre-existing agreement. As you noted, seniority has its privileges."

Doug and Josef watch the sun rise over the Cascade mountain range, portside, from the bow of a passenger ferry. Bundled against the winds of the Strait and sipping steaming coffee from insulated travel cups, they remain silent for much of the trip. Eventually, Josef surveys their surroundings for listeners before speaking. "Doug, you did well. You did very, very well. No hesitation, like a seasoned professional. I'm proud of you. And I didn't manipulate you."

Doug sighs. "Well, you did, but I'm not mad." Smiling.

Josef stares with a knowing expression.

Scouring the Hatchet

"Next phase, Douglas."

That evening, back home at the kitchen table, Josef plops down a thick manila envelope in front of his grandson, along with a top-bound legal pad and a variety of pens and markers. "This packet contains a fictional target list, all within a twenty-mile radius of an urban center, with an intelligence packet for each target - their home, their workplace, details about their personal life. You will:

One: Define your team needs

Two: Define your equipment needs

Three: Define your logistical needs – transport, lodging, expenses, and so forth.

Four: Define your operational plan – where you'd take them, when, and why that approach.

"To make it simple, we posit a one-time supply of equipment. You and your team are operating without support other than infiltration and extraction. You have neither support from local government, nor a network to rely upon. In reality, we don't want to be in that position, but this will keep your mind sharp and avoid Rambo scenarios. Any questions?"

Doug sits back, looking to the ceiling to gather his thoughts. "America? Europe? Where?"

Josef nods. "That's defined in the packet. Canada, specifically Toronto. To keep this straightforward, let's avoid getting too fictional and keep your team requirements to numbers, instead of getting into language skills and anything exotic."

Doug opens the envelope, spreading the paper-clipped packets out and unfolding a large map of the Toronto metro area. "Can I specify gender of team members?"

Josef shrugs. "Sure, that's worth considering."

"Okay. Any limitations on hardware?"

"Keep it straightforward," Josef says. "Real-world, and feasible. Nothing experimental if it can't be whipped up by a standard machine shop, or its equivalent isn't available on the global market. Let's say nothing exotic or theoretical."

Doug spends Friday and Saturday developing his mission plan, turning in the work Sunday morning after performing a final review over two cups of coffee and a light breakfast. Josef reviews the plan, presented in outline form, in his favorite chair while listening to Chopin's Nocturnes, marking up the document with red ink. Doug hops down the stairs and places his overnight bag next to the front door, then approaches Josef.

"Pops, I should get back. I have a big assignment due tomorrow. Any initial feedback?" Doug asks.

Josef looks up from behind his reading glasses. "Pretty good so far. Take this with you and put together an intel packet using the university library. Just avoid creating an electronic footprint. Do NOT use your account." Josef picks up a letter-sized envelope from the side table and holds it between his index and middle fingers.

Doug takes it. "Who is it?"

Josef smiles. "Okay. Sit down a minute, son." Doug sits on the couch beneath the bay window, holding the envelope in both hands. "Our people cut me off from researching the men who killed your dad. Right away. They were concerned about blowback, conflict with other factions within the government. As you saw in that report – read it again, in depth – it was a casual team of FBI and DEA working together, but not operating within the usual command structure. Do you remember the event report, what they said about your dad?"

Doug cocks his mouth sideways while recalling the text. "Yeah. The DEA believed that he was working with drug traffickers, including Steve's dad and uncle, or, at minimum, looking the other way. But the FBI exonerated him."

Josef leans forward. "Connect the dots, Douglas. WAS he doing that?"

Doug opens his mouth slightly, eyes wide.

"Correct." Josef pushes himself out of his chair and walks a short loop in the living room, lecturing. "It was a warning, a shot across the bow. Our faction has been involved in covert operations since the 1930s. What do all of the academics say goes hand in hand with intelligence operations?"

Doug leaned back into the cushions for support. "Drugs. Crime."

"They're somewhat correct. They exaggerate, but it's somewhat correct. Intelligence work often relies on criminals. Much of what we do, even with government sanction, is technically illegal, thus it must be deniable. So you have cut-out companies and shady people running things, and lines become blurred." Josef points to the envelope in Doug's hand. "Back to reality. You father wasn't a drug dealer; he wasn't involved in our activities. Well, hadn't been for several years. He was going easy on, in his words, people in the community who made mistakes. His leniency brought the ire of the DEA, and frankly, the more information I've gotten, the more I believe that he was killed by another government faction to handcuff me and our activities. And we have to do something about it."

Doug stands, fuming. "I feel like you're dragging me into a vortex, Pops."

Josef puts his hands up. "Doug, read the packet. It's in the names. From your father's friend Hopkins, the handlers, the leadership. The foot soldiers were within their jurisdiction, but the people at the top give it away. Between Hopkins and that envelope, it draws a picture. And I think we can get them. If we can make a case within the realm of feasibility, and with my vote, I'm positive we can get consensus to act. To punish them for what they did to your dad, and to you."

Doug tears the envelope open, pausing, calming himself. "You could have just spoken to me about this in a straightforward way. You're hiding things. You've always been direct with me. Was I supposed to call you on the phone, freaking out?"

"I'm sorry, Doug. I'm upset, too. Another friend of your father's gave me that information. He just retired. Judge Lee, who worked with Sheriffs Bryce and the coroner. Those are his uncensored notes from the investigation. He recorded names, dates, phone numbers of every discussion he had, every intervention. Federal authorities instructed the coroner to revise the report you read earlier. I wanted you to see the official story, and then see the truth. Well. It's time for you to hit the road. Want a coffee to go? Drive safe, son. There's a lot of work ahead."

Josef reviews Doug's mission plan once more, nodding with approval. The weapons detailed in the plan were all available in their basement armory, and relatively common in the open market.

Mission Plan:

Five targets within 25-mile radius in area of Toronto, Ontario, Canada

Target summary:

47 year old male, lawyer

Work place: Weingarten LLP, Adelaide St E and Yonge St, #3400, Toronto

Residence: Lakefront home Hubbard Blvd & Hammersmith Ave, "The Beach" neighborhood, Toronto

Automobile: 1992 BMW M3, black

Relations: live-in boyfriend, no children

62 year old male, Editor, Toronto Globe and Mail

Work place: 444 Front St West

Residence: Melita Place, Brampton. Doug's handwriting notes "Borders Hilldale Park"

Automobile: 1985 Saab 900, green

Relations: wife, 58 years old, 3 grown children, do not live in the home

41 year old male, Police detective, Toronto Police Service

Work place: 22 Division, 3699 Bloor St W, Toronto

Residence: Guernsey Dr, Etobicoke. Noted, "Densely populated neighborhood"

Automobile: 1990 Ford Taurus SHO, bronze

Relations: 36 year old wife, 2 young children in home

54 year old female, University Administrator

Work place: UT St. George, Knox College, #307 (office)

Residence: 200 block of College St, Toronto – noted, "secure building, second floor"

Automobile: none

Relations: none

34 year old female, City Councilor #19, Trinity – Spadina ward

Work place: 226 Bathurst St A, Toronto – noted, "ward office"

Residence: 1000 block Queen St W, Toronto – noted, "apartment, secure building"

Automobile: 1981 Volvo wagon, silver

Relations: 41 year old boyfriend, no children

Team: Req. 4 men, 3 minimum.

Equipment:

Due to urban environment and nature of targets, team will employ only suppressed, compact weapons.

4 gun belts.

2 suppressed .32 ACP handguns. Preferred system is Beretta 82BB with safety/decocker modified to allow single shots from locked slide for silence and case retention. Suppressors are compact wet environment cans using wipes, ~4" length. Alternatively, single stack Model 85 .380 with same mods. Holsters for each, one spare magazine each with pocket carrier. Subsonic hardcast lead flat nose cartridges.

2 suppressed 9mm handguns. Preferred system is original Beretta 92 with frame mounted thumb safety. Alternatively, Taurus PT-92 series. Suppressors are wet environment cans using wipes, ~6" length. Holsters for each. Two spare magazines each with belt carrier. Subsonic 147 grain hollowpoint cartridges.

1 Thompson/Center Contender, 10" barrel in .300 Whisper with 8" long 1.5" diameter suppressor, aluminum body. Fitted with Choate side-folding stock and a 4x scope. Briefcase bag for storage / transport. Ammunition –both subsonic and supersonic projectiles.

2 leather saps or blackjacks.

4 Motorola radios with earpiece and throat mic.

2 police scanners modified for cellular bands.

4 utility pocket knives.

2 sets of lock picks.

2 1' long pry bars.

2 pairs of 18" bolt cutters.

4 Surefire flashlights, batteries.

4 pairs police leather gloves.

4 balaclavas.

8 coveralls.

2 high visibility safety vests.

2 safety helmets.

2 compact toolboxes, 21" length.

2 rolls thick moisture barrier.

4 monthly bus passes.

4 pagers.

2 Nokia mobile phones, one for team lead and one floating.

<u>Logistics</u>:

Two vehicles, preferably one panel van and one sedan. Sedan used for scouting, tailing, C&C, day to day use. Van for operations.

Apartment or rental house for 2-3 weeks. Time allows for familiarity with region, traffic, observation of target routines as not included in packet, and operations.

Expenses –

2 rolls of coins for telephone calls and small purchases per person per week.

$100CD per person per day, $500CD/week other expenses held by team lead for fuel, incidentals.

Operations Plan & Assumptions:

- Target at home. Snatch & grab possible.

- Surveil and determine approach. Home has easy approach, but spouse likely present. Car park at office, or potentially office itself, or during commute. Snatch & grab possible.

- Surveil and determine approach. Home is off limits due to family presence, neighborhood density. Workplace is equally challenging. Plan: take during commute or work hours using two vehicles and full team. Snatch & grab highly unlikely.

- Surveil and determine approach. Lives and works in heavily populated, high traffic area with restricted auto access. Assume operations require foot team supported by van.

- Plan for snatch & grab, most likely at residence, which is on the edge of a commercial district. Assuming late night opportunities based on implied lifestyle.

Josef adds notes in the margins while reading, circling entries and adding questions, then sets the document and pen on an end table. He slowly rises out of his chair, creaking and straining, and grabs a hand-carved wooden cane from an umbrella holder to steady himself. He moves slowly through the hallway to a small closet. Josef puts his left index finger into the hole in the doorframe's strike plate, pushes a switch, and then presses the right side wall, which swings open to reveal a lit staircase. He works his way down the stairs, slowly, holding the handrail in a death grip for each step. At the bottom of the stairs he enters a code into a vault door's keypad lock, then steps into a large, brightly lit, well ventilated concrete room crammed with racks, filing cabinets and shelves neatly but tightly packed with firearms and crates. Josef dons gloves and moves down the left row to a large drawer system neatly labeled with makes and models, stopping at the BERETTA drawer. He opens it and transfers four small black handguns, several magazines, holsters, magazine carriers and suppressors to an empty desk on the north end of the room. He returns to the same drawer, this time withdrawing several older Beretta 92 pistols and accoutrements.

Josef closes the drawer then moves to a middle aisle rich with submachine guns on one side and scoped precision rifles on the other. At the far end of the row, he selects two short single shot rifles with scopes and suppressors, one of them with a folding stock and one with a quick detachable fixed stock. He places them on the worktable and returns to the same spot, selecting eight 20-round boxes of ammunition, two slings and two ammunition pouches from a cubbyhole.

Back at the worktable, Josef stretches his back briefly, then begins sorting the equipment into two identical groups of two of the small Model 82s, two Model 92s, and the T/C Contender carbine, along with their supporting material. Finally, he selects two medium-sized gym bags and a handful of ditty bags for sorting the accessories and packs the kits, testing the heft of the bags, guessing each bag weighs no more than 15 pounds. He selects a clipboard mounted to one of the shelf ends and scribbles out "4 B Md 82, 4 B Md 92, 2 T/C. Re-up" on a new line of other notes about weapons and equipment, noting the date. He pauses briefly before moving to another crowded shelf to his left, selecting a 1' x 1' olive drab plastic crate emblazoned with white Dutch script. Unlocking the crate, he looks inside, removing a dozen of the same type of tiny golf-ball sized grenades Doug used in Victoria. He grabs from another box two thick, screw-together watertight plastic canisters and places six of the grenades in each before sealing them and adding the two canisters to the gym bags.

His work complete, Josef slings a bag over each shoulder and slowly moves back up the steep stairs, gripping the handrails on each side fiercely, before shutting the thick hidden door with a thump, the overhead lights blinking out.

Learning is Fun-damental

Doug arrives at his apartment minutes after 4 p.m., just in time to feel good about the $50/month fee he pays for a parking spot in the tiny secure garage beneath the building, as 15th Ave NE and the surrounding streets are crammed with the cars of students and other residents home for the week. He focuses his thoughts walking up the stairwell, repeating his plan like a mantra. Get to work. Call Cathy. Definitely call Cathy, put together a timeline, then get to work. He drifts down the hallway, greeting the neighboring party girls outside their door who call out to him. Doug unlocks the door to his apartment as quickly and smoothly as possible to escape before the girls interpret Mike's pot smoke as an invitation to come in.

"Hey, dude," he says, blowing past Mike, who is eating cereal in front of the TV. No bongs are presently lit, but smoke lingers in the room, and the windows are shut.

"Hey, man, where ya been?" asks Mike, standing, nearly dropping his large bowl of cereal, cursing and shifting it within his hands to not spill milk. "Is your gramps OK?"

Doug pauses. Protocol. "He's better. Neighbors are back and can check in on him. Did I miss anything good?"

Mike shakes his head. "Some chick called a few times for you. Didn't leave a message. Got a girl on the hook, buddy?" He grins, bits of cereal in his teeth.

Doug laughs. "You crack me up, dude. Sorry if I've been stand-offish lately. Worried about gramps. Whatcha watching? I have to write a paper... uh and make a call...." His eyes drift towards the hallway and his room.

Mike shakes his head. "Do your shit, but let's hang out tonight if you can. New Simpsons tonight."

Doug nods and smiles. "Sounds good. I need to decompress. Later."

That night, Doug and Cathy sit across from each other in a dingy diner southeast of 45th and Highway 99, sipping coffee and pouring over their Anthropology notes.

Despite the events two Fridays ago, Doug reverts to his usual stand-offish lack of forthrightness with females, the likely cause of the end of his one and only lasting previous relationship. Thus, a late night study ruse.

Cathy, on the other hand, isn't having it.

"How's your grandfather doing?" she asks.

Doug leans back in his chair and stirs his coffee mindlessly, locking eyes with her. "He's OK. The issue is that he's a stubborn old man in denial of his age. He's nearly eighty, and on his own when I'm not there. I feel bad." Doug sips his coffee, slumping slowly in his chair.

"You don't have any other family out there who can help him?" Cathy asks. "Liz told me that your parents are gone. I'm sorry to hear that."

Doug shrugs. "I barely remember my mother, photos aside. I was two when she left. My dad died when I was seven. It's been me and pops since then. I spent a bunch of summers in Spain with some cousins as a kid, but that's it. Pops insisted that I not stick around the Peninsula when I turned eighteen, but it kills me every time I turn my back on him. He has friends in the area, but he's not the most social guy." Doug smiles. "A neighbor lady fed us at least three meals a week for most of my life, and he still eats at their house at least that often. It's hard to describe the little community we have there, which I didn't even understand until I came here. People on the end of the world, taking care of each other. I don't know." He notices his slump, smiles and sits up, leans forward and puts out a hand. Cathy takes it. "Sorry; I don't want to bum you out. It's good to see you."

"It's good to see you, too." Cathy smiles and rubs that back of his hand with her thumb. "What a night. I'm glad that you're the kind of guy who is close with his family, as small as it might be. I can tell..." she pauses. "Don't be mad. I can tell you're holding something back, but I won't push you to say anything you're not comfortable with." She squeezes his hand.

"No, it's fair for you to have questions. Do you want the Reader's Digest version?"

She nods, "Sure, whatever that means."

Doug laughs. "It means the short version. I'm sure Liz has filled you in on my family drama. My dad was a cop, killed in the line of duty when I was a kid. Pretty bad, actually. But between church, scouting, sports, grandpa, and a lot of people looking out for me, here I am. How about you?"

Cathy shrugs. "It's not that odd to me, Doug. Basically every guy in my family was a soldier or a cop. Both of my grandfathers fought with the Americans against the Japanese during World War Two. They brought the family to California in the seventies, dragging a huge family around as migrants. All the boys went into the military. I have three brothers and a thousand aunts, uncles and cousins. My brother and some cousins are Seattle cops. Be warned, when I tell them formally that we're dating, they are going to look into you." She smiles. "It comes with the territory."

"No, that makes sense. I'm pretty old fashioned, believe it or not." Doug waves to the matronly waitress for more coffee. "Do you want anything else? I'm hungry."

Cathy shakes her head. "I'm good. OK, here's the thing I need to get out of the way. We got a little crazy at the rave, and you might think I'm a hypocrite, but I'm not going to give it up right away. I hope it's not a deal breaker."

Doug smiles. "Alright, but can you be less hot, then? That'll help, thanks."

Cathy laughs, her eyes bright. "You dork. So when did you learn kali?"

Doug shakes his head. "I learned from an escrima guy. Family friend. I didn't know some of what you were doing but just went with it. Did your family teach you?"

"Yeah. I wanted to learn what my brothers were doing with my dad and uncles, and I grew up in sort of a rough area." She focuses on the swirling vortex of her coffee, turning a spoon round and round. "Do you think that's weird?"

Doug shakes his head. "Doesn't bother me. I smelled like gunpowder that time because I spent the whole weekend shooting with my pops."

Cathy nods. "Lots of girls at school would be freaked out by that."

Doug grins a goofy grin. "Luckily I'm not interested in lots of girls."

Doug deposits Cathy at her front door with a hug and a warm kiss, tears himself away, and wishes her goodnight. As he drives to campus, his head is the clearest it has felt since his early teens. While he still lacks the laser focus of childhood – and assumes it will never return, now that he lives in reality – he feels something taking over within him, like a subroutine in the corner of his mind, drawing up plans and checklists.

A thought nags Doug as he moves through the night – his grandfather's quest for vengeance is like Orobouros, a serpent eating its own tail. The faction had developed organically, but evolved into a self-sustaining entity full of its own internal intrigues and power struggles. Charles McIntyre, still running the show at Vanguard after all these years, was their only verifiably genuine ally. Doug realizes that the best path forward is to present himself to McIntyre, of his own volition, bend the knee, and secure a mutual pact.

Still, to take control and prevent Josef from going on hits, the mission must continue, but directed by Doug. Thus, the trip to the Suzzallo and Allen libraries late at night with a purloined student ID. The microfiche newspaper archives and database terminals are accessible to any student, but due to the required ID swipe to access them, Doug suspects that an access log persists somewhere in the university network. Weeks ago – it seemed like a year – he'd pulled up the LA Times article his grandfather had mentioned at a terminal in the library, but hadn't dug any further. Well, now was the time.

Doug parks behind a nearby building, vacant due to the late weekend hour, and swipes through the library turnstile with his secondhand ID. He'd found it outside of a bar on the Ave one night, and recent checks of the student listing had revealed that "Jeff Davis" was still enrolled. Sorry not sorry, Jeff!

University of Washington libraries were always busy, even at 11 p.m. on a Sunday night. Weaving through a mass of students chatting in the lobby, Doug swipes Jeff Davis' ID at the turnstile sensor, then makes his way down a stairwell to Suzzalo's subterranean media center. Another swipe at the secure door and Doug sticks the ID in his jean coin pocket face-in, displaying the presence of an ID yet hiding the details from staff. He approaches the center's receptionist, a slim, pale, frizzy-haired grad student in her mid-20s reading a ridiculously thick, yellow-bound ironic postmodernist novel. Doug clears his throat; she glances up over her problem glasses.

"Hi, I'm working on a project for my journalism class, and need to use both the newspaper archives as well as LexisNexis to get current contact information. I've not used them before. Can you direct me to them?" Doug asks.

Frizzy manages not to sigh as she places a bookmark into her book and pushes herself up from the desk. She gives Doug a once-over and cracks the start of a grin. "Sure, c'mere." She turns while keeping her eyes on him.

Doug follows. He notices something off about Frizzy's physiology, although on paper she is passable. She stops at a microfiche station next to an enormous grid of drawers, each labeled alpha-numerically. Three bound folders labeled A-J, K-R and S-Z sit on the station's counter. Frizzy points. "These tell you the drawer, section and roll. Obviously, those are the drawers. Have you set up microfiche before?"

Doug nodds. "Yes, but not here. Can you give me a hand with the first one?" Laying it on a little thick.

"Sure." She puts her hand out, which Doug fills with his notepad, which begins:

LA Times
James Hopkins
October 22, 1982

Frizzy places the notepad on the counter and grabs the K-R folder. "Easy." She flips through to the LA Times section, October 1982. Doug leans in to watch her finger slide along the page. "LA Times has two rolls per year, so we'll just grab the second roll, which is in... drawer L12, section 7, roll 2." She steps over to the drawer and quickly finds the roll, then steps to the station and pops the microfiche container open. "It just drops into this drawer; line up like so – it'll click in and feed automatically." She powers up the viewer and turns the large central dial multiple times until she lands on the October 22nd edition. "OK, you're all set. Press this button here when you're done with the roll and are ready to put it back into the container."

Doug smiles. "Thanks, I appreciate it. I'll holler when I'm ready for the LexisNexis system."

Frizzy nods and bounces back to the reception desk, glancing at him and leaning across the desk to give him a view. Good God, Doug thinks, those late night library stories are real. At least she's helpful. He glances again at his purloined ID. Jeff Davis doesn't look much like him – at least the hair color somewhat matches - but was normal-looking enough that she might not be able to tell the difference if questioned a few months from now. He'd just have to be brusque if she continues to come onto him, or whatever she's doing. She's probably just bored.

Doug lands on his story almost immediately, A3, nearly half a page describing the fiery crash of Justice Department official Jim Hopkins. He zooms and prints the page, retrieves the print-out and marks it up with a highlighter. He ejects the microfiche cartridge and replaces it in its container, which he re-files. Scribbling out names and dates from the article on his notepad, Doug quickly develops an outline of his research sequence for LexisNexis. He glances at Frizzy, who is deep in her book, puffs up his chest a little, and moves to the LexisNexis terminal, which is locked behind a login. Crap.

Doug blanks out his face. "Pardon me, can you help me get set up on LexisNexis?"

Frizzy pushes off the desk again and strolls over to him, now chewing gum. She leans down over his shoulder and begins typing. He watches her fingers, not the screen.

"Sure. I'm Rebecca, by the way."

Username: SUZMED04

Password: login123. You're kidding me.

"Thanks, Rebecca, I'm Jeff." Her chin is an inch from his left eye.

"I know. Undergrad?" She glances down, a touch of disappointment in her voice.

"Yeah. You?"

She purses her lips. "Post. Journalism?" She glances at his print-out, the marquee image firefighters putting out a flaming car. "Well, looks like someone had a bad day."

"Yeah, a UW graduate wrote this story; I'm interviewing him for an article. Thanks for your help. So I just enter the search type into the command line, then fill out the search fields?" Doug elaborately directs Frizzy – Rebecca – to the screen and away from his face.

"Yep." His small talk deflection succeeds. "Let me know if you need anything else; I'm just reading." She peels off, as Doug's eyes watch the cursor blink on the command line beneath a selection of search types and their numeric labels. He enters "4," for person lookup, and hits return. Person Lookup populates with first, middle and last name fields, birth date, date of death, location, and keywords. Doug begins by entering James Hopkins and prints out all hits, which in LexisNexis includes residences, employment, and media mentions. He then collects other names that appear in the article, just to be thorough. Finally, he withdraws a carefully folded, aged photocopy of the incident report of his father's death and enters the names of the federal agents present. Levin. Vickers. Martinelli. A fount of data pours forth: locations, names, articles. Doug prints it all, underlining new cross-references and source material, then scans to plan his next move.

Levin left the FBI in 1989 for a judicial appointment, and is currently serving as a judge for the Western District of Washington. His home is on Queen Anne hill, on the southeastern slope. A rich array of local and national news articles refer to Levin, several with inflammatory titles. This should be interesting.

Vickers appears to still be serving with the DEA, lives in San Francisco and represents the Drug Enforcement Agency on Western United States multi-jurisdictional task forces in an executive role. Based on the relations report, two children and three divorces. A real Agency man.

Antonio Martinelli. SAC, Seattle office. All still within reach.

Doug sits back, reviewing the printouts scrawled with his notes and highlights, then numbers the article cites in a logical sequence. He logs out of the LexisNexis machine and stands, pushing the chair in like a gentleman. Back at the microfiche catalog, he marks up his article notes with information from the article catalog, spending the next hour retrieving and printing articles. Eventually Frizzy taps him on the shoulder, pointing to the clock. "Dude, it's almost two. I have to shut everything down in three minutes."

Doug survives his classes Monday thanks to high caffeine intake and selective attendance. He can't face the girls, so he blows off Anthro and spends the hour in an Allen library back corner next to a south-facing window, sketching out an increasingly convoluted and troubling picture about the men who, he now believes sincerely, murdered his father.

Over twenty dead in raids led by these men, disappearing witnesses, and a consistent focus on mid-sized drug operations plying the British Columbia – Washington border. While a joint FBI-DEA task force operating out Seattle would logically include this beat, the lack of variance is astonishing. Levin transferred to Los Angeles less than a month after the death of Sheriff Paul Shea, and participated in the "investigation" into Hopkins' death. He reappeared in Seattle in 1985. Doug had heard whisperings through the stoner grapevine, and had read about, very large, professional trafficking organizations that were seemingly impenetrable – one biker gang in particular, and a rumored crew founded by Vietnam vets that had gone completely white collar.

Vietnam vets.

Doug flips through his printouts. Levin, considerably younger than Vickers and Martinelli, was not a military veteran, and earned an undergrad degree from Yale in 1978 and a law degree from Columbia. Vickers and Martinelli were both Air Force veterans, stationed in Southeast Asia, Vickers an officer in an airlift unit and Martinelli an enlisted man in security. Both were assigned to Nakhon Phanom Air Base in Thailand during a common period, 1972 to 1974. Vickers left the Air Force for the DEA in 1975, while Martinelli stayed in until 1976, earned a degree from UCLA in 1979, then joined the FBI. His first assignment was in Seattle.

Doug flips back to Vickers' file. DEA assignments before Seattle: Virginia from 1975-1977, Los Angeles 1977-1979, then Seattle. A pattern. Levin's first assignment was Seattle, 1981. So. Vickers and Martinelli are joined at the hip, despite being in separate alphabet agencies. What was the common thread?

Air Force Vietnam vets. Doug sits up and re-sorts his documents into distinct bundles, sliding the groups into separate folders, then zips them into his bag. He makes his way to a library terminal and enters a Boolean search, VIETNAM AND "AIR FORCE" AND DRUGS. Several books come up immediately; Doug scrawls out the top two titles and author names on a piece of scrap paper.

The Politics of Heroin in Southeast Asia by Alfred W. McCoy

The Great Heroin Coup: Drugs, Intelligence & International Fascism by Henrik Krüger and Jerry Meldon

Doug modifies his search terms based on the text descriptions – CIA AND "DRUG TRAFFICKING" – this returns many of the same books, as well as new ones covering South and Central American operations. As a news junkie, Doug is familiar with the Iran / Contra scandal and its implications, as well as rumors about Contras smuggling cocaine into the US in the 80s, but has only a cursory familiarity with the material. He checks out several books using his pilfered student ID and heads back to his apartment for some speed reading.

Awaken From Your Dreams

A pattern emerges late that night, while Doug sips his fifth cup of coffee and peruses Usenet conspiracy and political discussion threads after skimming four books and jotting a dozen pages of notes. His stereo plays ambient music from the college radio station, nearly indistinguishable from background noise.

Doug balances a notepad on his leg and organizes his thoughts.

The Central Intelligence Agency is known for looking the other way when governments or non-state actors they support participate in criminal activity, whether as official policy or via individual decision-making.

The Royal Lao Government, for example, had collected opium as a form of tax from the hill tribes for hundreds of years. When the French colonized Indochina in the 19th century, this tax levy remained in place, with the Lao government passing a portion of the opium on to the French government, the remaining revenue covering most local government expenses.

The French government distributed their cut of the opium "legitimately," to their credit, although there was substantial evidence that individuals in this network were also involved in illicit traffic. When the French left Indochina, the government opium tax remained in place, as did the networks, both legitimate and illicit.

As the CIA developed anti-communist forces in Laos in the 1950s, they disregarded the local opium trade, as well as heroin processing by the government and specific government factions. Undermining this revenue resource would weaken support for US representatives and policies.

Investigators had uncovered rumors, as well as evidence, that individual employees of, and agents contracted to, or directed by, the CIA had personally participated in drug trafficking. This activity, however, was unsanctioned and unofficial. During the Vietnam War, several drug trafficking networks were established by American servicemen, the most sophisticated and farthest-reaching within the U.S. Air Force, for obvious logistical reasons.

Doug scribbles a large "DUH" beneath the last point, underlines it thrice, then throws his notepad against the wall. He stands, pacing the small room as much as possible – four steps in each direction.

"Fuck it." He grabs a large canvas gym bag from the closet, throwing his arm through the handle, then walks into the living room to find Mike asleep in front of the TV, his largest bong tipped precariously against the couch where he snores. Doug leans over, grabs the bong and moves it into a more protected nook, then enters Mike's room, wheeling his mountain bike out into the living room then out the front door.

An hour before sunrise, the cloudless sky slowly brightening to a steel grey, Doug sits on a steep hillside staircase on Queen Anne Hill, surrounded by overgrown boxwood, and stares at the front door of an imposing turn of the century pseudo-Victorian home with a commanding view of Elliott Bay. Mike's bike is wedged between the enormous boxwood and the handrail at the base of the stairs, waiting. Doug had changed out his clothes in his Bronco for two disposable layers – a base layer of long underwear, a coverall, and a windbreaker with a hood, as well as a knit cap and a riding mask to both protect against the November cold and conceal his face. A pair of oversized boots are tightened over four layers of socks, slightly awkward but tolerable. A small backpack is slung backwards across his chest, the top partly unzipped.

It's Tuesday, so barring a major change of plans, The Honorable Eric Levin will begin his day at a reasonable hour to allow for the scheduled 8 a.m. opening of his courtroom. He will either back his car out of the retrofit garage twenty feet to the left of the front door, or catch the downtown bus a block away. Doug holds a paper bus schedule up to catch a sliver of streetlight from the road above, comparing it against his watch's tritium dial. The next bus comes in twelve minutes, then twenty-seven minutes, every fifteen like clockwork.

Three minutes later the garage door swings up slowly. There he is, Judge Levin, dressed in gym clothes and holding a small satchel, walking past a Jaguar coupe to a Mercedes Benz sedan. Now. Doug draws a suppressed Skorpion machine pistol from the backpack, chambers a round and flips the stock down, then sprints across the traffic-free street. He crosses the cobblestone driveway and strides right to the edge of the garage, gun up in both hands and stock pressed tightly against his shoulder. Levin looks up in surprise.

Doug speaks one word: "Levin." He loses all discipline and empties the twenty round magazine into the man, clak-ak-ak-ak-ak-ak, right into the center of his chest, following Levin with a stream of bullets as he collapses to the ground. Levin's body settles awkwardly to rest, his head and left arm against the edge of the car in the tight garage, a pool of blood spreading quickly beneath the thoroughly dead judge. Doug reloads, running to the garage door opener by the entry to the house; he stuffs the Skorpion into the backpack and presses the garage door button. He sprints out beneath the closing door, stepping over where he assumes a safety sensor beam would be, then crosses the street and grabs the bicycle, hopping on it and zipping down the street for several blocks before veering directly south down a steep, straight lane. Half a mile later, he finds his Bronco parked beside a heavily wooded greenbelt. He throws the bike in the back before closing up the tailgate, then changes out of his disposable clothes back into his usual wear, removing the boots and all but one layer of socks, then dons sneakers. All of the clothing from the job goes into the satchel, which Doug rests on the passenger seat as he calmly drives east towards home, then disposes of the bag in an alley dumpster in Lower Queen Anne.

I'm not going to be able to do that again, Doug thinks to himself, as his mind races, analyzing the job. Levin was the softest target of the three, and with him down, the others will likely be suspicious. Although a U.S. District Court Judge would have a lot of potential enemies. But how many would be in danger of being sprayed with a submachine gun? Shit. Twenty rounds from a .32 is obvious. Shit. I used the same type of weapon in Victoria a few weeks ago, as well. Double shit.

On one hand, I'll need this weapon more than ever. On the other hand, it's a giant, radioactive liability, so even if I re-cache it, that cache is also tied to the murder of a federal judge. I have to ditch this thing. I probably have to shed myself of all connections to Skorpions and .32 ACP handguns. I'm an idiot.

As he drives on, considering his options for safe disposal of an illegal fully automatic murder weapon, it occurs to Doug that their entire faction would automatically assume he had wasted Levin, and law enforcement in B.C. and the US – possibly even INTERPOL – would tie Levin's murder to the Victoria operation. No illusions that they have some loyalty to him and his father. Time to bend the knee.

Niche weapon, in an increasingly marginalized chambering – a giant strobing signature. Way to go, dipshit.

Two hours later, Doug stands before the impressive tropical hardwood reception installation within Vanguard Industries' offices at the Port of Seattle. He had showered, shaved, and pressed and donned his best white collared shirt, accenting his light grey wool suit with a red and gold striped club tie.

"Yes, may I help you?" asks the receptionist, a petite, curly haired redhead of his own age. She looks him over for a response with her bright green eyes. Doug had steeled himself with a shot of whiskey and a No-Doz before leaving his apartment, vanquishing doubt. Doubt? No way to move but forward.

Doug puts on his most charming and confident façade. "Hi, Douglas Shea. I'm here to see Mr. McIntyre."

The receptionist smiles with slight surprise, glancing down at the calendar blotter on her desk, then back to Doug and rises from her chair. "Yes, uh, Mr. Shea, please come with me." She gestures to the smaller hidden door to the right of the Vanguard Industries sign on the wall behind her. To the left is a large, hardwood double door, which leads to conference rooms and other offices; the right leads directly to McIntyre's private reception area and office. Doug follows, distracted by the receptionist. She holds open the door, waving him in. "Would you like a cup of coffee, or some water, while you wait for Mr. McIntyre?" Her eye contact is excellent.

Doug shakes his head. "No, thank you." He enters the room, noticing the floor to ceiling windows looking out over the port, a luxurious brown leather sofa, tropical hardwood coffee table, and two other doors. The door ahead leads to McIntrye's office, the other to a conference room. He turns to the receptionist, who stands by the door, waiting and observing him. "My appointment was somewhat last minute. Do you know if he'll be long? Not that I mind waiting."

She shakes her head, smiling. "No, Mr., ah, Shea, he should be in the office momentarily. It's not quite 8 a.m. yet." She lets the door close behind her before leaning against it. "I know who you are."

"Oh?" Doug reacts a little more than planned.

Her smile grows larger. Her skin is very fair, but clear and healthy-looking, with a scattering of freckles across the bridge of her nose. Cute. "Yes, I've met and spoken with your grandfather several times. He's very nice. Mr. McIntyre told me that he's a part owner of Vanguard. From the description, I expected you to be, ah, a little less... what's the word?" She looks him over.

He takes a risk. "Handsome?" Smiling.

She laughs, blushing. "I'd better get back up front, ah, Mr. Shea."

Doug can't stop smiling. "Then you'd better go. Call me Doug."

She shakes her head. "No, I'd better call you Mr. Shea. Bye," dragging out the last syllable as she steps backwards through the door, watching him.

Doug adjusts his belt and clears his throat, looking around the room again, then spots a black Town Car through the window, pulling into a parking space below. McIntyre. A Driver, in the professional sense, steps out of the front seat, opening the rear passenger door, and out steps Charles McIntyre, dressed in what appears to be the prototypical immaculate dark grey suit, blue shirt and black tie Doug always remembered him in. They disappear from view; two minutes later the door to McIntyre's office swings open, and a fit forty-something woman in an on-point skirted suit enters the room. "Mr. McIntyre will see you now, Doug," she says, grinning knowingly.

"Thank you." Doug searches his memory for the woman's face but can't place her. Of course, she's probably a senior secretary, executive assistant, whatever, and would know all of McIntyre's business. He enters the office, an extremely formal room with deep green carpet, dark formal hardwood paneling on the walls, and a massive matching desk, recalling to Doug an "English private library." Through another door, in steps Charles McIntyre, large and still imposing in his eighties, grinning like a long-lost great uncle. He walks quickly to Doug, chuckling, his arms out for a bear hug, which Doug accepts.

"Douglas, Douglas, so good to see you. You look like quite the gentleman." McIntyre steps back at arm's length, evaluating him. "Ah, yes, it's been too long. Have you been thinking about my offer?"

Doug nods, somewhat surprised. Ah, the secretary. "Yessir, I have."

McIntyre looks to the secretary. "Marcia." She nods, leaving the room. "Douglas, please, sit down," gesturing to a substantial chair in front of the desk. Doug sits.

"Douglas, your grandfather tells me that all went well on your sailing trip. That you performed admirably. I trust Josef Shea with my life, and have long looked forward to the day when I could bring you into our world." McIntyre leans across his desk, opens a burl humidor, then turns the assortment of large cigars towards Doug. Doug shakes his head. "To offer you some shelter from the storm. Especially relevant nowadays. If I may be candid, you've met some men with whom Josef has found himself engaged, in lieu of their sponsor; men who have, I believe, gone off-script."

Doug nods. "I'm not sure it's my place to comment, sir."

McIntyre sits and waves dismissively, sparking an enormous flame from a desk lighter that appears to be set within a gold nugget. Several draws later, a puff of smoke and a cherry going, he leans back in his chair and fixes his eyes with Doug's. "Nonsense; you're a sensible man. So you want to come work for Vanguard. A condition of employment is candor. Tell me, what was your impression of the two men who visited you? I am familiar with them, and have my own opinions."

Doug, still unsure of the play, decides he has nothing more that isn't already on the table. "Well, sir, they come off as... unseemly. The young guy, the black guy, Green, he has the air of a soldier, but ambitious. I don't trust him. Miller, he strikes me as a company man. And considering the company, sir, I don't trust him, either. They were leaning on my grandfather. Sir," he concludes, sitting back.

McIntyre nods, waving his cigar. "And for good reason. I'm going to be open with you, Douglas. There may be rare occasions when I don't tell you the whole story, but I'll inform you upfront. It's often to your benefit to have as little information as possible. Not where it would endanger you, of course. Regardless,

Miller and Green report to the son of an old comrade of your grandfather's – and mine – whose interests have evolved. Personally, I've not had any business dealings with him for some time. Josef remained engaged with him, I suspect due to loyalties arising from his father's shared Balkan experience, and the goings-on there now. Hence." He beams, knowingly.

Doug nods. "I wasn't wild about it, sir, but felt I owed it to my grandfather to join him. Now it feels like the brakes have been taken off a train. I told him that they have a careless air about them, like they're just using us, and we need help. Well, here we are."

McIntyre stands carefully, places his cigar in a burlwood ashtray, and walks around to the front of his desk, leaning against it and looking down at Doug. "Yes, here we are. Here's what I'd like to do. I'd very much like for you to begin working with me immediately. I have a man who can get you up to speed. Furthermore, please feel free to reach out any time you'd like to talk. I wish that your grandfather did not live at the end of the world. I suspect that some of his choices are influenced by isolation. But, it was an excellent place for you to grow up. Just look at you. Healthy, robust. You see the difference between yourself and many of your classmates at university, do you not? Anyhow. Call the office at any time; we have a service, and you will be directed to me if I am available. I'd also like to host you for dinner at my home. Soon. Early next week, perhaps?" He stands and proffers his hand.

Doug stands and accepts it. "Excellent, sir. Monday or Tuesday would work well. I'll be there."

"Good, good." McIntyre embraces him, patting his back with vigor. "Welcome to your birthright. Marcia will contact you to arrange dinner, as well as your start date. I presume you're back to school?" McIntyre walks Doug back to the waiting room and the lobby door.

"Yessir." Doug nods. "I've missed class a bit lately, with everything going on. I have to buckle down and finish the quarter strong or my grades will take a hit."

"Well then. Best be off. Thank you, Douglas. Welcome aboard." McIntyre holds the door for him as Doug walks into the lobby, turning and nodding. The receptionist, speaking animatedly on a headset, glances up at him, smiling and giving a little wave, as he walks by. Holy shit, Doug asks himself. What just happened?

While he had foregone his earliest two classes for the meeting with Charles McIntyre, Doug urgently needed normalcy, so he drives straight to campus through a light rain and pays $6 to park onsite. He enters his Anthropology class in his suit, slightly damp. Doug generally holds umbrellas in disdain, like all proud mossbacks, but acknowledges their sensibility in this garb. His appearance garners a whistle from an anonymous classmate as he makes his way directly to a beaming Cathy. Liz is her usual casual self, wearing an open zip hoodie and a form fitting flannel shirt and jeans with Converse sneakers; Cathy is dressed down similarly, but with her silky black hair pulled up into a tight, striking bun. "Whoa, look at this handsome stranger," Liz asks Cathy. "Do you recognize him?"

Cathy sits back, patting the chair next to her. "Where were you yesterday?"

Doug sits and turns to the girls while hauling out a notepad and pen. "My granddad isn't doing so great. I had to go see a friend of his this morning to ask for help with some things. He's a pretty old-fashioned guy, thus," he gestures to his suit. "Gotta say, I see the appeal."

Cathy pinches his collar lightly, running her hand up and down it. "Nice fabric. I like it." She rests her hand on his left forearm. "Sorry to hear about your grandfather."

"Thanks." Doug rests his right hand on hers. "Sorry for the disappearing act."

Their disheveled-as-usual professor stumbles into the room, officially starting the class. They sit back and begin taking notes. Doug's mind drifts frequently, exhaustion taking hold as the caffeine wears off, and he sees, over and over in his mind's eye, a storm of lead carving out the chest of the Honorable Eric Levin, who had been younger and more athletic than Doug had expected, if shorter.

Late Thursday night. Doug sits at his desk, typing a half-formed essay for Anthropology, searching for a thesis. His battered old desktop phone rings on the second line. Doug lifts the receiver, adjusting the cord around the desk to speak. "Hello?"

From a million miles away, faint and scratchy. "Doug." Josef.

"Hi, pops." Doug puts the handset against his shoulder and leans into it, closing his eyes. "How are you doing?"

"Well, better now." Silence. Doug waits. "Seen the news?"

Doug shrugs. "I don't watch the news, but might know what you're talking about."

Josef laughs through the line, mechanically. "Well done. I spoke with Charles as well. I'm very happy that you reached out to him. This is gonna be good, kid. Any chance you can come visit this weekend?"

Doug leans back. "Sorry. I should probably stay in town this weekend. I'm digging my way out of a classwork hole. Next week I was planning on heading home late Tuesday night for Thanksgiving. I'll bring the turkey from that farm up north and head over on the ferry. I'm having dinner at Mr. McIntyre's Monday. Any chance you could come in for that? He'd really like to see you."

A pause. "I might. You know, I'll do that. I'll give him a call. That sounds tremendous. OK, Doug. I'll see you then. Be well."

"Goodnight, pops. Love ya." Doug hangs up the receiver with a clang. Well, that was quick. A tremor goes up his back. He slides open his drawer and brings out his father's service revolver, a glistening dark blue five inch barreled .41 Magnum with cocobolo grips and a bobbed hammer. He swings open the cylinder to confirm its loaded condition, then places it next to him on the desk along with two speedloaders stoked with lead hollow-point handloads. He pauses, then steps to his closet, slides it open, and removes a set of concealable body armor, which he places on the bed. OK, back to homework.

Levin did not appear for his thrice-weekly pedaling class that morning, and was a no-show at work. In the early afternoon, his office contacted his girlfriend, a City of Seattle employee in her thirties, who drove to his Queen Anne home, where she found him shot to pieces in the garage. A visibly shaken, yet furious, Special Agent in Charge Tony Martinelli, hair thinning and face sagging, a little soft around the middle but still tough-looking, conducts a press conference that Tuesday afternoon regarding the murder and investigation, emphasizing the resources being committed. "We protect our own, and we will bring the perpetrators of this crime to justice," Martinelli barks at the cameras, as he announces a task force of over sixty agents investigating the judge's murder. There is not yet a single hint of the investigation stretching out to their faction - Josef receives no word, nor does Charles McIntyre, and Miller and Green remain silent. Doug realizes that Miller and Green would likely not express their displeasure verbally, and thus takes to wearing his body armor and carrying firearms to school, specifically a snub-nose revolver and his father's hard chromed Browning Hi Power.

Vanguard Industries turns out to be exactly what he'd imagined, an import-export company with extensive global connections, which he finds engaging. The junior executive he'd been assigned to, one Jake Steiner, is competent, fun to talk to, and a good trainer. Doug jumps immediately into market analysis and corporate intelligence gathering, surprising Jake with his speed of uptake, and he commits to working three days a week and occasional bonus days. The farce that college students lack free time is not news to Jake, who gives Doug stretch goals after assessing his workflow capacity.

On Saturday, Doug and Cathy have a real date; Doug watches in amusement as she eats nearly twice as much seafood as he, despite her hundred and five pound frame. Doug inflicts a cyberpunk anime on her at a Capitol Hill art theater as a true test of their compatibility; to his surprise, they share a two-hour discussion over coffee and dessert – for him – about the ramifications of artificial intelligence and globalism. As Cathy breaks down the paradox of ultimate freedom from personal responsibility within the box of limited political and economic freedoms, he imagines an alicorn sprouting from her forehead. He delivers her that night to her parents' home above Rainier Valley, situated on the southwest side of Graham Hill at the end of a long, straight dead-end street, an oasis of calm and security in a busy, often higher-crime area. Cathy reports that most of the neighbors are Filipino, a third of them blood relations, her grandparents the first to settle the block. As it is late, Doug is not invited in, and Cathy escapes out the door without a kiss, wishing him luck in preparation for his mid-terms Monday and Tuesday.

Doug retires at a reasonable hour, spending two tossing and turning, torn between unchaste thoughts of Cathy and darker memories. Eventually he walks to the kitchen, swallows two ibuprofen and three slugs of bourbon, and passes out on the couch.

He rises early on Sunday and spends two hours in the on-campus gym. At home he inhales five over-easy eggs and a cup of coffee, along with several bottles of water. He spends the rest of the day reviewing notes and texts for his mid-terms, completing the last of his anthropology essay. At five, Mike begins his countdown to the Simpsons from the living room, from which drift female voices and marijuana smoke. Doug gives in, bringing bottles of water, venison jerky and raw vegetables for Mike and the stoner girls from down the hall. Bowing to ritual, Doug does several bong rips during a Sideshow Bob rerun episode. Oblivious Mike has his eyes glued to the TV, repeating the dialogue of the long-ago memorized show, while What's-Her-Name, the taller and horsier girl, attempts flirting with him. Doug and Allie, the tomboyish pigtailed blonde in overalls and a white tee, glance knowingly at each other. Allie only flirts with the bong, loading it over and over from the endless jar of hairy, frosty, orange-tinted nugs that Mike will be burning through for another month. Doug glances at her feet, gripping the edge of the coffee table between her toes, which are more than a little rough, evidencing long periods of going barefoot, or wearing only flip-flops, a little silver pinky toe ring glinting mere inches from the nug jar. Awful.

Doug feels a heavy wave wash over him, separating him emotionally from the room and the people in it, driving him farther out to sea as each moment swirls by. Pot is no escape, but an anchor, a fuzzy, resiny anchor, blurring his thoughts and trending them underwater. He recalls a time when it was fun, light, filled with laughter and fresh insights, and not jagged, geometric wallowing with mere spikes of buoyance. His reading on the subject suggests that the thin, lower-yield, sunny climate Sativas are more enjoyable, the dense, squat, shorter cycle, high yield Indicas being stonier, body-heavy. In the words of a vibrant friend from his teenage years, "no fun." Perhaps. But this is no way to spend the limited time he has in this world. College often feels like an inevitability to him, a series of labors, but oblivion is no answer, distraction no solution.

Doug stands slowly, seeing Mike engage with the horsey girl more, as they laugh at the morphing primary colors and ironic dialogue coming from the TV, while tragic Allie nestles deeper still into the collapsing couch, her eyes turned to slits. Doug grabs a water bottle and inches out of the room. In his bedroom, he changes into long underwear and a jogging suit, pulls a knit cap down to his eyes and slings a Discman into a narrow backpack. Before he leaves his room he pauses, walking back to his desk and retrieves the Browning Hi Power and two magazines, which he stuffs into panels within the running pack.

Doug leaves his building, surveying the area, accepting his inability to spot all but the most obvious observation, the thread of paranoia re-entering his mind. Late November in Seattle brings, no surprise, drizzle in the dark, each drop a near-freezing payload, homing in on exposed skin. He steers north, running several blocks to Ravenna-Cowen Park, an urban arboreal oasis of snaking trails through the shallow, winding ravines separating several residential neighborhoods and the University District. The fairly well-lit paved paths offer yellow-orange waypoints for his run. The illumination from lampposts in the park, along roads bordering the park and bridges overhead, provides both excellent visibility and countless opportunities for concealment. Doug decides that he should begin exploring additional locations for equipment caches in the park, as his escalation has increased the likelihood of an escape and evasion situation. This urban forest is still the best caching location within range of his place, and while he had two caches in this park already, he could easily add several well-chosen sites without increasing the risk of discovery. As he runs, he mentally marks out an area to explore on his return run, deep in rhododendron tangles near a large, distinct fir. At the northeastern end of the park, which opens out of the trees and into a sports field complex, he turns back, driving several dozen yards off-trail and into the rhododendron forest, without finding evidence of human habitation, more common under the bridges bordering the park. All of the noted sites are easy enough to get to, but lacking game trails, yet have enough room within which to work and dig without being visible from any of the paths or roadways around. Illumination is poor without a flashlight, such as the tiny AAA-battery-powered keychain light Doug uses to examine the ground back in the dense foliage; he figures that dawn is the best time to work. Yes, any of these spots will do fine.

With energy to spare, and wanting to be anywhere but home, Doug runs back to the southwest corner of the park and Ravenna Boulevard, then jogs several blocks west through piles of rotting leaves in the broad median lined with enormous mature deciduous trees. At least a dozen inhabited buses and vans line the road, which Doug has always noticed but not paid great attention to. The "residents" congregate in the park on dry days, or at a few bars and mini-marts at the north end of the Ave; in student lore, they serve as a likely source for hippie-centric drugs. At 45th Avenue, he turns south, and contemplates the distance of his run. He is tempted to hit the green space bordering the Cut to the south, a strip of water connecting Lake Washington to the east and Lake Union to the west, and the southernmost border of the University District. The weather gets angrier, the rain falling harder and colder, with more wind, as he runs in the open with only low homes to each side, and he expects it to be no better down by the open water of the channels and cuts. The cache site he pictures in is mind is about two miles to the south, near the Fisheries center along the water, surrounded by nicer student housing, computer labs and other mixed-use buildings. Twenty minutes later he finds it – four hundred-plus-foot tall pines spread their broad lower branches out over a sheltered span of bare earth, each tree offering a ten-foot space where he can walk without hunching over. He is astonished that no homeless have set up here, but perhaps campus police patrol the area. His best bet for setting up the cache would be late at night on an actual holiday. He could brush needles onto a tarp, dig out a section for a supply tube, carry the soil out in a large pack, and sweep the ground before spreading the needles back across the area to conceal the change to the surface. Besides, UW Police don't search for underground caches; they search for campers, and he will be done in twenty minutes.

Doug lies down on the fairly dry ground, peeking out from under the tips of the branches, and searches for signs of campus police. Finding none, he grits his teeth and sprints out from under the tree, headed to the nearest north-south street. He soon passes Cathy and Liz's apartment building, new and shiny, and wonders how quickly the dilapidated hundred year old houses around will fall to development and density. He moves north into commercial buildings, crossing 45th Avenue in a gap in traffic, and pushes back into the small homes on the northwest side of the U District before turning east and sprinting several blocks up to his apartment building on 15th Avenue. Approaching from the rear, outside the parking garage, he examines the power and telephone lines running into the building and the corners of other buildings, making mental notes for future reference. He circles the building and comes up through the alley to the front, wishing that he did not live on a dynamically changing street where the vehicles parked out front change every day. What are you gonna do.

Thoroughly soaked, he draws his keys from the outer pocket of his backpack, noting that the pack kept the Browning pistol in its holster nicely oriented for a quick draw, not shifting in the least. He enters the building, climbs the stairs to the fourth floor, and approaches his apartment with a combination of relief and dread, the hallway feeling narrow and low, but at least not noisy. Crossing the threshold into his apartment, he's punched in the face with pot smoke and Alice in Chains, Mike and horsey face looking back over the couch at him, Allie gladly home. Mike waves, Doug waves, then storms into the bathroom and strips out of his saturated clothes for a warm shower and, soon, deep sleep.

Monday is a blur – early morning calculus exam, deliver Anthro essay to a teaching assistant, who frees the class to leave as they wish, brief chat with Cathy, who kisses him lingeringly in the hallway. She blushes, fleeing the scene; Doug plods home. He attempts to nap for a few hours, but he's too well-rested, so visits the gym after speaking with his grandfather by phone, who will be hitching a ride with a neighbor into town. "I'll see you at McIntyre's at 5 p.m., Doug – I'm looking forward to it." After a push session, Doug showers at home, shaves, then heads to Vanguard for a few hours. The traffic from the Port to McIntyre's house in Magnolia is lighter than expected, and he arrives twenty minutes early, pulling up along the curb in front of a long line of boxwood, some three hundred feet before the next house. An ornate gate bars the entrance.

McIntyre's driver, the stone-faced Mr. Evans, exits the grounds via a port door in the fence and knocks on Doug's hood. He has the dark-suit-white-shirt-bushy-black-moustache look down pat. "Hey, kid, I'ma open the gate; you pull up in the turnabout. Parking's on the east side – EAST, this way – facing out. See ya in a minute." He turns and runs back through the port door. The gate grinds to life, swinging out. Doug drives through, nodding to Evans, and comes up a two-hundred-foot driveway with a long hedge to the right, bordering the north edge of the property. Left, a sprawling, precisely manicured Japanese-style landscaped yard, sloping gently southeast with a spectacular view of Queen Anne Hill, downtown Seattle, Elliott Bay and the Cascade mountain range beyond. The border hedges are at least ten feet high along the north and east edges of the property, which edge Discovery Park, and slightly lower to the south to preserve the view. He circles the driveway turnabout, parks his Bronco facing north, and hops out, surveying the property, whistling in spite of himself. This side of the property is nearly four acres, centering on a sprawling complex of single story buildings with an impressive amount of roof surface, suggesting both Japanese and Northwest longhouse style, in dark stained wood siding. Doug vaguely recalls visiting the house as a child, only remembering the indoor swimming pool, a trophy room with dozens of African animals – including an elephant – and an outdoor koi pond. He turns about, absorbing the scene, and Evans approaches, the crack of a smile beneath his moustache.

"Aright, kid, let's go," Evans says, walking towards the large, intricately carved double doors, a Southeast Asian portrayal of Hindu epic in dark tropical hardwood. Stepping through the doorway onto a colorful doormat of silk rag, atop an expansive single slab of rough slate, Evans whistles for Doug's attention, then removes his own shoes and sets them on a shoe rack. "Shoes off," he commands, and Doug obeys. This is the entryway to the house, decorated mostly in Southeast Asian style. McIntyre spent the forties through the sixties in Asia, Doug recalled, first with the OSS, then the CIA, finally riding the intersection of intelligence and commerce as president of Vanguard.

The usually standoffish Evans curls his finger to Doug, beckoning. "C'mere, kid, let me show you something." He leads him into an adjoining room heavy with incense and flicks on very dim, indirect lights, revealing a Theravada style altar with a seated golden Buddha, smiling a flat smile, one hand turned up and the other pointed skyward. They look at the scene for a few moments, Evans nudging him finally. "Ain't that something? Mrs. McIntyre's family altar, removed before the communists took over. If you're good, you can use the room." He winks and turns, tugging Doug's arm, guiding him down a long hallway with a massive, commercial-grade kitchen on one side and a casual dining area on the other. Beyond that, they pass a formal dining room, then arrive at a lounge decorated in dark hardwoods and deep leather matching Mr. McIntyre's office. Josef and McIntyre sit in two of the four deep lounge chairs, chuckling about something; Evans gives Doug a pat on his back and clicks his tongue before disappearing.

Doug enters the room, thinking about what to do with his hands. He decides to walk forward and get their attention, hoping his voice doesn't crack. "Hi gramps; Mr. McIntyre. Sir, you have an amazing home." From the center of the room he takes in view to the west, through floor to ceiling glass panes, of another five to six sloping acres of landscaped grounds, a long, low building down by the edge of the property, and the Puget Sound, shimmering in the sunset, the imposing Olympic mountain range beyond. Doug realizes that he's been staring out the window for nearly a minute, entranced.

Hours blur by as the three converse over glasses of fine whiskey and a straightforward but masterfully prepared venison shank served with an array of wild mushrooms and root vegetables. Doug participates by mostly listening to the two looming giants of his life and their when-we, whatever-happened-to tales. The seemingly apocryphal Mrs. McIntyre, eldest daughter of the equivalent of an earl of a defunct Southeast Asian nation, is visiting her sister in Hawaii, to be joined by Mr. McIntyre in time for the Thanksgiving holiday. The weather turns during their meal, treating them to a view of a thunderstorm moving up Puget Sound from the southwest, slowly blotting out the lights of Vashon Island, West Seattle, and Bainbridge before reaching them. Josef announces that he will spend the night in one of McIntyre's several guest rooms before accompanying Doug on their circuitous trip back to the Peninsula tomorrow.

Over digestives for the older men – too sweet, and Doug will be driving shortly – McIntyre presents Josef with an engraved FN Model 1922 in .32 ACP, resting on purple silk in a simple but perfectly executed wooden display box of oceans-deep burl. The men gush over it, their preferred handgun in times past. Doug's mind slips back to a framed photo in his room of faded sepia, two young men wearing flat caps and Basque shirts in the scorching Spanish sun, FN .32s stuffed into their waistbands over leather cartridge boxes, C-96 Broomhandle machine pistols in their hands. His grandmother, who he knows only from photographs and stories, to their right, staring out from black curls under a white shawl, her peasant dress and apron stylishly accented by a slung Mauser rifle.

Wednesday afternoon, Doug and Josef sit in the Bronco at the foredeck of a ferry cutting across the channel between Whidbey Island and Port Townsend, a route the pair chose for variety's sake. The storm that swept into the region last night has not abated, and the channel is rough and windy, with great washes of saltwater blowing across their windshield. Doug tunes in from distant thoughts to his grandfather, who has been speaking for some time.

"I should be concerned that you acted without consultation, or even recklessly, lacking regard for the wheels set in motion, but I would be lying if I claimed to have some master plan. I'm glad he's been punished for his part in your daddy's death, and that you executed seamlessly. Now, I am a bit concerned at the response, but it would not have been any different with any of the men involved, given their positions." He pauses, studying the side of Doug's face.

Doug turns to face him directly. "I screwed up. I used a Skorpion. Not our handloads, but the hot Czech ammo. It would be the easiest thing in the world to tie the Victoria job to Levin, once forensics are in, which I'm sure they are."

Josef doesn't respond, studying Doug through a squint. He blinks, observing, his preferred "talk out your own solution" tactic.

Doug shrugs. "That said, I'm retiring the Skorpions for the time being, and the only people who would know it was me, or would suspect me, are Miller, Green and McReady, plus anyone else in the faction privy to the particulars. Canadian and US law enforcement, really, they'd only be able to connect the dots if there were an informant, or I were caught red-handed with a Skorpion. It's too rare of a weapon; I should have known better."

Josef puts his hand on Doug's shoulder, patting it. "It'll be fine. You're over-thinking things."

Doug exhales a long breath. "I'm not so sure. Miller and Green, I don't trust them. They could turn us over for their own advantage. I knew I'd made a mistake right away. I should have just used a disposable 9. Sticking to the same MO was a bad move."

Josef clears his throat, turning to look through the windshield as the ferry dock loomed ahead of them, the massive boat's reverse turbines rumbling to life. "That thought had occurred to me, of course. Let's wait and see. Now that you're operational, you're far more useful to them under our existing agreement. Put those thoughts out of your head. Let's talk about something else. This girl that you're seeing, I want to know more about her." Doug contains the rising paranoia - no, panic - in his chest, and forces a grin.

Doug gives thanks for the opportunity to get away from his mundane life for a few days to help Josef prepare their property for the winter, clearing dead brush and fallen leaves from around the house and hiking the trails that lead into the mountains. Several sections of trail in their valley show damage from heavy rains, as is expected, and he spends two days making repairs. He visits his caches on the mountainside and breaks in a new pair of side-zip all-season boots, which will reside in the hall closet next to his bug-out bag.

Thanksgiving morning, Doug rises early with Josef to get started cooking, but they receive several invitations to dinner, so instead spend the afternoon and evening visiting with neighbors and old friends, reserving their carefully prepared turkey and sides for leftovers. Josef and Doug spend most of Friday in the armory and shop, preparing an order of small arms and ammunition for field deployment. Josef looks over the weapons, mostly compact Yugoslav AKs, and a number of Czech 9mm handguns fitted with suppressors. "Balkans," Josef observes, "has to be. A long way to go just to turn back 'round. What a shame."

"What do you mean, pops?" Doug asks.

Josef's shoulders slump a bit, and he exhales loudly. "Nobody is an angel there, but the United States is definitely not on the side of the angels. The fucking Turk." He spits on the floor.

While perusing the deep storage stacks for the order, Doug finds an olive drab plastic crate with Spanish markings leaning against the wall, recognizing the logo of the Infantería de Marina, the Spanish Marines, and 5.56mm labels. "Go ahead, those are ours to do with as we please," Josef says to Doug upon his inquiry. With the order completed, Doug digs into the Spanish crate and finds four rarities he'd only seen line drawings of, the green, short-barreled Ameli Squad Automatic Weapon, which looks to him like a shrunken MG-3 from WWII. As they examine a sample up on its bipod, Josef explains its provenance.

"Your cousin Marceo set these aside for the faction. The Spanish Marines love the Ameli, and dedicated substantial resources to improving them, after the army had decided to scrap them over manufacturing flaws that led to short service lives. This is their product-improved variant, with an optics mount and some improved internals. We have more in Spain in a Vanguard warehouse, but only this crate here stateside. It's belt-fed, but you have these boxes that snap onto the frame," gesturing to a stack of 100 and 200 round boxes in the crate, "and you're gonna need 'em, because it has an extremely high rate of fire. Finally, the reason we snapped them up – watch this." Josef pushes several retaining pins out in various locations and breaks the weapon down into two foot long segments. "You can get it all into a small backpack or suitcase. I figure they'll run well with a nice, robust suppressor if it has enough volume. Let's give it a whirl."

Doug glances at his watch, a cheap but reliable Casio G-Shock with a web wrist strap. 3:20 p.m. "You got it. I promised Cathy I'd call her at 5 p.m., so I'll work quickly." Doug focuses on the disassembled miniature machine gun, stripping it of its long term preservative grease, which goes much more quickly than with the old commie guns. He flips through the Spanish-language user manual after snapping it back together, lubricates the bolt path and several other indicated areas, then finds a case of appropriate ammunition, SS109 spec 5.56mm in M27 disintegrating belts, the NATO standard. He packs up 800 rounds in a mix of 100 and 200 round boxes, which fit neatly into a range bag with ear and eye protection. Doug hauls the entire heap to their outdoor range for a familiarization session.

Late that night, Doug enjoys on beer and reheated turkey while chatting with Josef in the living room, listening to whatever musical surprise awaits. Tonight, it's Afro-Cuban jazz, spun on Josef's well-cared-for forty year old stereo system, which they enjoy beside the roaring fireplace.

"We need a dog," says Doug, as he sets his frosty beer bottle on a coaster on the end table. "This place doesn't seem the same without a dog."

Josef glances at him from over his reading glasses, without bringing his head up from his book, a German historical philosopher Doug isn't familiar with. "You're telling me that I need a dog."

Doug laughs. "That's fair. Wouldn't it be fun to have a dog again? You're by yourself all the time."

Josef sighs. "I don't dislike dogs, but it's nice to not have to worry about anyone other than you and me. Dog wouldn't get enough exercise, either. I'm fine, Douglas. You needn't worry about me feeling lonely."

Doug smiles sheepishly. "I want a dog, I just can't have one now. I know people who have dogs with them at college, and it's borderline cruel."

Josef sets down his book. "Now isn't the time for you to be a family guy with family type attachments, Doug. It's normal to have a girlfriend, but this life is hard on relationships, and the last thing you want is to be worried about an animal. Believe me."

"Jeez, grandpa."

Josef sighs. "You shot a federal judge two weeks ago, and here you are lecturing me about pets. When the police raid a place, who gets shot right off the bat? The dog. Anyhow. I've been thinking about what you said about Miller and Green the other day. Charles is going up the chain to get them out of our hair. They're supposed to keep him informed as to their activities with us, but apparently that's not happening. Don't go getting any ideas – we're simply going to avoid them."

Doug crinkles his eyes. "I thought they reported to McIntyre."

Josef shakes his head. "That's what I'm saying. They're not in his chain of command per se, though they were supposed to do so when they set up shop in the Seattle area. Zero loyalty to Charles or us; they're flunkies for Brooks' son." He raises his hands. "These things are much tidier in the first generation."

"So who is Brooks?" Doug asks. "I feel like I need a diagram. Was this something we covered, or was I not paying attention?"

Josef waves dismissively. "Let me lay it all out." He grabs a notepad and pencil and draws an umbrella with four points at the top:

SHEA   MCINTYRE   DYER   BROOKS

"Dyer and Brooks were OSS hands we worked with during the War. Brooks died nearly twenty years ago, lung cancer. A good man. The best, actually. His son, Aaron, was CIA. Took over. A competent man, but he has no ideology save for power. He'll work with anyone. Men like him are how U.S. foreign policy has become so bent. Dyer was with State, recently retired, but still has his fingers in all sorts of pies. He was our man in the bureaucracy. Frankly, that wing is pretty much gone; though there are some who still have his loyalty, it ain't what it used to be. Miller works for Aaron Brooks."

Doug leans in. "And Green works for Miller."

Josef nods. "Look, Doug, that's a man with a chip on his shoulder if I've ever seen one. Miller isn't a killer; he has his dirty work done for him. Green looks like a gang kid who has moved on to the big leagues. Young, hungry guys like that will do anything – anything."

Doug passes the bottle of beer back and forth in his hands, watching it carefully. He looks up and speaks. "I have an idea. Tell me what you think." He takes a swig and swallows quickly, standing and pacing. "Green and I are supposed to check in with each other, as the guys on the ground. He made a joke about me hooking him up with college girls. I'm not going to do that, but he doesn't know that. What if I were to reach out to him, act cagey, a little concerned, but say nothing is wrong, that I just want to talk to him."

Josef leans back in his chair. "Like you want to confide in him, but aren't ready yet."

"Yeah." Doug sets his beer back down on the coaster, then stretches. "I'll play the soft white boy from a rich family, and he'll be the hungry, smarter guy who can manipulate me. I'll see if he lets anything slip. Maybe they know about Levin. Maybe they don't. I want to get a feel for the guy. Maybe we can use him. Maybe I can get him to consider teaming up with us and McIntyre. Or maybe he'll tip his hand. What's the worst that could happen?"

Josef narrows his eyes. "Fine with me, I trust you. Just be careful."

Doug shrugs. "Alright, we have a plan." He picks up his beer, nursing it while looking out the window at the rain in the spill of the porch lights.

Josef pushes himself up out of his chair with significant effort. "I'm off to bed. Tomorrow we're spending some more time in the shop. You need your manufacturing skills bumped up a notch. Goodnight."

"G'night, pops." Josef pats Doug on the shoulder and walks down the hall to his bedroom, clicking off lights along the way, and Doug feeds a new log into the wood stove, along with the faction org chart from the notepad and the four pages beneath it for good measure.

After a vegetable juice and six-egg breakfast, Doug and Josef spend the morning on the shop lathe, machining dies for forming suppressor baffles from sheet metal, covering materials, dimensional calculations, and then using the dies to form baffles on the simple shop press brake. They then use the lathe to practice machining precision baffles and suppressor endcaps, carefully drilling centers and threading them to interface with the thread pitches of different barrels. Finally, Josef hands Doug a simple Hungarian blowback .32 ACP handgun, a rudimentary but well-made copy of the classic Walther PP design, along with a box of ammunition, instructing him to modify the weapon to accept a suppressor and then build a suppressor for it. "Do whatever you want, go with whatever design you prefer; this is a learning experience. I'm gonna read and have another cup of coffee. Take your time."

Doug strips the handgun on a workbench and looks it over, then grabs a pair of precision calipers from a tool drawer, along with a legal size notepad, pencil and ruler. He takes internal and external measurements on both ends of the barrel and scrawls out notes detailing his planned modifications. Doug raids Josef's raw materials and selects a foot long, 1.25" external diameter aluminum tube, and a solid round bar of aluminum, slightly larger than the internal diameter of the tube. He sketches out a simple suppressor design based on Josef's tried and true two-wipe variant, five inches in overall length, then draws two different baffle stacks, one press-formed and the other machined. Because of the two-wipe design, the end caps will need to be able to screw out in the field without tools, so Doug designs them with ¼" exposed knurling. His penultimate sketch is of the threaded barrel extension the pistol will need to accept the suppressor, then finally on the other end, cutting a ring inside weapon's chamber to give the brass something to expand into, extending dwell time. As working with an existing object is the most complicated and involved, Doug decides to modify the barrel first, and then build the suppressor.

After several hours in the shop, some false starts and redos, Doug admires the modified pistol and sleek suppressor he's machined by hand and anodized in matte black, happy with the results. Testing each piece along the way, and measuring multiple times before each cut, he built a hearing-safe suppressor that did not affect the reliability of the host weapon. While it may not be exotic or professional-grade, it makes an adequate disposable assassination pistol. He leaves the pistol on the workbench and goes into the house for lunch, letting his grandfather know that the weapon is ready for inspection.

After a turkey sandwich and a bottle of water, Doug packs up for his trip back to school. Josef glides into the room with the suppressed .32 in a ziplock bag, sprayed with oil. "Pass!" he declares, tossing the pistol into Doug's bag. "And you'll need this," adding a sandwich bag with two fifty-round boxes of European commercial ammunition. "Let's do two more assignments." Josef sets down a large hardback book, a heavily illustrated tome on submachine guns and machine pistols. "I was reading about some of the European Personal Defense Weapon concepts, and the specialized hardware being produced in that framework. I photocopied a few articles and put them in the book, along with your assignments. Design a single, multi-use insurgency weapon as a low cost, but modern conceptual replacement for the Liberator pistol. You know my love of Broomhandles. The PDWs are in that niche; our pistol projects and this book make me think we can find something that will cover a wide variety of roles, as we were always trying to find in the sixties and seventies. I have an idea, but would like your input."

"Sure, pops." Doug looks the book over, and flips through the print-outs, covering submachine guns with shrunken rifle cartridges and often unusual weapon layouts. "What's number two?" he asks, while examining the hand-written assignment page.

Josef stretches his right shoulder. "Canada job, but using locally sourced weapons. Because of Canadian firearms restrictions, you'll be constrained to bolt action rifles or shotguns. A good thought exercise. Anyhow. You have a safe trip back. Don't let this thing dog you; you'll be fine. I'm sure of it. But if anything sets off alarm bells, stick to process."

"You got it, pops. Will the feeling going up my neck ever go away?" Doug asks sheepishly.

Joseph pauses, a slight smile on his face, and puts his hand on his grandson's shoulder. "That feeling has saved my life many times. Trust it."

Doug stands and hugs his grandfather. "No regrets. I'll trust it." He leans back and stares into his grandfather's eyes – he's a rock. "Thanks. I'll hit the road."

"Call if you need to, Doug." Josef steps back. "Now get going. You got a sweet young thing waiting on you; best not dilly dally. But don't come off as too eager, either. Anyhow. Please lock the door; I'm beat. It's going to be an early night for me."

Doug grins, then slides his reading material into his duffel bag, which he scoops up by its handles. "Back to the belly of the beast. Love ya, pops." He steps into the hallway, turning to watch his grandfather survey the room – emptied of many of his youthful decorations, it seems bare and sad – smiles, then pivots on his heel, trotting down the stairs with a combination of enthusiasm and regret.

Tuesday, noon, Doug sits alone at a window table perched high above Lake Union in a tasteful glass-and-cedar seafood restaurant, sipping excellent black coffee and watching another late fall storm elbow its way through the city and parts beyond. He's ten minutes early to the restaurant, after spending twenty minutes looping the blocks around by car and on foot. True to form, he has parked two blocks away at the mouth of an onramp to Highway 99 northbound in case things go sideways. In honor of the establishment, and adjusting to the dress code of his new employer and station, he's selected a dark grey wool suit, a white cotton shirt and a dark green silk tie, plus a heavier black wool topcoat and matching wool flat cap, now hung on a hook at the coat check. As he still hasn't fully adjusted to dress shoes, especially the mobility aspect, his feet are shod in black leather boots developed for urban police officers, as in city, not African-American. They are light and fast, with only mid-thickness soles, but keep him warm and dry in the rain.

Green responded positively to his Sunday afternoon call, suggesting a meet Monday; Doug countered with Tuesday to set the frame. Green, possibly sensing his maneuvering, suggested this restaurant, part of a well-established local chain that remained popular, yet not hip. Doug knew he'd be ordering the salmon, but wondered what Green, not from around these parts, would have – a burger? A sandwich? If fish – often not popular with inlanders – saltwater? Freshwater?

And there he is. Doug watches as Green steps in, talking to the hostess, obviously laying it on a little thick even from this distance. So he's got a bit of a chip on his shoulder, as expected. The hostess gestures towards Doug, escorting Green in his direction after taking his coat and fedora – a nice touch.

Doug stands, processing all data points quickly. While Doug does not consider himself a capital-R "Racist," his experience with black people, given where he grew up, has been limited to University of Washington administrative personnel, a handful of students, and various street personalities. Most of those black students are athletes moderately interested in academics, save one particularly sharp linebacker in the business school whom Doug has seen at several anime showings at an art house theater on the Ave, and sat with once. Were Doug a certain type of white guy, he'd regale every person he could with tales of this individual, inflate their relationship, and present it as proof positive that he is a non-racist who just believes in everything that Martin Luther King, Jr. stood for. He's not that kind of guy.

It is through this filter that Doug Shea processes what he knows about Lawrence Green, Jr.: entered the US Army at age 18, earned a GED while a corporal in the 75th Ranger battalion, re-upped and transferred to the Intelligence and Security

Command, specifically the Army Operations Group. An army spook. Now in the private sector, working with dirty government factions and criminal networks. Not a dumb guy, but Doug finds it harder to judge people accurately when they belong to different ethnicities and social groups, regardless of national boundaries. Green moves like a professional, subtly scanning the room while appearing to be looking at his destination, chatting with the hostess, a young blonde upper middle class woman who obviously finds him somewhat charming.

"Thanks, hon. Hey, Doug," Green says, locking eyes; their height is nearly identical, though Green has a slightly smaller head and neck, so he seems taller. They shake hands cordially, watching each other carefully. OK, good, Doug thinks, he doesn't think I'm a chump.

Doug gestures to the table. "Have a seat. I just got here myself."

They sit, Green leaning back. "Naw, you got here about thirty minutes ago. It's cool." Waving his hand dismissively. "I like your truck. Not really my style, but useful. I have something similar, but newer, leather seats, street tires. Truck like that makes sense for where you're from." A waitress pounces, as the restaurant fills up, taking drink orders to keep things humming. Doug sticks to water; Green gets Glenlivet 18 year, rocks, "big cubes only."

"The salmon is good here, wild-caught, none of that farm crap." Doug nods to the kitchen with his chin. "Trout, too."

"Mmmm." Green rests his chin in his hand with a finger cocked over his mouth. "I usually go higher protein. They'll actually prepare a steak here the way you order it, and I'm starving from my workout this morning. Yeah, I'll get a steak."

Doug puts down his menu. "If you like red meat, I'll hook you up with some elk steaks. I didn't get a chance to get out this season, with school and all, but our neighbors gave us a bunch. Pops is a venison evangelist."

Green sips water seemingly absent-mindedly, while looking out the window. "Yeah, you got plenty of hunting in already." His eyes drift back to Doug.

Doug smiles. "Might as well, if you got a tag. Otherwise that's food off the table."

"Mmmm, mmmm." Their waitress arrives with Green's drink, which he fusses over a bit before graciously accepting as-is. They order, Green going to great lengths to explain his preferences for doneness of the meat and the sides. As the waitress walks away, Doug follows her with his eyes theatrically, positioning a male bonding moment.

"I know, right?" Green asks gratuitously. "Women in this town dress like they're in Nome, Alaska, or on the DMZ. Gore-Tex and polar fleece. So when they dress well, I can't help but like it."

Doug laughs. "College is largely about watching people stop grooming themselves and gain weight. It's pretty disgusting. My grandfather always stressed a need to dress well, and I don't think of it as a pain in the ass anymore. One benefit of the military is the grooming standard that gets drilled into you, I'd think."

Green nods. "So you've done your homework. Good. You're not a dumb, spoiled hick after all."

Doug narrows his eyes, acting offended, then laughs jovially. "Family-run businesses are often a disaster, I get it. But there's something to be said for people raised for a gig from birth. A caste thing. But unlike you, I'm behind the curve, because it's been all theory for me, until recently."

Green shrugs. "Look, let's just be straight with each other, and quit the maneuvering. It's tiresome. We're working together, and it's going to be fruitful. It's going to be productive. I'm no dummy, and you're no dummy. I'm not going to be able to hide anything from you, and you're not going to be able to hide anything from me. Such as... extra-curricular activities. It might not be a big deal where you're from, but it is to me. I have to pretend I have no idea what is going on, which isn't a good feeling. So stop it. I'll let this one go, but that's it. Okay? Even if it is your granddad's idea." Green catches himself leaning across the table and relaxes, fluidly grabbing up his scotch. "Not that it means anything to me. I wasn't a fan." He pulls a swig of the scotch into his mouth, swirling it and swallowing it slowly.

Doug maintains his expression. "I'll talk to pops about cutting off that sideline."

Green flashes a disappointed smirk. "Come on, man, use your head. You can't stick to an MO and pretend you don't know what I'm talking about. This is bigger than you. If you can't be honest with me, we can't work together. If we can't work together, that's a really big problem for you and your grandfather. I don't think it needs to be, so just drop it. Alright?"

Doug nods. "Alright." He sips water, looking out the window and points toward downtown. "There's a lot of guys running around out there right now. It already got back to you?"

Green looks at the table, steering the ring of condensation from his glass around on the light lacquered cedar with his left index finger. "There ya go. Of course. Things work a certain way; when they don't work smoothly, people talk, different people with different interests and needs. Like I said, I don't like pretending I don't know what's going on, and Miller and I know what's going on. It's stopped there, but it doesn't have to, and if you guys are fucking around on us, causing problems, all it takes is a phone call, my man." Green makes an X with the condensation against the lacquered sheen of the table. "I foresee a nice partnership, Doug, though Miller is less bullish on you guys; has been for decades." He locks eyes with Doug. "Decades."

Doug nods. "Roger. I'm on board. Any other decision-makers I should be aware of?"

Green shakes his head. "It's not for you to know about decision-makers; you're a doer. Part of being a doer is knowing your place, and your role, and right now your role is to learn and do whatever you're instructed to do; no more, no less. Your grandfather and McIntyre might command the respect of the old school dudes, but I gotta tell ya, there's a lot of senior guys who want that generation out of the way. Guys our dads' ages are running things now, and they're done with the old rules. Me? I'm a fan of the old rules. Well, some of them." He sips his scotch again, savoring it, looking towards the busy kitchen and other tables being served, then back to Doug and swallowing. "Food should be ready real soon. I'm starving."

Doug scans the restaurant theatrically. "I'm gonna wash my hands before the food comes. I'll be right back." He pushes his chair back and nods to Green, then turns and heads to the restroom, where he relieves himself and washes his hands twice, looking at himself in the mirror and feeling a deep sense of dread. I could waste him and bail, but then there's Miller, and I have no idea where Miller is. That'd be a disaster. No, he's trying to keep us on the reservation is all. I fucked up, big league.

He returns to the table to find lunch served. Green graciously waited for him before eating – such a gentleman! Doug sits and puts his napkin in his lap, examining the salmon, cooked pink and just beginning to fall apart, not too heavily seasoned. Some lame rice pilaf is on the side, next to roasted vegetables, happily not soaked in oil. Green's steak looks amazing, sixteen ounces and aged over a month, cooked to the lower edge of medium rare as requested, lightly spiced, with horseradish sauce on the side and vegetables cooked and seasoned to his precise specifications. Green closes his eyes as he chews the first bite of steak, nodding his head and chewing, nodding and chewing.

"Your steak looks killer," Doug notes after swallowing his first bite of perfectly prepared Coho. "I just eat salmon so rarely these days that I get it when I can."

Green says, "I don't like fish much, but I can tell they didn't ruin yours. This place is alright, huh?" They spend some time in silence, chewing and swallowing, looking around, nodding at each other, the tension fading. Green points towards the University District to the northeast. "You like school? It's so damn big. I hear it's impersonal."

Doug nods. "It'd be easy for someone who isn't a go-getter to just drift into the crowd and not get out of it what they want. Just navigating the place is a pain in the ass. I think that's the biggest problem. Plus, their resources are oriented towards graduate students, who are a fraction of attendees. That said, if you know what you want, you can get it there, and there are some great staff and programs. It is what it is."

Green shrugs. "One of the myths about the army is that you're just a number. I mean, you are, but people take care of each other and teach the new guys the ropes. Seems like a waste to have a bunch of eighteen, nineteen year olds flailing on their own. Too much booze and drugs, sex, right when they should be focusing on getting through it. Sounds fun, until you realize what a waste it is for so many people. I don't know. I need to graduate – I put three years under my belt when I was in the Army – but this isn't really the city for me, you know? I don't know."

Doug watches him, trying to gauge the statement. Green looks up at him over his meal, a big hunk of meat on his fork, poised in the air. "You know what I mean, right?" He leans over the plate, pulling the meat from his fork swiftly, chewing with his mouth closed, watching.

Doug points out the window at the grey downpour. "Takes a certain kind of person to put up with the weather. Insular; cold on the outside, warm if you make it into the inner circle. The Seattle Chill."

Green nods, his eyes closed, chewing faster and swallowing. He points to Doug with his knife. "There ya go. I heard about that before I got here, and it's real. I thought it was just 'cuz I was black, but people talk about it; it's a thing. Though I doubt being black helps with some folks."

Doug smiles understandingly. "Part of it is that everyone holes up eight months out of the year, so if you don't know them from work, or church, or school, you're not going to get to know them. That leads to indoor habits in general. I suspect it'll be more of a problem as more people move here from other places, not used to the weather, and less people going to church, meaning we're going to have a society where you only meet people at school, work or bars. I don't know; I'm used to it. Where are you from originally?"

Green shakes his head a bit. "Houston. You know it's 74 degrees right now down there? I didn't even know the term 'sun break' was a thing until two years ago. Goddamn."

Doug laughs; Green smiles and they return to eating for several minutes, enjoying their meal. Green finally breaks the silence, putting down his knife on his plate loudly, the steak consumed. "Look, man, I know why it happened, and I sympathize, but we can't have any of that. If things change in the future, maybe I can help you out a little with that side project. I'm not gonna say shit – for now. Let's keep this an amicable working relationship. Every once in a while I'll have something for you." Fuh-you. "I'll need you to funnel information my way. We'll do that face to face, until we get a system worked out. Part of this meeting was to judge your level of discretion; you passed. Any questions?"

Doug chews his last bite of salmon, moving a thin bone to the front of his mouth with his tongue; he pulls it from between pursed lips, then swallows before placing the bone on his plate. Green shakes his head in amazement that a person would bother eating such things. Doug places his elbows on the table and hands together, leaning forward. "Comms?"

Green nods and pulls a small pager from his pants pocket, placing it in the middle of the table. "Pager. I'm not giving you the number; I'll be the only one leaving messages. You don't need to wear it; you can keep it at home. But take it with you when you go to your granddad's. It'll give you a phone number to call, that's it. Different voicemail drops or my number. Do NOT use your home phone or the same phone twice. Carry a roll of quarters for payphones, and plan out routes to all the pay phones in your area. Passcode for the voicemail drops will always be '187.' Got it?"

Doug grimaces. "Smartass."

Green laughs. "You're up on things, that's for sure. Alright, Doug. Anything else?"

Doug shrugs, depositing the pager in his pants pocket. "I'm good. How do I reach you?"

Green shakes his head. "Can't be like that right now; maybe later. Bet you most of the old white dudes eating here assume we're drug dealers. Or car salesmen. Some shit like that. We have to maintain our official distance, so no calls going back and forth. Signals, man, signals. Anyway, let's wrap it up. I got the check, you can skip. Got it?"

"Yeah, I got it. Thanks, man." Doug stands, offering his hand. Green rises and shakes Doug's hand earnestly. "Until next time, Mr. Green."

"Until next time, Mr. Shea. Until next time." Green raises his hand, getting the waitress' attention, and nods. "Won't be long."

Doug turns and glances about the restaurant. Despite Green's proclamation, he sees nobody paying them any mind as he heads to the coat check. Donning his jacket and cap, he tips the girl a $5, turning before she can respond, and strides out into the rain as he buttons his jacket. The wind from the south has picked up, and he has a tracking device sitting in his pocket. Whatever; it beats two bullets in the head. He goes home.

The Afghan Whigs steadily assail Doug's ears as he sits on his bed, back against the wall, flipping through his grandfather's assigned reading on the Personal Defense Weapon concept. The notepad on the bed fills up with ideas and sketches as solutions form in his mind. No school until tomorrow; Vanguard is closed for the rest of the week, as McIntyre believes in long holiday breaks, and grants the same to his staff. With no responsibilities or sense of motivation, Doug sparks up a joint and takes several draws, but stubs it out and opens the window to the rain and wind, bored and curiously disappointed in himself.

Too much dreariness, nihilism. He grabs his stereo remote control and changes discs, settling on Bjork's Debut. There. Cathy has promised to call him this afternoon when she's free, but the day is dragging and the room feels smaller and smaller. He is primed, ready to explode, and the chill won't leave his neck and shoulders, that someone is watching, that something horrible is about to happen. *What am I doing, trying to have a normal life?* He stands up, feeling cornered, grabs the stubbed-out joint from his desk and pops it into his mouth as he pockets his keys and wallet. He selects his snubby revolver from a drawer to carry in his coat, plus two reloading speed strips, which go into his left front pocket. Doug flees the apartment while slipping into his coat and a knit cap, tying his running shoes in the hall. He palms the joint and exits the building via the west alley, lighting up as he walks south. The rain strikes his face, stopping at his tight upturned collar, and the joint is exhausted within two blocks. Marijuana doesn't improve his mood; Doug finds himself dreading every alley and street, watching every corner and doorway, checking his back theatrically every few strides.

What now? A beacon to the south – Cathy and Liz's apartment. It's okay to be vulnerable, and right now, he's vulnerable, having walked down the street smoking a joint while carrying a revolver. Genius! Never break more than one law at a time, Josef always lectured; drive the speed limit with hands at ten and two when anything illicit is in the truck. Engagement with law enforcement would not go well right now. Way to go, Douglas.

Doug lengthens his stride to a run and arrives at the secured doorway of the girls' building minutes later, as if time has barely passed, the interim forgotten. His finger finds their apartment number and mashes the intercom button, and he starts talking before – click. "Hello?" Cathy.

"Hey, Cathy, it's Doug. Can I come in?" Trying to slow his voice and failing.

"Yeah, come in!" The door buzzes, he grabs the handle and flings it open like a snatch with a five-pound weight. He sprints up the stairs to the girls' floor, steadying himself against the wall as his still-increasing highness sends him surging wildly in his head. Okay, that's the right door, right? No? The next door opens, and Cathy pokes her head out, long, damp, silken black hair hanging straight down. Doug laughs and charges up to her, her eyes going wide, and he scoops her up in a bear hug, holding her tight, plopping her down, shedding rain all over her sweatshirt and face. Cathy steps back, eyeing him carefully. "What's going on? I was getting ready to call you."

He slows his breathing further, holding a finger in the air. "Sorry. I ran here. I don't know what to say. I wanted to see you, couldn't wait anymore." He pauses, watching her unchanging face. "I hope that's okay."

She beckons him into the apartment, closing the door behind him. "Take off your shoes and coat; you're soaked." Doug obediently pulls off his shoes, leaving them next to several other pairs by the door, and hangs his coat on a hook on the wall, then removes his knit cap, sliding it into a jacket pocket. Cathy leans against the wall, watching him critically, her arms crossed. He turns to her, looking at her, and smiles. Her expression softens into an annoyed grin, and she shakes her head. "What the hell, Doug."

"I'm sorry." Doug decides to go for it. He steps carefully up to her, stunned by how he towers over her, although he never felt particularly tall, and carefully puts his arms around her, crossing at the small of her back. She obligingly steps into him on her own, placing her arms behind his neck. "I probably look like a lunatic."

"Your breath smells like weed," Cathy says, bemused. "I thought you always waited until 'your shit was done,'" chiding. "It's like three o'clock."

"My shit is done." Doug laughs. "Come here." He leans in and kisses her, carefully, then commits. They pull apart after a few moments, heat rising within them.

"What the hell," Liz calls from the living room couch, looking up from a book. "You got a room, Cathy, use it."

Brotherly Love

Evans, McIntyre's driver, spends Wednesday with Doug developing three Vanguard employee profiles, two American and one Canadian, and provides driver's licenses, passports, and supporting ID for each. Doug stores the material for two of the profiles in a safe at Vanguard, but brings one American profile set home and assembles them in a wallet with five hundred dollars cash. These go into the concealment waist belt in his bug out bag, stored in his closet floor safe, in case of disaster. In the Vanguard computer system, these profiles are flagged with a filter that allow executive level employees to call them up by name with a passcode, but are not output in wildcard searches or lower level employee account searches. The American profiles are assigned to the Vanguard Barcelona office, reporting to his cousin Marceo, the Canadian to Vanguard Toronto. Evans and Jake plan a visit for Jake and Doug to the Toronto office in January, making use of the Martin Luther King, Jr. holiday.

Doug, of course, suspects that the Toronto visit and Josef's mission analysis assignment are related.

They are.

The story develops; Miller and Green's employer, Brooks, has interests extending to Toronto and its suburbs, with a small network of local influence peddlers suppressing an investigation into a drug trafficking organization originating in Kosovo and Albania with ties to anti-Serbian mujahedeen supported by the United States. Josef and McIntyre have concluded that Brooks' helping hand in the region must be severed, one way or another. Jake will serve as team leader for the operation. He shares with Doug more about his background one brilliant cloudless day in mid-December in the Vanguard boardroom, as Elliott Bay sparkles iridescent behind him. ROTC, University of Washington. Army, Ranger battalion. Assigned to a team training Croatian Army units during the Yugoslavian severance, spotted by a Vanguard talent scout filling a State Department logistical support contract.

Rather than treating the job as a nail with only one corresponding tool – a bullet festival – Jake and Doug whiteboard their analysis of who is likely to respond to a night letter. The "night letter," a classic form of correspondence, consists of a simple explanation of the why's and wherefores of a situation, such as, here are photos of you with person X, here's some money, shut up or we publish it, or worse.

Jake and Doug, being nice guys at heart, decide that the fate of any parents will be decided later. Clearly the lawyer has to go – removing him will take a tool out of Brooks' toolbox and paradoxically reduce the scope of potential anti-Brooks informants. This pressure release valve should neutralize Brooks' need for a violent response in the area, as well as his ability to coordinate it. As the lawyer is the key fixer who works directly with Brooks' Canadian lieutenants, the folks farther down the chain will remain vulnerable and in the dark longer.

The Cat Lady at the university, sad to say, serves no social use, and is the most ideologically committed member of the network, securing fake enrollments at the University of Toronto for Albanian jihadis engaging in drug trafficking, the shittiest refuse Jake and Doug can imagine being inflicted upon the fine people of Canada. While a clean removal would make the most sense, they decide it would be hilarious for her death to be a public and gory message to the other conspirators.

The young city counsellor is too pretty for the boys to slaughter, even though her balding, effete, leather-elbowed-sweater-wearing boyfriend has Jake ranting about vegetarian diets and communist indoctrination. A nice night letter after Cat Lady, with whom she co-chairs a local refugee settlement committee, gets smoked should suffice.

Doug decides that the editor has to go. His kids are grown, and his wife will manage without him. Jake signs off – the editor is a zealot, whose death will send up smoke signals. That leaves the police lieutenant, a clearly corrupt, tough street fighter, who rose meteorically within anti-narcotics and organized crime task forces. Doesn't feel good, to take out a man with a family, but they can't imagine changing his direction without stirring up a hornet's nest. Better safe than sorry. Regardless, he will be taken care of away from the home, and a snatch of a man like that is nigh impossible. A messy job.

The weapons will be issued mostly as requested, with four Beretta handguns available onsite via Vanguard. To teach a lesson in onsite improvisation, a local Vanguard employee will facilitate the modification of a locally-procured, unpapered Lee-Enfield .303 rifle into a suppressed urban sniping weapon. Doug's Canadian improvisation essay is employed in the design. No need to spray up the scene – Doug and Jake will use less men, more powerful shit for their team.

Christmas and New Year's pass, a blur. Doug goes out with the girls on New Year's, a bit disappointed that the ladies grind up a Ritalin and snort it to fuel hours of dancing, although they didn't behave unusually. Whatever – Doug can't claim to be a saint. He asks Jake about Ritalin, and Jake thrills him with tales of using what is essentially methamphetamine while on missions to maintain focus and performance over long periods with no sleep. "Whatever; don't worry about it, dude, unless she keeps doing it," Jake explains, which seems like a reasonable approach.

The day arrives. Doug rises extra early and retrieves Jake from his Belltown condo, arriving at security in SeaTac forty-five minutes before their flight, plenty of time at 5 a.m. On the drive to the airport, Jake explains the security signature concept. "These burner IDs will probably be done for – we won't be able to travel so openly for these types of jobs much longer. The networks are too ubiquitous. Had we gone through customs and flown directly to Toronto, we'd be radioactive. But, as we'll be infiltrating, we won't even have our faces photographed by Canadian customs."

The flight goes smoothly. Doug listens to several mix CDs Cathy burned for him on his Discman, emphasizing retro electronica, most of which he finds surprisingly good, though he dozes while attempting to read. Once on the ground in Buffalo they meet one their Vanguard contacts, Ed Roy, whose grandfather worked with Josef in Spain during and after the war. Doug would happily put Ed on a military educational poster as a template of Canadianness – mid-thirties, sandy blonde hair a little thin in front, fair skinned and lightly freckled, manly but pleasant. "This Man Is Canadian. He Fights For Freedom." He and his older brother, Tommy, will make all arrangements and do the driving for Doug and Jake through the snow and ice of a Lake Ontario winter.

They cross Lake Ontario after midnight on the back of snowmobiles piloted by Ed and an unnamed conspirator, blasting across the January ice cover without running lights, bound up in arctic-grade gear for the sub-zero temperatures. The city lights from both the Canadian and U.S. sides of the lake brighten the cloud-covered sky and illuminate the ice cover in dirty yellow-gray for the entire jarring and terrifying thirty-plus mile journey. Although Ed planned their route using National Oceanic and Atmospheric Administration maps, updated daily, and tested the route the night before, Doug is unable to shake the thought of hitting a thin patch at fifty miles per hour and plunging beneath the ice sheet with a shattered spine.

Ed deposits the pair at a marina an easy three-block stroll from their luxuriously furnished safe house on the lake, just down the road from their first target in the neighborhood known as "The Beach," with a promise to see them at 8 a.m. the following morning. No weaponry or operational equipment is stored at this location, in case the team is tracked during infiltration. Doug realizes the wisdom of this approach – during the War, Josef had to assume that actual eyeballs were on him during infiltrations, operations and exfiltrations; rendezvous and resupplies were only carried out after significant backtracking and re-routing. He'd read of recent tests of airborne observation of key smuggling routes by the U.S. Border Patrol, night and day, along the Mexican border; straight lines are the enemy.

Doug and Jake rise at 6:30 a.m. for vigorous calisthenics and stretching led by Jake, then dress in polos and jeans covered by workmen's insulated coveralls before an egg-and-coffee breakfast prepared by Jake, a protein fanatic. "Doug, do yourself a favor and focus on nutrition, minimizing grains and sugar, and your physique will improve over the years, rather than deteriorating," Jake lectures at the breakfast nook in their retro-modern kitchen, all high-end stainless steel and dark stained woods, gesturing with his fork. "The modern diet will kill you. Eating at restaurants will kill you. Noodles and shit." He shudders. "You eat a lot of venison, right? I didn't grow up hunting; never done it."

Doug nods. "I didn't get out this year, but it's hard to not bag an elk and a few deer up where I grew up. I can probably get a nice fifty-pound haunch for you, if you're interested."

"Hell yeah." Jake beams. "Good, clean meat, no hormones or cannibal slurry animal feed." He checks his watch, a throwaway Casio G-Shock, provided by Ed to each of them. The clothing and accessories they wore for the trip from Seattle are stored back in Buffalo, along with their carry-on luggage. "We got three minutes." They wolf down their food and Doug collects their plates before lightly scrubbing them in the sink and placing them in the dishwasher. As he dries his hands, Jake says from the front room, "Saddle up."

They both slip into side-zip work boots, put on wool knit caps and grab heavy wool jackets more appropriate for the downtown office set. Jake walks to the panel van waiting in the driveway, chatting with Ed in the passenger seat as Doug arms the security system and locks the front door. In the van, Ed introduces the pair to Tommy, the driver; they shake hands and look each other over as they pull out. Tommy looks like a slightly older, slightly balder, more pugnacious iteration of Ed, but he's all business as they explore their new area of operations by vehicle and on foot, covering the areas around their targets' residences and employers. The team covers "The Beach" through downtown until noon traffic grinds everything to a halt; they break for lunch at an Italian deli not far from UT St. George for sandwiches and steaming-hot Americanos.

"I gotta tell you guys," Doug says to the others at the last table before the restrooms in the rear of the deli, "I thought Mount Olympus – that's in Washington – in a snowstorm in February was cold. But this is COLD. Is it always like this during winter here?"

Ed and Tommy shrug. Tommy puts down his half-eaten sub and wipes his mouth, raising a finger as he chews and swallows. "Yeah, our winters are pretty rough. You have to remember that it's relatively flat here, I mean the terrain, and where there are hills and mountains, they generally go north-south."

Ed interjects, "And you got the lakes –"

Tommy nods. "The lakes, the flats, you got crazy arctic winds coming down from the north, you got the plains – which stretch across the middle of the States as well as Canada – you just get crazy winds. It's what, negative thirty right now."

Ed nods. "Negative thirty if you count wind chill, although that's not even bad, relatively speaking."

Jake shakes his head. "I grew up mostly in Minnesota. Every time I complain about the winters in Seattle – boys, you know the whole rain deal – I just remember a snow camping trip when I was a Scout, thought my fingers and toes were gonna fall off, actually had to get medical treatment."

Tommy gestures with his sandwich. "Yeah, but the weather does move on. We have a lot of snow and ice, wind, but you can see the sun at least half the winter. I hear that's not the case out there, at least from my guys in Vancouver."

Doug finishes his sandwich, and then stands. "Here the weather kills you. There, you kill yourself because of the weather."

The team spends the rest of the short, miserable afternoon scouting the homes and workplaces of their targets, scribbling out notes vague on details, grouped only by a number for each target. Doug and Jake patrol on foot as much as possible, having a rougher go of that in the suburbs than the city due to lingering snow from a recent storm. They decide to split into two teams, Jake and Tommy working the west side of downtown, Doug and Ed the east, for the evening patrols. A member of Ed's network delivers a three-year-old dark blue Crown Victoria sedan to a pizza restaurant's parking lot, handing Ed the keys inside before disappearing, while Doug is in the restroom. Their first stop is College Street – the university admin.

Doug finds Ed to be congenial yet professional, casually conducting a personality analysis as they navigate the city. At a red light several blocks from their destination, Ed turns and speaks openly. "So, Doug, don't get me wrong, but you seem like a nice kid. I know who you are, I mean, but are you really up for this?"

Doug returns his assessing gaze coolly. "Don't worry about it, I won't choke. Without getting into it, this isn't my first rodeo."

Ed laughs. "I spent a lot of time as a kid on my granddad's ranch in Alberta. I know a little about that."

Doug laughs. "I haven't ridden a horse since preschool. Hey, did you guys get more than one rifle up and running?"

Ed nods as the light turns green. "That your design? Seemed bizarre to me, but damned if it isn't slick. Built one and tested it out at the farm last week. Real small.

A shame to chop up an Enfield like that, but it fits in a tiny gym bag now, real accurate out to 300 meters. Didn't try any farther. Wouldn't shoot the subsonics past that. I have the mil dot holdover notes with the rifle for the subsonic loads."

"Great." Doug points through the windshield to their target's apartment building, coming up a block ahead on the left. "Look; totally different environment at night. Lots of little hidey-holes and shadow. Nice."

Ed narrows his eyes, nodding to the apartment as they drive past. "Her schedule over the past few weeks has been busiest Thursday and Friday nights. Gets home late, around ten, ten thirty. From that direction," pointing east. "So, tomorrow and the next night. The rest of the time she gets home with take-out by seven, then watches TV. Thursday and Friday, she does her jihadi social club outreach bullshit."

"So we smoke her tomorrow or Friday. Works for me." Doug points to a street parking spot in front of another apartment building, which Ed slides into deftly.

Ed throws the car into park and turns to Doug. "What say we do this together. I'll take this side of the street; you scope out the apartment. I have an idea; see that campus office building up there, with the open street-side stairwell?"

"Nice." Doug nods. "I'll wait a minute to get out."

Ed checks the side mirror before stepping out into the street and closing the door. He walks around the back of the sedan and steps over a short bank of snow onto the sidewalk, then strides carefully towards his destination. The sidewalk appears bare and salted, but patches of sheen inspire caution. Doug watches Ed through the side mirror as he walks to the end of the block, crosses a single-lane access road, and disappears into the open lobby of the office building.

Doug pushes his door open to get out, but it travels mere inches before stopping in a crunch. He looks down; the low snowbank along the edge of the road blocks the bottom two inches of the door. "Shit." He closes the door carefully, knocking only a little snow into the car, then crawls across the driver's seat, waits for several cars to pass, and exits. The street has remnants of slush amongst the scattered salt; he runs across all four lanes during a gap in traffic. On the north side, he steps over puddles in the accumulated snow between long-parked cars, crosses the steeper snowbank, then stomps the crusted snow from the soles of his boots. The locals are clearly comfortable in this weather; there's still quite a bit of foot traffic, with students, staff and yuppies out and about for the evening or heading home. He moves southwest, glancing periodically towards Ed's position, the sidewalk, and ahead to the apartment building.

The central courtyard of the U-shaped apartment building, a three story mid-century institutional-looking structure of sandy brick with small windows, is barred behind a four-foot tall wrought-iron fence. The gate is secured with a keypad lock; Doug punches in the four-digit code, procured by the Roys, and enters the wide courtyard, noting the landscape, areas of concealment, and the approaches to each building. No cameras, as reported – Doug chuckles, figuring they will be here soon enough. Steps ascend about six feet from the courtyard to the doorway on the target's side of the building, on his left; an identical approach is opposite, serving the other side. He looks up to the target's window on the second floor, then across the street to the office building where Ed went. Eight months out of the year, the foliage of the large trees lining College Street would block visibility beyond the curb, but he can clearly see Ed between bare branches. Ed waves. Doug steps back, performs one last look about, then walks out through the courtyard and across the street. The office building is set back about thirty yards from the sidewalk, ten or more feet higher than street level. Two large, mature deciduous trees with thick, snaking branches flank the broad walkway to the entrance. Atop the paved stairs of the walkway, he turns, looking back to the courtyard, then glances up at the third floor where Ed waits, looking down at him over a chest-high concrete slab. He bounds up the stairwell to meet Ed in a surprisingly narrow hallway, cringing at the sickly yellow overhead lights and soulless institutional grey concrete "architecture" typical of 1950s officialdom.

"Good God, is this building horrific," Doug comments, walking partway down the hallway to see if there are any occupants. He walks back to the stairwell landing, where Ed leans on his elbows and gazes across the street to the courtyard.

"I already checked it out," Ed states levelly. "Nobody home. These professors, they're not exactly burning the midnight oil. This is all commie poly sci types, here, this building." Ed shakes his head. "We have a nice perch here. It's about seventy meters to the middle of that courtyard, right where the path makes a T. Wanna hear my idea?"

Doug nods, leaning against the concrete slab with his arms crossed. "Shoot."

Ed smiles. "We got a guy up here. Workman. Got his tools out, a big tool bag and a toolbox, set up right here, the rifle all assembled and ready to go, safety on. Earpiece. He's fixing this stupid light, or something." One of the big faded-yellow-housing florescent lights behind them blinks every few seconds. He turns to Doug, waiting for a cue. Doug nods his head in the affirmative. "Alright. We got the van parked down around the block to the right, doesn't really matter where. We got two guys on foot to track her, one behind, one in front; they'll let us know when she's coming so the guy up here can pick her out. Finally." He takes a pack of cigarettes out of his coverall's chest zip pocket, draws a green Bic lighter from within the pack and pops a cigarette between his lips. He holds the pack out, offering one to Doug, who declines. He shrugs, lights the smoke, and returns the lighter to the pack, the pack to his pocket. After a long draw, he removes the cigarette from his mouth between his left index and middle fingers with a casual flourish, he breathes a heavy stream of smoke from between his nostrils. "Mmmm. It's an easy shot – you got this slab, a foot thick, perfect height, just brace on your elbows, ZAP. Slide the rifle into the bag, bag over the shoulder, grab the tool case, you're gone. Ground team can confirm she's wasted from down there," pointing with his cigarette hand to the sidewalk in front of the courtyard, "walk up and around the corner to the van. Everyone gets in, we're gone." Ed turns his head, watching Doug's face as he plays the scenario out in his mind.

"Good plan." Doug gestures with his chin across the street. "That's a shit area for a close-up job. Too many windows, not enough cover, too many ways for it to go bad. I'm in. Let's walk around this part of campus, see what we can see."

Ed points behind them with his thumb. "There's a stairwell back there, looks just like this one. It lets out on a nice path behind these buildings, up to the street I had in mind."

"Let's do it." They push off the wall and walk through the dingy hallway, then slap their boots down the concrete stairwell, exiting onto a cozy path in a deserted campus courtyard, lit by handsome black iron streetlamps. The older buildings in this part of the campus suggest Doug's favorite part of the UW campus, the Quad, a sort of Beaux-Arts filtered 19th century gothic, but here having a more directly medieval feel. Another mid-century institutional nightmare looms ahead on the left, ruining the experience.

"Here we are," Ed notes, as they leave the courtyard via a narrow gap between the obvious administrative building and a more evocative structure, meeting the sidewalk of a narrow street sparsely occupied with parallel-parked cars. "I feel calmer already." He gestures up and down the street. "We'll slap a parking permit in the rear window of the van and call it good. It's early in the term. This place will fill up in a couple of weeks as the pace picks up. I graduated from here, oh, a decade ago. Doesn't seem that long ago, but a lot has changed." A group of four Asian students dressed in massive parkas strolls around them, heading towards College Street, chattering in Mandarin. Ed smiles knowingly to Doug.

Ed and Doug arrive at the safe house thirty minutes before Tommy and Jake, and use the time to enjoy the view from the patio - the lights of Toronto and the American side of the lake - while Ed chain-smokes and rants. "I'm trying to quit. These damn things. Tommy quit; won't let me smoke in the car. It makes sense – these'll kill ya, they killed my grandfather and my dad both – but man, when things ratchet up, nothing like nicotine to smooth it over. I've smoked more in the last three hours than in a week." He stubs out the cigarette in a brick planter box, paces a bit, then lights another.

"Are you nervous?" Doug asks. Ed has been calm all day with the group, but has been getting antsy since the drive back from the university.

"Eh." Ed shrugs. "I always get a little jittery before a job. I just want it to go well. Don't worry, I'll be cool as a cucumber." He seems to realize that he's making Doug nervous, and slows his breathing. "Maybe I need to quit smoking; it could be the nicotine." They hear Tommy and Jake pull into the driveway in the van, doors slamming, and head in to meet with them.

It's only 9 p.m., so the team decides they'll plot out the next day before getting some sleep. Ed grinds some coffee beans and preps the pot before Tommy tells him to save it for the morning. Ed concedes, instead brewing decaffeinated tea, which the Americans are less enthusiastic about, but find soothing.

Jake takes over as team lead, running the meeting, offering team members veto power if they can justify any argument against a suggested plan. He plops a white legal pad down on the dining table in the kitchen, encouraging everyone to crowd around. The team sips their steaming tea and go over their scouting missions, referring to intel packets, and offering suggestions for each action.

Doug and Ed go first, starting with the lawyer. Their idea is straightforward – walk right up off the walking path on the lakefront to his breakfast nook and blast him through the window in the kitchen. His "partner," a twenty-five-year-old bartender with a party lifestyle, usually gets home after 4 a.m., while the lawyer rises at 5 a.m. to go to the gym before starting work promptly at 7:30 a.m. His partner probably won't suspect a thing until he walks downstairs around noon and feels the cold winter air through the broken window.

Other witnesses aren't a concern, either, as the lawyer's lot is one of the few beachfront properties in the area and has very tall hedges for privacy against the small apartment building to the east and houses to the west. The house is separated from the beach boardwalk and biking paths by a long lot as well as a full lot side yard, a good eighty feet from theoretical foot traffic, beautifully landscaped even in frost-bitten Toronto winters, with a covered patio for the approach. As Ed notes, nobody is crazy enough to jog in -30C temperatures at 4:30 a.m., not even Torontans.

Ed suggests that the lawyer go first, since he's the common link between all the targets, as well as the rest of Brooks' organization. Further, he rises earliest in the morning, and will – likely – be the target discovered last. Jake raises his hand, silencing everyone, and suggests that they focus on each target analysis before defining an overall operational plan. "OK, Doug, Ed, what about the cat lady?"

Ed and Tommy look at each other quizzically. Jake explains. "'Cat lady' is a pejorative term applied to older, single, childless women who project their unused maternal instincts on society at large rather than where God intended, their own family." The table erupts into laughter.

Doug leans in. "I wasn't real happy with the options until Ed here found a perfect sniper's nest. It'll be a semi-public job, of course, but with the rifle and the cover of night, it should be a while before anyone catches on. All we need is one or two minutes. No way are we getting into her apartment, way too hairy. At her job, no way, way too many people, no privacy. On the street? Too difficult to do cleanly.

So, single shot from, what, seventy-five, eighty meters, drop her in the middle of the apartment courtyard."

Jake cringes. "Really?"

Doug smiles. "Hey, you wanted to send a message, right, make it a little splashy?" He frames an imaginary newspaper in the air between his hands, "publishing" a headline. "'Jihadi Enabler Whore Blown Away In Public.' All caps. Hilarious. Any other scenario turns into too many witnesses at the time the bullet hits the bone, possible interference, big trouble. Too risky."

Ed points to Doug. "Golden Earring, nice."

Jake shrugs. "Yeah, I don't like the idea of the daylight university option. Too many kids around." The team agrees, and moves on to Jake and Tommy. As Jake is running the meeting, Tommy explains their recommendations.

"The police detective. This is a hard-charging guy, armed, real rough, does hits for Brooks' organization. We can't give him a hint that anything is going on. I know we're not talking ops planning yet, but Jake and I agree that we have to take him close to his house, first thing in the morning, before the blood is pumping, and before anybody else turns up missing or dead. He works late, gets home at random times, but always leaves the house around 6 a.m. His neighborhood is a nightmare, real narrow streets and tightly packed houses, small yards, fences everywhere, a real eyesore. But," Tommy pauses, then grabs another legal pad and begins sketching out a street layout, "there's only one way in and out of his neighborhood, here. Here, a block away, is the main drag towards downtown, with a no-turns-on-red street light, and you can park all the way up to here," drawing a crosswalk and curbs. "There aren't houses here, just a commercial building on the left, and a park on the right. Park here, backseater blasts him in his car from five feet away, pull out, you're good. Another commuter finds his car running, oh dear, checks, the guy is toast."

Doug asks, "So someone's gonna blast him with 9mm subsonics through the passenger side window? Pretty confident that you can stop him so quickly?"

Jake responds. "That's fair. That's what magazines are for. Another alternative is to block the street with the van at the light, while someone on foot blasts him, or both. Not a lot of other good options. No way are we doing it at the police station, and I'm not doing it in front of his house where his wife and kids will find him."

Doug and Ed look at each other. Ed takes out a cigarette, but Tommy gives him the stink-eye. He puts the cigarette on the table. Tommy picks it up and throws it across the room. Ed opens his mouth, then closes it. Doug blurts out, "Alright, so we're talking lots of bullets."

Jake looks at the two brothers while responding to Doug. "He goes to a commercial gym in the morning, every weekday morning, so he shouldn't be wearing a vest."

Doug counters, "Why not take him at the gym, when he's getting out of the car?"

Jake sits back, looking a little annoyed, but pondering it. "Doug, no matter what, this is gonna be what you call a bullet festival. I'm willing to take the chance on an imperfect hit at the best place to do it, versus rolling the dice elsewhere where there are more witnesses, more ways to screw up."

Tommy leans towards Doug, his hands wide, magnanimously. "We don't like it much, either, but it's the best opportunity given what we have to work with. I figure, shoot him up, we got the drop on him, it's worth a bit of a gamble, and not even much of one at that."

Doug sits back. "Sure, just wanted to talk it over."

"Alright." Jake moves on to the next point. "The Editor. This guy is our softest target. His house, couple of acres, backing to a wooded park, he wakes up, tools around a little, checks email, reads in the kitchen while eating too much breakfast, then drives down to work at the paper. His wife, I was inclined to spare her a horrorshow, but she has a bunch of pet lefty causes, real hard left, and not in the way that is about taking care of regular people, you know? I say blast him through the window with the rifle, or we can blast him in the garage," looking over at Doug, who swallows uncomfortably, "with the Berettas. Or we can cap him in the parking lot at the paper. He has a reserved spot. I think it'd be hilarious to shoot a journalist in the head where his fellow slanderers will find his body."

"Tell us how you really feel, Jake," says Ed, chortling. "Jeez," taking his pack of cigarettes from his chest pocket.

Tommy palms the cigarette pack and smashes it into Ed's chest, rubbing back and forth, sending flakes of tobacco into his lap. "Stop. With. The. Cigarettes," he says, punctuating each word with a push. "You're acting like an amateur." He sits back in the chair, folding his arms.

Jake shakes his head. "Tommy, can the health lectures resume after the job is done? A little bullying is OK, but I don't want him going through withdrawals this week. Let the guy have a cigarette." Ed walks over to the kitchen, removes a fresh pack from a drawer, and steps outside to light up, giving Tommy a dirty look.

"Sorry, Jake. I can't take him bitching about how hard it is to quit smoking." Tommy slumps in his chair, clearly exhausted.

"Don't worry about it." Jake drinks the rest of his tea, grimacing as he swallows the tails, then pushes the cup out of the way. "I like the paper. We just have to go on foot, van a few blocks away, do another car switch somewhere. None of these journalist faggots are going to chase us down or anything."

Tommy nods. "Yeah, we'll use our storage unit over on Adelaide. Real close."

"Alright." Jake clears his throat. He beckons out the window to Ed, who stubs out the remains of his cigarette, then re-enters the house and sits with them. Jake waits a beat, then continues. "OK, so we'll take him at the paper. Finally, the cute city councilor. We're gonna do a night letter, and leave it at that. I figure, access her building at night after the cat lady gets smoked, 'Quit and disappear or you're next,' real gentle like. If we have reason to believe she needs to go, you guys can take care of it in the future. What do you think?" Ed and Doug shrug. Tommy looks at Jake with a funny expression. After a beat, Jake asks, "What?"

Tommy lets Jake stew in silence, a flat smile on his face, before exhaling theatrically. "Jake likes hippie chicks. Never would have believed it."

Jake crosses his arms. "I just don't see why she needs to go. I have no evidence that she's doing anything that any dumb girl between six and sixty wouldn't fall for, without the guiding influence of an actual man."

"Oh, shit." Tommy shrugs exaggeratedly. "Whatever, softie."

Jake huffs, and the group breaks down laughing. "Alright, guys, we're getting delirious. It's been a long day. Let's put together our operational plan. So. With all of the above – timelines?"

The team debates for several minutes, drawing out lists and times, but ultimately settle on the following timeline:

The lawyer. 5 a.m., at home. Team of two – Doug and Ed.

The detective. 6 a.m., at the intersection. Team of two – Jake and Tommy.

The editor. 9 a.m., parking garage of the newspaper office. Jake and Ed on foot, Doug as backup, Tommy driving.

The cat lady. 10 p.m., from the office across the street from her apartment. Doug will shoot, Ed and Jake will track her on foot, Tommy with the van. This drives the most debate – will she show up to her community meeting that night, once word gets out that the lawyer – her connection to Brooks' organization – has been murdered, along with a known left wing editor, and a dirty cop? It's worth a gamble, they decide – she doesn't own a car, she doesn't have a lot of options. If she heads straight home from work and holes up or gets out of town, they can take her out in the future, if they feel the need.

The city councilor, night letter after midnight.

The most important logistical element will be vehicular – the team has been driving around all day in a pair of vehicles, now parked in the driveway of their safe house. A van full of their equipment for tomorrow is parked several blocks away in a parking garage owned by a Vanguard subsidiary, so Tommy will load the gear into his van and bring it back to the house tonight. Tomorrow, Tommy and Jake will use the new van, and Ed and Doug will swap to another car after they do the lawyer and head downtown. Ed telephones an associate using the kitchen wall phone, requesting delivery of a sedan tonight to Lee Avenue, across from Beaches Park, two blocks from the target house. The associate will leave the keys in an undercarriage magnetic key box, and retrieve the Crown Vic from the same space tomorrow night.

Tommy leaves to retrieve the equipment, and the rest of the team showers and shaves for the next day, which will begin in less than five hours. Freshly scrubbed and polished, Doug selects garments for the following day:

Heavy insulated light grey coveralls over wool long underwear, with a lightweight dark gray coverall over it, which he'll shed before they transfer cars. Black leather gloves. Heavy black wool knit cap. Thick black wool socks. Brown leather heavy insulated winter work boots.

His upper-middle class college student guise, a ski jacket, green wool sweater, grey wool Swedish army surplus cargo pants, thick black wool socks and insulated Doc Marten boots, black leather, natch. This collection goes into a garbage bag from the kitchen, then into a gym bag emblazoned with a European sportswear logo.

Tommy returns, carrying a large duffel bag in each hand and a blue-green hard plastic reciprocating saw case slung over his shoulder. "Ta-daaaaa," he announces, holding up the bags. "Let's split up the gear and get fitted." Off the top of one bag, Tommy draws four pairs of black leather police gloves, which they will wear when handling their equipment and for the duration of the operation tomorrow.

The equipment provided is a light interpretation of that specified in Doug's mission briefing. Each two-man team gets one Beretta .32 ACP pistol and one Beretta 9mm, modified per Doug's design requirements, along with holsters, gun belts, magazine carriers, and a suppressor for each firearm, with its own belt pouch. Doug takes the .32 ACP, Ed the 9mm. The holsters are minimalistic, made with an inexpensive thermoplastic, and designed to cover the trigger guard and attach to the belt via a tether, with no other frills. They each select an encrypted Motorola radio with an earpiece and a mic key that fits down a sleeve, a small Surefire flashlight with fresh batteries, an 8 power monocular with a belt mounted case, and a balaclava. The belts are pre-mounted with a black leather sheath containing a Swiss Army knife – the small Tinker – and a small pocket pry bar in a thermoplastic sleeve. Also standard are a yellow safety helmet – a hard-hat – as well as a high visibility safety vest, safety glasses, and a clipboard with several blank work order tickets to complete the utility worker disguise. "Seems like we'd be drawing attention to ourselves," Ed comments.

"Not at all," Doug says. "The FBI recently published a study of witness descriptions. They found that specifics about perps are much more challenging when they wear an iconic uniform - they look like they belong there. For example: military camouflage in the city sticks out like a sore thumb; wear this getup and carry a clipboard or tool bag, and you are practically invisible everywhere, even if you're sneaking around in alleys or office building back hallways. The description is rarely better than 'white male utility worker.'" The brothers shrug, while Jake looks at Doug with an approving smile.

Each driver selects a handheld scanner capable of accessing police and cellular bands, as well as a Nokia mobile phone, along with batteries yet to be installed. "The phones are tested, but we don't want them to connect to the network until we're well away from this safe house, or any other location linked to us or Vanguard," Tommy explains. "We'll incinerate them after the job."

Finally, Tommy flips open the twenty-six-inch-long blue-green tool case, revealing a cut-down Lee-Enfield No. 4 Mk I in a fitted foam bed. The Lee-Enfield is the iconic British Commonwealth rifle of World War II, commonly found in Canadian homes, but this one has a barrel abbreviated to 12" and threaded, with a matching shop-made high-volume suppressor furnished. The rear iron sight is gone, replaced by a low-power pistol scope mounted over the barrel, forward of the receiver. The stock is also modified, with the forend cut off two inches behind the end of the barrel, a sling mount attached at terminus, and the butt removed and replaced with a pistol grip and side-folding stock, machined using a simple design published in a gun magazine. 190 grain bullets are used in special subsonic loads charged with bulky shotgun powder. Conventional supersonic cartridges are also included. Tommy remarks that the sound reduction is impressive.

The Lee-Enfield, arguably the best bolt-action rifle ever issued by a military, has a ten round magazine that can be quickly topped off via five-round stripper clips, which take up far less room than spare magazines. Following Doug's specs, Tommy has included in the package an original issue two-cell web stripper clip pouch, which Doug will mount on the front of his belt, left side, with subsonics in the left cell and supersonics to the right. There are twenty additional rounds of ammunition loaded into stripper clips in the case, along with notes about hold-over for subsonic ammunition using the Mil-Dot scope reticle. Doug is a little disappointed that they'll only be physically removing one of their targets with this slick number, but at least he gets to be the trigger man.

The last item issued to each man is a money clip with an inset liquid compass, containing $500 Canadian dollars in various denominations, a prepaid phone card, a pocket map of the Toronto area, and a Toronto Transit Commission weekly pass. "This is if the shit completely hits the fan, boys," Jake notes. "If we get separated, or worse. Each job has a rally point, which you've discussed, but each sector of town has a transit hub that we'll use as a fallback. Let's standardize on meeting one block west of the southwestern corner of each transit hub." Jake opens his own map, pointing out the secondary rally points for each region. "Call the voicemail box written on the back of your phone card to check in. If you're burned, or under surveillance, say, 'The Leafs blew it.' Otherwise, just name the station, and we'll meet you at the rally point on the soonest hour. If we can't get there, don't hang out, just meet on the next hour. Have a cup of coffee or something. Finally, we're going to use simple identifiers on the radio. Team One is me and Tommy. Ed, Doug, you're team Two. The team leads are 'One.' Therefore, I'm One-One. Tommy is One-Two. Ed, you're Two-One. Doug is Two-Two. Simple?" The team agrees. "Finally, if we have to change channels, I'll call the change, and give you a number three higher than the actual channel we'll use. Alright? We'll start with channel five."

They test their Motorola radios around the house, each man already familiar with radio protocol, so it goes quickly. Finally, exhausted, the team retires to their bedrooms, setting alarms for 3 a.m. Doug is up not long after 2 a.m., unable to sleep, so he hits the safe house's adequately equipped basement gym to get his blood flowing, then showers again for good measure. He still has enough time to assist Ed with breakfast – eggs, ham, hash browns, and coffee – before Jake and Tommy join them. They are, to a man, tooled up and ready to go, their equipment concealed beneath their insulated coveralls, thin coveralls over those. At the kitchen table, Jake stands, tapping the steaming coffee cup in his hand with a fork. "A toast!" The team stands, raising their own coffee cups. "We have a busy day ahead of us, and a team up to the task. Let's execute perfectly. Stay calm, stay focused, stay alert. Above all, communicate – communicate – communicate. If something isn't going to work, we switch to plan B. No cowboy shit. None of these people are invincible, but if something looks bad, trust your instinct, and we'll get 'em later. To victory!"

"To victory!" goes up the chorus, and the four men click their mugs together, then sip the scalding coffee, laughing and sitting down to eat. There's very little small-talk, each pair focusing on their partner, switching into mission mode. They wrap up quickly, discarding the plates in the dishwasher, Ed preparing four thermos bottles of coffee – in the old green steel bottles, not the new cheap Chinese plastic ones – and issuing one per man, along with a large disposable bottle of water and commercial protein bars. They check their clock – still just before 4 a.m. – and shake hands, wishing each other luck in battle, then head out to their vehicles, each with a gym bag containing their gear, Doug carrying the rifle in its tool case. Tommy and Jake have the longest drive, nearly an hour to their target in the western suburbs, while Doug and Ed make the short drive to the eastern edge of Beaches Park. There they find the nondescript sedan left there by Ed's associate, a tan Mercury Grand Marquis, and fortuitously slide into an open spot less than fifty feet up the road. They exit their Crown Vic with their equipment, and Ed places the car's ignition key in a magnetic box in the undercarriage beneath the driver's seat.

They retrieve a key from the same location under the Grand Marquis, then place their extra gear in the trunk. The equipment needs for the lawyer are minimal. Ed puts a small can of black spray paint into Doug's hand; Doug slides it in his rear pocket.

On the walk to the lawyer's lakefront home, Doug nudges Ed. "You seem to like these big road sofas. Why not a truck, or a more compact car, for maneuverability?"

Ed shakes his head. "Both of these things are basically police pursuit vehicles that look at home in someone's grandma's driveway," he explains. "They each have the V8, rear wheel drive, extra handling package, heavy duty suspension, beefier rear axles, dual exhaust, a more nimble transmission, et cetera. They're fast as hell and can ram through most cars, if you know what you're doing. Besides, you notice the snow and ice? You don't want to be driving around in a little shitbox in this weather."

Doug nods. "I gotcha. Your roads are a lot better around here than where I grew up, where we're on dirt or gravel, mountains, super steep hills, and so on. We default to trucks. Makes sense. A truck identifies you as a type of person. Sedans are boring and invisible."

"Exactly." Ed draws a pack of cigarettes from his coveralls as they cross the street towards the lake, a frigid breeze hitting them in the face. "I'm gonna smoke. Since I got overwatch, screw it, I'm gonna have a smoke." He turns, ducking his head down into his chest and cups a cigarette in his palm, lighting it with his Bic. The cherry flares, and a puff of smoke drifts back to the street; Ed returns the lighter to the pack and stuffs it back into his coverall chest pocket. They continue walking into the wind, grateful that there is no precipitation. Doug rolls down his balaclava to insulate himself from the -20 C blast as they turn east onto the walking path that runs between the beach and the small cluster of houses and apartment buildings in this section of The Beach, their target looming ahead. Ed checks his watch; 4:18 a.m. "We're early," he notes.

"That's fine," Doug notes as the wind picks up, buffeting the pair. Ed stubs out his cigarette on his boot, slides the remnants into his left front pocket, and rolls down his balaclava. They walk to the end of the block, past the target house beckoning on their left, to look up Hammersmith Avenue for any signs of foot traffic or law enforcement captured in the streetlights. None.

"If it were summer, there'd be joggers out, even at this hour," Ed notes. "Alright. I'll set up on that bench like we discussed – I can watch all the way down the trail to the west or east, and up Hammersmith, as well as scope out these apartments. I'm gonna be chain smoking. Let's do our radio check." Ed keys his radio, "Two-One, check, check."

Doug nods, keying his own radio with his left hand. "Two-Two, check, check."

Ed nods. "We're good to go. Get moving, Doug, and Godspeed."

"OK, this is it." They shake hands, then Doug strolls back to the west, passing the brick apartment building and approaching the lawyer's home, the wind blasting his back. The beach trail runs right up to the home's low wrought iron fence, which Doug hops at the corner, next to the brick apartment building. Visibility is quite good due to the reflection of city lights off of the cloudy skies, but Doug does not skulk, as that would be more suspicious to a third party watching him. He scans the windows of the home, which are unlit, then closes his right eye and carefully walks up to the raised deck, drawing the spray can from his rear pocket and shakes it gently. A motion sensor light flips on, bathing the deck in bright white light; Doug sprays the two exposed bulbs and motion sensor in thick black enamel, then pockets the spray can. Once again in darkness, he opens his right eye; within twenty seconds, his left eye has readjusted to the dark.

Doug squats and carefully scans the interior of the lawyer's house through the windows and floor to ceiling sliding glass double doors. The kitchen and dining table are to his left, a living room with two low leather couches and a rear projection TV to the right, beside a fireplace. And there, on one of the couches, lies the lawyer's blonde boyfriend, nearly naked under a blanket, snoring away.

Shit. Above him, a light goes on upstairs, softly illuminating the outer reaches of the deck. The lawyer is awake. Gentle sounds drift down – a closet door sliding open, feet plodding, another door opening. Doug moves left to right, attempting to find the best angle for an accurate shot into the kitchen and the boyfriend on the right, not finding anything promising. He notes in one of the reclining deck chairs' arms a mostly empty bottle of Moosehead and an ashtray with several cigarettes and joints stubbed out in it. Clothes are scattered between the sliding glass door and the couch. He reconstructs the boyfriend's journey home last night from his bar, with a nightcap on the deck before crawling in to pass out. It's worth a shot. Doug unzips his coverall to his waist and draws the Beretta .32 ACP pistol with suppressor already attached, unsnapping it gently from the thermoplastic holster, then zips his coverall closed. He checks the former "safety" lever, now the slide lock, with his thumb; it's disengaged. He straightens his right arm with the pistol locked tightly in a firing grip in his hand, finger off the trigger and held along the frame – safety first! – then squats slightly and extends his left hand forward, resting it on the right sliding door's handle, then pushes to the left. The door silently glides open several inches.

Drawn forward as if by a grappling hook in his chest, he carefully steps into the house, onto the boyfriend's shirt which lies barely over the threshold, then ever so slowly slides the door shut behind him. Gently, Doug rubs his boots into the shirt, then picks up the shirt with his left hand, rolling it into a tube and sliding it into his left front pocket. He points his pistol at the head of the sleeping boyfriend on the couch in a two-handed grip, listening carefully for sounds of life upstairs. A glance at the microwave in the kitchen shows the time, 4:33 a.m. The lawyer should come downstairs within the next few minutes. Doug reluctantly steps over to the edge of the couch, looking down at the sleeping, snoring form of the handsome young man drooling on a throw pillow, flips the slide lock into place, and fires a single lead bullet into the boyfriend's brain stem. The thump of the bullet striking the skull is shockingly loud, far louder than the discharge of the weapon, thanks to the slide lock and wipe-based suppressor design. Doug picks up another throw pillow from the other couch, positions it over the boyfriend's head to hide the horrific mess, then pulls the blanket up to cover him as he lets out a final sigh.

Oh, well. Flickers of guilt peck at his mind as Doug unlocks the slide and manually cycles the pistol, catching the spent .32 ACP case and slipping it into his right front pocket, then de-cocks the pistol and re-engages the slide lock. He plods carefully around the couch to the hall-side wall and leans against it, pistol in his right hand. Checking the microwave clock again, the time is 4:35 a.m. An eternity of waiting, with a man he killed lying on the couch twelve feet away, bowels voided and beginning to reek. A light goes on in the stairwell beyond the hall, and feet carefully patter down, something fabric and something firm being set down at the bottom of the stairs. The same feet carefully slip down the hallway, socks swip-swipping against the smooth hardwood, and the lawyer, tall, scrawny, bald-pated, wearing a grey track suit and awful glasses, shimmies into the room. "Richard? Richard?" the lawyer asks in an unseemly accent that Doug can't quite put his thumb on. "Oh, no, did you do it again?" His voice is effeminate in the stereotypical way but with another edge, not the usual Canadian lilt, more Northeastern American. Ah, that's what it is. Doug extends his pistol forward in a two handed stance and fires a single round into the base of the lawyer's skull, while noting this time, backlit from the hallway, a light sooty mist spraying out of the muzzle of the suppressor. The wire pulling gel ablative. Again, the impact of the bullet is far louder than the report of the pistol – a cracking thump – and the lawyer collapses like a marionette whose strings have been severed, over the body of his young boy toy. Following the same manual cycling procedure, and stepping right to avoid any lingering ablative mist, Doug walks around to the back of the couch, grabs the lawyer's scrawny arm and turns him over. Morbidly curious, he examines the gunshot wound, which smoothly pumps blood out at fifty beats per minute. A cardio guy, Doug thinks, dropping the corpse.

Mission accomplished, Doug unzips his coverall and slides the pistol back into its holster, zips the coverall closed, and walks out the sliding glass door, back into the wind. No movement, though the apartment building has one window lit up behind an opaque curtain. He keys his radio mic and says, "Two-Two returning, over."

His own earpiece squawks with Ed's voice, "Roger, Two-One moving, over." Doug walks carefully through the backyard, opens the wrought iron gate and gently closes it behind him, then joins Ed. "Let's roll," Ed says, and they move at a brisk walking pace with the wind at their backs for the two blocks to Lee Avenue. The town is coming slowly to life, with the occasional early morning commuter car out on the nearby streets, but no foot traffic. Under the street lamps and bare-branched deciduous trees along Alfresco Lawn, Ed asks, "How'd it go?" as he draws a fresh cigarette from his pack.

Doug doesn't answer immediately, but rolls up his balaclava and gestures to Ed for a cigarette. Ed hands him one, lighting it as Doug cups his hand over it in his mouth. The cigarette flares bright, and Doug's lungs fill partway with caustic smoke, but he holds it for a count of ten before exhaling.

"That bad?" Ed asks, matter of factly.

"Mmmm." Doug looks about, but there is nobody around. He takes another drag, more slowly this time, then expels it. He begins walking again, and Ed goes with him. "The boyfriend. He was downstairs. Had to do him. No other way about it." He turns as they walk, examining Ed's face carefully.

"Oh, well." Ed smokes aggressively, sucking down a quarter of the cigarette in a few drags. "Dude was a convicted child rapist. Buttfucked a bunch of thirteen, fourteen year old boys. Didn't see that in the intel packet you read? 'Cuz I made the original packet."

"Naw." Doug nods, walking and smoking. "Naw, that wasn't in there. Fuck it. I'm glad I greased him."

"You and me both, pal." They get to the Chrysler, as ridiculously long as when they left it, and strip off their thin outer coveralls, revealing the thick, gray insulated ones underneath. The outer coveralls go into a garbage bag in the trunk. Doug brings their gym bags into the passenger seat as Ed warms up the car, then pours each of them a cup of coffee from his thermos. Ed holds his cup up toward Doug, looking him in the eye with a smile; they click cups and drink the still raging hot coffee, letting its warmth spread throughout their bodies. After a few moments of comfort, Ed says, "Damn, I can make a good cup of coffee. Alright, let's roll. Turn on that cell phone, see if we got any action yet."

"You got it." Doug snaps one of the two battery packs into the Nokia, pulls up the antenna, and powers it on, waiting through startup as Ed pulls the land yacht out onto the road and executes a U turn, then heads north toward the arterial, Queen Street.

"How'd that little .32 work?" Ed asks, theatrically putting another cigarette into his mouth while turning the large steering wheel over and over and over to the left, sliding them through a wide turn.

"It did the job. I wouldn't want to be popping off shots against armed and moving targets, but for this it's more than enough. They used 'em for this during the war, and CIA still used .32s into the 70s." Doug squints in the intermittent street light at the screen of the cell phone as it comes online, finally connecting to the cellular network. "No calls."

"Good, wouldn't have expected any," Ed notes as they cruise down Queen. Doug looks out the window at workers waiting at a bus stop, a redheaded barista unlocking the door of a coffee shop, a young man pulling up alongside them at a stoplight behind the wheel of an old International Scout flecked with rust and corrosion around the wheel wells. Doug laughs. "Glad you're perking up, Doug," says Ed, rolling his window down and turning the heat up to high with a click. He lights yet another cigarette off the remnants of the other, gesturing with his right hand for Doug to roll the window down. He does. "Ya know, it's not like we're in a war, where you say, 'there's the enemy,'" pointing out the windshield with his right hand, "'he's trying to kill you, go kill him.' It's not like that." He puts the cigarette back in his mouth and drives forward as the light turns green, and talks with the cigarette clamped between his lips as he steers the car onto the expressway. "I don't wanna get too personal, but I thought your granddad, who I love by the way, was asking a lot from you to get you into this. But, you're the right guy for the job. You're a soldier." Ed takes the cigarette out of his mouth, exhaling sideways out the window, and looks steadily at Doug for a moment before extending his right hand. Doug accepts it. "Alright," Ed declares, turning his attention back to driving as they roar down the highway, the bay on their left, Old Toronto to their right. "We got some time to kill – ha! – so let's just head to the west side of town and support Jake and my brother, in case they need it. We'll hang out as a reaction force, as it were."

"Works for me." Doug drinks some more coffee and nibbles on a protein bar. "You were in the Canadian Forces, right?"

Ed glances at him. "Yeah, still a reservist. What of?"

"Did you think you'd be doing this in your own town?" Doug asks.

"Pffft." Ed rises up in his seat, laughing. "I joined the army because I wanted the training needed to clean up my town, and to join my dad and brother in the family business. Look, this place is a mess, Doug. Corrupt as hell, which is easy to sweep under the rug when it's just the nice domestic Canadians. It's steadily getting worse as things change. Mark my words – in twenty years, nobody will recognize the place, and it'll be run by foreigners. And I'm not talking about folks from the States, Doug. Like that scumbag lawyer you wasted. The Prime Minister should give you a medal."

The pair drives for another fifteen minutes before exits for Etobicoke appear, the sky lightening despite the cloud cover. "We'll take the 427; that'll drop us off right around the corner from this scroat. I got an idea," Ed says, and seven minutes later they pass a commercial gym on Burnhamthorpe Road, ascend a slight hill and pull into a housing development-to-be on the right, with streets paved and curbs in place, but no homes or utilities in evidence. Ed steers the Mercury down the fresh blacktop, says, "This should do," and pulls to the right, up into a vacant lot with a territorial view of the area, still covered with several inches of snow. Ed gets out of the car and pulls his monocular from its belt pouch, scoping the parking lot of the gym. Doug joins him, sitting on the front bumper and examining the view. "See all of this construction? Where are the people? Why do they know so many people are going to be living here? Who are those people? Who do you think, Doug?"

Doug looks out over the area under the thinning grey clouds, gaps showing pink, orange, and red sky between them, and the steady grid of residential development all around, a smattering of commercial buildings and cleared development sites along the highways, arterials and to the south in Islington and Etobicoke. Just to their northwest is Toronto Pearson International Airport, the second busiest airport in North America. A steady stream of aircraft circle overhead, intermittently flying in, others departing every few minutes. Ed points just to their northeast, less than a mile away, a dense residential cluster glowing yellow in a tangle of street and porch lights. "Jake and Tommy are right over there, waiting. I'll let 'em know we're here." Ed clears his throat, then keys his mic and says, "Two-One to One-One, in pos two, got your back, over."

Ten seconds later, Jake's voice beams into their earpieces. "One-One, roger, thanks, all is well, will confirm, over."

Doug and Ed glance at each other. Ed crunches through the still-soft snow to the trunk and removes the sawzall case and places it on the back seat. "This is just over a hundred meters; you ready to shoot if it comes to it, or should I?" Ed asks.

Doug shrugs. "I'm cool with you having a turn, Ed," laughing.

Ed smiles. "My dad slotted a lot of guys with a Lee-Enfield during the war, and then again in Korea. I'm half hoping Jake and Tommy abort, and I get to use this baby. She doesn't look like much, but she shoots sweet. You're crazy, man," laughing. He opens the sawzall case, unfolds the rifle's stock, and opens the bolt, placing a five round stripper clip of subsonic loads into the stripper clip guide, but not yet loading. He pushes the spring loaded scope cover release buttons, popping the covers open. He steps back, watches the main road for a bit, then checks his watch, walks back to the front of the car and sits on the hood, getting out another cigarette, first offering the pack to Doug, who declines.

Jake's voice comes over the earpiece. "Two-One, Two-Two moving out, rally point three, over."

Ed deflates a bit. "Two-One, roger, Two moving out; well done, over." He sighs, and walks back to the rear seat, leans into the car and clears the rifle and prepares it for travel, locking the case closed and returning it to the trunk, which he slams shut. He and Doug take their seats in the car, which Ed starts up, backing out of the snowy lot and coasting to the arterial.

Doug turns to Ed. "Why don't you take the Cat Lady? I don't mind."

Ed shrugs. "Eh."

Doug punches Ed lightly on his right shoulder. "You take the Cat Lady. You're missing out."

Ed returns Doug's gaze, perkier. "Really? Let's play it by ear. I guess I do have the most range time with the rifle, not that it's a big deal."

Doug nods. "See, that's a good point. I'd just be trusting that I've been given correct information about an unfamiliar weapon. You actually put a bunch of rounds through it. You take the Cat Lady. C'mon, it'll be fun."

Ed chuckles. "We sound like a couple of ghouls."

They proceed towards rally point three, back in Toronto proper, merging into the escalating early morning commuter traffic that flows from arterial, to highway, to expressway. The sun breaks over the eastern horizon, bright and glaring; Ed directs Doug to the glovebox, where he retrieves several pairs of cheap sunglasses for them. Doug turns to Ed, head tilted back, and says sardonically, "We're on a mission from God."

They arrive at their rally point at 6:52 a.m., the parking lot of a ground floor laundromat in a remodeled warehouse turned condominium block, six blocks northwest of their third target's newspaper building, in an area showing fits and starts of a rise out of industrial decline. The first clear skies since Doug and Jake's arrival to the region cheer the group up; they greet each other when Jake and Tommy emerge from a new panel van, this one a dark blue Chevy, with enthusiastic handshakes and smiles between the four men in coveralls, knit caps and work boots.

"How'd it go?" Doug asks Jake. Jake glances around the otherwise-vacant lot before turning back to speak.

"Like clockwork." Jake's energy is still up, and he's stepping from foot to foot. "Pulls up at the stop sign, right next to us, window partway down, pop pop pop, then an anchor shot. Done and done. You guys?"

Ed steps in. "Doug took care of two problems, not just one. Hey, Jake, why did you edit the packet about the boyfriend?"

Jake squints, processing the question, then straightens. "Oh. Well, that wasn't relevant to the job. Didn't want anyone taking risks to go above and beyond the primary target."

Doug shrugs. "That's fair. I didn't really have a choice, but I would have felt better knowing that in advance. Whatever; that's done."

Tommy gestures to the laundromat. "I'm gonna drop this package off for my guy," patting his hip pocket. "We've got a good hour and a half before we need to be in place. What do you guys wanna do?"

Jake is still stepping from foot to foot. "I dunno, go for a walk? I have way too much energy, I can't sit down or eat or anything. What about you guys?"

Tommy starts walking toward the laundromat. "C'mon, anyone who wants to can hit the head. I'll be quick." Doug stays with Ed in the parking lot next to the van for another cigarette. Doug feels the same sense of calm and camaraderie as in high school wrestling tournaments between matches, hanging out with his teammates shooting the breeze and laughing at stupid jokes.

"It's something to do with dopamine," Ed says, examining Doug through narrowed eyes.

"What?" Doug asks.

Ed mumbles, cigarette in mouth. "Dopamine." He removes the cigarette, exhaling a cloud into the sun-warmed air. "It's a neurotransmitter. It reinforces self-efficacy by flooding the reward centers of the brain. You're hitting on all cylinders, and you know it, so you get a little hit of dopamine."

"Didn't know that." Doug watches the sky continue to brighten, little wispy clouds banished to the periphery of the southwestern horizon. "What a beautiful day. It's warming up."

Ed nods. "They're saying it'll hit negative twelve today, first day in a while. That's over zero in Fahrenheit, I dunno exactly."

Doug calculates in his head. "Around ten degrees. Still cold as hell."

Ed shrugs. "I'll take it, brother."

Jake and Tommy exit the laundromat, striding across the parking lot to the pair. Jake appears to be his normal self.

"You just had to pee, Jake," says Doug. The group laughs.

"Yeah, yeah." Jake grins ear to ear. "Thinking it over, it'd be sensible to get to the paper before it gets too busy. Let's head on down there and get into position. Leave the car. You guys ready to roll?"

Ed and Doug grab their gym bags from the Mercury and leave the rifle in its case in the trunk, along with their coffee thermoses. They pile into the back of the blue panel van, sitting on a horizontal bench facing racks of electrician's equipment. Jake slides into the shotgun seat and Tommy starts the van up, engine roaring as he revs the cold engine to heat up the cab. They pull out onto the street in the increasing traffic, and slowly travel a quarter mile to Stewart Street, an area of older row houses and small light industrial buildings, lined with bare-branched trees farther west. They see several demolition projects along the way, which Ed points out, nudging Doug frequently.

"Ed, you got a family?" Doug asks.

Ed pauses, a blank expression giving way to something else. Dejection? "No. No, not now. I want one. My dad was pretty old before I was born, and you can't be doing this shit with a wife and kids at home. It's not fair to them. Someday, man, someday."

Doug nods. "My dad passed away when I was nine. That was bad enough. I can't imagine the other way. That's a good call."

Ed leans in close to Doug, inches from his face, and speaks into his ear, barely above a whisper. "If you hold ambitions, consider them in all things. All. Things. Start planning now. Someday it'll happen. But I'll probably be on the other side of the world before then." He cocks his head toward his brother in the driver's seat. Doug nods.

Tommy backs the van into a gap between two parallel-parked cars; after engaging the parking break, he places a cell phone and a map on the dashboard, along with his coffee thermos. Jake turns in his seat to face everyone. "Alright, Tommy stays here until we call. Target gets to the office between eight thirty and nine every morning, right?"

"Every morning," says Tommy. "Like clockwork."

Jake points to Tommy. "OK, so that's what we do. Doug, Ed, which of you will be on street watch?"

Doug raises his hand. "Yo."

Jake points to him, then to Ed. "OK, Ed, you're with me in the parking lot, just like we went over. We'll do a radio check on our way. You guys got your shit?"

Doug and Ed each grab a toolbox from the van's bottom shelf and rotate equipment into it – a clipboard, safety helmet, and commercial respirators from the rack. Jake joins them in the back of the van, and they each slip into a light outer coverall, blue with a company logo emblazoned in yellow across the back, then don electricians' tool belts to complete the disguise. Finally, Jake encourages a weapons check. Doug drops the magazine from his Beretta, now three cartridges lighter, and replaces it with a fully loaded magazine from his belt pouch, where he returns the first magazine. Finally, he thumbs up the safety lever, decocking the weapon, then clicks the lever back down to "off," and replaces the pistol – complete with mounted suppressor – in the inside the waistband holster.

Jake nods to Doug's pistol. "That thirty two do the job?" Jake refreshes his magazine via the same process with his own Beretta 9mm.

Doug grins as he zips up his coverall. "Sure did."

"Good hunting, boys," calls Tommy as they slide the cargo door open and exit onto the sidewalk in sunglasses. They wave back to him and slam the sliding door shut, then walk towards the sun. Turning to the southeast onto Portland Street, an area of newer apartment buildings and hundred-year-old red brick housing converted into retail shops, Ed points out a soulless white concrete building being erected across the street with an outer wall six inches from a classic brick and stone house.

"Look at that shit," he gestures with his right hand, getting out a cigarette. "Unbelievable."

Jake glances at Doug with a hard, questioning expression; Doug nods casually back, quickly returning his glance to the sidewalk. Their destination lies just ahead; Toronto's largest newspaper's atrocious-looking "basement in the air," a low, boxy turd deposited just north of the rail yard in the 1950s, which peeks at them as they round Wellington. To the east looms the iconic CN Tower, which Doug can't help but compare to the Space Needle, a tall, pointless but visually interesting relic of mid-century retro-futuristic design. To Doug, the Space Needle looks like a UFO atop a skinny, elongated white-framed Eiffel Tower; the CN Tower looks like a baseball shoved partway down a syringe.

"OK, guys," Jake announces in a low voice, as they filter through drifts of commuters headed towards work or the transit hub of Spadina Avenue, "that's her." A small four story brick apartment building blocks part of their view of the sprawling off-white façade of their destination, 444 Front Street West, surrounded by parking lots on the Wellington side, the north side of which is packed tight with various eras of brick apartments, commercial buildings and once-fine homes converted into multi-unit buildings. "Doug, you're going to set up at the table in front of that building and keep an eye out for our guy, while Ed and I head into the parking structure. Remind me of the car you're looking out for."

Doug repeats from memory, "Green soft top Saab 9000, 1985. Can't miss it."

Jake nods. "Yeah, try not to." He glances at his disposable Casio G-Shok watch. "We have at least twenty minutes until he arrives, up to fifty. Ed, let's patrol the parking area and perimeter wall, focusing on the electrical conduit." They stop across the street from the building, pretending to consult the work order clipped to Jake's clipboard, while watching the flow of traffic around the building. An obvious hierarchy materializes, with lower rung workers arriving via transit to the east – and probably south, on Front Street, blocked by the building – or parking in the open lots bordering the east and west sides of the building. The small parking structure before them scarcely earns the title – there is a ramp on the east side up to the roof, where senior employees have assigned parking spots, while a large loading dock takes up the ground floor, next to visitor parking.

"Quick radio check." The team steps several paces apart, and Jake starts the cycle. "One-One, check, check, over." Doug and Ed nod to Jake.

Their earpieces squawk again. "One-Two, check check, over."

Ed responds. "One-Two, roger, this is Two-One, check check, over."

Doug ends the ritual. "Two-Two, check check, over."

Jake points to the sky and swirls his hand clockwise, and the trio splits, Jake and Ed heading across the street to the ramp, which has a four inch high, two foot wide curb on the left, bordered by a waist-high railing. Doug watches the pair don their respirators as they walk up the ramp on their narrow walkway, checking his watch, before moving over to the green rubber-coated steel picnic bench bordering a commercial building's small parking lot. Doug sets his toolbox on the tabletop next to him and turns to face the newspaper building, looking up and down the street intermittently. After ten or so minutes, Jake comes over the earpiece. "One-Two, be ready, over."

Tommy returns the call. "Roger, One-Two moving, over."

Doug watches Ed cross the parking level to the edge of the building, follow a conduit pipe to a junction box, and set his toolbox atop it. A green Saab soft top appears at the far west end of Wellington, headed their way. Doug keys his mic and says, "Two-two; head's up, the puck is in play, over."

Jake responds: "Roger, Two-Two, over." Ed straightens up, grabs his toolbox and partially unzips his coverall. The Saab's right hand turn signal flicks on, blinking for a hundred feet as the car slows, and there he is, the Editor, all two hundred forty pounds of sloppy, bespectacled communist, cranking his steering wheel hard to make the turn into the newspaper's lot. He slows to a roll for the abrupt transition to the parking ramp then accelerates gently. He may be a subversive on the payroll of a global criminal organization, Doug notes, but at least he is a careful driver.

The Saab turns right at the top of the ramp, and then disappears from Doug's view. Nothing happens for a tense minute while Doug waits. Tommy should be moving the van to the alley forty feet to the east, he thinks. Doug stands and grabs his toolbox, then walks to the sidewalk bordering the alley. Jake and Ed appear at the top of the parking ramp, walking quickly his way, and step onto the narrow walkway to make way for a silver BMW M3 headed a little too fast up the ramp. They maintain their steady pace and hit the north side of Wellington's sidewalk before a high-pitched shout goes up from the rooftop, a female voice – "Oh, my God!"

The trio walk quickly into the alley, between the hundred-year-old brick building on the left and a nine-story modern brick monstrosity to the right, several delivery trucks and vans crowding the narrow lane. They pick up their pace when they see the back end of their blue van thirty yards ahead on the right – Tommy backed in for an easy exit. Ed and Jake remove their respirators as the three men walk quickly to the van then pile in, Doug and Ed again in the rear, Jake in the shotgun seat. Tommy is moving before the doors are fully closed, pulling the van out quickly onto westbound King Street, goosing the engine; after two short blocks they duck into a single lane side street packed with turn of the century row houses and old brick carriage houses festooned with "colorful" graffiti. Newer glass and steel condominiums crammed between soulless seventies and eighties apartments loom over them a block to the east, and they're gone, the van moving a little swifter than Doug would be confident driving, squeezing between dumpsters and double parked delivery trucks. Ahead, a turn of the century brick warehouse with a loading dock aimed right at them; Tommy slows the van and rolls into the transition to a steep ramp, hits a garage door control clipped to his visor, and the metal gate rolls up. Tommy drives the van through the gate and into a twenty-foot-square room with a high ceiling supporting dusty, yellowed florescent lights, thick timber beams framing the room. Tommy throws the van in park, then kills the engine, removes the keys, and clicks the garage door control again; the rumbling door closes with a rattling thud. He turns to the team, a smile on his face, all of them waking from their passive spectator roles and beginning to stretch their limbs.

Jake throws his door open and exits the van, removing his safety helmet and placing it on the ground; the room is completely barren save for a coat hanger and rack of keys by the door to the hallway. He removes his sunglasses and coveralls, then draws his pistol, unlocking the slide and cycling the action, removing a spent cartridge from the chamber. He decocks the pistol and returns it to his waistband, then places the spent casing into the pocket of the discarded blue coverall.

"OK, guys, let's sanitize," Jake commands. Doug and Ed remove their coveralls and add them to the pile; Ed collects the toolboxes, flipping through them, then returns them to the van, sans respirators, which also go on the pile. Doug remembers to check the pocket of his coveralls and finds the spent casings he had removed from his pistol there. Jake nods. "Leave it there; it's all going in an incinerator." Jake adds his ball cap to the pile. Ed stuffs everything into a black trash bag, which he ties off and places next to the door. Jake orders, "Ed, get the street clothes," and starts unlacing his boots. Ed grabs the four duffle bags from the back of the van, peeking inside and handing them to their owners; the team changes into their street clothes, Doug donning his "middle class university student" garb, adding his boots and coveralls to the duffle bag.

Ed addresses the group. "Add your gloves to your bag. We'll each carry our bag to the laundromat, where they'll be burned in the incinerator. Potential forensic evidence. This van is getting chopped as well. I've got new gloves for everyone here." He retrieves a Ziploc gallon sized bag with four sets of brown leather police gloves from the van and hands each man a pair, then dons his own, stuffing the Ziploc in his duffle bag. "Everyone needs to wash up at the laundromat as well, faces, necks and hands. Oh, yeah." Ed runs into the van and retrieves sunglasses left on the dashboard, adding them to his duffle bag. "Are we forgetting anything?"

Jake raises his right hand to get everyone's attention. "Ideally we'd have different weapons for every job, but let's take a vote. The only two weapons fired today were my nine and Doug's thirty-two. We have more than enough for the next job, but I want to see if you guys are comfortable if we dump these and have two guys go unheeled for the rest of the day."

Doug shrugs. "I'm cool dumping my pistol. We can just redistribute weapons for the Cat Lady job."

Jake shakes his head. "Think about it, though. If we pick up heat, theoretically, we're carrying identical weapons to those used this morning, with two guys unable to slug it out. These things will be slag before sunrise tomorrow, but I'd be more comfortable operationally having two more guns until the job is complete."

Tommy tilts his head towards Jake. "I think our team leader has made the right decision. Let's roll."

The four men file out of the room into a narrow, dusty hallway, while Ed locks the door behind them. They exit the building out onto Adelaide, a broad, three-lane one-way street, and make their way west on foot toward the laundromat, the sun casting their shadows in front of them. Doug checks his watch – 9:21 a.m. He speeds his pace and draws parallel to Jake, trailing just behind Ed and Tommy, and says, "Can we get a bite next? I'm starving."

Tommy and Ed consult each other, then Ed casts over his shoulder, "Sure, how about Irish stew and a pint? A pint, not several," smiling to Jake.

Jake says, "Irish stew and a pint, it is."

They arrive back at the laundromat, the Mercury now surrounded by a relatively full parking lot, and stroll through the front door. An array of faces, mostly foreign women bundled up in massive parkas, look up at them briefly before returning to their clothing. Small children run about aimlessly, colliding with people. Nobody apologizes. The team penetrates the dingy cacophony and goes through a battered door marked EMPLOYEES ONLY. A heavyset, hard-looking mountain of a man wearing a wool flat cap and a heavy blue ski jacket slumps on a stool reading a newspaper emblazoned in Cyrillic, carelessly smoking an unaromatic brown cigarette. He nods to Tommy and Ed, ignoring the rest of the group. Tommy waves them back around a corner office to a turn of the century cast iron blast furnace, once painted white, and opens the large door, which groans on its hinges to reveal a raging coal fire. "Throw 'em in," he commands; each man tosses his bag into the maw of the incinerator. Tommy swings the door shut with a shuddering thump, then brings the handle down ninety degrees, locking it. He steps back and points back towards where they came in. "We'll wash up in the bathroom there; it has two sinks."

Ed leads them to the bathroom. Doug pockets his gloves and washes his hands, forearms, face and neck thoroughly with the gritty pink institutional grade soap, which reminds him of elementary school. He rinses off in the steaming hot water, then dries himself with several handfuls of paper towel, taking extra care dabbing around his neck and collar. Jake points to Doug's ear, which Doug wipes clean with the towel while looking carefully in the mirror, squinting in the dim light, clearing out little bits of the powdered soap tucked into the folds of his ear. Done, he steps back, looking around the dingy room, overlaid with the leavings of several technological epochs. He asks Ed, first of the brothers to finish washing, "Does Vanguard own this place?"

Ed shakes his head. "No, Tommy and I do. We own the building. This is the old coal furnace, which we crank up on occasion. It still plugs into the HVAC system here; gas prices fluctuate quite a bit due to the exchange rate; it's a good economic move. OK; ready to eat?"

Doug has the best restaurant-made shepherd's pie of his life at a seventy-year-old Irish pub around the corner from the laundromat, made even better by the alcoholic liquid bread known as Guinness. He is still several months from his twenty-first birthday, which is not an issue in Canada, due to the legal drinking age of nineteen. Doug is not much of a drinker; between the meal, several days of little sleep and a morning filled with adrenaline dumps, he passes out in the passenger seat of the Mercury, his face pressed against the window. He jolts awake as the car hits a pavement seam on Gardiner Expressway, looks about in confusion and searches for his pistol with his hand.

"Doug, relax; you just fell asleep," Ed soothes, rolling down his window and drawing a cigarette. He offers one to Doug, who declines. Ed lights up, returning the lighter to the cigarette pack and sliding the bundle into an inner pocket of his jacket. "Mind some music?" He turns on the stereo, flipping through stations until he lands on a rock station, playing something vaguely familiar. "Alright! You know these guys?"

Doug can't place it. "I think I've heard it on the Victoria station; I know they're Canadian."

Ed shakes his head. "You gotta pick this album up. Splendor Solis. The Tea Party. A classic. A CLASSIC. The River. Love this song." They rocket eastward, Doug looking out the window between buildings and parks to Lake Ontario, the unpaved landscape layered in the brilliant white of snow and ice under a dazzling light blue sky. The sunlight brings a life to the landscape that he hasn't seen during his visit, a promise that winter is temporary, that the bitter cold will be gone...

sometime. He sits up, wipes a bit of drool from his cheek, and listens to the music, the guitar winding his mind around a center, then flinging him off, over and over.

"Where are Jake and Tommy?" asks Doug.

Ed takes the cigarette from his mouth, blowing smoke out the window. "Dropped them off at the other van just a couple minutes after you passed out. Don't worry, I'm beat, too. We're headed back to the house for some Zs. Not sure the Guinness was a great idea, but it sure took the edge off. We probably all need a shower – you can smell adrenaline on a guy. This car stinks, no offense."

"Mmmm." Doug straightens up, grabs his coffee thermos and swallows a few sips. His head is still cloudy. The song goes into a guitar duel, a crunching low rhythm track met with a wavy, North African vibe. "These guys are great."

"Told ya. Seen 'em live a bunch of times. I love live music, but the concert thing isn't for me anymore, unless I'm sitting in a chair with a beer. One grows old, Doug." Ed chuckles and holds his cigarette out the window, pinches off the cherry, and examines the butt before flicking it out into the air. At the Don River, Ed steers the Mercury off the Expressway onto Lake Shore Boulevard, passing the Port Lands on their right.

"We're ditching the car, right?" Doug asks as they pass a water treatment plant and the Lake lurches back into view, both sides of the Boulevard surrounded by large parks.

Ed taps another cigarette out of his dwindling pack, thinks better of it, and puts the pack back in his jacket. "I gotta quit smoking; this is ridiculous. Yeah, we're gonna leave it in the parking garage on Queen Street and walk back to the house. I don't want to be anywhere NEAR any place we set foot today, but we don't have any choice." Ed sweeps the steering wheel to the left as Lakeshore turns north in a wide curve onto Woodbine. The signal at Queen Street is red; they sit patiently behind a bus, their turn signal tick-tocking.

"I got that icy finger going up my back, Ed," Doug says casually.

"Alright, how do you deal with it, then?" Ed asks.

Doug performs an inventory of his thoughts, the entire day, especially this morning, the scene of the crime mere blocks away as they head east on Queen, passing Beaches Park and Lee Avenue, where they left their car and picked up this Mercury. He couldn't think of a single misstep, other than perhaps the highly illegal silenced murder weapon he was wearing in a concealed holster in his waistband. He laughs. "Stop freaking out and just breathe. Keep my eyes peeled for trouble, and don't act suspicious."

"There ya go," says Ed. "That's your mind telling you not to slip up, to keep your shit wired tight. You gotta find a way to relax, to let it go, and I'm not talking about booze or weed. A discipline. Don't laugh, but I do yoga, meditation. A little. Sometimes after a drink or smoking a little weed."

They laugh together, glancing between each other and the road, Doug spotting Hammersmith Avenue ahead and craning his neck to the right, looking down the narrow tree-lined lane packed tight with houses; he can see a flash of the beach park at the end, but no obvious police activity. He checks his watch – not even noon yet. "Someone's gotta be checking in on those guys by now."

Ed shrugs. "Who knows. Who cares. You executed perfectly. They don't have shit on you, Doug." They ride in silence, and near the end of Queen Street, Ed signals left for a parking garage bordering an animal hospital. At the barrier arm, he draws a long term parking card from the glove box, which he slides in and out of the pedestal, driving forward after the arm raises. He swings the Mercury in a wide right turn, then puts the car into reverse, turns in his seat, and steers backwards into an open parking spot next to Tommy's van. Throwing the car into park, and engaging the hand brake, he places the parking card on the dash and removes the keys from the ignition. Ed turns and looks at Doug. "Let's roll. Leave the thermoses; we'll get the rifle later, too."

They exit the car and head south on Munro Park Avenue towards the safe house, marveling at a bank's blinking LED sign declaring the temperature to be 3 degrees Celsius. "Positively balmy," Ed comments, as Doug stretches his limbs and picks up his pace to match. They carefully approach the safe house, looping around the block together and casually inspecting ingress and egress routes, before walking up the drive to the front door. Ed taps in the entry code on the keypad and they enter, scanning the room, but see nothing amiss. Ed slips off his boots, leaving them by the door, and collapses onto a couch in the living room. After a beat he removes his equipment and places it on the coffee table in a heap, the butt of his Beretta 9mm oriented towards him. Doug sits in a voluminous recliner, removing his boots as well, and leans all the way back, drawing his pistol and placing it on the coffee table in front of him. They look at each other, communicating exhaustion with a glance. Ed closes his eyes. "I'm gonna sleep right here, I don't care. I should have passed out the pep pills. Whatever. I'm beat. Say hi to my brother and Jake."

Doug hears an engine on the road and stands, picking up his pistol as he moves to the window. Jake and Tommy pull into the driveway in their clean van, and then spill out. Doug opens the door as they approach, peeking his head out for their verification. Jake comes up the walk first while Tommy locks up, and surveys the room inside, glancing at Ed, who opens his eyes briefly and gives a wave. Tommy follows up, and Doug closes and latches the door.

Jake pats Doug's shoulder. "Don't worry about falling asleep; I figure we ought to nap in a rotation. I'm still a little wired, so I'll take first watch, catch a little TV to see what they're saying about today, and plan for tonight."

Doug bends down and grabs his boots. "Cool, I'll sleep in my room. Since I already slept a little, grab me for next watch. When will that be?"

Jake shrugs. "Maybe two, three hours? Depends on when I'm nodding off."

"You got it, boss," Doug says. "See ya then." He walks upstairs to his room, briefly considering brushes his teeth, and decides to rinse with mouthwash for now. The lingering tastes of tobacco, coffee and Guinness coat his mouth. Disgusting. A few rinse cycles and he decides to brush anyway, scouring his tongue and the roof of his mouth as much as his teeth. His teeth seem to pulse, not in pain, but probably overstimulation from the cigarettes. A nasty habit, he thinks. After a more thorough than planned shower, he leaves the bathroom and lies down on his bed with his pistol next to him, his boots next to the door, and stares at the ceiling for a few minutes, playing out the day in his head. Firing a single shot into the skull of a sleeping man two feet from him, the cracking sound of the bullet impact, driving through his brain and exiting, forcing itself down into the couch. The sound of the blood pumping out of the wound, soaking the fabric, the smell of his bowels emptying. Ugh. Not my finest hour. But this was not a normal man, not like a family man, not a man who had any reason to go on living, a "man" who had sex with vulnerable young boys. Fuck him. And the lawyer, a wizened buzzard, big beak and awful withered hands. Do they both have AIDS? Why would the guy shit his pants regularly? Doug thinks about it – OH. Truly disgusting.

Think about something other than that. Anything. His mind drifts to his life back home; his grandfather, seated on the tattered throne of an invisible kingdom at the end of the world, as Charles McIntyre had put it; his roommate, Mike, the lovable zero. Cathy and Liz; Cathy, who left his heart in flames, every time. Day three, and he was sick with absence. How do soldiers do this, for a year at a time?

"Doug." Suddenly, there was Jake, in the doorway. Doug sits up, swinging his feet out and onto the floor, rubbing his face and looking at the clock. 3:32 p.m. "You got watch. Let me fill you in. Come over to my room."

Doug follows, picking up his pistol and clicking it into its holster, which he then slides back into his waistband. In Jake's room, appointed nearly identically to his – a queen bed with an excessively large dark wood frame, dark blue high thread count sheets, and a small TV on a matching dresser – Jake mutes the television, turned to a news station. "Check it out," he says, scooting into the middle of the bed and leaning against the pillows and headrest.

A female Asian talking head with big, permed hair is nodding seriously while an older man in a grey suit jabbers on, conveying his disappointment in the world, as a map of Toronto flashes onscreen, and two cartoonish revolver icons appear, one in Etobicoke and the other downtown on Front Street. "The lawyer isn't part of the story. Either the police don't know yet, or they aren't talking," Jake notes, holding his remote up and – click – the TV blinks off. "I dropped a line to our guys monitoring chatter, and as far as we can tell, the hooks we have in Brooks' org aren't giving off any indicators. When they lawyer is found, all bets are off; my guess is it lights up like a Christmas tree. Whatever; we're a go for tonight."

"We have signals guys?" Doug asks.

Jake nods. "Yep, through Vanguard. Don't worry, they're loyal."

Doug scratches behind his ear. "Do they know who is on this op?" he asks.

Jake thinks. "They know I'm on this op. You're not named explicitly, although they might have access to the Vanguard employee database, and have determined that you might be active, based on the profiles we set up. I don't know, that's inference. Maybe. Why?"

"Just curious." Doug leans against the doorframe. "If you trust them, and McIntyre trusts them, I'm sure they're solid."

Jake shimmies down into bed, leaning his head against an overstuffed pillow. "Well, just in case, my main guy in that crew is Owens, out of our LA office. Just in case. I'm gonna crash."

"G'night," Doug says reflexively. "Whatever. See you in a few hours." He closes the door most of the way, then walks downstairs, where Ed and Tommy are sacked out on the couches, and enters the kitchen, grabbing the ever-brewing coffee pot and pouring himself a cup.

That night, after Ed prepares a surprisingly tasty meal of spaghetti with meat and vegetable sauce – Jake's request for a salad is nixed, because Tommy doesn't want anyone "feeling regular until after midnight" – the team re-deploys to the periphery of the University of Toronto after picking up a new operations van in the parking garage. Ed distributes fresh coveralls and boots to the entire team, which the passengers change into while Tommy steers the van through the tail end of rush hour traffic. Toronto is one of those towns where a significant portion of the population commutes to work in the suburbs, particularly the southwest, yet live in the city, so Tommy fights congestion all the way up Spadina, a major thoroughfare on the western edge of downtown proper.

Jake talks through their deployment plan for the night. "Cat Lady runs a weekly orientation for new 'refugee' arrivals at Toronto General Hospital, getting them plugged into the healthcare system. Surprise, surprise, a bunch of the 'refugees' in her program are jihadis coming out of the Balkan war. The editor squashed a story about it, and fired the reporter investigating her for supposed malfeasance. He was blackballed from the industry."

"What a prick!" Doug exclaims.

"Not anymore," says Jake.

"Toronto General is just a few blocks from her apartment," Tommy notes. "She'll walk down College after the meeting, same as every time we surveilled her."

Jake points to Doug and Ed from the shotgun seat, Ed holding the disguised rifle case vertically between his legs. "I like your plan, so we'll stick to it. College is too busy for a snatch, and while I want fore and aft tails on her, dropping her in the courtyard, at range, is both safest for us, and most photogenic. 'Propaganda by deed,' as the commies say."

Doug ticks off the fingers of his left hand. "Jake and I pick her up at the hospital, and work the tail. Ed sets up across from her apartment at the admin building. Tommy's taxi. When she enters the courtyard, Jake and I confirm Ed's shot, then we move up College two blocks – what's the street on the north side?"

Ed says, "Huron."

Doug nods, ticking off his index finger. "We all rendezvous on Huron, cruise through campus northbound, and we're gone."

Jake holds a finger up in the air. "This is our most exposed job, spread out over the widest area. A lot can go wrong. Stay cool, and remember, if we have to abort, we abort. I expect a lot more talk on the radio. Let's all set up on channel four." The team stuffs fresh batteries into their radios, then switch over to the new channel; Tommy engages the police scanner and turns up the volume at a red light in Chinatown. They perform a quick radio check, then Jake consults his watch.

"Her meeting starts in twenty minutes. I don't recommend spending much time wandering around the hospital; they have more surveillance than anything short of a police building or defense contractor. Fortunately, this NGO uses a meeting room in the second floor of an admin wing on the west side of the hospital, which has light traffic after hours. Jake, you're going to eyeball her in the hospital, right?"

Jake nods. "Yep, then I'll take up aft tail, with Doug in the lead, a block ahead of us on College. Everyone ready?"

Several minutes later Tommy turns the van onto eastbound College Street, two blocks west of their target's apartment, and drops Ed at a streetcar stop. Ed casually salutes the team as they pull out, swings the covert rifle case onto his back and grabs another toolbox. They pass the target's apartment, Jake and Ed noting the well-lit courtyard, smiling to each other. At a red light at the intersection of College and McCaul, Tommy turns to Jake and Doug. "I want to drop you off on the next block, so that I can slide down a side street and loiter there. That way I can swing in and help you guys if you need it, or get Ed, without being all over the hospital's surveillance network. There's nowhere to do that on University."

Jake nods. "Works for me."

They turn right onto McCaul and Tommy pulls the van onto the low curb just before Orde Street. Tommy inclines his head towards Orde on the left. "There ya go. Two blocks to the hospital. Pull those caps down low and engage the light, boys, you'll be on Candid Camera once you hit University."

Jake hands Doug a red baseball cap with a tiny clip light under the brim and puts on his own, adjusting the fit. They shake hands with Tommy and step out of the van with their toolboxes, then head east on Orde, getting back into the world of high rises and no parking zones as they approach University. Before hitting the avenue, they click on the infrared lights clipped to their hats, which provide no visible illumination. They wait at a crosswalk for the walk sign, then in the median for the eastbound crosswalk to turn green. Jake points with his chin to an unattractive dirty-brick structure with steel and glass additions grafted to it. "Second floor," Jake notes as they walk down the wide sidewalk, alongside parallel-parked cars, Doug squinting and spotting cameras at every hospital entrance and corner, focusing on an awful sunbaked brick building eighty feet to the south.

They turn their faces toward the camera gazing down at them from the side door alcove as they enter the building, then walk up the stairwell on their immediate left to the next floor. Doug follows Jake down a deserted hallway lined with closed office doors to a wider north-south lane, busy with nurses and technicians in scrubs interspersed with visitors, nearly all headed somewhere else in the complex. Jake holds up his hand and points to a row of payphones down a side hallway; Doug steps over to one phone and sets his toolbox down, theatrically drawing quarters from his pocket and feeding the phone before partially dialing a number and holding the handset to his face in his gloved hand. After several minutes, Jake returns and inclines his head back towards the stairwell.

Doug walks alongside Jake, who says without turning his head, "She's there; small group today. They're already doing paperwork. You head across University to the corner, sit down at the streetcar station, and wait for my signal."

"You got it," Doug says, and heads down the stairs, out onto the street, and across the first crosswalk, passing the imposing curved glass wall of the Ontario Power Building as he moves north. At the corner of College and University, he leans against the tall polished stone retaining wall ten feet from the streetcar station, gazing in the general direction of the hospital, watching people go about their lives. At that moment, on the hub of this wide avenue of high rises, deep in an old, densely populated city, Doug finally feels foreign. Not in the residential streets, or the restaurants, or in a car on the highway, or a cozy house on the lake, but here. It occurs to him that, if he were arrested during this operation, he would spend the rest of his life in prison, enduring years of interrogation by Canadian and American law enforcement and intelligence agencies. Everyone connected to him would have their lives turned upside-down.

What was it the Cambodian royalist soldier told him in his Foreign Policy class, about the worst thing he saw during the war? Losing. Not the bombings, the acres of blasted trees strewn with pulverized bodies, soil turned to mud from the blood of hundreds of teenaged soldiers, or even the killing fields. Losing ushered in the latter. OK, so don't lose.

His earpiece crackles. "Two-Two, One-One, over."

Doug responds. "One-One, I read you, over."

"Moving; two uninvited guests accompanying, be warned, over."

What? Doug watches the hospital entryways around the admin building, but is unable to ID his target for several minutes, until he spots her across University almost parallel to him under the streetlight by the crosswalk, accompanied by two males, one much taller than her, the other around her height. They are wearing large parkas, one good old American woodland camouflage, the other a black commercial job, and he can see black beards on their faces. "One-One, I see 'em, moving west, over." Doug moves fluidly down the block, stepping behind the far edge of the Ontario Power Building's retaining wall on Murray Street and peeking back. The trio is crossing University, somewhat slowly.

"Roger." Jake's voice conveys rapid movement. "I'm crossing to the south. Two-One, you got about five to seven minutes, over."

Ed comes over Doug's earpiece. "Roger, Two-One in place."

Tommy comes onto the net. "One-One, cut up the side street; you can run and get a better position. I'm moving to the rendezvous, over."

Doug keys his mic. "Two-Two moving west to next loiter. Their pace is modest. One of these guys – ugh – can't keep his hands off of her. Uh, over."

Jake again, clearly running. "Two-Two, cut the details, over."

Doug walks casually westward, looking in the windows of a row of commercial buildings, eyeing a pho restaurant and the steaming hot soup bowls flowing from behind the counter. After a day of sun and clear skies, the temperature has plummeted again, with a bracing breeze intermittently coming in off the lake and still penetrating this far north. He glances left without turning his head to watch the trio move slowly towards him, the tall one playing up his passion for the formless blob of the Cat Lady, who he can hear laughing – "Oh, stop! Muhammad, stop!" and "resisting" his advances. The short one plods along, clearly frustrated, turning occasionally and gesturing ahead. They stop and confer for a bit, Cat Lady pointing to a shop on the next block. Doug crosses McCaul without waiting for the signal, then steps into a streetcar stop shelter where several students are clustered, and pretends to read the schedule. Looking to his left, he sees the short man split off from the other two and head into a kebab shop, while Cat Lady and her groper continue down College towards him.

Jake re-emerges on the net. "One-One, have visual on two, where is three? Over."

Doug walks out of the streetcar shelter and keys his mic, facing the street, and says softly, "Three went into the kebab shop. She's gonna have kebab three different ways tonight, over."

A long silence while Doug smiles, enjoying his joke, before he consults his watch and moves westward. Ed responds: "No, she's not. Over."

Jake keys in with a new plan. "One-One, hanging back for three. Two-Two, proceed. Over."

"Roger, over." Doug crosses Henry Street, and on the short block before Beverly, and the target's apartment, he steps behind a large, heavily pruned maple, which has pushed the sidewalk up at angles and split it. He turns and peeks from around the tree, watching the un-aesthetic, un-eugenic couple stumble towards him on the next block, kissing animalistically, the Cat Lady fully in the throes of this Albanian Lothario.

"I can't watch this shit." The disgust in Jake's voice is thick and visceral. "Three has his kebabs and booze. Didn't think the Mooz would sell it. Over."

"Mooz are the biggest hypocrites imaginable," Ed says calmly. "Especially in the west. You boys got me licking my lips. Over."

Tommy comes over the net. "Moving; about to pass you, Two-Two. Hi, Two-One." After several seconds, he returns. "Uh, change of plans. Rally point is blown. Cops and tow trucks. Fuck."

Jake responds. "Your call, Two-One. Over."

Ed says coolly, "I'm good to go, One-One. One-Two, let's push it two blocks north and west, over."

"Roger," Tommy says. "Boys, adjust rendezvous point north and west, two blocks EACH. They're weird blocks, up in student housing."

Jake's voice returns. "Roger, thanks for the details, but please spare them on the net. We can figure it out. Three is hustling. Two-Two, what's your status, over?"

Doug stands in the streetcar shelter in front of the target's apartment building, again "consulting the schedule," watching the Cat Lady fiddle with the locked gate to the apartment courtyard. She's even more formless and asexual looking in person, with a little streak of pink dye in her hair hanging down from an awful knit cap with a pom pom on top. The male is clearly an Albanian, a lanky, curly black haired and bearded stereotype, continually groping the Cat Lady under her lumpy garments. Three, the shorter man with a leadership vibe, has crossed Beverly and almost caught up, now twenty yards from Doug. Three is scanning the street as he walks; he sets eyes on Doug and stops.

Doug speaks softly while keying his mic. "One-One, you got this guy? I might be made." He slowly unzips his coverall and slides his hand over the butt of his pistol, thumbing the slide lock safety off, praying that the shelter blocks as much light from the street as it seems to. A quick glance reveals no civilians behind Three, thank God.

Three's head explodes, and he crumples into a heap where he stands, the tinkling of shattering glass muffled by the plastic bag as he drops his cargo to the pavement; an instant later a loud thump sounding from the couple falling to the ground just inside the courtyard. The wrought iron gate swings to a stop against the tall Albanian's prone head. "Three for two," says Ed in Doug's ear, "Confirm, over." Doug runs with his right hand inside his coverall, toolbox in his left, to the couple, who are both leaking blood from their chests, Cat Lady sucking air with eyes wide in panic, but unable to do more than twitch. The Albanian was dead before he hit the ground from a spine shot.

Twenty feet away, Jake kneels over the wreckage of Three and says into the mic, "Three is done. Two-Two?" before coming around the hedge entryway to the courtyard, his hand also in his coverall.

Doug straightens, zipping up his coverall, Jake following his lead. "Mission accomplished. Let's di-di. Nice work, Two-One! Over."

"Roger, I'm gone, over," says Ed. Doug and Jake head west on College, glancing briefly to the north as they cross Huron Street to their original rendezvous point, which seems to be in the throes of a vigorous parking enforcement operation. Jake slaps Doug on the shoulder and, after passing a clutch of eastbound Indian co-eds, they pick up their pace, hurrying to Spadina, which they cross swiftly during a break in traffic. On the other side, past a mini mart, they slow their stride, sparing their energy and trying not to stand out. At the Crescent roundabout, they cut west again past a wacky mid-century UFO-inspired campus building and into a classic densely-packed student housing district, stepping out into the street several times to move past clusters of students blocking the sidewalk and calling each other "Dude." Bending around to the north, on Robert Street, Jake points to a beacon of hope halfway up the block, Tommy's van, which they find parked across a driveway. They wave to Tommy, who unlocks the doors, and Jake enters the shotgun seat, Doug through the cargo door.

Tommy keys his mic and says aloud, "Two-One, what's your status, over?"

Several seconds pass, then there's a rap on Tommy's side window, Ed standing there. "Hey, guys."

"Get in the van," says Tommy, and Doug slides the street-side cargo door open, Ed coming around and hopping in, sliding the covert rifle case under the seat as Doug shuts the door. They buckle up and Tommy pulls out, headed south. The energy in the van is electric, and the team pat each other on the back and laugh while Tommy calmly drives them south.

Jake turns in his seat to face Doug. "Dude," putting on a falsetto voice, "'She's gonna have kebab three ways tonight,' what the fuck," laughing uproariously.

"No, she's not," says Ed, smirking.

"Nice shooting, man," says Doug, elbowing Ed in the arm. "I thought I was gonna have to turn that place into a bullet fest."

Ed fishes a cigarette out of his pack. "Tommy, I love ya, but I'm having a smoke," lighting it and throwing the now-empty pack up to Jake, who catches it and drops it onto his floormat.

"You deserve a smoke," says Jake. "You sure practiced with that rifle."

"The action is like butter, Jake. Like butter!" Ed declares.

"Ed and I have been hunting with Enfield rifles since we were, what, eleven years old?" says Tommy, turning into the Spadina Crescent and heading south. "Hey, should I turn left and check it out?" he asks innocently, to NO NO NOs from the rest of the team. He laughs. "Let's listen to the scanner," and he turns the volume up on the handheld scanner stuffed into the driver's side cup holder. As they cross College, everyone looks to their left to see two police cars pulled across the sidewalk at the scene, lights strobing and casting the block in blue-red.

"Bye-bye," says Jake, in a mock toddler's voice. "Bye-bye!"

"The price of horse is gonna go way up!" Ed quips.

"Or there'll be a street war with the Chinese," says Tommy.

Their final stop for the night is in the southwest part of town, near Queen Street and Ossington Avenue. Jake, as the biggest fan of the City Councilor they are granting a "night letter" rather than a bullet, declares himself deliveryman. He retrieves the night letter from the glove box, where it sits in a sealed and folded

Ziploc gallon bag, inside an unaddressed envelope. Two blocks from her apartment building, Jake steps out to the curb and tips his red cap to the team, then walks to the corner of Brookfield before activating the IR light clipped to his hat brim. From the Ziploc bag he draws a freshly-cut key, which Tommy and Ed prepared during their surveillance. He disappears into the building and emerges two minutes later, walking coolly to the west, the opposite direction of his approach, deactivates the IR light a block away, then cuts north into a neighborhood of row houses, stepping up into the waiting van halfway up the block. Tommy steers them north and west to Dufferin, then heads south, under the train lines and across the Gardiner expressway, winding through the parks and tourist-focused Exhibition Place to eastbound Lake Shore Boulevard, maintaining a leisurely pace.

"What was in the letter?" asks Doug.

Jake turns. "Ah, you know. I kept it pretty low key. Something like:

Dear baby,

You know we can get to them. You know we can get to you. Walk away, and we will, too.

P.S. I like you. Do you like me? Yes / No"

The team cracks up.

"Wanna eat at the yacht club?" Tommy asks.

"We're not really dressed for it," says Jake.

"Damn." Tommy points out Fort York, to the left. "Where we muster." To the right, the shore is lined with parks, Billy Bishop Toronto City Airport out in the bay in the Toronto Islands, lighting up the middle of the frozen lake. Tommy steers the van back onto the Gardiner Expressway for two miles, then back to Lake Shore towards The Beach. A feeling of climax, of completion, settles over Doug as he looks out over the same territory he examined earlier today in the glaring sunlight, this time seeing darkness with little bright spots of light smeared across the landscape, which dissipate as they hit Woodbine Park and the view of the Lake opens up. Before they turn north onto Woodbine Ave, for a brief twenty seconds all he sees are the distant lights above Rochester in the sky to the far southeast, with lesser points lining the shore, snaking westward, the Lake completely black.

"Can't see anything out there with the clouds gone," Doug says. "What are our prospects for a night crossing without the cloud cover?"

Tommy flicks his head over his shoulder briefly. "That's what running lights are for," he says. "You'll be surprised by the visibility. Don't worry about it."

Back at the house, Doug and Jake say goodbye to Tommy, who takes all of their operational equipment and clothing for disposal. They shake hands vigorously, patting each other's backs, and wishing each other well. Ed goes with Tommy, to meet his snowmobile handler; Doug and Jake will walk to the marina down the beach where they arrived only three nights ago to be picked up for the crossing. Over their Toronto street clothes from the morning's exfiltration, they don the thick armored snowmobile suits, carrying their helmets as they walk across the lakeside boardwalk and down the beach to the marina, flickering ahead against the black of the lake.

Doug turns to Jake. "Hell of a couple of days," he notes. "I like these guys."

Jake looks up into the cloudless sky, a mere handful of stars visible due to light pollution. "We'll be working with them a lot, I suspect," he says. "I'd work with those guys any day. And you. You make a hell of a soldier." He hammerfists Doug on the shoulder playfully. "For a civilian. You know what; I never did anyone before today." They walk in silence for a few moments, enjoying the view. "I thought I'd be more bothered by it, but I'm not. Probably because these people are scum, and we did it without any extra mess. I feel better about it than some of the 'peacekeeping' bullshit I did in the army, frankly."

Doug laughs. "Since we're talking about those feeling things, when I plugged that fuckboy this morning I felt terrible. I'm not one of those 'kill all the homos, raaaah' guys. I feel bad for them. Most of them are broken people. I'll grant that some might just be that way. But when Ed told me this guy's M.O., it's like God came down and wiped my conscience clean."

"Yeah," Jake says, as they step off the beach boardwalk on to the paved path snaking southeast to the marina's side entrance, "Like I said this morning, I pulled those details from the packet because it wasn't pertinent to the mission. Didn't want you taking extra risks to get him. That said, fuck him."

From the northeast they hear the whining grind of the snowmobiles before their headlights come into view. The two machines draw a wide arc around the marina and pull up in front of Doug and Jake on the beach, who don their helmets and climb onto the long seats behind the drivers. The snowmobiles jerk forward with a roar after they settle in, headed south. Visibility out on the ice is indeed acceptable, particularly with the enhanced headlights in place on each machine. Tonight's ride isn't much rougher than the trip north had been, which is not to say that it is comfortable in the least; Doug grips his oh shit handles, as he envisions they are named, intensely, losing awareness of his hands after several minutes, but not losing his hand strength. After an hour and a half of this madness, the ever-approaching coastline of the United States finally appears in detail in the headlights, and the lead snowmobile steers slightly east, slowing to tip up onto the beach and leveling out on a flat, snow-covered road running through a forest. The din of the engines seems as if it will never end, but after another fifteen or so eternal minutes, and countless twists and turns, the drivers pull the snowmobiles up at a lone metal building in a small clearing, a bare bulb dangling below a sheet aluminum reflective cone bolted above a garage door. The lead driver hops off his machine and steps through several inches of snow to the doorframe, where he flips up a keypad box and types in a code. The roll-up garage door shudders and rises, and the lead driver flips on an interior light, revealing a working garage with a wood stove, several bunk beds and a green classic 70s-era Bronco with a tasteful lift kit. The drivers steer their snowmobiles into the garage, finally killing the engines, and Doug takes his helmet off in relief.

The lead driver, who Jake rode with, removes his helmet – it's Ed. "I'll start a fire," he says, grabbing newspaper and kindling from the tinderbox next to the wood stove, and works deep within the wood stove with a lighter.

Jake, also helmet-free, pushes himself up off the snowmobile seat, expressing the deepness of his stretch with a roar, and says, "I don't wanna ride one of those things for a while, no offense."

"None taken," says Ed's mysterious colleague, who Doug has been riding with, a stout redhead with his hair pulled back into a ponytail and a thick, untamed beard to match. He's pulling water bottles from a refrigerator. "This here's my family's land. We're gonna stay here until morning, then get you fellas over to a hotel by the airport so you can wash up." He pronounces it "warsh."

Doug rises from his seat and approaches the redhead, extending his hand. The redhead accepts it with a vigorous shake. "Thanks for your assistance," Doug says earnestly.

"Oh, my pleasure," says the redhead, offering Doug a water bottle. He takes it, chugging down a third of it in one go. "It's not much, but we also need to get up pretty early, and sleeping deep doesn't happen around here," he adds with a grin.

Jake walks over to one of the bunks and pulls off his snowmobiling suit, which he rolls up and sets on the floor before kicking off his boots. "Guys, I'm beat; I'm going to sleep." He slides under the blanket and rolls over, and is out in minutes.

Ed points his water bottle at Jake. "That's a soldier, alright," he says.

Doug checks out the Bronco for a few minutes, talking to the redhead, who does not reveal his name. Doug does not ask. The wood stove slowly heats up the building as Ed feeds it wood, stuffing in several large logs before calling it good. Ed and the redhead sit by the woodstove, chatting, while Doug goes to sleep fitfully, first too hot, and then too cold, waking before sunrise to a dark room. He flashes on his pocket light, which he kept from the operational gear, to navigate out to the side of the building to take a leak in the snow. He soaks in the silence of this place, looking up to the sky out of the clearing to see more stars than when in town, but still catching light pollution on all horizons save for the south. Unable to sleep, he checks his watch – about twenty minutes until they were planning to rise anyway – and goes back inside, feeding the smoldering coals in the woodstove some branches, blowing until flame leaps back from the coals. He adds a log to the woodstove and swings it shut, then grabs his water bottle, finishing it in three gulps. He's been sweating like an animal for twenty-four hours, and reeks of adrenaline.

The morning is a blur. The redhead drives them in the Bronco – which feels crowded with all four of them inside it, Doug less than enthusiastic about riding behind the shotgun seat – to a motel bordering the Buffalo airport. They thank the redhead for his hospitality, and Ed gets out of the shotgun seat to help them with their luggage. He embraces Doug in a bear hug, patting his back roughly, promising, "If you ever need anything, call on me, brother," then passing on to Jake, "You, too." He hands Jake their room key. The three enter the room, Doug and Jake dropping their bags; they say goodbye to Ed, who talks up a storm as he walks out to the Bronco, waving.

Jake and Doug look at each other, alone in the hotel room, and Jake says, "You can shower first."

Doug, lacking social graces as per usual with only children, says, "Okay" without furnishing a counter-offer. He steps into the bathroom with his toiletries bag, where he takes a hot, bracing shower, scrubbing his body hard with a heavily soaped washcloth, and then shaves. He walks out in a towel, telling Jake, "You're up." Jake has the TV on, and the Toronto news station, slightly funny accents and all, is detailing a number of horrific murders committed the day before – authorities insist they are unrelated.

Jake tosses the remote control on the bed and grabs his toiletry bag. "They found the lawyer," he says, standing. "A neighbor was saying it could be revenge, a disgruntled family member of one of the boys they'd run through. All their dirty laundry is coming out! I feel like a saint." He walks into the steaming bathroom and shuts the door.

Doug dresses in his travel clothes – a suit minus the jacket – sets his wool topcoat on the bed and repacks his carry-on from the trip in. He flips through the Canadian and US morning news shows, looking for a common theme in the reporting on yesterday's deaths, and the anchors primarily fixate on organized crime. All of the targets were dirty as hell. An RCMP officer describes the Cat Lady as having been under investigation for engaging in visa fraud for an international drug trafficking syndicate. Too true, sir! Doug thinks.

Jake exits the bathroom and grabs his clothes, shutting the door again, then emerges, looking like his usual slick, processional self, full black suit cut form-fitted to him, bright red tie over a brilliant white shirt, framing his chiseled face and spiky dirty blonde hair. "Man, this feels good," he says; "Even in the army I got my issued uniforms tailored. Wearing that disposable clothing makes me feel like a slob; I can't help it." He slips on dress shoes from his overnight bag. "Pretty interesting, huh?" he asks, pointing to the TV.

Doug nods. "Organized crime. I guess it's sort of true."

Jake laughs. "Let's get out of here."

They cruise through security at the airport and sit down for a real breakfast at what Ed labelled "the one good restaurant" near their gate, focusing on consuming eggs and meat in bulk. Their flight home is uneventful; Doug sleeps during much of the trip, waking from time to time, worried that people are watching him, that people know. The pilot announces the approach to SeaTac in the mid-afternoon, one of those gorgeous, cloudless January days in Seattle, the Sound and Lake Washington shimmering like bejeweled surfaces below them. The snowy, blue-and-white Cascade and Olympic ranges frame the scene.

Evans, Charles McIntyre's black-suited driver, appears as they exit security, stopping them in the flow of people disgorging into Doug's homeland. "Please go directly to Mr. McIntyre's home; he and a guest will debrief you."

Doug replies, "My car is in long-term parking; should be able to get up there in about an hour, unless the Five is particularly bad."

Evans nods. "I'm sure it is. I'll let them know." He turns, joining them in their walk out to the parking garage complex, then splits left into short-term parking with a perfunctory wave. Doug and Jake spend the next forty-five minutes grinding through the afternoon traffic of I-5 North, exiting onto Mercer St and crawling all the way to Magnolia before hitting the speed limit for the first time mere blocks from McIntyre's urban estate. The estate gate opens before Doug rolls down his window at the terminal, and they cruise up the small hill to the parking roundabout at the home's entrance, then step out to enjoy the view of downtown while Elliott Bay turns orange-purple-red in the last light of the setting sun.

Jakes whistles. "Never been here before," he says. "I bet this place cost a fortune."

"That's the whole idea," Doug says, and they turn and head into the house, where Evans, who orders them to remove their shoes and don slippers, meets them. Jake continually slows his pace to take in the house, ultimately stopping in the hallway to admire a display of elaborate European and Southeast Asian swords illuminated behind glass.

"Is that carved elephant tusk?" he asks, pointing to a heavily gilt long-handled saber.

Evans stops and turns, walking back to the display. "Yes, Lan Xang, seventeenth century. Belonged to one of Mrs. McIntyre's ancestors, a member of the royal family. My favorite is this one, if you'll permit me," he says, stretching up and pointing to an odd long knife with wavy double edges and intricately-wrought hardwood handle jutting out at an irregular angle, layers upon layers of steel folded into it with seven gold layers for good measure. "It's an Indonesian keris, what they call a 'Manglar Manga,' not the Japanese comic books, with thirteen 'luks' or waves, and even the scabbard is invaluable. Notice the serpentine motif, beyond the normal floral work. I've studied silat, their martial art, and it makes perfect sense to me now. Mrs. McIntyre doesn't like it, says it's a magical item; it's supposed to protect against black magic. Mr. McIntyre has a local Indo shaman guy, although he's technically Muslim, anoint it to revitalize its powers every year." He turns and looks at Doug and Jake, examining their faces for a response, receiving none. "Alright, let's not keep the boss waiting," he says, pivoting and bringing them down the darkening hallway and into the study, where he announces them before disappearing into a side room. Doug and Jake step into the room and are met by Charles McIntyre, dressed splendidly as usual in a fine medium blue wool suit, tightly woven white shirt, and a light purple paisley neckerchief. At the window is Josef, somewhat hunched, holding his hands behind his back and enjoying the sunset over the Olympics.

After shaking hands with McIntyre, Doug introduces Jake and Josef. "Grandfather, this is Jake Steiner, my immediate supervisor here at Vanguard; Jake, this is my grandfather, Josef Shea."

They shake hands warmly, Josef patting Jake's upper arm with his left hand. "I've heard great things about you from Charles, young man. You were in the Battalion?"

"Yes, sir," answers Jake, ramrod-straight and resuming his classic formality. "I've been at Vanguard since '93. I hope to work there for a long time, sir."

McIntyre walks to the window clutching two carved crystal tumblers of Scotch, a single large ice cube in each glass, and hands them to Doug and Jake. McIntyre picks up his glass from the desk and raises it, followed by the other three, then says, "To success." The others repeat the toast; they clink glasses and drink.

Doug slips into passive observer mode, waiting to be called on. Jake, speaking in round, vague terms, explains their operational timeline. McIntyre and Josef observe, nodding, asking the occasional question. Josef finally asks, "How did the hardware treat you?"

Jake shrugs. "Pistols were fine. I like the slide lock option. I couldn't believe how quiet they were, in such a small package. Being able to retain your brass is great."

"I'm glad," says Josef. "Sounds like the long gun worked out, as well?" he asks, looking at Doug.

"They built it to spec. It saved us from, uh, things being more dramatic than intended," Doug says, looking at Jake.

McIntyre waves his hand. "We can speak candidly here, men. Just spit it out."

Jake looks to Doug, who nods to him. Jake takes in a large gulp of air. "Sir, the administrator didn't travel home alone that night, despite the pattern the Roy brothers reported in their packet. I'm not saying they did anything wrong; just reporting the facts. We had to improvise."

Doug says, "Ed Roy saved my ass, uh, sir; I got made on the street by one of the guys. I could have handled it myself, eventually, but it would have been a bullet festival. He took him out from across the street with a suppressed rifle from an overwatch position, then dropped the Cat Lady and the other guy with a single bullet."

McIntyre smiles. "'Bullet festival?'" He and Josef laugh.

Josef asks, "I assume you were using the thirty-two?"

Doug nods. "I had the thirty-two, which I used for the lawyer. Two Mooz left the meeting with the Cat Lady, uh, headed to her apartment." The two older men make disgusted faces. "Jake was aft tail, I was fore, and one of the guys, the leader, split off to get food and booze along the way. Originally, the plan was to drop her in the courtyard of her building, as a nice, splashy message. Because the third guy split off, Jake stayed back to follow him. He spotted me at the streetcar stop, and our eyes locked after he saw me. I messed up. If Jake had fired at him, that could have sent bullets my way, or down the street into an area filled with people. If I had fired at him, I'd have to trust that my little thirty-two would drop him quickly enough. But it worked out – Ed dropped him with a headshot, then cycled and shot the other Mooz in the spine, and that bullet did a through-and-through and killed the Cat Lady."

Josef puts his hand out to stop Doug. "Colorful nicknames aside – they're very evocative – all that matters is that the job is done, nobody was hurt, and you didn't leave operable evidence."

"Not a single casing hit the pavement," Jake says. "For the dirty cop, I fired from well inside the van, through the cargo door, and all of the brass stayed inside."

McIntyre addresses Jake. "How did your special lights work for you?"

Jake shrugs. "It's not really possible for us to know unless we can get info from inside RCMP, but there weren't even descriptions of us on TV, from what we could tell, but that doesn't mean much. I'd like to know; in testing, those little IR lights completely flare out a good one-foot diameter of low-light video."

McIntyre looks over his glass, poised at his mouth, to Doug and Jake. "At the very least it means there weren't any witnesses. Five people erased publically in Canada's most peaceful city, and no eyewitnesses talking to newsmen. Well done." He sips his whiskey, swallowing it soundlessly and lowering his glass. "Speaking of, tell me about that bastard editor."

Jake states, matter of factly, "I let him get partway out of his car, then gave him a single round in the head with my nine millimeter. Spilled him out in the parking lot right in front of the building entrance. The photos will be very dramatic and troubling, I'm sure."

"They are. What about the lawyer, Doug?" asks Josef, watching his face closely.

Doug swallows and sets down his glass on a coaster at the edge of McIntyre's desk, illustrating the scene with his hands. "Patio door was unlocked, so I took a chance and entered the house. The lawyer's f-, uh, boyfriend, was asleep on the couch. I couldn't change the whole plan, and didn't want to risk going upstairs and screwing up the ambush, so I plugged him, cycled the gun and pocketed the casing, then waited. When the lawyer came down, I put one into his brain, and bailed."

McIntyre takes another sip of his whiskey. "And the very attractive young lady City Councilor, you let her walk, correct?"

Jake nods. "That was my call. I couldn't find any evidence that she was critical to the operation, or involved in anything that would warrant violence. So we left her a night letter. If she doesn't lay off, I'll plug her myself."

"We're not animals, men," says Josef. "We're soldiers, who just happen to be deniable assets lacking uniforms. You successfully removed several major problems, which will simplify many, many things for many, many people. Speaking of: how was it, working with the Roy brothers?"

Jake, sipping whiskey, swallows before responding. "Completely solid. I'd go to war with them any day."

McIntyre interjects, "And one another?"

Doug and Jake look at each other. "Doug is solid," says Jake. "Solid."

"Jake is a hell of a team leader, sir," says Doug. "Between him and the Roys, we had every angle covered, and nobody took any stupid risks."

"Well, alright then," says McIntyre, pouring more whiskey for each man. "We'll have our signals team keep an eye out for any news, but otherwise, it looks like we can go back to business as usual. Take a few days off; I don't want to see you boys until next Wednesday. Go skiing, or something else you enjoy. Does that sound like an order you can handle?"

"Yes, sir," says Jake. Doug says nothing; they all look to him.

He sighs. "I have school."

Josef grins. "Doug has a young lady friend who he needs to check in on." The other men smile.

"Fine, Douglas, return to school; it's important. Try not to stress yourself out. And reach out if you need to talk about anything," McIntyre says. He gestures to the hallway. "Let's have dinner."

Gambit

Doug returns to his apartment after 8 p.m., exhausted, the caffeine he'd been propping himself up with for several days finally petering out. Mike is, for once, not in the apartment – possibly a good sign. He finds two messages blinking on his answering machine, both hang-ups. He checks his dedicated Cathy cell phone; she's left a voice mail.

"Hey, you. Just thinking about you. Call me when you get back, kay?"

His heart flutters.

The pager – damn. Doug forces himself off his bed, grabs a snub-nose revolver from his floor safe, and slips on running shoes at the door, leaving them unlaced. He enters the hall, passing the hippie girls' apartment down the hall, smelling weed. Mike? Doug continues to the stairwell and down to the garage, entering Cathy's pre-programmed number into the Nokia. She answers.

"Hey, it's me. I'm back." Doug exits into the parking garage, looking about the low, crowded space, and makes his way to the northwest corner, where the pager sits in its faraday bag on an I-beam in the ceiling.

"Hey." Cathy sounds cheery. "How was your trip? You get everything sorted out?"

"Yeah, it went well." Doug reaches up into the shadow of the dusty I-beam and withdraws the faraday bag containing the pager, his link to Green. "Pops has a lot of business interests I'm working with, before things are too far down the road to address them properly. Luckily I have some good people to work with, friends of his." Guilt over his omissions leave an actual taste in his mouth, despite the semi-truth of the statement.

"I'm glad." She pauses, kitchen noises in the background. "When can I see you?"

Doug sighs as he walks back to the stairwell. "I'm completely exhausted. Just got back home. Are you working after class tomorrow?"

"Yeah," she says, the disappointment thick in her voice. "But I get off at five. Let's hang out. I want to show you something. Can you pick me up at work?"

Doug leans against the orange stripe painted along the rough concrete wall of the parking garage, next to the stairwell. "You got it. Dress code?"

"Mmmm, we'll be outside. Bring some of your good little friends like we had that night, that'd be perfect. Alright?"

"Alright." Doug smiles, imagining Cathy's face on the other end, her hands holding the phone, twisting the cord around her finger, just as she has him. "See ya then. G'night."

"Goodnight." There's a rustling, echoing sound as Cathy hangs up the phone, followed by an electronic click, then silence. Doug looks at his phone, then the faraday bag containing the pager. Call from the phone? Or walk over to the grocery store and call from the payphone bank?

Supposedly, his cellular calls route through a box in the Regrade, and reflect caller ID from one of many numbers, but it would not take much research by a professional organization to match to the company. A fed with a warrant? Forget about it.

Doug walks upstairs to his room, grabs a jacket and his wallet, and walks through a light mist to a payphone bank on Brooklyn Avenue, under the overhanging roof of a grocery store. He removes the pager from its faraday bag and turns it on, checking his messages. Three messages, all from Green, beginning at 9:03 a.m. local time the day before, then 4 p.m., and finally this morning at 9 a.m.

Doug dials the pager number and keys in their response code for "call me back," and punches in the phone number of the pay phone. Three minutes later, the phone rings. He picks up the headset and brings it to his ear.

Green goes through their verification check, his line passing static and road noise. "Nice night for walk."

Doug responds. "Wash day tomorrow, nothing clean, right?"

Green responds in a casual tone. "Hey, welcome back."

"No, sorry, I was feeling paranoid and put this in a place I couldn't get to until tonight." Doug feels the cold finger at the back of his neck and turns around, studying the beggars in front of the grocery store, sitting on cardboard, watching him.

"Uh, huh. Look," and Green's phone rustles as he adjusts it, "we need to meet. I have to talk to you about something we got going on. Tonight."

Doug covers the mouthpiece of the phone with his hand, cursing, before bringing it back to his face. "I don't know; I've got a big project I'm working on that's due tomorrow. Tomorrow afternoon?"

"Yeah, about those big projects. You need to chill on those big projects, man. Let me come meet you; I'm less than twenty minutes from your place."

"Alright." Doug looks around, and focuses on an apartment building a block south. "Meet me on the southern corner of the Brooklyn side, on 47th."

"Don't try to play me, Doug. I'll meet you in front of YOUR building, not some imaginary bullshit apartment. We're friends, right? Don't make this seem more hostile than it is. I just need to check in with you." Witchoo. "I'll see you in fifteen. Late."

Doug slams the phone onto the hook and runs back to his building, storming up the stairs and into his apartment, still empty. He goes to his closet and slips on a set of soft body armor over his t-shirt, then covers it with a thick, voluminous green sweater. He threads a leather holster for his Browning Hi-Power onto his belt, along with a spare magazine, and grabs the suppressed .32 project automatic for good measure, stuffing it into the left side of his waistband, the can in his back pocket. He looks in the mirror mounted to his closet door, studying his face, then squats down to the floor safe and retrieves two of the tiny V-40 hand grenades, locks the safe and flips the carpet back into place.

Out in the front of his building, Doug stands at the curb, looking and up and down 15th Avenue, trying to spot Green. He imagines a car pulling up with its windows rolled down, him dying in a shower of bullets. He runs across the street in a gap in traffic and leans against the tailgate of a pickup truck, in the shadows between streetlights. He places his right hand on his belly, with the left hand on his belt buckle, to facilitate a quick draw.

Green pulls up in a black Range Rover a few minutes later, parking in the loading zone in front of his building, leaning forward and scanning for Doug. Doug runs across the street and raps on the driver's side window, making Green jump, before waving and walking around the back to the passenger door, which he swings open.

"Hey, Doug!" He hears Mike call his name behind him. Doug turns and looks at his roommate, ten feet away, walking with Allie and What's-Her-Name, the horsey-faced stoner girl from down the hall.

"Hey man," says Doug. "I'll see you in a bit." He looks in the back seat – empty – then hops up onto the black leather seat of Green's Range Rover, waves to the trio, and closes the door before sliding on his seatbelt. He turns to Green on his left, who is gripping the steering wheel tightly with his left hand, turned slightly towards him. Green is staring at him with dead eyes.

"Hey, Doug." He slowly offers his right hand. Doug takes it. "Where ya been?"

Doug shrugs. "Like I said, I put the pager in a hidden place in the parking garage, for safekeeping. They were doing some work down there, painting, and had the area blocked off with plastic sheets. Couldn't get to it until tonight."

"Uh huh." Green watches his left side mirror, then pulls the car out onto 15th, headed south. He stares dead ahead, focused on his driving, while he speaks. "It makes me nervous, you dropping off like that. What are we going to do if there is a problem?"

"What kind of a problem do you have in mind?" asks Doug.

Green remains silent for a few minutes as they drive past the University of Washington campus before turning west on Pacific, traveling along Portage Bay and under the University and Ship Canal bridges. A view of the bright downtown skyline appears to their left; Green turns left, into a parking spot looking out over Lake Union and the glittering areas ringing the water. Green turns on his stereo, the car shaking and windows rattling with the low thumping bass of a track by Method Man and the RZA.

Green points to his stereo. "You know this?"

Doug shakes his head. "Not really; I know it's that guy from Wu Tang Clan, that's it."

Green smirks. "So you kind of know it."

Doug sighs. "What are we talking about, Lawrence?"

Green eyeballs Doug silently for a few moments, then finally speaks. "Look, Douglas," emphasizing the last syllable, "Brooks' crew is onto you. Miller called me yesterday morning, told me about Toronto, to start doing some legwork. When you didn't get back to me before the end of the day, I knew you had something to do with it. There's no other crew up there that would have done this as clean. The Canadian groups would have shot up the whole place, like a bunch of amateurs. The cop threw them off. That was a good move."

Doug looks Green dead in the eye. "I don't know what you're talking about. Why are you telling me all this?"

Green chuckles. "Because you've had a pistol pointed at me from under that sweater since 45th."

Doug nods. "Indeed."

"And," Green adds, "I spent time in Bosnia. Those jihadis are shitty people. I don't want 'em here. To be honest with you, man, I don't like what is going on. We shouldn't be letting them in. And Brooks is not only letting them in, he's letting in the worst ones, and arming them."

"Alright," says Doug, "Then leave that crew and join ours."

Green deflates. "Easier said than done, man. I have some ideas, though. Hear me out?"

Doug nods. "Go." He notes that Green has been holding the steering wheel at 10 and 2 since they shook hands twenty minutes ago.

Green exhales. "Okay. First, I told Miller yesterday that you checked in. So I threw him a curveball there. You're welcome. Second, the crew we hit in Victoria, they were some of Brooks' imports who went independent. That's why we came to you with the job. Brooks thought he could build and control a network of imported operatives in North America, on very short leashes, but these guys don't work that way. They're zealots. Their identity is everything, all the way down to the regular guy running a gas station. They aren't part of us, they aren't with us, they're not going to take orders from us."

Doug nods along with Green, trying to figure out the play here. Is Green being straight? He says, "Ok, Lawrence –"

Green corrects him, benevolently. "Larry."

Doug nods. "Larry. I don't know about this Quebec business, or whatever, that you're talking about." Green shakes his head. "But I'm happy to work with you for our mutual benefit. I hope you understand that I have difficulty trusting you, because some guys from your faction murdered my dad thirteen years ago."

Green blinks. "I did not know that," he says slowly.

Doug shrugs. "I didn't know it until very recently, either."

Green asks, "Is that why you smoked the lawyer?"

Doug shakes his head. "I don't know what you're talking about."

"C'mon, dude." Green leans back in his seat, covering his face. "We have to be able to be honest with each other. I've gone out into No Man's Land for you."

"No, we have to be able to trust each other appropriately," says Doug. "I trust you as much as I can trust you. You've said some things, and I have to verify them. But I do want to work with you."

Green adjusts in his seat. "Can you take the gun off me?" Doug does not re-holster the pistol under his sweater, but brings his right hand out with a flourish and holds it up at shoulder height. "Thank you. So, here's the deal. We got a problem with another group of Albanians we set up, right here in Seattle."

Doug turns, looking into the back seat again, unable to shake that chill. "Marvelous."

Green puts his hands back on the steering wheel. "We got these guys; they're bad news. I want to prove to Miller and Brooks, all the guys above me, that we can't manage these animals. There's not a big Albanian population around here, but there are more and more Muslims every day, and the boys are getting squirrely. They've started attending a mosque in Northgate and networking. They're running heroin, God knows what else. Brooks set them up with a bunch of Eastern Bloc weapons, an order your grandfather fulfilled."

"Whoa, whoa, whoa." Doug puts up his hand. "Just a couple weeks ago? We thought those were going to Yugoslavia."

"Former Yugoslavia," Green emphasizes. "No, that went to this crew."

"Motherfucker. That's a lot of heavy hardware." A fire rises inside Doug's head. "This is a problem. He never would have done it if he knew it was for domestic distribution, especially to Albanians."

Green extends his hand. "Then let's work together. Let's erase these guys, get Miller and Brooks over a barrel."

Doug takes Green's hand and shakes it. "You got it, Larry."

Friday night, Doug picks Cathy up after work in front of a high-rise downtown on Fourth Avenue, watching her split off from a clutch of young women in skirts and topcoats, who stare, giggling, as she makes her way into his Bronco, waving to her. Doug grins and waves back to the girls.

"God, I'm so embarrassed," Cathy says, buckling her seatbelt.

"Hey, they just want to see your famous roughneck boyfriend. Hi ladies," Doug says, leaning over her, rolling down the window and waving again. "Hiiiiii."

"Knock it off," she laughs, elbowing him sharply in the ribs. "Get me home so I can get out of these clothes."

"That's a FANTASTIC idea," Doug says, as he pulls the Bronco out into traffic.

"Doug, that's not what I meant!" Cathy laughs.

"I know!" he returns. "But it's what I meant!" At the intersection, he turns to her, holding eye contact. "And don't you forget it."

She turns her head, looking out the window. "Hey, we have a party at my parents' house next Sunday. Do you think you can handle a dozen Filipinas feeling your muscles, critiquing you, and stuffing your face with their food, to see if you're worthy?"

"What are they going to be feeling?" he asks, turning towards the highway onramp and crawling through rush hour traffic. "I'd rather have you do the feeling, thanks."

"Jeez, quit it." She smacks his shoulder with a hammerfist, which also hurts, like her elbow.

"Just having fun. Good to see you." He leans over quickly and kisses her on the cheek while accelerating onto the highway, then braking when met by a sea of red taillights.

"What did you do back home?" she asks, watching him in the red light.

Doug turns to Cathy and shakes his head. "I had to go to the east coast, talk to some of my granddad's business partners. You don't know this, but I'll be inheriting a pretty big share of an established import-export company. That's where I work, Vanguard. We were talking to some lawyers and partners back east, in the snow. I'm pretty glad it's all over."

"You just made my job easier," Cathy says. "My mom'll only need you to go through confirmation, once she finds out you're rich."

Doug shakes his head. "No, most of the assets are tied up in the business. Pops kind of let his share lapse a bit, only doing a little here, a little there. That said, maybe we'll go up to Mr. McIntyre's house some time – his business partner – he has a huge place over in Magnolia, worth a few million bucks. His wife is from a royal family in Asia, or something."

"Is marrying an Asian girl a prerequisite for taking over the family business?" she teases. "Or do you actually like me?"

Doug leans over and takes her hand, resting it on her leg. "Stop it. Looks like we'll be back at your place in about ten minutes. Then you can, uh, change into something more comfortable. Where are you taking me again?"

"A place over by my parents' house," she says. "A park on the ridge above the lake. It's nice."

Doug points out the window to the right. "Look at that guy," and when Cathy turns her head, he adjusts the front of his pants. Better.

"I don't see anything."

"Never mind." After ten minutes they exit the express lanes in the lower lanes of the Ship Canal Bridge into the south end of the University District, arriving at Cathy's apartment a few minutes later.

"You stay here," says Cathy, hopping out of the Bronco in front of her apartment. "I'll be quick." She slams the door shut and runs to the door, unlocking it, smiling at him before disappearing inside.

"How am I going to stay here?" Doug asks himself, sitting in the middle of the road. He loops around the block four times before Cathy appears, wearing jeans, Doc Martens and a dark grey hooded windbreaker over a purple UW hoodie, head in a white knit cap. She jumps into the Bronco and Doug waits for her to buckle up, watching her, while a car honks behind him.

"You look super cute," he says to her, looking down. The car honks again, and someone yells out the window.

She blushes. "Come on." Doug accelerates, slowly, before steering around to the south and heading towards Montlake Boulevard.

They very slowly make their way through sluggish Friday night rush hour traffic, crawling along 23rd Avenue deep into the Central District before passing Garfield High School. Cathy directs him left on Alder, and they pass every American's favorite street to be on, Martin Luther King, Jr. Way, and drive uphill, over the ridge, and down a few blocks to the northwestern edge of the Leschi neighborhood.

"Park over here; there's a trailhead right there, into the park," Cathy says, pointing out a dark area free of streetlights.

"The thing that drives me crazy about Northwest winters in the city," Doug says, "is that you're always outside at night, in the car at night." He pulls forward, then backs into the widest slot on the block. "It can get old, but this is cool." He puts the Bronco into park and engages the parking break before shutting off the engine.

"C'mon," Cathy orders, and Doug follows, locking the Bronco and approaching a narrow, dimly lit trailhead, fortunately free of evergreen trees, so the light of the city is sufficient for navigation, once their eyes adjust. They walk slowly, holding hands, and then Cathy leads them down a steep hill to a rock outcropping looking down over Lake Dell Avenue. She sits, patting the rock next to her with her right hand. "Light it up. I have a bottle of water."

Doug obeys, drawing a tiny joint from his jacket's inner pocket, and lights it, puffing until the cherry is established. He passes the joint to Cathy, who takes two small drags. They settle into a rhythm, puff puff pass, and calmly watch the headlights of cars down on Lake Washington Boulevard and the buzzing flow of the I-90 bridge just to the south.

"This is a cool spot," Doug says, and puts his left arm around Cathy, who leans into him. Cathy finishes the joint, stubbing it out on the rock to her left.

"I'm glad you brought a small one," she says. "That big one you gave me and Liz was too much; we smoked half of it and nearly passed out."

"Most people smoke too much," says Doug. "I have to drive in a little bit, and I don't like driving stoned. I'd be curled up in a ball, overcome with paranoia, if we smoked a regular joint and I had to drive you home afterward."

They look out over the landscape, holding each other; Doug is overcome with the urge to let nature take its course. He resists.

"You're tense," Cathy says, turning and looking up at him.

He kisses her, then draws back mere millimeters from her lips. "No, just part of me is tense," he says, and kisses her again.

"Stop it," she says, hitting him, then kisses him back. They linger a moment before Cathy puts her hand on his chest and pushes them apart a few inches. "Down, boy," she says, but she's still close, grinning.

"Mmmmm, how are we going to do this?" Doug asks, his right hand on her bare hip under her hoodie.

Cathy scrunches her face up in an exaggerated expression of pensiveness. "Very." Then kisses him. "Carefully." She pushes him onto his back and stands up, laughing. "I want to show you something."

He stands. "I have something I want to show you, too." She throws another light slap to him, which he lets connect on his cheek, laughing.

Cathy lures him down the hill into what Doug immediately recognizes as a great position for an ambush – an old stone building with a long-gone roof, covered in graffiti and moss, built into the hillside, held up by a mortared stone retaining wall. "My brothers and I used to play here," she says, leaning against one of the walls. "I got stoned here with my cousin for the first time my senior year. Come in here and look up."

Doug stands next to her, and they lean against the high southern wall. Cathy points to a small one-foot square window up at the tip of the northern wall, framing a small spray of stars, the sky appearing darker through the aperture. "Come over here," she says, and they maneuver until Orion's Belt fits perfectly within the window frame.

"Whoa," Doug says.

"*Los Tres Reyes Magos*," Cathy says. "The Three Wise Men."

They enjoy the view for a few minutes, talking about nothing. Finally, Cathy begins grousing about hunger, so they head back to the Bronco, drive down to MLK and north a few blocks to a pho restaurant, where they both get small bowls with various cuts of beef, tendon, tripe and spongy meatballs. Cathy loads her bowl with sprouts and basil, adding a little heat with sauces and a single slice of jalapeño. Doug, as an outlander, isn't much of a spice fan; he holds on the peppers. It's the best bowl of soup he has eaten in a long time. His mind drifts to another pho restaurant, in Toronto, and the filth he helped kill two blocks away. He watches Cathy, so talkative and bubbly, across from him bundled up in her hoodies, her face framed in a white knit cap, eyes a little red, and smiles. Good riddance.

Wednesday afternoon, Doug, Jake, Evans and McIntyre meet in the main Vanguard conference room to discuss the matter of Lawrence Green, Miller, and the Brooks organization in general. After Doug's exposition on their past engagements, Jake raises his hand. "Hey, I know this guy. Not personally, but he was in our Bosnia contingent right before I rotated in. I've read his intelligence packets. He's sharp."

"It would be nice to know more about this man," adds Evans. Charles McIntyre invited Evans into the meeting unexpectedly, surprising Doug and Jake. "False sincerity and an expressed interest in serving as a double agent are common ruses. Sir?" he asks, turning to McIntyre.

McIntyre fiddles with a cigar, trimming the tip and punching a hole in the base with a golden implement. He lights the cigar, puffing until flame catches, and fills the room with a surprisingly pleasant aroma. He points to Doug with his cigar hand. "Douglas, do you believe him?"

Doug shrugs. "I have no idea, sir. I don't trust him, but that doesn't mean that he's not being honest. I have difficulty reading him. Like Jake said, he's a sharp guy, but he's like a brick wall to me. He's after something, but I don't know what it is."

Evans and Jake look at each other, grinning slightly. Evans nods back to Jake. Jake clears his throat. "One of the challenges in the modern military is the disparate backgrounds of the men you're working with," he opines. "For me, the hardest guys to anticipate with were black guys, even the top tier hard chargers in the Battalion. Not because they're black, but because, being black, when you're dealing with something political, they're just coming from somewhere else. It is what it is. Everyone has self-interest, but they may align with a shitbag co-racialist, or be ten times harder on an underperforming black guy, or more nurturing. I dunno."

Evans looks to McIntyre, who nods. Evans stands. "We don't want to bark orders at you guys, but Mr. McIntyre would prefer to come to a consensus, even if it's somewhat forced. Doug, you're sure you didn't give away the game to Green?"

"I'm positive, uh, sir," Doug says. "But it seems to me that we can use him. If he's trying to infiltrate, we can feed him info to drive a result. If he's being earnest, we can take apart the organization that much more efficiently."

McIntyre waves his hand. "Maybe he'd make a good asset. All that said, we only know that he's Brooks' man, thus a potential enemy. If it comes to it, don't hesitate to put him down. He seems to be making a big show of putting you on the spot, Douglas, and my loyalty to your family far exceeds that of some negro peacetime military veteran." He stands and walks out of the room, nodding to Evans.

Jake draws his hand across his brow, pressing his spiky hair down, and retrieves a handkerchief from his suit coat, rubbing his hand with it.

"Relax, Steiner," says Evans, walking around to the front of the room. He points to Doug. "Shea, continue to engage, but be on your toes. Keep us informed. If you see anything that spooks you, let us know. Immediately. Call my line, I'll answer. Any time. Any little thing. Steiner, we need to set you up with some gear. If you want to come along, Doug, you can. You might want to try something different from what your granddad is issuing. We're on a more modern tip."

Evans turns and beckons Doug and Jake to follow. They flow out into the executive hallway, then down a secure stairwell after Evans swipes an RFID card and punches in a code. At the bottom of the stairs, Evans enters another code, and they enter an armory that is the more-recently-painted spitting image of the one under Doug's house, but roughly ten times larger. Here, however, the majority of the equipment is in crates, which are sorted on labeled shelves. Evans wags his finger over his shoulder as he walks down one of the rows of shelves, stopping at a row of suppressed submachine guns and short-barreled rifles. He gestures to the weapons, waving his hand along the shelving, then grabs a stack of gloves from the shelf and hands them to the other men before donning his own pair. "These are samples of the weapons in the crates. We have MP5s of various flavors, including some of the FBI 10mm models. A couple of M-16 types in 9mm, .45 ACP and a thirty-caliber subsonic."

"Whisper?" asks Doug. "Take that one, Jake."

Evans picks up a short-barreled M-16 with what appears to be a stepped cylinder front end and a collapsing stock, the carry handle cut off in front of the rear sight and a short section of scope rail mounted to the top of the receiver. "I like this one," Evans says. "Uses standard M-16 magazines and a thirty-caliber round with heavy bullets. You can also shoot a supersonic load with AK ballistics and commercial hunting projectiles. This one has a ten-inch barrel, like the Commando, a free-floating handguard for accuracy, and of course a suppressor." He points to a switch poking out of a hole atop the handguard. "With this you can set the gas system for supersonic loads, subsonic loads, or cut off the gas entirely for silent single shots. Pop the pins and the whole thing fits into a backpack or toolbox."

Jake handles the rifle, adjusting the stock to fit him, and shoulders it when something catches his eye. "Hey, a Krinkov," Jake notes, passing the rifle back to Evans before selecting another, a stubby folding stock AK-47 with a large muzzle brake and a red dot sight mounted over the gas tube.

Evans picks up a suppressor from the shelf. "A Yugo variant in 5.56mm. The muzzle brake pops right off so that you can thread this on. There's a little dial on the gas block that allows tuning, like an FAL. Custom job." Jake grins. "Still," Evans continues, "I suggest that you stick to a platform you're familiar with."

Jake grins. "I was a Ranger, and I spent six months in Bosnia training their shitty Mooz army on the AK. I know this weapons platform."

Evans looks at him stone-faced. "It's your dance, Steiner." He looks at Doug. "Shea, you need anything?"

Doug drools over an MP5K with folding stock and threaded barrel. "Always wanted one of these. Granddad hate's 'em." Evans gestures to the MP5K and Doug picks it up, manipulating the stock, working the bolt, and admiring the tiny buzzsaw. "I even like the color."

Evans rolls his eyes. "OK, you two, outfit 'em and put 'em in a bag. I have a few pistols for you, Steiner, Berettas with cans. Shea, sorry to disappoint you, but Steiner is going to be responsible for these for the time being, given your living arrangement."

Doug nods. "Works for me."

Evans walks to the other side of the room. "I'll grab ammo for you guys. Pack 'em up."

Jake selects a wide, boxy but short padded soft case, unzips the top and holds his hand out for the MP5K. Doug hands it to him, and Jake straps it into a corner with the stock folded, then adds the AK, its stock also folded, into the other panel. They add magazines of varying lengths, suppressors, a universal cleaning kit, slings and small magazine-carrying chest rigs to the bag, then Evans returns, carrying mid-sized olive drab ammunition crates in each hand. "You have five hundred rounds of 5.56mm here," holding up the crate in his left hand, "and eight hundred rounds of 9mm here," holding up the right. Doug takes the ammunition, and together they carry the equipment to the next room, an indoor shooting range 25 meters long.

Evans laughs. "Have fun loading the magazines, guys! I'll set out some more ammunition by the door. Steiner, I expect those weapons to be clean before they leave the building. I'll bring in the pistols."

Doug and Jake spend nearly an hour familiarizing themselves with their new weapons, Jake showing Doug some tips about the MP5K. The handguns that Evans delivers to the pair are new Beretta 92FS models, with an added slide lock mechanism bolted to the frame, and a Special Forces issue Snap-On suppressor each, which uses wipes and an ablative gel. Jake is familiar with this variant, and explains its use to Doug. After shooting, they sit at a table in the armory, cleaning the weapons while wearing gloves. Jake and Doug conclude that Josef's Beretta 92s with frame-mounted safeties, as used in the Toronto mission, make for a superior, simpler slide lock design.

"Yeah, but I'll take it," says Jake, selecting a shoulder holster from the armory for each Beretta, along with magazine pouches and suppressor carriers. He offers a shoulder harness for the MP5K to Doug, who waves it off.

As Jake loads the weapons case, Doug says softly to Jake, "So, now that we've done a job together, are you open to extra-curricular work?"

Jake studies Doug's face carefully. "Go on."

"Oh, you know." Doug lays all of the magazines on the table before him, grouped by weapon, and begins loading the pistol magazines. "There are a few peripheral targets that the world would be better off without. Instead of slugging it out with the little guys, why not remove some higher-ups, who are the actual source of the problem?"

Jake looks at Doug skeptically. "And you know who they are?"

Doug nods. "If we are comfortable removing a facilitator in Canada, why would we not be comfortable removing one right here in Seattle?"

Jake squints, thinking.

"There are some men who are part of the Canada-U.S. trafficking network, hiding behind badges." Doug pauses, watching Jake. "I'll give you a packet, and let you decide for yourself. It's personal with me, but I'd feel better with someone competent tagging along."

"Why wouldn't McIntyre and Evans give us the assignment, if it's legit?" asks Jake.

Doug, having loaded the pistol magazines, moves on the longer, curved MP5 magazines. "A good question. Maybe McIntyre wants to jiggle the handle in a different way. My grandfather would have discussed this with him. That could be what this gear is for. Who knows?" Doug stands up, shuffling magazines and ammunition boxes to assist Jake in loading the larger AK magazines. He lets the silence between them linger until they have all the magazines loaded. Sliding the loaded AK magazines across the table to Jake, Doug asks, "How familiar are you with the Spanish Civil War, Jake?"

Jake shrugs. "I know that the Soviets supported the leftists, who called themselves Republicans. The Germans supported Franco, who won. I also know that Mr. McIntyre and your grandfather met during the war."

"Okay, the basics." Doug says. "Do you know why the Republicans lost?"

"No idea," says Jake.

"They didn't have a unifying ideology or identity. The communists and anarchists were subsumed by foreign, or at least non-Spanish, elements, and their morale fell to pieces because of atrocities committed by zealots and those non-Spanish groups hostile to Spanish culture. Nobody could surrender to the zealots – they'd be murdered. Nobody who questioned their ever-changing leadership could trust that they wouldn't be shot in the back of the head by a communist political officer." Doug pauses. "The Republic wasn't even a thing. It was a not-thing – not the monarchy. Why were the famous 'International Brigades' a thing?"

Jake shakes his head. "Hemingway?"

Doug nods. "Sure, there was romanticism there. 'Democracy.' But most of the people involved were just communists, and like I said, many were hostile to the traditional Spanish culture. A huge factor in that civil war was the same people behind the 1917 revolution in Russia, and the one quashed in Germany by the rise of the Nazis."

Jake asks, "How can the same people be in all of those places?"

Doug counters, "What's the one non-Christian ethnic group that has persisted in Europe since the fall of the Roman Empire?"

Jake leans back. "Ohhhhhhh. Gotcha. Doug, what's your point?"

Doug picks up Jake's compact AK and fiddles with it, examining folding stock mechanism and red dot sight. "It just occurred to me. I know why I work for Vanguard. It's partly my grandfather's operation. It's a part of my identity, a role I was raised to step into. That's a positive identity. Is ideology a part of it? I don't know. What's *your* role here at Vanguard?"

Jake nods. "You've never asked me why I quit the army after a mere five years active duty as an officer, which had been my life-long dream."

Doug says, "I'll bite. Jake, sir, why did you, a patriot and hard-charging guy, quit the army, when you could have had a long, lucrative career serving your country, with a long, comfortable retirement?"

Jake laughs. "Because, while I loved running and gunning, and the guys I served with – mostly – and grew up expecting to fight the Soviets, defending America, I found myself doing things that had nothing to do with defending America. We were supposedly 'defending America's interests,' or 'protecting emerging democracies,' but that was all bullshit. Every situation was about enforcing an agenda that the average American would hate. Real Americans, not the talking heads and bureaucrats. Like I told you before, in Bosnia, we built a Mooz army, and pushed out Christians with a historical claim to the country. Then I met some guys from Vanguard, who were able to fulfill State and DOD contracts by helping out only the people they wanted to help. There's a long history of US foreign policy being carried out by private companies of ex-military and ex-CIA guys, and you can get rich doing it."

Doug laughs. "There's that."

Jake stands up. "I'm down for whatever, if you can make a solid case that any op is on the side of the angels, and it's not against the interests of our employers. We have to do it right, though."

Doug offers his hand. "That's why I want you in. You're a great team leader and I value your advice."

Jake looks at Doug's hand for a moment before meeting his eyes and shaking on it. "OK, we need to do some whiteboarding. When can you get me that packet?"

Doug shrugs. "I'll make copies tonight, and can drop them off tonight at your place, or tomorrow here. I'm not working tomorrow because of school, though."

Jake says, "Make it tonight, and we'll whiteboard tomorrow night. Deal?"

"Deal."

Proditione

Doug and Jake walk out of Vanguard's office and into a light drizzle. Jake leads Doug through the secure parking lot to a silver late-model BMW M3 coupe, then turns to face him with a grin. Doug whistles as he walks around the car, peeking through the window at the glossy black leather interior, while Jake loads his bag of shiny new weapons into the trunk. The tires are unlike anything Doug, a truck guy, has seen before, giving off a racing vibe, though they run on unflashy rims.

"Nice ride," says Doug. "How fast is she?"

Jake pushes the trunk down gently until the latch clicks, then walks around to the driver side door. "Pretty fast. I had her imported from Germany; it's got a straight six and is really nimble. You don't need a massive engine for real driving. I've had my eye on an M5, which is a larger sedan built on the same concept, but the parking garage in my building is a little tight for that. The main thing about this car, from an operational perspective, is that it's a little light for ramming. Imagine a fleet of Vanguard guys with M5s."

Doug nods. "Ed Roy was expounding on the benefits of sedans with performance packages. The only problem with the BMWs, that I can see, is that you stick out like a sore thumb outside of the city, or even in most neighborhoods."

Jake shrugs. "Hillbilly. I'm a yuppie with a downtown Seattle condo and a BMW. Right? Pretty good camouflage."

Doug says, "Touché."

Jake extends his hand. "See ya tonight, Doug."

They shake on it; Doug follows Jake out of the secure employee parking lot in his Bronco, the automatic gate rumbling closed behind him. They both head north on 99, Jake waving back to Doug as he blasts ahead in the light mid-afternoon traffic; Doug veers onto the West Seattle Bridge eastbound. In his rearview mirror, Doug notes a pair of white sedans, screaming Rental Car, which pull out of the Port behind him, following two cars back. He moves into the left lane, for the I-5 North ramp; the Rental Cars follow suit. I-5 north is moving fairly smoothly, due to the hour, though each lane is crowded; Doug gooses his engine and speeds two lanes over, watching the Rental Cars; within the next quarter mile, they follow.

"Fuck." Doug draws his cell phone from the center console, removes it from its faraday bag and dials Evans' cell number. Evans answers in seconds.

"Yes." Silence.

"It's me," says Doug. "I picked up some tails leaving the office. Might want to reach out to Jake, give him a head's up."

A few seconds of silence. "He doesn't have a cellular. I'll leave a message for him at home. Thanks. Do you need a hand?"

Doug thinks for a beat. "I'm gonna lose them. If they are who I think they are, though, they might already have my home address."

Evans' obvious pedigree as an NCO emerges. "Give me everything you got, no filters. Now. Or I can't help you."

Doug sighs. He searches his mirrors and over his shoulders for the Rental Cars; one is three cars behind him in his lane, the other in the lane to his right, two cars back. Traffic slows, as is traditional, due to the upcoming I-90 interchange and downtown exits. He guns it, crossing all the way to the I-90 eastbound exit, eliciting honks from the cars he cuts off. One of the Rental Cars makes it to the ramp, the other just missing, slowing and heading north in the right lane.

Traffic on I-90 eastbound is light, so Doug floors it, pegging his engine at 64 mph. "No way is this an Imperial entanglement; it's JV all the way." He steers around slow cars in his lane, watching the one remaining Rental Car speed behind him to catch up. "Green's crew of Albanians from North Seattle, probably; I can't get a look at them, but I don't see who else would be tracking us. Looks like our questions about Green have been answered."

Evans' commanding voice sounds in his hear. "Try to ditch 'em, but if you can't, just get back here. Don't do anything you can't talk your way out of; I got a guy headed to Jake's, but he's coming from here. Might be time for you guys to go to ground."

"Fuck." Doug roars onto the Rainier Avenue South exit, passing a row of cars on the shoulder, then taps his brake and skips into southbound traffic. The Rental Car gets stuck behind several cars; Doug turns onto a side street after the Oberto Sausage plant and heads west twenty mph over the speed limit, up towards Beacon Hill, praying that no kids step out onto the street. "OK; I'll dial back with a status update. I'm gonna head to Jake's; I have a bad feeling about this."

Evans nearly shouts. "Be careful; I'll call my guy, but we have to avoid any blue on blue disasters."

Doug says, "Don't worry, I won't shoot any white people." He squashes the End Call button on his phone and tosses it onto the seat, then slows the roaring Bronco before pulling right into a side street, skipping back a block before heading uphill again. The Rental Car is gone. Now following the speed limit, Doug turns north onto 15th, passing the VA hospital, then crosses over I-90 on the 12th Avenue bridge, dipping down into the International District before heading west on Jackson to Alaskan under the viaduct, where he heads north towards Jake's Belltown condo. Crawling north in the growing rush hour traffic, Doug runs an inventory in his head of the weapons he has on tap in the car: the Browning Hi-Power, a lever-action .30-30, a handful of the little V-40 grenades, and a short lever-action .357 threaded for a suppressor, loaded with heavy subsonic bullets. Running through Belltown with long arms seems like a terrible idea, so Doug grabs the Browning and two magazines, sliding the pistol into his waistband and the mags into his left front pocket. He pounds the steering wheel as he inches forward at under 5 mph.

Finally emerging on the north end of the Viaduct, Doug turns right, uphill, onto Vine, parks in a loading zone just west of Western Avenue and hops out of his car, grabbing a baseball cap from the back seat and pulling it low across his face. He looks across Western to Jake's building and runs through the intersection to the parking garage gate, which appears to have been rammed. He slides his hand over the butt of his pistol, peers into the parking garage and sees Jake's BMW smashed into a concrete pillar, the engine still running, smoke rising from the hood. He runs down into the garage and around to the driver's side, shattered glass crunching under his feet, and sees Jake, or what is left of him, his face shot to pieces and a Glock pistol clutched in his hand, the slide locked back. Doug turns and examines the ground, spotting a spray of rifle casings, 7.62x39mm, and small holes perforating the side of the car. Sirens scream in the distance; Doug runs out of the parking garage into view of a cluster of bystanders across the street in front of a print shop, spots of setting sun showing between clumps of dark clouds behind them, a worker inside on a telephone, watching him, her lips moving.

Doug shouts, "Call an ambulance; there's been an accident!" He crosses the street and walks down to his Bronco, hopping in and roaring out onto the street, praying that the bystanders don't call it in and feeling like a fool for parking so close to the condo. He finally notices his tightening chest, his face squeezed tight; tears explode from the corners of his eyes and he sobs, coughing, steering on autopilot towards his apartment, squeezing the steering wheel until his hands ache. Getting himself under control, wiping tears and snot onto the sleeves of his shirt and controlling his breathing, he finally picks up the cell phone as he crosses Mercer on 99 north. He dials Evans.

"Go."

Doug exhales deeply, emotionally exhausted. "They got him. There are witnesses; police will be on the scene by now. I verified. The witnesses saw me; possibly saw my vehicle. I'm going to ground."

Evans sighs loudly. "OK. Get in here, we'll get you out. I don't want to lose another man today."

Doug shakes his head, pondering his words before responding. He looks to the northeast, across Lake Union. "I got something I gotta do first."

"Doug –"

Doug hangs up on Evans and pulls the battery from the cellular phone, considering his moves as he crests the high point of 99 on Queen Anne before the Aurora bridge, plotting his course and inventorying his options. Crossing over the Fremont Canal, he exits onto Bridge Way and heads due east, watching the I-5 Ship Canal Bridge loom closer and closer, passing under it and emerging into the lower University District. He turns north on 7th, then right on 43rd, moving towards Cathy's apartment on 42nd. He checks his watch – 4:50 p.m. Will she even be home? He looks to his cell phone and plugs in the battery. He parks the Bronco in an alley a block from the apartment, thinks for a moment, and crawls into the back of the Bronco. From the lock box in the bed he grabs and dons gloves, then fills a pocket with several of the tiny grenades. He curses himself for forgetting the weapons in Jake's trunk, then selects his .30-30, jacking a round into the chamber, mounting a leather cartridge carrier to his belt. He slides a cartridge from the carrier into the loading gate, then decocks the hammer before wrapping the rifle in a light wool blanket. Topping that off with a pouch of goodies from the center console, he crawls back out of the Bronco and locks the door behind him, headed towards the girls' apartment. He pulls up Cathy's number on the cellular phone and dials.

It rings twice before Liz picks up. "Hello?"

"Liz, it's Doug. Is Cathy there?" Doug has the phone in his left hand, the blanket-wrapped rifle in his right, as he scans the darkening alley, the dumpy houses and apartment buildings around him offering innumerable ambush points. He walks through the yard of a house towards the girls' apartment building, glad for the cover of darkness.

"She should be home soon; she didn't work today, and was studying at the library. What's up?" Liz's casual attitude makes Doug want to scream. He controls himself, trying not to sound panicked.

"I was thinking of coming by. I'll head over your way. Just… stay inside. See you soon." He hangs up the phone before Liz can respond, and slides the phone into his coat pocket, transferring the rifle to his left hand and keeping his right hovering near the Browning. He notices that he is damp; the drizzle is transitioning to a downpour. His element.

Doug loops around the apartment building in an elliptical orbit, passing close behind the rear and sides of the building before expanding out a few houses to check the street in front, scanning for parked cars with occupants – that aren't obviously car campers, an endemic issue around UW – particularly the Rental Cars or other vehicles that don't belong. Finally, at the end of the block, he sees it – a blue Ford Taurus, brand new, completely inappropriate for the area, with two heads silhouetted inside by car headlights. Passing behind them at the crosswalk, he notes their perfect view of the entrance to the girls' apartment building, three driveways away. Moving down the next block, then coming up the side street, there it is, one of the white Rental Cars, with two people inside conferring with two standing on the sidewalk. Doug crosses the street and squats down at a rusty old Chevy Suburban, bringing only his left eye around the corner to watch them. From this distance, in this poor light – streetlights are sparse in this old neighborhood – he can't get a good look at the men. Doug leans the blanket-wrapped rifle against the Suburban's tire and removes his goodie pouch from his jacket pocket and withdraws an 8x power monocular, which gives him a better view of the men across the street. The two in the car have long, curly black hair and beards, big beaks but slightly European features. Albanians or Turks. On the sidewalk, another of the same and – Doug stops – Green.

Motherfucker.

Doug is tempted to shoot them down right here, but pauses, assessing his options.

Green had obviously been tracking him for weeks. Doug's countermeasures assumed a stranger starting at zero, not someone with prepared intelligence. Green already knew everything about him before they met for lunch; the rest was a ruse.

Whatever Green's stated intentions, or portrayed conflict, here he is, waiting outside Cathy's apartment for him. Or Cathy.

Green and the others pause, two putting their hands over an ear; they all look up towards the apartment. Green and the other man spread out, moving towards 42nd rapidly. Doug pockets the monocular and pouch and picks up the blanket-wrapped rifle, remaining in a low crouch, and cuts through a side yard to an alley parallel to his street, then runs up to 42nd. At the corner of a house he scans the street and sees another white Rental Car parked not ten feet from him, and Cathy on the other side of 42nd. Doug looks right and watches Green walk up to the front of the apartment building, pretending to scan the call box directory. The other man on foot stops at the corner on Doug's side of the street, obtusely watching Cathy directly, and the blue Taurus from the end of the block crawls slowly down the street towards them. The passenger door of the nearby Rental Car swings open and another Albanian steps out, this one in a mismatched Adidas track suit, and looks Doug right in the eye.

"Cathy!" Doug shouts, throwing an armed V-40 mini grenade into the Rental Car, striking the driver in the shoulder, and draws his Browning Hi-Power, firing eight shots into the nearby Albanian and the one in the driver seat of the Rental Car. He pivots right, hitting the man on the corner, now armed, with two shots before crouching to reload. The grenade explodes with a surprisingly loud but low-pitched WHOMP, blowing glass and fragments of the driver out of the Rental Car. Doug stuffs the pistol into his holster and transitions to his lever action rifle, dropping the blanket to the sidewalk while scanning for Green, who has disappeared somewhere across the street, most likely behind parked cars. Doug spots Cathy, her head peeking up across the street, behind the trunk of a Honda, and shouts to her again. "Cathy! Get out of here!" She ducks down again, out of his sight.

Doug curses and steps into the street, moving towards Cathy, scanning the street with his rifle. The blue Taurus stops and the doors swing open; he jacks multiple shots into the driver area of the windshield, then puts several more of the heavy 190 grain solids into the passenger area. The car continues to roll forward slowly; Doug slides more cartridges through the rifle's loading gate, scanning the street for the other men and Green. Now at the rear of the Honda, Doug steps left, onto the sidewalk, his barrel aimed above shoulder level to avoid pointing the rifle at Cathy, but she's two car lengths away now. Green steps out from behind another car quickly and grabs her by the hair with his left hand, cursing as he lifts her off her feet, compressing his body behind hers, pointing a SIG Sauer pistol at her head. Green peeks from around Cathy, who has ceased struggling as he barks orders at her, emphasizing each statement with a tug of her hair. Her right cheek has a slowly bleeding cut from the front sight of Green's pistol. Doug aims his rifle just to the right of her head, looking for a clear shot.

Green's cold words cut through the drizzle. "Slow your roll, Doug; let's find something that works for both of us. You might get me, but I'll get your girl here." Green's trigger finger is applying pressure, the hammer back most of its travel distance.

"Cath-" Doug starts, but Cathy moves, bringing her feet up so her entire body weight goes straight down, while simultaneously jamming a large stainless steel folding knife into Green's thigh, gouging out a wound four inches deep and six inches long, curving the blade inward as she drops. Doug, watching, fires, striking Green high in the right side of his chest, while Green fires a single shot in front of his own face, screaming in agony. Cathy scrambles out of the way and behind Doug. Doug chambers another round in the rifle and scans the street, watching the last of the white Rental Cars squeal on the wet pavement in reverse and scream out of the area. Doug crouches and fires two shots down the block, skipping bullets off the sidewalk and putting at least one into the chest of a man from the Taurus, peeking out from behind a truck's rear tire with a pistol in his hand; he collapses.

Forty seconds have elapsed since Doug threw the grenade.

Cathy, crouching behind Doug, shakes, emitting animal sounds, somewhere in the crossroads of terror and rage. Green lies flat on his back, blood frothing from the hole in his lungs and pouring from the wound in his leg. Several inches of femoral artery were simply removed by Cathy's wickedly serrated knife; he struggles for air. He blinks, looking up at Doug and Cathy.

"Nothing... personal...." Green chokes out. "Thought I backed the... winning horse."

Doug looks to Cathy, reaching out his hand. She draws back sharply, and shouts, her face contorted. "Don't touch me!"

"Baby, get in the apartment, or go to your parents. You don't want to be anywhere near here. I'm sorry." Doug steps forward, his ears ringing wildly, watching Green die, and steps on Green's right hand, eliciting a low moan. "Get going. Get to your family; they'll protect you."

Cathy looks at him, all recognition and surety gone, leaving only a dull, stunned expression of fight or flight. She looks down at the knife in her hand; a gory mess. She squats over Green's lower leg and wipes the blood from the blade, then her hands, pockets the knife and stands. She blinks, looking up at Doug, and to his agony, turns and runs to the apartment door, unlocking it and sprinting up the stairwell.

Doug looks Green in the eyes. "Nothing personal?" He fires the .30-30 into Green's forehead, which explodes upward and out, the bullet ricocheting off into the University District sky. Doug runs behind the apartment building into the alley and sprints back to his Bronco. He drives due north at the speed limit, avoiding arterials, parking in the alley behind his apartment and storming up the stairs, Browning in hand; nobody greets him. He runs into his apartment, not removing his shoes, and grabs two go bags from his room and several photographs, and disconnects his desktop computer from all of its peripherals, stuffing it into a duffel bag. He is piling all of his gear by the door when Mike comes out from his room.

"Hey, man! What's going on?" Mike asks, an as-usual concerned-but-not-really expression on his face.

"I'm gonna be gone for a while, dude." Doug is happy to be telling the truth. "Let me give you the rest of my weed."

"Whoa!" Mike's eyes light up. "Thanks, man! Who was that guy the other night, the black guy? A big connect?"

Doug looks at Mike, stone-faced. "Sure, you could say that." He turns and walks back into his room, grabbing family photos and all of the contents of the floor safe and lock box – cash, documents, guns. He hands the bags of marijuana to Mike, who watches in confusion as Doug stuffs his gear into backpacks and duffles.

"Hey, you're going for good, aren't you?" Mike stands in the doorway, crestfallen, then sets down the weed.

Doug picks up two duffle bags, stacking them in Mike's hands. "Yep. Let me give you some cash for rent. Uh, also, get all of your drugs and illegal shit out of the place, just in case." Doug pauses, seeing an angle. "That guy may have been a narc; get the shit out of here AND make yourself scarce for a while. Go to your parents, or something."

Doug pushes past Mike into the hallway, slinging all of his bags onto himself, adding more for Mike, and leads him out into the hallway and down the stairs, eliciting complaints and "whoas." Doug piles it all unartfully in the back of his Bronco, heading back up for one more trip.

Doug hugs Mike in the doorway, handing him a wad of cash as promised, then grabs his last two bags and a favorite jacket from the hall closet. "See ya, man. Good luck." Mike follows him into the hallway, watching with his mouth open, as Doug disappears into the stairwell and out of his life forever.

Alpenfestung

Doug drives at the exact speed limit through side roads and only minor arterials, avoiding major intersections, on a snaking southerly route all the way to his private garage in Georgetown, arriving after nearly an hour, a small backpack open on the passenger seat containing his collection of V-40 hand grenades, the .30-30 covered by a jacket in the footwell. He rolls open the garage door, one of thirty set into a crumbling once-white-washed cinderblock wall, and pulls the Bronco into the left slot, the right occupied by a ten year old Ford F-150 4x4 with a canopy, heavy steel tube bumpers and grill guard, and an off-road package. Rolling the garage door closed, Doug transfers his gear to the floor of the garage and performs an inventory.

1. Photos and street clothes. He consolidates these into a single bag.

2. Computer. He removes the hard drive for careful disposal. He'll simply throw the case into the nearby Duwamish river and dump the hard drive into another body of water.

3. Bug-Out. He has two bags from his apartment, one urban-oriented, the other rural-, along with food and water.

4. Wilderness gear. The Bronco has more water, an axe, a small chainsaw, a tent, a shovel, emergency food, fire starter, and its own bug-out tools, as does the truck.

5. Cash. Between his bug-out bags, the garage safe, and what he brought from his apartment, Doug has a little over $12,000 in 20s and 100s. He leaves $8k in the garage safe.

6. Weapons. Doug is blessed with an abundance of firearms, though he recognizes that they are, in fact, a nearly incoherent jumble of calibers and overlapping uses. At least he has significant stockpiles of ammunition for each.

From his Bronco:

a. Marlin .30-30 lever-action rifle
b. Marlin .357 lever-action carbine with suppressor
c. Browning Hi-Power 9mm pistol
d. Smith & Wesson .38 snub-nose revolver
e. Smith & Wesson .41 Magnum revolver
f. .32 ACP Walther PP knockoff with suppressor
g. Eleven V-40 miniature hand grenades

In the garage safe:

h. Remington 7mm Magnum bolt action rifle
i. Springfield Armory M-1A .308 rifle
j. Skorpion vz.61 .32 ACP machine pistol with suppressor
k. Ameli Squad Automatic Weapon, 5.56mm
l. Beretta 92 9mm with Shea modifications and suppressor

Doug scratches his head. What to do, what to do. He feels an urge to get out of town immediately, head home, call in the cavalry, maybe hop the border, but there is no use in putting all of his eggs in one basket. He may need this place in the future, and he pre-paid the rent through 1998. Why not?

Doug leaves everything save the Browning Hi-Power, snubby, and 7mm Mag in the safe, and divides the V-40s nearly in two, keeping five and leaving six, and leaves most of the food and water. There's more at home, and even if he is interdicted on the way, on foot, he can't carry much. He replaces his wilderness gear in the Bronco, along with the urban bug-out bag and personal items, and transfers the computer onto the passenger seat of the truck. All tidied up, Doug surveys the garage, which contains a small shop – drill press, manual hydraulic press, small welder and grinder – and a beat-up kayak and its gear, all left by a previous tenant and included in the rent for an extra $1k. Well, so long, maybe I'll see you again, he thinks, as he rolls up the garage door, backs the F-150 out, and closes up again before heading out, stopping at the Duwamish waterway under the 509 bridge to dump his computer into the water – sorry, fish! – and makes his second to last call on this cell phone while headed south to the I-5 interchange.

Evans answers before the first ring is complete. "You're still here," Evans says, relief in his voice.

"Not for long," says Doug. "Hitting the old dusty trail."

Evans softens his tone. "Come on in; it'll be easier for everyone that way. No need to be out there on your own. We'll take care of you and your grandfather."

Doug remains silent for a few beats as he drives, turning the offer over in his head. "You know, you're probably right, but I have to get to him myself; we'll go from there. I hope you understand. He's an old man, set in his ways. If you can get there before me, do it."

"I understand," says Evans. "I'll get someone up there. With all that's happened, we can't go with our usual guys across the Strait. It might be tomorrow morning before we have a solid plan."

Doug says, "That'll work. Good luck."

"Good luck, Doug." Click.

Doug separates his phone and its battery, leaving both on the passenger seat for the long drive home. Just before Olympia he pitches his hard drive out the window and into a waterway, then takes the next exit to stop at a gas station. Fuel, bathroom break, caffeine and beef jerky, then back on the road, not pausing his drive until two hours later for another top-off in Quilcene. At the gas station he loads the battery back into his phone and dials home, figuring that they're burned anyway.

"This is Josef," his grandfather answers, groggily.

"Grandpa! I'm headed your way." Doug checks his watch – nearly 11 p.m.

"Okay," says Josef, somewhat suspiciously. "Why now?"

Doug employs one of their codes. "How's hunting?"

"Roger." Josef goes with the code. "Talked to the guys in our party a few hours ago, and it looks like our permits were good."

Doug shakes his head. "I don't think so. I had a run in with some JV fish cops. Our party is headed back to camp to lay low for a bit, less a man. Might want to turn on the TV, then take an extra look at the salt licks along the road. I'll be there in a little over an hour."

Josef sighs. "I copy. Have a safe trip up."

Doug discards the battery from his phone in a trash can at the gas station and gets back onto 101 Northbound, pausing a mile north to step out of the truck into the rain and throw the cellular phone into the creek below, hearing a splash in the darkness.

Doug encounters nothing suspicious on his rainy drive home, though he becomes increasingly agitated on the approach. After pulling off 101 onto the poorly-paved service road heading south into the foothills, he finally winds his way through their property gate, his mind alive with paranoia. He pulls his truck right up to the front steps of the house and storms up to the door, where Josef meets him with a hug.

"Calm down," says Josef. "It's okay. What happened?"

Doug shakes his head, kicking off his shoes and entering the living room, where he collapses onto the couch, then stands again, pacing. "No, it's not. We got tailed, one of our guys – Jake – got smoked in the parking garage of his apartment. They tried to ambush my girlfriend. Fucking Green and seven guys. Albanians or whatever. I killed all but two or three of them."

"Whoa, whoa," Josef says, bringing his hands up. "Is she okay?"

"Well, she's not hurt, if that's what you mean, but it was ugly." Doug stops, putting his hand out in a hushing motion. "What's that sound?"

A low, gradual thrumming of motors, whump whump whump, echoes through the hills outside, steadily growing in noise as they approach.

"Helicopters," Josef spits out. "Doug, go."

"Fucking helicopters? The Albanians have helicopters?" Doug follows Josef, nearly running, down the hall to his office, where he slides open the security panel to display their camera network monitors. At the outermost camera, three hundred yards down the road from the edge of their property, a line of ten sets of headlights are oncoming in a dense convoy. Doug stares, his mouth open.

Josef turns to him. "You tangled with the JV team, well, now they're sending in the Varsity squad." He stabs a finger out towards the hallway like a rapier. "Grab your bug-out gear from the closet and go."

Doug runs into the hall and opens the closet, slipping into a camouflage winter-weight coverall and grabbing a dark green backpack, which he slips onto his shoulders. He pulls on side-zip boots and zips in. Josef picks up a rifle from the closet, a long, wood stocked M-14 with a scope and a pistol grip, placing it in Doug's hands.

Doug grabs a matching coverall from the closet, zips it open and holds it out for Josef. "Come on."

Josef shakes his head. "I'm an old man. I'd just slow you down. Those whirlybirds are getting closer," pointing at the ceiling as the whump-whump-whump grows louder and louder, beginning to rattle the windows of the house.

Doug shakes his head, the reality of the situation bearing down on him. "No. Come on. Let's get out of here and hole up until they're gone!"

Josef hugs him tight. "Son, I have to sanitize this place. Get to the stronghold. The weather will cover your tracks. Don't worry. They won't get me. You have no time." Josef pushes Doug bodily to the back door of the house. "GO."

Tears well up in Doug's eyes as he shakes his head. "Dammit. I did this."

Josef calmly shakes his head and embraces his grandson one last time. "No, you didn't. I did. I love you, Doug. Now go. That's an order." Josef swings the door open and pushes Doug out onto the porch. Searchlights from the overhead helicopters switch on and begin playing across the other side of the house, the trees shaking violently in the rotor wash.

Doug wipes tears from his eyes. "I love you, too. I promise...." He takes one last look at his grandfather before turning around and sprinting into the trees and to the path up the hillside, into the Olympic National Park wilderness. Josef watches until he disappears, closes the door and locks it, then turns off the hall light and walks calmly into his office, where he sits at his desk and watches the monitors. He opens a desk drawer and removes a handgun, the presentation-grade FN Model 1922 Charles McIntyre gave him at Thanksgiving, chambers a round, and places the pistol on the desk.

On the bank of screens the convoy of cars arrives at the gate, the lead vehicle, a large four-wheeled armored car, rams the gate off its hinges, and the convoy rumbles into the winding woodland driveway.

"Run, Doug," Josef whispers. He pivots in his chair and keys a combination into a wall panel, swinging it open to reveal a tangle of capped wires, switches and buttons. Josef removes the caps on two wires, then punches them into an electrical panel and throws a switch to power the lines. He powers up a strip of switches and buttons, then toggles another switch on each panel, the red display lights flipping from red to green.

Josef picks up his desk phone and dials a local number. His hands hover over the panel as he waits. A male voice comes on the line. "Hello?"

Josef stares at the monitors. "Martin, it's Josef. I don't have much time. They're here. Blow it all out."

From the other end of the line, a gasp. Sheriff Martin Bryce says softly, "Oh, God. Josef...."

Josef transitions the handset to his other ear, emotion causing his jaw to shudder. "And look out for Doug. That's all." He pauses, swallowing. "Goodbye, Martin. You've been a dear friend to us."

Josef hangs up the phone and throws a toggle switch on one of the wall panels. On the monitor, in black and white infrared, a massive flash in the middle of the road flips the lead armored car in the convoy head over heels, dropping it on top of the Suburban behind it. The blast of the explosion echoes up the hillside, shaking the house for a moment. The drone of three helicopters, two large Blackhawks and a small spotter, thump directly overhead.

Josef points to one of the monitors aimed into the clearing and watches as one of the Blackhawks attempts to land by the range. It smoothly descends until something goes terribly wrong; it jerks, seeming to bounce upwards several inches, then tips to its side and the tail swings violently upward, the craft nosediving into the greenhouse; the earth shudders. Josef smiles, searching the cameras for the other craft, which he can hear reorient themselves overhead – the larger of the remaining craft moving away from the house and pausing at a higher altitude.

Josef whispers, "Run, boy."

The monitor displaying the shop view from the house shows seven men fast rope into the clearing where they split, three lining up against the shop wall, the others stomping up the stairs to the porch. They wave hand signs at each other. Josef smiles and throws another switch; the walls of the shop buckle inwards, the earth shaking as thermite charges in the armory beneath the shop go off and melt the stockpiles of arms into slag and cook off hundreds of thousands of small arms rounds. The stack collapses and the men run away from the shop towards the house, as Josef feels the boots of the stack on the deck shake the house as well, their shouts from fifty feet away cutting through the helicopter noise. He picks up a framed photograph from the desk and places it in his lap – a sharp black and white image of himself as a young man smiling, holding his grinning wife, his son Paul, a toddler, in her arms. He sighs, touching his family with his left hand, and flips a switch on the wall panel with his right.

The interior of the Bell Jet Ranger circling above is chaos, the pilots cringing with the screams and feedback in their headsets from the explosions and dying men below, maintaining distance from the Blackhawk drawing upwards after deploying fast-ropers. The co-pilot has all but given up their primary mission of scanning the house and surrounding area with the Forward Looking Infrared camera mounted to the nose. The FLIR screen is filled with white – intense, screaming white – as the shop erupts in molten flame.

"Holy shit!" shouts the co-pilot, as Claymore mines explode at waist height around the house, eviscerating the Hostage Rescue Team lined up below, the heat of their bodies giving him witness to their deaths and dismemberment before intense flames shoot out of each corner of the house. The roof goes up like a tinderbox and within minutes, as the Jet Ranger circles above, the house collapses inwards on itself, the distinct structural elements succumbing to flames.

FBI Special Agent in Charge Antonio Martinelli leans in from the back seat and slaps the pilot and co-pilot on their shoulders, commanding, "Enough of this shit show. Scan the area, and see if anyone made it out alive. You're wasting valuable seconds." He leans back in his seat and nudges the HRT sniper beside him, who slides open the side door and begins scanning the woods below through the night vision scope of a long, suppressed bolt action rifle.

Doug squints as the explosions reach his ears, slowing to look back. Their valley is crowned with a radiant halo, its substance fed by an ever-rising pillar of thickening smoke. His knuckles go white as he tightens his grip on the stock of his M-14, pushing back grief for another time. There is no doubt that his grandfather has fallen, one way or another.

He drives on, shins burning, using the light from the flames while he can, driving out the darkness in the landscape and his mind. Gaining altitude, the rain transitioning to sleet, he continues checking his tail, wary of the aircraft circling. At least one of the helicopters he saw was a Blackhawk, most likely carrying another team of hunters, ready to disgorge them upon their prey. Doug recognized the FLIR pods slung under its nose; at this range, the trees would shelter him from their gaze, but as the landscape opens further with each step uphill, he must carefully consider his next path. Between the weather and his countermeasures, pursuers might be delayed long enough for him to disappear into the Olympics. Might. Doug removes a small bundle from his coverall pocket, places it in the middle of the trail and pulls a pin, before turning and marching south.

Within minutes, the crunch of dirt, gravel, and pine needles under his feet are joined by a low whup-whup-whup behind him – one of the helicopters, approaching. He turns and crouches, releasing his rifle to hang by its sling while he unrolls the sniper's veil on the top of his pack. A combination of an olive drab emergency blanket and brown mesh with shredded burlap strips, he prays that the veil will disrupt his heat signature enough that the FLIR unit won't be able to pick him up. He figures that, if spotted, two minutes will separate him from a squad of armed men eagerly seeking vengeance in the remaining Blackhawk.

At the top of a rise, Josef's favorite viewpoint of their valley, Doug nestles into position amidst an outcropping of granite. From his roost, a Blackhawk and a smaller helicopter appear to be heading directly towards him at eye level, homing in on the smoldering chunk of trioxane he left to confuse their infra-red unit. He pulls his M-14 in tight to his shoulder and flips open the caps on his scope, then settles in. Thirty seconds to range. He dials the scope to 6x magnification and gets his breathing under control. The white Vs of the pilot and co-pilot's chins and necks in the Blackhawk are visible due to light splash from their instruments. The

Leupold scope shows a fairly bright, crisp picture as the craft's nose comes up and its tail swings around clockwise, gently locking into a holding pattern over a meadow two hundred meters past their infrared target, as the remaining men inside throw down their fast ropes.

Now. Doug places the crosshairs above the pilot's illuminated chin and squeezes the trigger. The M-14's buttplate pushes into his shoulder firmly, but he is back on target in a fraction of a second. A second shot, loud but with no discernible flash. He immediately swings slightly right and fires tap-tap-tap-tap-tap at the cargo area and the mass of men inside; he relaxes slightly and watches the action. Nothing to do now but wait for the reaction from the scout helicopter.

Inside the cockpit, the pilot bucks involuntarily against his safety harness as his co-pilot's head blows apart and showers him with a red mist. He has enough time to register the event before a second slug tears into his chest. He slumps to his right. Men behind him begin shouting as the Blackhawk lolls around, its nose rising as the tail swings sharply to the left, spinning and spinning.

One hundred meters to the south, SAC Martinelli shouts at his pilot and commands him to hold back. "What the fuck is going on?" asks the sniper. "I thought this was just one old man and a college boy." Martinelli grimaces at the man and keys his mic. "This is Martinelli. We have another chopper down. I want local law enforcement mobilized and the Seattle field office alerted. He's heading into the mountains, and the weather is getting worse. Get me on the ground, now."

Doug smiles at the crunching impact of the Blackhawk, but knows that his stunt has merely prolonged the inevitable. As the scout helicopter heads back north, he knows that his only chance of surviving is remaining concealed in the hills until he can get to a safe haven, of which he is considering three. It finally dawns on him that he could have died several times tonight. Many of the men he'd just killed were likely good men, simply pawns of those he was trying to exact vengeance upon. No matter – can't think about that now. He pushes southeast, moving farther up into the hills, eventually hitting his old Boy Scout trailhead. As the snow deepens he dons snowshoes, and withdraws a small plastic vial from his breast pocket. He pops the top, easing out a tiny white pill that he chews and swallows dry, leaving a bitter, alkaline taste in his mouth. If I can put ten miles behind me by dawn, he thinks, there's hope.

Drive on.

SAC Martinelli is livid. Twenty-seven Bureau men were dead; a simple hit that he had hoped to disguise as a raid on a "white supremacist militia" had devolved into something out of an action movie. The old man and college boy, who he had assumed would be easy pickings, had erased most of his command. The Federal Bureau of Investigation of legend was developing a reputation as a farce, a joke, a corrupt bureaucracy of incompetent faggots, and now their latest debacle hung squarely around his neck. At least they had the kid on several homicides. The challenge, which he turned over in his mind, was in pushing the McIntyre/Vanguard element out of this, lest surviving members of their faction bring the house down around him.

With hours until sunup, and a steady downpour turning the site into mud, a search of the property — as in, the areas not currently burning like a chemical plant — was not yet feasible. The remains of the house, garage, and metal framed outbuilding were unapproachable. The local volunteer fire department was busily fighting the spread of the flames, though explosions and the crackle of burning ammunition sounded from time to time.

The Bell Jet Ranger had set Martinelli on the ground and was again airborne, scanning the nearby area with its infrared, but hours had passed, the weather worsened to the south, and he had lost hope of finding the kid tonight. Search and rescue teams had been called up, but they were either afraid of the kid's rifle, or hostile towards the agents. Imagine!

A clusterfuck. The original plan was to kill the suspects and recover incriminating evidence from the site, but the intensity of the chemical fires left him suspecting they would find only molten steel.

Agent Harris – his first name escapes Martinelli – young, handsome, clean-cut, recently ex-military – approaches him reluctantly with a cellular phone in his right hand. "Sir, ah, it's DC. An AD, actually." He holds the phone out at arm's length, visibly cringing.

Martinelli's frown tightens. "Fine." He takes the phone and brings it to his ear. "Yes sir, this is Martinelli." The earpiece explodes in a flurry of profanity. Martinelli throws the phone into the mud and walks to a black Suburban. "Harris, this is yours. I'm headed to Seattle. Report to the AD. That is all."

FBI Special Agent Brian Harris feels his soul begin leaving his body mere minutes into his first briefing of local community leaders and reporters. Soon after what passes for "sunrise" on a foggy, damp January morning, Harris fights to gain control of the narrative in a hastily erected GP tent in the field outside what he has been instructed to refer to as the Shea "compound." His boss, The Bitch Supervisory Agent Martinez, tasked him with handling all extra-agency inquiries from anybody lower in rank than a Senator or Representative. Now that role means convincing a local volunteer Search and Rescue team to begin the search for Douglas Shea in the foothills of the Olympic mountain range, where he escaped last night, without revealing more than three sentences about last night's catastrophic operation.

Once the professional PR team and other west coast federal law enforcement teams arrive, he'll be able to escape to a nearby motel to get some sleep, or, more likely, stare at the ceiling and process the horror of his colleagues being blown or burned to pieces.

Amidst a flurry of shouted questions and pointed fingers, his savior arrives in the form of the local Sheriff, whose name escapes Harris for the moment. The sheriff has removed his tan ten-gallon hat and placed it on the folding table beside the regional and area-specific topographical maps sprawled across it. A robust, early middle-aged man with slightly shaggy light brown hair and a bushy moustache, the Sheriff has raised his hands and faced the audience to calm them. The assembly goes quiet, save for the whir of a Seattle affiliate news camera.

"Now, folks, let's keep in mind that Agent Harris here is a representative, and we're all working in partnership together to find out what is going on and how to proceed. There will be plenty of time for questions after we brief the Search and Rescue team, and coordinate the local and federal teams for the search. Bob," the Sheriff nods to a wiry fellow in a hunting coverall that reminds Harris of his Scout Master back home in Whitesville, Illinois, "let's go over this again. Our job right now is to divvy up teams and assign them to agents, assigned to different sectors for the search. The Forest Service and Park Rangers are en route, and we're coordinating available air assets between multiple agencies, with more on the way from other parts of the state."

Bob, the wiry Scout Master, speaks in a clearly measured, controlled tone, though anger clearly bubbles beneath the surface. "Martin, you know what the FBI did in Idaho and Texas, and what happened to Paul. What you're telling me is that I'm supposed to take a group of Douglas Shea's neighbors into the mountains, in winter, on behalf of these federal agents who murdered his father and grandfather?"

Agent Harris starts; the assembly erupts in shouts and questions; Sheriff Martin Bryce briefly slaps his right hand across his face before raising his hands again. "Okay, okay, okay. Bob, you're out of here. We'll talk later. You get with your guys and decide if you're going to contribute or not, but I won't handle any more disruption." He points to the tent flap; Bob the Scout Master storms out with two team members, followed by half of the reporters, who are showering him with questions. As the furor dies down, Sheriff Bryce turns to Agent Harris and shrugs. He addresses the remaining crowd.

"Now, with that out of the way. One question at a time. You." Sheriff Bryce points to a blonde, late twenties reporterette from a Seattle news station, shrouded in a large blue ski jacket. A videographer rotates to the sheriff's side to film her.

The reporterette smiles smugly. "Agent Harris, Janet Howle, KRTY 8 News. Do you have any comments regarding the documents faxed to several news agencies, and posted on the internet, last night, that suggest a cabal of FBI and DEA agents murdered Clallam County Sheriff Paul Shea and another local in 1982? One of those agents was Eric Levin, the federal judge recently murdered in Seattle. And..."

Agent Harris' face goes white. Sheriff Bryce smiles and interrupts the reporter. "Miss Howle, perhaps I can assist with that question. My office also received those documents last night. While they appear to be legitimate, I'd rather leave that to investigators. My agency will cooperate to the fullest extent; Sheriff Paul Shea was both my mentor and friend. Bob Lundegaard and I," and he gestures out the tent flap to indicate the departed Search and Rescue leader, "roamed these hills with Doug for a decade in Boy Scouts. And now we have to go get him, without any further bloodshed. So. Agent Harris, any comment from the FBI?" The Sheriff turns, smiling conspiratorially.

Harris does not speak for several beats, processing the exchange, before returning to his script. "Uh, nearly a hundred FBI, Drug Enforcement Administration and Bureau of Alcohol, Tobacco and Firearms agents are en route from across the western United States to assist with the investigation and manhunt, and we will bring this danger to the community to justice. We will be sharing more information as events unfold, I assure you."

Another female reporter cuts in, this one Asian, with a sly expression on her face, speaking in an odd sing-song tone. "Agent Harris, Kathy Chen, KDTV News, Channel 3. We understand that the Seattle Office Special Agent In Charge Anthony Martinelli is implicated in the murder of Sheriff Paul Shea. He headed this operation, is that not the case? Can we speak with him?" The group erupts again.

Agent Harris throws up his hands. "That's all for now, folks, thank you; Sheriff Bryce, can you come with me, please?" He gestures behind him to another tent flap, directing the Sheriff out. Sheriff Bryce scoops up his hat and follows Harris through the mud to another GP tent in the FBI staging area. Harris' supervisor greets them with a scowl; Agent Martinez, a raven-haired Latina still wearing a blue FBI blazer over her tactical suit from last night's operation.

Agent Martinez shakes her head, a steaming travel cup of coffee in her hand as she stands in the midst of a slowly assembling command center, agents and lackeys having arrived from Seattle with computers and communications equipment. "Harris, what the hell?" she asks, upon seeing the Sheriff.

"Uh, we have a problem, ma'am," says Harris. "The press isn't even asking about the search; they're talking about Agent Martinelli and some supposed murder here ten years ago! The Search and Rescue team won't cooperate. I pulled the plug. Sheriff Bryce here can explain. I'm heading back." He turns and walks out of the GP tent in a huff; Martinez turns to Bryce, fire behind her eyes.

"Sheriff, are you refusing to cooperate with an FBI investigation? I can make all sorts of trouble for you if that's the case," she sneers.

Bryce looks down at her casually, unruffled. "I'm sure you could, but that's not what's happening. My S and R guys are volunteers; I can't force them up into those hills after a marksman with a rifle who plugged a bunch of your guys. That's for the law enforcement professionals," he adds, sliding his hat back on.

Martinez trembles, her black eyes flaring, but she contains herself. She spits out, "Speak more respectfully of my team, Sheriff; twenty-seven cops were murdered by your pal last night, and I was there. I'll fucking...." She contains herself as SAC Martinelli steps into the tent and to her side. Compared to the petite, career-girl-looking Latina, Special Agent in Charge Martinelli presents a more authoritative figure to Sheriff Bryce, two inches or so taller than his own six feet, powerful and imposing, with an edge of violence to his demeanor, despite his muddy dress shoes and pantcuffs. Martinelli removes his uniform standard Ray Ban sunglasses and tucks them into his coat chest pocket.

"So we meet again," drawls Sheriff Bryce, extending his hand to Martinelli. "Clallam County Sheriff Martin Bryce."

Martinelli looks at the Sheriff's hand, slowly accepting it. "Have we met before, Sheriff?" he asks, stepping closer so that Bryce must look upwards to maintain eye contact.

"Indeed, in 1982. You went on a job with my boss; you came back, he didn't. I was a deputy at the time. Do you remember now?"

SAC Martinelli stares at him without blinking. "Nope. Can't recall ever meeting you."

The sneering Latina agent pipes up from the side. "Boss, the Sheriff is being uncooperative. We need to sideline him, let professionals take over from the yokels."

Martinelli looks down at Bryce, a smug half-grin spreading across his face. "Do we, now?"

Bryce steps back and takes the coffee from Martinez' hand. "Thanks, hon. Can the men talk? Bye, now."

Martinez begins puffing up her chest, and her mouth opens, but SAC Martinelli waves her away. She dutifully shrinks, leaving the GP tent. The other agents take their cue and skulk out. Martinelli shakes his head, tsk tsking. "Male chauvinism and racism. Can't have that in today's law enforcement agencies. Who do you report to? I'm inclined to file a report."

Bryce shoves his thumbs into his duty belt, shifting his jacket around the butt of his holstered handgun, a hard matte-chromed slide Glock 21 .45 ACP, flashing it for the SAC. "Elected by the people of Clallam County. And I carry a lot more water here than you do. Have you read this report that your agents are talking about? I'm sure you have, although it's been a while. You and your crew killed my boss and one of my citizens, all to cover up connections for a border-hopping drug gang. It's all over the wires."

Martinelli shrugs casually. "Internet bullshit. Conspiracy theory. Much easier for us to leak the fact that Josef Shea was involved in illegal business dealings; his son was abusing his law enforcement authority to cover it up, and poor little Doug got involved, too. We have two witnesses who will testify to Douglas and Josef Shea doing a drug hit in Victoria a few months ago. There would be three, but your boy murdered him in Seattle last night. And who leaked the documents? We have no idea, but based on your demeanor, I suspect you already knew about them."

Bryce rocks on his heels, smiling. "Whoever did it, it's not much of a crime, if any. In the meantime, your name is all over murder, drug trafficking, extortion, overseas bank accounts. And you guys suppressed the forensics report regarding Paul's murder, falsified evidence implicating a dead man. Want to know something else, Martinelli?"

Martinelli glances about the empty, damp tent. He lowers his face into Bryce's and pokes him in the chest. "Try me."

Bryce doesn't move, though a tremor runs through his body. "You aren't gonna catch Doug Shea. He's up in his old stomping grounds; your shiny toys, your helicopters and FLIR, can't handle the weather, and there are all kinds of Scout caches and shelters that he can take advantage of. Oh, I'll cooperate, mark 'em on the map, but I don't see you folks finding him. You'll have to get on the ground. And besides." He pauses, watching Martinelli.

Martinelli doesn't bat an eye. "And besides?"

Bryce shrugs. "And besides, Josef Shea had friends in high places. Those friends will be drawing knives on you and your bosses right about now, especially given this new information. I'm sure you'll be taken off the case, someone else will come in to lead it, and you'll be out there, wondering when Doug Shea will come by for a visit."

Martinelli feigns boredom. "Thank you, Sheriff; show Agent Martinez where these caches and shelters are. If you're fucking with us, I'll have you prosecuted. Now get out of here."

Sheriff Bryce tips his ten-gallon hat. "Until we meet again, Martinelli."

Just before dawn, a hint of light from the east, above dense, low clouds. With a diminishing supply of chemical help, Doug pushes through sheer exhaustion and continues his one-two step through deepening, softening snow over a fold in the mountain, a blizzard blasting him in the face. He reorients to the southeast, adjusting the sling of his M-14 and pulling ski goggles down over his eyes. Two hundred yards or so – there – along the knife-edge ridgeline and the rock outcropping, and a small cave, shelter, and food. Fifty yards from his destination he drops to his knees and crawls, the wind too strong to stand against, or him too depleted. With some effort, Doug uses his snowshoes to scrape snow back from the mouth of the cave, then crawls into the space, the size of a small master bedroom but with a ceiling low enough to require a crouch save for the middle. He sheds his pack and rifle before pushing more snow to the edge of the cave's mouth, blocking the wind. This complete, he collapses onto his back, breathing for several seconds, before forcing himself onto his hands and knees and crawling to the cache.

He finds the expected small stock of firewood next to a box of tinder, hand-painted with the Boy Scout fleur-de-lis, maintained by his troop for several decades. Doug prepares the fire pit, adjusting some shifted rocks, stacking the tinder and starter branches in a cone, braced on three sides by a triangle of medium sized branches. First drawing his sniper veil from his pack, he spreads this over the entrance to the cave. He then opens one of two small waterproof canisters from the tinderbox, removing a cottonball covered in petroleum jelly, which he pulls apart into a spidery expanse, rubbing the jelly all over the cotton, placing this at the base of the fire pit tinder cone. From the other canister he draws a windproof match, which he scrapes across the flint rod at the bottom of the canister. The match catches, flaring and sparking brightly, caustic smoke puffing out in the confines of the small cave. Doug slowly places the flaming match beneath the fuel-soaked cotton ball, which flares up in blue and yellow flame. Flicking the match into the rest of the dry tinder, adjusting the twigs and small shaved pieces of cedar, the fire is burning steadily in minutes, the smoke rising into cracks in the rock and dissipating. Doug sets his watch for 2 p.m., spreads his sleeping bag out several feet from the fire, then grabs the stainless cooking cup from his canteen and fills it with snow from the mouth of the cave, setting it next to the fire to melt, before collapsing into a restless, dreamless sleep.

That afternoon, Sheriff Bryce walks into the snow-blown Olympic National Park Ranger Headquarters, Heart O' The Hills, stomping out his boots before introducing himself to rangers and FBI agents consulting topographical and relief maps. A sheepish Agent Harris sidles up to him, offering a cup of steaming hot coffee.

Bryce accepts the coffee with a nod. "Agent Harris. How does it look?"

Harris shrugs. "The snow is easing up, just in time for nightfall, but the search area is massive, and winds are still really bad up on the mountain." He directs Sheriff Bryce to the large relief map table in the middle of the room, strung with yellow thread in a circle emanating from the Shea homestead. "Current search zone. Even conservatively, they figure he could have cleared fifteen miles last night, another twenty during the day, given the storm and visibility, though the rangers figure that's less likely."

Bryce shakes his head. "I don't see it. Fifteen, twenty miles is more like it. And knowing our boy, he's going deep. I'd focus on the northwest slope, talk to family friends in that area, but who knows. Any air get up at all?"

Harris shakes his head. "Not yet; we got five Blackhawks and three Jet Rangers, all with FLIR, and some National Guard attached Chinooks to help move us up there, shooting for setting up several base camps within the hour. The FLIR choppers will be radiating around the base camps; we're trying to cut some areas off at the pass, get men along these areas," pointing to ridges and passes around the Olympic mountain massif, "but we can't focus too exclusively on one area or another. We have SAR teams from other communities who are chipping in," giving Bryce a slightly dirty look, eliciting a bemused expression, "but that's still a massive, massive search area. We're hoping and praying for a clear day tomorrow, sunshine, and to be able to track his footprints from the air, but with the wind...."

Bryce sips his coffee with a knowing expression on his face. "What kind of gun teams you got up there?"

Harris ticks off his fingers. "Four SRT teams, howling for blood. Nearly two hundred FBI agents, though not many with rifles, mostly the MP5 10mm, which isn't good beyond 100 meters, but within it?" He whistles. "I'm not gonna lie, most of us are city hunters, but up in the snow, not so much, unless he walks right by and they can pot him."

Bryce winces slightly. "Howling for blood. I hope you can keep a leash on these guys. We're doing everything we can to keep the locals out of your hair, but this isn't a compound in the desert, Harris."

Harris responds matter-of-factly. "Believe me, I know. We have a senator and a couple of state reps down the hill in Port Angeles, demanding access to the operations room. Martinelli got spooked by the Internet thing, headed back to Seattle. The DEA has some hotshot teams on loan out here, too, and your State Patrol has three, four dozen SWAT guys assigned to us. Most are serving as rapid response teams or manning checkpoints around here," indicating Highway 101 to the north and east, as well as the scattered roads and trails leading into the park.

"Do you think you can get him without a bloodbath?" asks Bryce.

Harris shrugs. "You know about some of our other recent manhunts. Most of the time, we're dependent upon our target slipping up, getting seen by locals, running out of supplies. Speaking of, thanks for the supply cache tips; they'll be our focus with the FLIR choppers."

Bryce nods. "My deputies are making the rounds, talking to neighbors and classmates, teachers and the like; I don't think we're going to get a lot of help there, but we'll possibly turn up some new names to look into."

Harris moves to a coffee dispenser, gesturing for Bryce to follow. "If he has a support network, it's all about combing through his communications and their communications. Phone records, now you have email, which we're working on getting from the U, people talking. It's going to take a few days just to wrap our arms around that. Don't hold your breath, Sheriff."

"Let me ask you something, Agent Harris." Bryce hooks a thumb in his belt, resting his left elbow on it, his chin in his upturned hand, stroking his moustache. "Why did this operation go down like it did? If the Sheas are such bad guys, why not pick them up quietly, or come by my office, go up there with me?"

Harris glances around the room, then directs Bryce to an unoccupied corner of the room, before lowering his head and voice. "This was originally written up as an information-gathering raid on a solitary Josef Shea; didn't expect any trouble, a simple search for evidence."

"With a few dozen agents?" asks Bryce. "Helicopters? The same thing went down in Waco; you could have picked up your man on a drive into town, instead, nearly a hundred people died."

Harris winces. "Those days are over for us, unfortunately. 'In the interests of officer safety,' you know the drill."

Bryce shakes his head. "If you treat people like enemy soldiers, don't be surprised if they see you the same way. I would have told you to expect exactly this type of response. Shit, Joe Shea was ex-CIA, OSS, a volunteer in Spain. He had a bunch of weapons licenses that I can't even understand. And he's still connected."

Harris nods. "We know that they were both employed by a company in Seattle that is a suspected CIA front. The current administration is attempting to clean up that sort of thing, but it's difficult for obvious reasons. One of their employees was shot to pieces yesterday afternoon. We're dealing with an army of lawyers right now to get a search warrant, records; the company's, State Department. We didn't find anything at Shea the younger's apartment, save for a pot pipe his roommate had in a drawer."

A gaggle of armed Rangers enters the room, calling out for Harris; he turns to Bryce, extending his hand. They shake. "Thanks, Sheriff; looks like our briefing is about to begin. Let's keep in touch, and don't skimp on any details your deputies turn up. Thank you." He walks to the Rangers, greeting them; Sheriff Bryce sips his coffee, steps over to the Olympic National Park relief map, and stares at the terminus of a long, unmarked ridgeline at the northeastern edge of the park, seven miles due south of the town of Sequim.

Doug is awakened from oblivion by the incessant beep-beep of his digital watch, though wakefulness comes to him slowly, the fog in his head telling him to continue sleeping. He pats about his chest pockets before finding a small clip-on keychain flashlight with a red lens attachment, then scans around his confines, the memory of his last waking hours catching up. The Big Cave, as his Scout crew knew it, on the tip of the most spectacular navigable ridgeline this side of the Mountain. He reaches for the canteen cup in the embers of last night's fire, tapping it carefully; it's slightly warm. He sips the water, gratefully, then peeks through the corner of his sniper veil, out into the world. The snowfall has stopped, and dry powder has piled up several inches at the edge of the cave's mouth, blown by a moderate, steady breeze up the slope. It's still light, though today that means grey, dense clouds, and visibility of no more than three hundred yards, a manageable rifle shot for any semi-competent marksman. Doug searches the sky through the drawn corner of his sniper veil, seeing no gaps in the clouds, but no indications of storm, or likely precipitation. He checks his watch again, downing the rest of his lukewarm water, and considers the night ahead, drawing a topographical map from his coverall's breast pocket and spreading it out on his sleeping bag. He figures he'll move at 4 p.m., heading partially up the Mt. Townsend north ridge to his east, then branching off into the next valley, which will be an easy downhill walk through dense trees. At this point, his biggest danger is vehicle intercept, meaning trucks on the road, or helicopters with thermal imaging, though his sniper veil and a shelter rolled up and strapped to his pack hold a surprise.

Doug stretches his legs out before standing, squatting up and down, getting his blood flowing, before sitting Indian style and preparing his evening victuals. Popping open a side panel of his pack, Doug removes a screw-top thermos and plastic food storage box, containing a variety of Ziploc bags, several hexamine fuel tabs and a lighter. He grabs his canteen and partially fills his canteen cup with water, folds down the leg stands and sticks a hex tab on the platform of one leg, touching it with the flame of the lighter. He draws back his hand as the hex tab flares up, sending up a bit of noxious smoke. To escape the worst of the smoke, Doug lies down on his stomach, unscrews the thermos, and pours the contents of two Ziplocs into it – instant rice, dehydrated meat and vegetables, a dash of spices and a chicken bouillon cube. The canteen cup of water bubbles lightly, sufficient for his needs; he pours most of the water into the thermos, stirs it briefly with a titanium spork and screws the lid on tight, shaking it a bit before setting it on its side. Doug flicks the hex tab into his fire pit, squashing it out with a rock and grinding it into the dirt, before brushing an inch of dirt atop it and placing the rock back into position. He folds the canteen cup's leg stands back into place, then pours the contents of another Food Saver-sealed packet from a Ziploc into his cup – Tang mixed with four hundred milligrams of ibuprofen powder and a crushed amphetamine tablet. Mmm, alkaline and delicious.

Doug uses his time to perform an inventory check, locking the switch of a two cell flashlight to "on" and shoving it into a ceiling crack to aim it at the floor of the cave. He's carrying entirely too much stuff, in too many layers; his hips and waistband area feel raw. He opens his pack, spreading out the equipment, and sheds his coverall to get access to his inner layers, which he wore on the drive up from Seattle. He strips naked and rolls his street clothes into a bundle, which he shoves deep into his pack; they reek of sweat, adrenaline and amphetamine. Starting afresh, he dons wool long underwear, then fresh thin wool undersocks, adding medium weight boot socks over them. Next, the coverall, which is heavy enough for a man on the move, and a knit cap. He sets aside a pair of leather mittens with trigger fingers, with their thin wool liners, as well as a pair of leather shooting gloves.

His backpack harness serves double duty as webbing for his rifle and front line gear, and includes a holstered Glock 17 9mm pistol, a pouch for miscellaneous gear, a compass in its pouch, his canteen, a fixed blade knife, and two M-14 magazine two-cell pouches. The backpack itself contains more food, cash, a water bladder, rifle and pistol ammunition, a compact liquid fuel stove, B&E tools, wire cutters, a small folding saw, a night vision scope for his rifle in an armored tube, and spare wool layers for fixed positions. Strapped to the pack he has a small hatchet, a camouflaged thermal tarp, a first aid / personal care pouch, and a place for his sleeping bag in its stuff sack. Finally, he has his wallet, another packet of IDs, his Browning pistol with two magazines, a folding knife, his .38, and six of the V-40 mini grenades all of which he had worn under his coverall for the first few miles of his escape. His chafed body reminds him of the escape, the moment he no longer heard the choppers or saw the glow of the fires, when he transferred his gun belt and pistols into his backpack and coverall.

The fires. Cathy. Jake. Grandpa. Doug lowers his head, puts his dirty hands over his face, and weeps.

Sheriff Bryce dines with his family that evening after showering and shaving, announcing at the table that he'll be heading back to the office for an overnighter. His thirteen-year-old son, who idolizes Doug Shea from his years as a leader in Scouting, assails him with a flurry of questions about the night before, the constant beat of helicopters all day, the phone ringing off the hook, federal law enforcement everywhere. His younger daughter looks on dolefully while poking at her chicken and vegetables, focusing on the interaction between him and his wife, who has put her best foot forward but is obviously beside herself. Paul Shea had been a stand-out lineman as a senior at Port Angeles High School when Martin and Judy were in middle school; he had always known that she fancied Paul, although it remained unspoken. The slow destruction of the Shea family was wearing on her, no matter the official story and rumors; her glances told him everything he needed to know.

He manages to extricate himself, promising to discuss the situation with the family in detail as he learns more. "We're safe; I'm safe; don't worry; I'll check in before bedtime, honey."

Sheriff Bryce catches several catnaps on his office couch that night, between check-in calls with the FBI, other Sheriffs of counties in the search area, and escalated calls from community members passed on by the gals at the switchboard. He's nearly surprised by the overwhelmingly negative response to the federal forces – nearly. His own investigators and select deputies, as well as members of neighboring law enforcement organizations, are busy visiting an ever-expanding network of teachers, classmates, youth sports team members and Boy Scouts. He perused the incoming reports, skimming for interesting details, and learned that the FBI forensics team had discovered hundreds of recently fired .32 caliber handgun bullets of various configurations in the Shea's private range backstop, the only hard evidence so far linking the Sheas to actual crimes, and were broadcasting this detail aggressively via the media.

The federal, state and local law enforcement teams scouring the Olympic National Park, along with their limited air assets, had so far turned up nothing, not even Doug Shea's footprints. Despite his insistence upon a western egress point, and the misdirection of provided Boy Scouts troop caches, the FBI teams were focusing on the eastern edge of the Park and peripheral roadways, although the weather in the foothills necessitated that. Coastal winds were dying down, so they expected better penetration of the mountains by helicopter that night.

And one more time, Sheriff Bryce prays for Doug Shea and his soul.

E & E

TAP TAP TAP TAP TAP TAP TAP TAP TAP

Joshua Fekete looks up from the stainless steel tray in his lap where he picks seeds from a large marijuana cola. He squints and glances around the small sunroom of his beach shack, out onto the sunlight-fading view of the northeast side of Hood Canal, three miles south of Quilcene, scanning all of the many windows left to right. He places the tray onto the battered olive drab footlocker that serves as his coffee table and takes two steps to the stereo to pause Ween's discordant cacophony.

TAP TAP TAP TAP TAP

There – a finger raps on the deck door's bottom left window pane. Josh walks slowly over to the door, reluctantly, then peeks over the side of the window.

"What the fuck?" He unlatches the deadbolt and swings the door open. "Doug!" Though he doesn't have neighbors for hundreds of feet, out of instinct Josh lowers his voice to a whisper. "What are you doing lying on the ground?" He runs his hand through his tousled, nearly-shoulder-length brown hair. Doug looks up at him from his back in a mud-smeared camouflage coverall and boots, camouflage paint on his face and neck, one hand tucked behind his back.

"Hey, dude. Can I come in?" Doug grins awkwardly, blowing a bit of dried vegetation from his lower lip.

"Come around to the mudroom on the south side. That way, by the dock. What the hell are you doing?" Josh crinkles his face in utter bewilderment.

"Long story," Doug says, still smiling. "Close the door and go inside, and draw the side window blinds. I'll be over there in a few minutes." He shuffles on his back toward the front of the small house as Josh shuts the door and throws the bolt closed. Josh drops his blinds on the north side, twisting them closed, then scans along the shoreline and trees of his family property. He looks out over the Canal, where he sees no boat traffic, only a seal backstroking between the oyster posts; he draws the southern blinds closed and walks back to the mudroom door, which he unlocks and opens slightly. He looks around and grabs an old, heavy short-barreled revolver from the top of his refrigerator and slips it into his waistband, flipping his Danzig tour t-shirt over the butt. He hears the mudroom door swing open gently and peeks around the corner to watch his old friend Doug Shea enter on his stomach, waddling quickly, before closing the door and standing to latch it.

Josh shakes his head. "Dude, not a good look. You're lucky Em and the baby aren't here; she'd be freaking out." Doug zips out of his boots and steps to a utility sink surrounded by black and orange foul weather fishing raingear hung on hooks; he removes a chrome plated automatic from his pocket, looking benignly at Josh, and sets it on the counter next to the sink. He zips out of his coveralls, which he holds in a wad in two hands at waist level, wearing only socks, long underwear and a knit cap.

Josh points to the sink. "You can put 'em in there. We'll want to hose everything off first. We'll go through the pockets first, I'm guessing?"

Doug nods. "I left all of the rest of my gear in the work shack over here. I knocked here first but you didn't hear me."

Josh points his thumb into the house. "Why don't you shower; I'll grab you some clothes. Em and the baby are at her mom's tonight. I'll load 'em. You look tore up."

Doug grins, looking exhausted. "Thanks, man. I'll explain."

Josh shakes his head. "Don't say shit until you're clean and have a meal in your belly."

Doug nods. "Sounds good. Thanks." He picks up his pistol by the slide and hands it, butt-first, to Josh, who takes it and slips it into his left jeans pocket. He leads Doug to a bathroom. Fifteen minutes later, Doug emerges from the steamy bathroom refreshed, shaven, hair combed, wearing a Faith No More zip-up hoodie and black jeans to match Josh's. He walks into the kitchen and stares with animal hunger as Josh stirs a pot full of noodles.

"Hey, want some ramen?" Josh asks.

"Yeah, I've been living off bouillon cubes and water for two days. I don't recommend it." Doug shakes his head, grabbing an apple from a hanging fruit basket. "Nice."

"Yeah, Em has made this place fit for humans. So, Doug," Josh asks, as he turns and chops vegetables and cold baked chicken, "what brings you to my door at twilight on a Wednesday night, looking like you belly-crawled through a drainage ditch?" He loads two bowls with noodles, pours in the broth, then adds the chopped goods from the cutting board, sliding chopsticks into each bowl and picking them up with one hand each. "Let's sit on the couch. It's been a long day and you interrupted me."

Doug takes one of the bowls and opens the fridge, scanning for beverages. Josh points to a cluster of beer bottles, Henry's; Doug grabs two by the neck with his left hand and closes the door, following Josh out to the sunroom, where he sees all of the blinds closed. They set their bowls down on the footlocker and pop the caps from their beers as they sit on the futon sofa, clinking the beers together.

"Cheers." Josh takes a swig of beer, swallowing contentedly, and tucks into his ramen. Doug follows suit, setting down the beer and eating the perfectly cooked ramen with great enthusiasm, finishing it off in two minutes.

Josh watches with detached interest as Doug wipes broth from his chin before guzzling his beer in three long pulls. Josh smiles, eating slowly, enjoying the show. Doug sets down his empty beer bottle, gasps, exhales loudly, and leans back into the futon, breathing hard.

Josh pokes Doug in the leg with an extended finger. "Dude, you don't look so good. What's going on?"

Doug shakes his head. "Where to begin?" He emits a near-laugh, which turns to a sigh, his face losing color as he stares off into the distance.

Josh grimaces and leans to his left, pulls Doug's Browning Hi Power from his waistband and sets it on the footlocker in front of Doug. "Will this make you feel any better?"

Doug nods and picks up the pistol, looking it over, before removing the magazine, thumbing off the safety, and racking the slide to remove the round from the chamber, all of which he sets on the footlocker. "It's nice to not feel like I need it. Thanks. So, have you seen anything out on 101 or on TV, or heard anything on the radio?"

Josh smirks. "I've been out on the Canal, working the beds with my brother and some of our guys. And you know I don't listen to commercial radio. Please." He sips his beer, looking sidewise at Doug, then walks over to the stereo, turning it back on, but dialing down the volume. The cacophony returns.

Doug shakes his head. "Still reppin' early Ween. I like the newer stuff better."

Josh nods. "Oh, I like the new stuff fine, but you know me." He sits back down on the couch and selects a marble-sized marijuana nug from his stainless tray, holding it in front of Doug. "Check it out; orange hairs and heavy crystals. Smell it."

Doug obliges. "Nice."

Josh smiles. "You can have a smoke if you want. This is for a big order of pre-rolls; tech guys in Seattle who buy oysters from us for parties pay a premium for completed product. I only smoke at harvest time now, to test it. Can't be high when I'm out on the water all day and all night. Besides, I have a family now. Remember the parties we used to have here?"

Doug looks around the small cabin, noting its cleanliness and the obvious female touches. "It looks great. I bet nobody over the age of two has puked here for a couple of years."

Josh laughs. "Besides Em, when she was pregnant." He stands up, walks to the window, and peeks through the blinds out at Hood Canal, now swathed in darkness, little points of light from homes, buoys, and the occasional car on the other shore. "I love it. Being a dad is awesome. Which reminds me. As a responsible dad, I have to ask you if the helicopters swirling around here for the past few days have anything to do with you belly-crawling into my house." He pulls his finger back, snapping the blinds closed, and turns. "Not that I care; I just want to know where we stand. You get popped moving weed?"

Doug exhales, a long, tired exhale, and nods his head gently in silence, pondering his response. Josh watches, silently. A minute passes before Doug speaks. "Remember what my granddad does for a living?"

Josh says, "How could I forget? Your basement blew my mind."

Doug nods. "I've been working with him and his guys for a bit. Everything was going well, until it wasn't. Now a friend of mine is dead, I had to shoot a bunch of terrorists, and feds are swarming all over Seattle and the Peninsula looking for me. They raided our place and my granddad blew the whole fucking place sky high." He pauses, collecting himself. "That was almost five nights ago. I went up into the mountains, moved through some of our old Scouting hides, using the weather to cover my tracks. I headed east as soon as I could, but kept running into search teams and helicopters with infrared, so had to lay low. The first night I covered like twelve miles, the second about ten, but since then I've been zigzagging, hiding under my IR shelter, crawling up and down hills."

Josh blinks, processing his friend's comments, then returns to the couch and continues breaking down the marijuana cola on the tray. "I'll play along. Why not let 'em arrest you, have the government guys explain who you are?"

Doug shakes his head. "No, we're super extra-curricular, off books. We have friends, but are formally deniable. A group we worked with left us out to dry; no, they flipped on us. They were coming in hot, to kill." He walks to the kitchen and grabs a glass from a cabinet, filling it with water from the tap and drinking. "Your spring water is even better than ours." He returns to the couch. "It took me two days to cross the clearings around 101, traveling inches at a time; went under the road through a three foot culvert. I'm amazed that I didn't get caught, or shot. I spent all day this side of 101 on my belly; moved less than two miles. Thank God for all of the drainage ditches along the highway and side roads; nobody seems to look in them. So, you could say I had a couple of rough days. Oh, yeah, my girlfriend broke up with me because she had to stab a guy. Um, I think that's it."

Josh stares, expressionless.

Doug points to a TV in the corner of the room. "Turn it on, I'm sure you'll see a story about me within a few minutes."

Josh shakes his head. "It'd just be lies. Anything I know about in real life that I've ever seen on TV, or read about in a newspaper, is bullshit. Besides, we don't get a signal here; we just use it for DVDs and tapes. I believe you."

Doug stands up and stretches. "I'd be asleep if it weren't for those little white pills. I'm beat to shit. Well, here's the deal; I don't want to make you an accessory, so I'll head out tonight. It'd probably be a good idea to inform on me, if you can wait a few hours, and say you just threw me out. You got a family to worry about."

Josh shakes his head again. "Yeah, that's not gonna happen. Think about it. Did you come here because we talked all the time, on the phone, like I'd be in your phone records? We've probably never talked on the phone. Who would say we were pals? You swing by here once or twice a year when you're driving by, just popping in, because I keep the welcome mat out. I graduated from high school two years before you, and we haven't been in Scouting together since I was sixteen. That was six, almost seven years ago. We're not exactly burning up the radar screen, Doug."

Doug thinks this over. "Makes sense. But like I said, I'm sure someone will knock on your door, and I don't want to cause trouble for you guys."

The phone mounted to the wall next to the kitchen rings; both men freeze. Doug loads his pistol in haste and steps towards the mudroom. Josh walks to the phone, calmly, and answers. "Hello? Hey, babe." All the tension runs out of the room. Josh listens in silence. "Sounds good. Just had dinner, gonna hit the hay for an early morning tour of the beds. Can I talk to the dude?" Josh pauses, then dives headlong into baby talk. The domestic normalcy is a dagger thrust into Doug's heart. He steadies himself in the doorway with his left hand, looks down at the pistol in his right, and returns it to his waistband. Grief hammers him; he turns to the mudroom sink and splashes cold water on his face, drying up as his friend concludes his conversation. They return to the couch, Josh picking up a nug from the tray and holding it out to Doug. "You're up."

Doug waves it off. "I'm a wreck. That sounds like a really bad idea. No offense."

Josh shrugs. "None taken. Like I said, I don't smoke recreationally anymore. We're touring the beds tonight." He goes back to picking the cured marijuana flower from the stem.

"What you mean 'we,' Kemosabe?" asks Doug. "I'm gonna bail. I don't want to make trouble for you."

Josh shakes his head, talking while he works. "This is how you're gonna bail. Where do you need to go? I have an excuse to travel anywhere on the western hook of Hood Canal, up into the Sound, all the way down to Vashon, and parts between. You got anywhere to go? I'm not letting you leave on your own two feet, my man." He extends his hand. Doug takes it, and they shake on it.

Doug sighs with relief. "Thank you. That means a lot to me. I have some people to call. They'll tell me where I can go. If I'm on my own," he pauses, "well, I didn't really plan for that. I have some money, alternative ID, and will go from there. That's in south Seattle."

Josh picks the last bits of flower from the main stem and rolls the smaller nugs between his thumb and fingertips, separating out small woody stems from the remaining flower, and speaks without breaking eye contact from his task. "I know you're not making any calls from this house, but there's a marina a little ways south, just past that point, with a 24 hour mini mart. They sell this local honey that Em likes." He carries the tray to the kitchen, placing it on the counter, and removes a coffee grinder from a cabinet, placing it beside the tray. "You can use the payphone there, then we'll plan next steps. Hey, one thing."

"Anything," Doug says.

"Can I get one of your grandpa's machine guns?" Josh takes the stubby revolver from his waistband and holds it up casually. "I like this, but it lacks pizazz."

Josh and Doug retrieve Doug's pack and M-14 from the oyster shack an hour after sunset, moving them to the floating dock and the small, partially enclosed pilot house of a twenty-eight foot long, ten-foot beam, aluminum-hulled oyster boat. Doug whistles as they step onboard. "Is this yours?" he asks. EMILY - QUILCENE, WA graces the rear of the hull, just forward of dual 250 hp outboards.

Josh shrugs. "Sort of. It's our company's boat; that means me and my brother now. My parents are pretty much retired, though they are still getting about half the cream. Pretty sweet, huh?"

Doug surveys the four-seat cabin. "I thought I was gonna be bouncing around in an inflatable."

Josh shakes his head. "No, the RIB out there is just for quick hops. We big-time now. Let's hit the hay. We're rolling out early."

Doug falls asleep surprisingly quickly, waking at 4 a.m. to Josh's greeting – "Rise and shine, per'fesser!" Josh provides Doug with his laundered clothing and boots in a kitchen trash bag, as well as foul weather boating gear to go over his borrowed clothing – bright orange bib pants, insulated wader boots, and a heavy hooded rain jacket. Doug covers his head with his brown wool knit cap, hand-rinsed that night and dried by the wood stove. Josh prepares instant oatmeal and three fried eggs each, which they eat quickly at the kitchen table out of small melamine plates and bowls emblazoned with childrens' television characters, sipping coffee from to-go thermoses. Josh rinses the dishes quickly in the sink before they leave the house, and bolts the door; Doug feels the tingling up his spine as they walk through a frosty mist and down the now-steep free-floating dock ramp to their transportation, the tide now nearing its lowest point for the day. Josh directs Doug to the pilothouse and instructs him to sit while he starts up his boat's outboards, warming them up before settling into an idle, the diesel fumes sharp in the still, frigid air. Josh hops onto the dock to untie the bow and stern lines from their cleats, then bounds back into the boat with a push that drives the aluminum-hulled craft clear of the dock. He leans against his seat in the pilothouse and scans starboard, applies a touch of throttle, and aims the bow to the southeast, between buoy lights in the darkness. He clears the buoys and taps the throttle to half power, sending the outboards into a roar and lifting the nose up and out of the light rollers at twenty knots.

Doug grabs a helpful handle and stands next to Josh, shouting, "She's fast!"

Josh shakes his head, an expression of casual competence on his face. "Once we get out of the bay I'll open her up. She can do fifty knots, easy, without any cargo. After we fuel up, and you make your call, we'll be wherever you need to go on the Sound within an hour and a half."

Doug watches his friend at work, remembering the day they met. Doug was a first year Boy Scout, after years in Cubs. Josh Fekete was two grades ahead of him, and proved himself a quiet, competent leader who did well with both younger boys and adults. Josh got Doug into wrestling in high school, and while neither of them were particularly competitive, they were both competent. Josh's family had been oystermen on Puget Sound for four generations, his father and uncle expanding their operation up into the Strait when Josh was in elementary school. Josh had always been a middling student, but hard worker, always out on the water with his family; after high school, he leaped at the opportunity to move into his great-grandfather's old cabin on the edge of Dabob Bay and work the oyster farms. "College," Josh had said confidently, "is not for me."

They had partied from time to time, taking advantage of the remote cabin lacking parental supervision, but Josh always kept it at a dull roar, constantly considering his sleep and work schedules, proving to be the most responsible stoner that Doug had ever met. No, not even a stoner, but someone who used drugs and alcohol occasionally and sparingly, his primary interests lying elsewhere. When Josh confided in Doug two summers ago, during the break between his freshman and sophomore years at UW, that he had gotten Emily Anderson pregnant and they were to be married, it never seemed anything but logical and appropriate.

"There it is," says Josh, pointing at a cluster of bright lights ahead of them as they round a point and break out of the mist. "Two miles south. I'm gonna open her up; hang on." Doug complies, tightening his grip on the stainless steel rail bolted to the wall, as Josh pushes the throttle all the way forward. The boat levels out and gravity pulls Doug rearwards as they skip across the surface of the water, the screws of the outboards the primary point of contact in the water. Doug searches the illuminated dials of the dash for the speedometer, finding it reading 47 knots. After a mere minute and a half, Josh reduces the throttle, sliding back down to fifteen knots, then ten, then four, coasting past the marina's 5 knot no-wake zone buoy marker and easing into a fueling slip effortlessly. Doug hops out of the bow with a line and ties a cleat hitch, then does the same with the aft line, pulling the hull all the way into the bumpers. Josh kills the outboards and joins him on the dock, checking the lines in their tethers, nodding his approval to Doug. "You remembered. Alright, I'm gonna join you up at the shop there," pointing to a well-lit marina store up the dock ramp, "to pay for fuel. You can use the payphone on the other side, by the gas station. You know, for cars. Need any quarters?"

Doug points to Josh's green meshback sportsball cap; Josh takes it off, hands it to Doug, and takes Doug's knit cap. Doug pulls the brim down low over his eyes, then shakes his head. "No, I'm good, thanks." He opens his wallet and removes a $100 bill. "For gas."

Josh looks at it for a second, clearly debating with himself, then shakes his head. "No, it's going on the company account, and will have a receipt. This is a completely routine trip, remember?"

Doug pushes the bill down into the left breast pocket of Josh's wool shirt. "OK, then grab me a bunch of jerky and granola bars, and a few bottles of water. And some gummi bears."

Josh gives him a thumbs up. "Let's roll."

Doug sees no obvious cameras outside of the store by the payphone, but is nervous nonetheless as he feeds four quarters into the beat-up payphone and dials Evans' emergency voicemail box, a 206 number. He keys in the payphone's 360 prefix number, hangs up, and waits. Three minutes later, the payphone rings, mechanical and abrasive; he answers. Evans' familiar voice, seemingly far away, says, "One Adam Twelve."

Doug responds. "We got whores in the city."

Evans closes the circuit. "'Settle down, Beavis.' That's so damn dumb. I can't believe I signed off on that exchange."

Doug smiles. "That's why I picked it. If we were burned, nobody would believe you'd go for it."

Evans continues, a touch of something resembling warmth in his voice. "It's good to hear from you, kid. We've been worried."

Doug asks, "Got any good news?"

There's a pause before Evans answers. "It could be better; it could be worse. An army of lawyers is doing our fighting for us right now. What can I do for you?"

Doug scratches his head behind his right ear, under the cap. "I gotta make next steps. Where can I meet you? Just you, nobody else."

Evans sighs. "Depends. I can guess generally where you're at. Some places are better than others. What if I said I was a little north of the last place we saw each other. Could you get here, if I gave you coordinates?"

Doug says, "Sure. Let's say I was a Marine. Tell me where you'd tell the Navy to drop off the Marines. I can be there in an hour."

"Copy," says Evans. "Alright, in that case, I'm giving you a coordinate. I'm going to add a modifier – this'll take a second, I have to do this with pencil and paper." Evans makes clicking sounds occasionally, but comes back on the line after about a minute. "Can you write this down?"

"Go for it." Doug has his Rite in the Rain pen and notepad out, three pages torn out and placed against the cover.

Evans recites a long number string, pauses, then recites another. "Repeat it back to me." Doug does so. "Okay, now divide that by the number of guys you were in a van with – including yourself – and that's it. I'm going to signal you before you approach. Two colors – the colors of the thing I showed you from that cabinet. Got it?"

Doug confirms, "Got it."

"Alright, I want you to signal me first when you're a mile out. You know Morse code?"

Doug grins. "Of course. I'll blink out the last thing you put in my hands."

Evans says, "It's a plan. Okay. I can be there in fifteen minutes. How long for you, did you say an hour?"

Doug shrugs. "Supposedly, yeah, seems correct."

"I'll get down there early and wait. Just be there before sunrise," Evans says. "And be discreet. Good luck." There's a rattling of plastic, then a dial tone. Doug hangs up the phone, then pockets his pen, notepad and writing sheet, before crumpling up the two blank pages and throwing them into a garbage can. He peeks into the mini mart, where an older woman wearing a grey Seahawks hoodie restocks cigarettes behind the counter. He walks down to the fueling slip where Josh stands by his boat, still fueling.

Josh watches Doug walk down the ramp to the dock before speaking. "Looks like you got ahold of someone?"

Doug nods. "All set. We have to calculate this coordinate. I'll do it in the cab."

Josh shakes his head. "Pilothouse. I got a bag of goodies in there for you on the bench."

Doug smiles. "Whatever." He enters the pilothouse and divides the number strings Evans provided by four, the number of team members in the Toronto operation. He watches Josh return the fuel nozzle to the pump, close up his fuel tanks and untie the boat from the dock cleats. Josh tosses the lines into the boat, then pushes the hull away from the slip before hopping aboard. He steps into the pilothouse and turns the ignition, the outboards burbling to life, and putters away from the dock at low speed to the northeast.

"OK, where are we going?" asks Josh, looking at Doug's scribbles.

Doug points to the calculated string on his scrap of paper. "He gave me some number strings, and I ran them using a figure only I'd know the answer to. Of course, a person listening could just guess and look for a match in the area. Probably not the best scheme, but we had to wing it."

"That's in the Sound, alright, either north of Seattle or the very north end. Let's look." Josh draws a bound and laminated book of charts from a drawer and examines the master chart grid, then flips to page 38, points a finger at a line on the grid and drags it down the page, stopping at a crescent-shaped section of pebbly beach abutting a rail line. "Yep, Innis Arden Reserve Park. This is the exact spot. I can get there in thirty minutes if I put the hammer down. When did you say we could be there?" Josh pulls his cap off Doug's head, and Doug's knit cap from his own, and swaps them.

Doug shrugs. "I said we could be there within an hour, based on what you said. We have a signal plan worked out. Morse code with lights on our approach. Can we use your spotlight?" he asks, pointing to a foot-diameter spotlight mounted on the left side of the pilothouse.

"Hell yeah; it's remote controlled from in here. Just flip the switch to punch out your code." Josh squints at the chart. "I don't know about bringing the boat up to the beach in the dark, Doug, but the approach looks nice and smooth; charts indicate it should be OK, but look, I'm not keen to fuck up my hull."

Doug nods. "Or you can put me in somewhere else and I'll just walk down."

Josh nods, point to a spot on the beach a quarter mile to the south of the coordinate. "This looks better. Hell, we got the spotlight, let's check it out. If I know my Seattle parks, there won't be anyone there. Some of the houses up on the bluff could see us, but given the time," tapping on the dashboard clock showing 4:58 a.m., "we should be fine. He's probably just walking you up to the street to a vehicle. Railroad shouldn't be an issue; the trains have to go through there nice and slow."

Doug looks at his gear in the corner of the pilothouse, his backpack and the M-14 rifle. "I'm not getting out with this rifle. You want it? Maybe you shouldn't keep it at home – it's full auto, highly illegal – probably best to cache it, or throw it over the side. I'll get you another machine gun."

Josh whistles. "I'll keep it. I got a place where it won't be found. My uncle had something like that in Vietnam. Pull those mag pouches off your pack and we're good." He extends his hand, and they shake on it. "Alright, enough sentiment. Get your gear squared away and I'm going to punch it up to a cruising speed of forty knots. We'll be approaching in about forty five minutes."

Forty minutes later, Josh reduces the throttle and taps Doug on the shoulder, handing him a pair of large Steiner binoculars. "We're almost there. Scan the horizon for other watercraft; I don't see anything between the ferries to the north and south. Focus on lights, but see if there is anything near the beach. And for God's sake, put the straps over your head; if those go into the drink, that's eight hundred bucks."

Doug steps out of the pilothouse, looping his right arm around a post to steady himself, and locks his shoulders and elbows to steady the binoculars. He scans north to south, seeking moving lights on the water, but sees only buoys, street lights, house lights and blinking red lights along the railway. The tide is still mostly out, two feet above low tide, and the beach ahead is a fairly steep gravel wall. To the south he spots Josh's alternative site, a much more gradual slope. Doug leans into the pilothouse and shouts, "It's gonna be the alternate. The beach is really steep."

Josh replies, "OK. Time to do your signal. I'll aim it right to the landing point and then give you the controls." He powers up the spotlight, turns it on, and points the blinding white beam like a laser at the shore, aiming it at the approximate coordinate. He waves Doug over. Doug takes out his scrap paper and scrawls out his message, then writes the Morse code for the letters beneath it.

"MP5? Like the gun?" asks Josh with bemusement.

Doug shrugs. He keys in the code on the light controls, the beam blinking long and short characters for several seconds. "Use the binocs; check the shoreline. This thing is so bright you might not be able to pick out handheld lights without letting your night vision recover."

Doug scans the shore. "Nothing. Let's wait a few minutes."

The boat, now barely drifting forward from momentum, is now rocking in the waves of the open Sound. The sky lightens to a deep blue to the east, dead ahead; Josh grows visibly nervous. "Okay, we're still an hour out from sunup, but I'm starting to get a bad feeling about this. This boat has registration marks and all its running lights; anybody takes notes and they're coming right to me." He steers the rudder to keep the boat oriented toward shore, then gives the engine a little power to reduce the rocking. "I'm going to ease in a little closer; we're still about three quarters of a mile out."

Josh waits for two minutes then says, "Close your eyes," does the same, and keys the Morse code characters into the spotlight. "Done," Josh notes. The pair open their eyes, and Doug steps out of the pilothouse to scan the shore with the binoculars. This time, two lights separated by a touch of blackness blink back at him, one yellow, one white, returning the MP5 code.

"That's him," says Doug. "Gold and white. Let's spotlight the alternative landing point for a second. Any thoughts on how to do that?"

Josh nods in the affirmative; "I'm going to spotlight the original point, then drag the beam over to the new point, and blink a few times." He does so – Doug watches the spot where the lights were, which blink back, 10-4.

Doug laughs. "OK, he copies. Let's go."

"OK." Josh pushes the throttle forward, bringing the bow out of the waves, and steers slightly to the south before reorienting towards the landing spot, reducing speed as they approach. The waves are carrying them forward, along with their momentum; Josh balances the throttle to a near idle, occasionally adding a touch of back thrust, allowing the boat to drift into the shallow shore gently. Doug watches over the side, using a powerful handheld flashlight from the pilothouse to watch the bottom, calling back his observations occasionally. "You're good; the bow should touch, without the motors hitting anything."

Josh says, "Fuck it," and throws a lever, which brings the outboards up out of the water. "We'll drift in. The hull will be fine." They rock in the waves, moving forward foot by foot. Josh hands Doug a long aluminum pole. "Get up in the bow with your pack. Use this rod to spear into the shore. When that's done, hop out with the pack, leave the rod in the boat, and give me a push back out. Keep the foul weather gear."

Doug goes in for a hug; Josh pats his back hard, squeezing him tight. "I owe you, big league," says Doug.

Josh pats him a few more times, then pushes him back. "Never. Get moving, man. Happy hunting." He winks. Doug grabs his pack, now free of .308 ammunition, magazines and sundries for his rifle, and drags it up to the bow by the top frame handle, along with the line rod. He squats at the bow and watches the shore approach slowly, foot by foot, testing the water depth with the line rod. A three-foot swell comes from behind, picking up the craft and pushing it towards the shore in a rush; the hull beneath the bow crunches softly in the gravel. Doug slides the pole back towards the pilothouse and stands straight, saluting Josh and holding it; Josh returns the salute. Doug waves, scoops up his pack, flings it ten feet up the beach, and hops from the bow onto the coarse gravel shore, then turns and pushes with all his might against the boat, stepping into the water. The gravel slurps at his boots, giving him a moment of panic, but he controls himself and, with one more hard push, frees the hull from the bottom, the outboards burbling in the water and drawing the boat rearward under power. Josh leans out of the pilothouse window; "Semper fi!" They wave at each other for a moment, then Doug turns and slogs up the gravel incline to his pack, throwing it over his shoulders. He trots up to the railroad grade, looking each way, before stepping onto the tracks and hastily marching towards the original rally point. The signal light blinks from the trees; Doug turns towards the light and stomps forward, the beach's surface lit adequately by traces of light from the houses and streets on the hills above. Evans holds a signal light under his face and flashes the light on, quickly; Doug sighs with relief in recognition, but keeps his hand on the pistol in his waistband.

The gravel crunching under his feet softens as the surface transitions into beach grasses along the perimeter of the trees. Evans speaks in a whisper. "That was something. C'mon, we gotta get out of here."

Doug catches up to him, walking along a single-lane road open to the sky above, the trees trimmed back from this railroad service road and the surrounding deciduous trees leafless. "We Marines now. Having a Navy is pretty sweet."

Evans' voice remains steady on the march, cardio being another one of his many strengths. "I'm parked a block and a half from the trailhead, and we have a few exit points. It's just me. I'm staying in an investment property two miles from here. I want to debrief you as soon as you've had some rest."

Doug shakes his head in the dark. "No, I'm refreshed; let's get started right away. I'll tell you everything."

The two men sit at a long dining table of recovered cedar, looking through a forty-foot long floor to ceiling window. Beyond, the Puget Sound slowly brightens, the sky lightening from purple to magenta to some other girl color as the sun rises over the Cascades behind them. Doug sips steaming coffee from a black mug, still wearing Josh's borrowed clothes. He sees an expression of what appears to be actual respect in Evans' steel grey eyes as they discuss the events of the past week, Evans occasionally interrupting with a pointed question.

Doug wraps up by explaining his relationship with Josh, and the relative security of their connection. Evans finally puts up his hands. "So what I'm trying to figure out is how all of this information about your dad's murder and the investigation into the Brooks faction got out. That's the only thing that doesn't make sense."

"I have no idea," says Doug. "My grandfather must have made a call. I remember him saying that certain people had this information. You guys, and Sheriff Bryce." He pauses. "It must have been Bryce. Has to be."

Evans leans forward in his chair and picks up a piece of jerky from a tray of meat and vegetables. "Your dad's understudy. I hope it doesn't come back to haunt him."

Doug shakes his head. "I can't see anything happening to him. He's too well-known, well-liked."

"They did your dad the same way," says Evans. "We're going to have to deal with these people, Doug. Every last one of them. These tickles out on the periphery of their organization are over. Or else, we are."

Doug sighs, leans back in his chair and looks at the ceiling – more recovered cedar beams and slats from a 19th century warehouse. "I need a break. I can't even think about that right now. I feel like my emotions have been burned in a funeral pyre. Speaking of; my grandfather."

Evans stands, looking out over the Sound. "Scarcely any remains were found, and the feds appear to not be cooperating with the county coroner. There's no living estate; your grandfather had everything wrapped up in trusts, in your name. One of our lawyers has everything under control, though the feds are trying to get their mitts on it. But they don't have a leg to stand on. Their warrants were bullshit, and aside from you being suspected of slaughtering two dozen of them before disappearing off the face of the earth, they have no hard evidence on you."

Doug, now hunched over the table, stares into the last three inches of coffee in his cup, trying to center the reflection from an overhead light in the middle of the sea of black. "Mmmm. I was thinking more of honoring the dead."

Evans turns. "That's going to be something you figure out how to do on your own. I think you've done a damn sight better than any funeral by slipping through their fingers."

"I wonder how Cathy is," Doug wonders aloud.

Evans raises an eyebrow. "Let me know if you need anybody checked on. Nothing in the papers or investigation notes we've gotten through channels mentioned her, despite what went down in Seattle. That's promising."

Doug slumps back in his chair. "I had a system to keep her signal low. Obviously not good enough; Green and his guys probably just tailed me. Guaranteed she hates me. 'Hey, sorry about that, wanna still be my girlfriend, even though the feds say I'm the worst person on the planet?'"

Evans shakes his head. "Look, this isn't going to help you now, but you'll remember it later. It'll get better. I've been divorced twice. I finally learned my lesson. The first one was an on-again, off-again relationship when I was a young grunt. She hated the life of a military wife, and whipped off a letter when I was off doing 'man stuff,' as she put it, in a then-obscure place called Vietnam. It broke me, and I barely made it out of that tour alive. But you know what? We didn't have kids, and in time, when I did have kids, I realized it wasn't a big deal. Look, you saved her ass; she'll understand that some day."

"Her ass wouldn't have been in trouble if it weren't for me," Doug says coldly. "She killed Green, though I finished the job."

Evans grins. "See? She's a tough cookie. She'll be fine; a story to tell her kids."

Doug groans. "Thanks for cheering me up."

"Look, kid," says Evans. "I spent thirty years in the army. You signed on for the same life, whether you understood it or not. Get with it: relationships with women are disposable, until they're not. You just have to figure it out for yourself. Now, about this Douglas Shea person."

Doug brings his head up. "What do you mean?"

Evans grins. "He doesn't exist anymore. You're going to switch to an alternate. Now; where do you want to go? Thailand? Spain? Canada?"

Doug shrugs. "Do I have to decide now?"

Evans laughs. "You're going to take a vacation, then we'll set you up somewhere. Look, you have over twenty million dollars in liquid assets from your grandfather, another twenty-five tied up in various business interests. You can do pretty much whatever you want, and the way he set his shit up, they're not going to be able to tie you to anything. Your Spanish is good, right?"

Doug shrugs. "I spent a bunch of summers there with my cousins outside Barcelona. I can swing Castilian Spanish, and my Catalan is rusty, but okay."

Evans nods. "Latin America is a great place to lay low. How many people know you used to go to Spain? Ever talk about it at school, with friends?"

Doug thinks. "Yes. I wrote papers about Catalonia, the Civil War, gave presentations, talked about my family connection. I'm sure they've talked to teachers by now."

Evans says, "See? That's off the list, for now; maybe not forever, but definitely now. In fact, I think a nice trip to Thailand, soaking up the sun on remote beaches, and playing with Western girls on vacation will get you mission capable again. Face it, Doug; this is you, and these guys aren't going to stop, even after the government does. You understand that, don't you?"

Doug nods. "I do. I can't handle it right now – I feel like I'm going to explode – but I get it. So. R&R. I have my alternate ID in a private garage in SoDo, not counting the stuff you held onto for me."

Evans asks, "Private garage. The people who run it, they've seen your face, right?"

Doug shrugs. "Yeah, but the owner is this autistic Korean guy. I'm paid up for like two more years, and all he ever watches is Korean TV when I'm in there, no American shows, and he barely speaks English. No fucking way does he say anything to the feds to draw attention to himself, even if he does see a story about me. He probably just sees anonymous white guy when he thinks of me. I mean, I'll stay away from there for a while, but all I have to do is float fifteen hundred bucks a year his way and it's mine forever. I have the keys in my bag," he says, thumbing towards his bedroom down the hall.

"Then it's settled." Evans slaps his hand on the table. Doug jumps in his seat. "You're headed out of this dreary winter wonderland to chill on a beach in Pattaya, collecting notches until you're bored with it, then it's on to another wacky adventure, wherever we find a good slot for you. Deal?"

Doug nods. "Deal."

Return to Ithaca

Six months later, a bearded, deeply tanned and blonde-ponytailed Doug Shea rolls open the door of his South Seattle storage unit, stepping into the cool shade of the interior. He turns, scanning outside, focusing on streetlights and rooflines, still unsure, after a day of observation and hunting for surveillance devices, that Evans' team is correct in their all-clear assessment. He flips the lights and rolls the door closed, examining the garage, which he last saw that night in January.

Doug enters the combination to the safe first and examines its contents, which are as he remembered. The same is true for the truck as well as the rest of the garage – no evidence of disturbance, which comforts him. He relaxes slightly, and proceeds with his work.

That evening, Officer Remy Ruiz of the Seattle Police Department sits in the driver seat of his Crown Victoria Interceptor, windows down, completing a stack of incident reports from earlier in his shift. His patrol car occupies the loading zone of a hundred year old brick apartment building on First Hill, pointed east, and he uses the last rays of the setting sun to illuminate his work. His radio crackles periodically at low volume, blurring into background noise.

"Hello, officer; pardon me, sir," says a tentative voice to his right. He looks up and out the passenger window, and finds a slightly shaggy but clean white male in his twenties – dirty blonde hair pulled back tightly, brown beard, white collared button-up short sleeve shirt and brown pants, boots. He has an edge of athleticism and health to him, unlike many of the dregs of this area who he might be mistaken for in a casual description.

Ruiz relaxes slightly, peeking over his sunglasses. "How can I help you?" His piercing brown eyes scan his target from a blocky, muscular face, cheekbones that could cut Arctic ice, glowing with masculine energy.

The young man takes two steps forward before squatting down to look through the window, maintaining several feet of distance. Ruiz realizes he's intentionally keeping himself visible. Smart. The young man takes a deep breath then says calmly, "Hey, you don't know me, but I know Cathy."

Ruiz's senses go on high alert. His left hand, concealed by his paperwork, smoothly flows to the corner of his seat, where he finds a small blowback .380 pistol. He grips the gun and points it beneath the clipboard towards the window. "Yeah? So?"

The young man puts his hands up next to his face, fingers splayed out. "I'm taking a risk, but to me it's worth it. She disappeared in January; I figure that her family was taking care of her, but I wanted to be sure. And if she's still around, I'd like to talk to her. If she wants to."

Ruiz's face hardens, the skin on his scalp bunching up beneath his shiny black flat-top. "And you are...?"

Doug smiles. "I think you know who I am. I'm not armed, but I can't say the same for my buddies across the street. The last thing I want is an accident, so let's stay cool. If you can pass on a message, or if you have one for me, that'd be great. If not, I understand. I'll drop it."

Ruiz turns, looking around him; while he doesn't see any obvious signs of being watched, there are a dozen potential places to escape his gaze. He relaxes, sliding the pistol back into its holster alongside his seat, and places his bundle of paperwork on the dash of his car. He splays his own fingers out and displays his empty hands to Doug. "As a matter of fact, we were wondering when you'd show up. Do you want to go for a ride?"

Doug laughs. "Not really; any alternatives?"

Ruiz looks at him coolly. "Got a number I can reach you at?"

Doug slowly reaches into the breast pocket of his shirt with two splayed fingers, and withdraws a small folded piece of paper. He extends it over the windowsill of the patrol car and drops it onto the passenger seat. "Leave a voicemail here. I've been to your parents' house. I was supposed to meet them for formal introductions until, well, everything happened. That seems like a safe place for everyone. I'll put myself into your hands there, or a public place, but nowhere else. Deal?"

Ruiz picks up the paper quickly, maintaining eye contact. "You're not in a position to be making terms, guy."

Doug shrugs, dropping his hands from view. "I know that. I'm allergic to uniforms with nametags other than 'Ruiz' right now. But I feel like this is something I have to make right before I can move on. And even if nothing happens after this, can you tell her that I never intended for this to happen, and I hope the best for her?"

Ruiz nods. "Best move along. I'll follow up." He throws the car into gear and zips out onto the street, accelerating smoothly, disappearing to the right at the next block. Doug straightens up, scratches his head and surveys the buildings around him before turning and walking east, downhill and downtown.

Two nights later, Doug hops out of a white panel van on a side street off Rainier Avenue South, waving to Evans in the driver's seat and one of Evans' guys, a former Marine NCO who works for a Vanguard-satellite tugboat company. Evans drives the van up South Morgan Street towards their overwatch position, while Doug cuts north to Graham through a busy cross street. The sun is down, it's a summer weeknight, and Doug is amazed at the amount of noise on this residential street. A group of teens approaches him mid-block, paralleling him on the other side of the street, challenging him loudly; Doug tells them to fuck off. They do, theatrically talking shit as they fade back.

Orienting himself uphill, he settles into a moderate pace for the ascent. He crests a little rise and finds the Ruiz family's block, just west of Wilson Avenue. He presses the illumination button on his digital watch, verifying that he's two minutes early, before stepping onto Cathy's family street. He sees the cherry of a cigarette flair on a porch to his left, a wrinkled, Asian male face behind it, watching him from a bench, a thin rod poking up over the porch rail, probably a rifle barrel. At the next house on the right, another Asian male, this one younger, probably thirties, maybe not, with a full head of black hair pulled into a ponytail, leaning against a ten year old Toyota pickup bed, his arm over the side, tracking him. Doug waves and continues forward. I get it, he thinks, you're watching me. The air is alive with cigarette smoke, silent watchers at seven of the ten houses in the cul de sac, Cathy's brother's patrol car parked in the driveway of their grandparents' rambler at the end of the street. On cue, Remy Ruiz exits the driver door in uniform, watches Doug approach, and gestures to him as Doug steps onto the driveway.

"Hands on the trunk," says Remy. "Do everything slow."

Doug walks to the trunk and plants his hands, leaning slightly. "I'm not armed."

Remy applies his left hand to Doug's back, between the shoulder blades, as he pats him down with his right. Doug notices that Remy is larger than he expected; probably about five foot ten, two inches shorter than Doug, but with a large upper body, big, cabled forearms, and he moves deftly. On the legs, Remy transitions to a two-handed pat-down, finding nothing. He pats Doug on the back twice, then says loudly, "Clear." More quietly, "Not even a wallet. Okay, come on in. You first."

Weaving along a paved walkway through a yard densely landscaped with shrubs and dwarf maple trees to the front door, Doug passes two more Asian men of indeterminate age, fifties-to-eighties, one smoking a cigarette, the other not, clutching WWII-era M-1 Carbines, wood stocked with thirty round magazines. The door opens, and an ancient man with thin silver hair and a lined face stands in the doorway, indirectly lit from a room to the right, a large leaf-bladed knife hanging in a wooden sheath from his belt beside a 1911 pistol shoved in his waistband, cocked and locked. He beckons; Doug enters a large open living room, stopping to zip out of his boots as directed. Remy converses with this man briefly in a language Doug doesn't understand, a smattering of English and Spanish words with something else – Tagalog?

The home smells of a busy kitchen - roast pork, citrus and not unpleasant fryer oil. Doug's mouth waters immediately. The living room is nearly thirty feet by thirty feet, devoid of furniture save for two low tables against a wall, and woven floor mats; a raised dais at the back frames white blinds that Doug guesses hide sliding glass doors that exit onto a rear patio. Two more M-1 Carbines lean against the corner. On the dais sit two men Indian style, one about sixty with salt and pepper hair and the other much older, both wearing white casual barong shirts with vertical embroidering. Remy steps around Doug, having shed his patrol boots, and speaks again in what Doug guesses is Tagalog, saying "Douglas Shea" more than once. Remy sits against the wall to the side, just below the dais.

Doug stands, hands at his sides, looking from Remy to the other men. He assumes the men before him are Cathy's father and grandfather. He searches for obvious familial traits in their faces, but gives up. He tilts his head forward slightly, knowing only that Filipino formality is completely different from the rest of Asia, but never learned much from his esgrima instructor not pertinent to the art. He tries to avoid clearing his throat audibly, then says, "Sirs. I am Douglas Shea." He holds his slight nod, feeling like a fool, then straightens.

The younger man on the left gestures to the floor before him, grinning slightly. "Please, sit." The older man watches impassively.

Doug lowers himself to the floor, glancing to Remy briefly; Remy watches him, expressionless. Doug orients his attention to the two men, who look down on him from their slightly higher position, blinking, waiting. Doug recalls reading an article about American business executives in Asia stumbling all over themselves when met with silence during meetings, betraying their standing. He waits, silently, watching.

After a minute, the older man cracks a smile, and mutters gently to his compatriot, who laughs. "Yes, Douglas Shea, we see why my daughter liked you," he says with a mild accent, a slight sing-song to his voice as he beams with a friendly smile. "But you look messier than she described."

"I'm sorry, sir, it's sort of a disguise since I'm back in town briefly. I normally look much cleaner." Doug allows a slight grin, but forces himself back into a neutral-friendly expression.

"Yes, self-control in one so young, especially, you know, an American." The two older men chuckle, while Remy looks on, stone-faced. He must be a hit at parties, Doug thinks.

"Mr. Ruiz, sir, is she OK? She looked unhurt, when I last saw her, but it was a bad situation. I heard that she left school," Doug says. "I've had my own problems, but I just wanted to tell her that I was sorry; that I didn't mean for any of this to happen."

The older man begins speaking, Cathy's father turning to watch him as he carries on in Tagalog for some time. He wraps up with what sounds like a question. Doug nods to him, then looks to Mr. Ruiz and Remy. Mr. Ruiz thinks, glancing up to the ceiling, before he begins speaking. "Our family has been through much worse; my father and mother were separated for five years during the Japanese occupation. My father described how I was born; my mother was injured in Manila when she was pregnant with me, and went to the countryside with her family; my father was in the jungle with McArthur's men. Do you know this story?"

Doug shakes his head. "Cathy didn't tell me about it, but I'm familiar with World War Two in the Philippines. My family story is similar, but in Europe."

The older men confer in Tagalog, the eldest nodding and addressing Doug in English for the first time, more heavily accented but clear. "You understand. Not easy, but we do what we must." He raises a finger to the air. "I ask you one thing. You understand me?"

Doug nods. "Yes, sir."

Cathy's grandfather collects his thoughts for a moment as the room watches him. He finally speaks. "What is one thing when it becomes two?"

Doug thinks for a moment, in silence, as their eyes bore into him. He wasn't expecting riddles. Doug holds his hands up, fingers curled, two loosely-held fists pressed together. He separates them, relaxing his wrists, miming a stone being split in two. He speaks. "Broken?"

The older men confer in Tagalog, then Cathy's grandfather points to Doug. "Yes. It is not good for one thing to become two. Understand that, and you will understand us." He pats his son on his shoulder, stands, and walks out of the room.

Doug looks to Remy, whose stares at him with hard eyes. Doug has to look away. Fortunately, Mr. Ruiz's expression is gentler. He sighs. "I can tell that you are a good boy. You would not be here if you were not. But you should not be here. You should be far away, safe. This is not a good place for you. Nor is it a good place for my daughter."

Doug swallows, sensing a hardening of the mood.

Mr. Ruiz beams graciously, lifting open hands. "I will send your good wishes to my daughter. She is somewhere safe. She will be fine. She will return to school, somewhere, and have a good life. Without you." He raises a finger in the air, then slowly points to the floor, and brings his finger down. "My daughter is my daughter. She knows who she is. You are who you are. You are broken, but still you know who you are. You cannot be together. Any life you make would be broken. You are trouble for her, and for all of us. Now go with my son; now you are safe, but do not return, or you will not be."

Remy stands, as does Mr. Ruiz, who fires a quick burst of Tagalog to Remy. Remy leaves the room quickly, then returns, holding a CD case. Doug stands and accepts the CD, a burned disc scrawled with Cathy's floral handwriting in purple ink. Doug swallows, hard.

"My daughter asked me to give this to you. She said it would say what she wanted to say." Mr. Ruiz looks up at Doug; he is six inches shorter, but radiates dominance. He steps to the side and pats Doug on the back. "Go with God, Douglas Shea; we will pray for you." Doug follows Remy to the doorway, where they don their footwear and cross the threshold back out into Seattle, the pair of guards nowhere to be seen.

Remy beckons Doug towards his patrol car, patting the hood next to him, where they both lean. He crosses his arms high on his chest, above the equipment on his belt. "Let's have our own talk," he says, in what Doug mentally labels a 'cop voice.' "I think you understand the risk we're taking even talking to you. On paper, I should have you cuffed and stuffed in the back of this car."

Doug nods. "I understand that. Thank you."

Remy gestures towards the neighborhood. "You see all these guys out here? Neighborhood watch. Based on my grandfather's old guerrilla group. When they came to the U.S. they stuck to the old ways. We solve our own problems. They started with a dozen carbines they bought from the government in the early seventies; everyone chips in, annual dues. Membership comes with rights and obligations. The orders they have are, thirty minutes from now, you show up anywhere, you get handed to the police or you die resisting. That's it."

Doug returns Remy's gaze coolly. "I wouldn't expect anything else."

Remy cracks a grin. "Look, I'm not as old school as the elders. I don't care if my sister dates a white guy. But they wouldn't have accepted you, and you would have gotten sick of it and bailed. I've seen it plenty of times. Anyway." He waves a hand. "Get out of town. If my dad hadn't told me months ago that we owed you for protecting Cathy, you'd be in federal lock-up, getting worked over. I don't like it, but it is what it is. Do you need a ride anywhere?"

Doug shakes his head. "No, I'll walk."

Remy narrows his eyes. "Same crew from the other day?"

Doug nods. "Yep. Thanks, Remy." He extends his hand. Remy accepts it, and they shake firmly. "You won't ever see me again." He pushes himself up from the car, turns, and walks down the middle of the street, away from this strange island, and disappears into the cacophony of the Rainier Valley; he doesn't look back.

Like a Hawk Taking a Bird

Doug sits at attention on the rear bench seat of Evans' panel van, swaying on the balls of his feet to stabilize himself as they wind through potholed pavement laid over pioneers' cartpaths, staring straight ahead through the narrow aperture of the windshield. Within ten minutes they enter a long, straight tunnel, a tube of glaring yet dirty yellow light, other cars whipping past them on the left and right. The pressure in his head drops as they emerge onto the long, vastly wide deck of the I-90 bridge span, angling down towards the surface of Lake Washington, where the concrete deck levels and points, arrow-straight, towards the mountain of light that is Mercer Island. Doug connects the human sounds from the front of the van with voices and words, and realizes that Evans has been attempting to speak with him for some time.

"Sorry, you were saying?" Doug asks.

Evans turns, casting his voice more directly. "Can you hear me now? You OK?"

Doug responds. "I'll be fine. I'm just tired."

"Okay. Almost there." Evans focuses on the road while his man, the Marine NCO, glances back with a worried expression. Doug zones out for the remainder of the ride, reading Cathy's scrawled messages on the CD and its jewel case over and over. The ride ends in the gravel driveway of a small A-frame cabin set deep in a deciduous forest, the only lights visible beaming from the front of the van. "We're here," Evans says. They all exit the van, Doug scanning the land around, seeing only a moderate incline that he guesses leads to the lake shore, with glimpses of light through the trees from all points. Evans leaves the headlights on and runs to the door of the cabin, his feet tromping across the rotting wooden deck; the door creaks open and he flips on interior and exterior lights, which reveal a clean but run-down house with little furniture.

Doug steps up onto the wood deck, which sags under his feet. He walks carefully to the door, peeking in. "What is this place?"

Evans stands by the door, the NCO removing bags from the rear of the van. "Original owners bought five acres before the bridge span was connected to Bellevue in the seventies. They kept the land after buying a bigger house on the west side of the island because their son loved playing in the woods here. He struggled with leukemia for years; after he died in the early eighties, his father couldn't bring himself to sell it. The father died last year; the mother sold the property to a developer, a shell company owned by someone you know."

"Sheesh, Evans," Doug says, flinching. "That's the saddest thing I've heard in a long time."

Evans steadies his gaze. "Good; quit feeling sorry for yourself." He walks to the van, gesturing to Doug to follow him. "Alright; fridge is stocked, no booze, and we got the gear you wanted." They each grab a large duffle bag from the eroded gravel driveway and carry them into the house, placing them next to a standalone wood stove, its chimney projecting straight up through the roof. Evans points around the cabin. "Sleeping loft upstairs, bathroom and kitchen downstairs. The couch is probably more comfortable than the bed," gesturing to an impressive but ugly low sectional couch upholstered in fuzzy orange-brown. "Workbench is over there for your little project," pointing to a long, institutional-looking steel desk. "Don't blow yourself up."

Doug shakes his head. "We'll be good. It's still looking like tomorrow?" He tests the couch, pushing down on a broad, thin cushion with his hands; it barely flexes.

Evans nods. "Tomorrow it is. We'll get you early. Early bird gets the worm, and we have a ways to go."

"Until then." Doug shakes hands with Evans and the Marine NCO, who regards him with an understanding gaze. "I'm sorry, I completely forgot your name. I'm Doug."

The Marine nods; in a deep, slightly raspy voice, he says, "Don't worry about it; name's Murphy." His enormous mitt wraps around Doug's with gentle pressure; Doug's hand is shaken.

"Goodnight, Murphy. See you tomorrow." The two men nod and walk to the van, reversing in a broad U, and crunch down the gravel drive, their taillights disappearing in the trees. Doug sighs, locks the door, and digs into his equipment bags. One carries his street clothing and toiletries, along with a day pack and a larger mountaineer's rucksack, both commercial but in subdued colors. He places this bag on the couch. Another bag contains their clothing and support gear for tomorrow. They're sticking to the construction worker look; had he used this gambit locally, he would go with another. The last bag is a wonderland, a veritable John Woo sack-o'-gats – the Ameli light machine gun with three hundred rounds, a suppressed 9mm Taurus, as their stock of vintage Berettas were now slag, and three small project boxes filled with new in wrap equipment, including the tools Doug will use to make them operational.

Doug walks through the house, opening windows to freshen the air; down here in the trees, there is little residual heat from the summer day, but preferences are preferences. He props the front door open, its screen door remaining latched shut, before running the sink and filling an old gas station animated character glass with cool water. Doug sips the water, gasping at its freshness; the bottled water he'd been drinking for the last six months in Thailand was sterile and dull, lacking the vibrance of Northwest tap. He dons rubber gloves and gets to work.

Doug places his equipment atop the desk, segregated by project stage. Four plastic-sealed six-ounce wads of commercial blasting explosive are placed atop the battered Danish modern coffee table; they'll be assembled in the field tomorrow. He's selected a binary explosive recently approved by the Bureau of Alcohol, Tobacco and Firearms for recreational shooting, which is also easily mixed at home from simple ingredients available commercially by anyone capable of following directions and safety protocols. Doug unrolls a work mat on the desk, and frames it with a soldering iron and solder. He plugs the iron into the wall, letting it heat on his stand, and lays out the components for the first build: a blocky, previous-generation Nokia cell phone, along with its service booklet, several sections of medium-gauge electrical, a male and female wire snap connection set, and a silver commercial electric blasting cap slightly larger than a .22 Magnum cartridge.

First, Doug builds out a test rig, which consists of the male side of the wire snap connection set, soldered on one end of a two-inch section of the medium-gauge wire, the other end bearing a tiny lightbulb socket and bulb. Following the directions in the Nokia service booklet, he removes the rear of the phone casing, and disconnects the ringer alarm from its circuit board with carefully applied heat, plucking it out with assembly-grade tweezers. Then he gently solders the female wire snap connection in place of the ringer alarm. He assembles the phone and realizes, battery in hand, that testing the phone in this cabin will result in a triangulated position associated with the device during a forensics investigation. Double shit. He'll have to test elsewhere. Cursing under his breath, he builds out three of the phone devices, as well as three male connections to the blasting cap. He looks at the thin black plastic project boxes and places the phones inside, applying a little epoxy to bond each phone inside the box, while orienting them to be easily accessed in case he's made an error.

The first stages complete, Doug places all three of the devices, along with the explosives, within a foam-lined tool box, retaining the blasting cap components in their original protective cases the size of film canisters. He turns the wire over carefully to prevent bending and crimping.

Bored, and disappointed with himself in not considering test protocol, Doug cleans the Ameli, then assembles and disassembles it for time, eventually getting down to thirty-two seconds for the former, forty six seconds for the latter. He examines the Taurus pistol, finding it to be of slightly lesser finish quality than the vintage Berettas, yet acceptable enough and with a slightly better trigger. They are also far less expensive, as the factory in Brazil is still churning them out on authentic Beretta tooling. That does it, then – the Taurus is adequate. Doug makes a mental note to continue Josef's Modern Liberator project based on the Taurus... once his life is under control.

Restless, Doug searches the cabin for a CD player, but finds no audio equipment more recent than his own birth date. He spends an hour walking around the property in the dark, enjoying the tranquility and pleasant Northwest summer evening vibe, a welcome break from the oft-oppressive swamp furnace he's been marinating in for the past months, before collapsing into a restless sleep on the couch.

"Here we go." After two hours of too-early-to-be-rush-hour traffic, Evans steers a blue panel van – exchanged for the white van in a parking lot, just off the highway in Federal Way – into the subterranean garage of a down on its luck, sixties-era downtown Tacoma high-rise.

"Are you good to set everything up?" asks Doug, donning an orange hard hat, clad in white coveralls and a tool belt. He drags an increasingly heavy two-foot long toolbox to the van's side door. "I can do it, if you'd prefer."

Evans shakes his head. "No, you get upstairs. Your job is primary. This is secondary." He picks up the small duffle bag containing the cellular devices and pats them. "Murph is on overwatch. I'd prefer two-man teams, but..."

Doug shrugs. "Fuck it. Okay, good luck." They exit the van, Doug hefting his toolbox and slamming the door shut before turning and walking through the dark, sparsely populated parking garage to a freight elevator. He remembers his earpiece mic and turns to test it. "One-one, check check, over."

"One-one, this is one-two, copy, over," replies Evans from twenty feet away. "I'm out." Evans waves and walks to a stairwell on the north side of the garage and disappears up it, moving towards his destination across the street.

The freight elevator rumbles into place, and Doug steps in, keeping his head bent forward. The night before he combed blonde hair dye into his beard to disrupt his appearance, though he will continue to avoid cameras. He punches the button for the 16th floor and whispers two verses cribbed from a Catholic prayer book as he ascends, clutching his clipboard with a phony work order like a shield.

God of power and mercy,
maker and lover of peace,

to know you is to live,
and to serve you is to reign.

Through the intercession of St. Michael, the archangel,
be our protection in battle against all evil.
Help us to overcome war and violence
and to establish your law of love and justice.
Grant this through Christ our Lord.

A sense of righteousness wars with his natural revulsion to hypocrisy as Doug chants under his breath. The elevator doors creak open in the midst of his third recitation; he continues the prayer as he exits onto a gutted office floor, walls downed, ceiling panels mostly gone, wires and other residue dangling from overhead or strewn about the floor. He trods across several years' thickness of dust, then dons a disposable facemask and orients himself toward the north side of the building.

There; the battered olive green filing cabinet that Evans described is right where he expects it, twenty feet from the windows, dead center of the floor. Out the window, across a narrow fifty-foot gap, is another office building of similar vintage, this one occupied on every floor. The Tacoma commercial property market being what it is, he could have selected several vacant offices with a view of his target, but this is the only building with a commanding, upfront view of the entirety of Joint Task Force Echo's operations center, established in a regional Department of Justice office with plenty of room to spare. Here, under the gaze of the allegedly unbiased DOJ, dozens of agents are hard at work to destroy what they are now, for reasons unknown, calling a violent white supremacist network, radiating outward from one Josef Shea.

Doug sits on the floor, shielded from the windows by the filing cabinet, and assembles his video monitoring unit – a camera, a cable, a folding monitor with an AC/DC adaptor – before crawling across the floor to the window, placing the camera into position, and returning to his hide behind the filing cabinet. On-screen there is a slight gold tint from the opposite building's windows, but he can clearly see beyond. As the sun gets higher – current time, 8:17 a.m. – the picture should be clearer, with less reflected glare from the treated windows. Doug only needs to identify one man before proceeding.

He keys his mic – "One-one, in place, over."

Evans chimes in. "One-two, packages in place, over. Returning to pos."

Finally, Murphy. "One-three, all quiet, over."

Doug watches the monitor, stroking his beard. "One-one, will check in when the party starts; over and out."

Evans and Murphy copy, leaving Doug alone with his thoughts once again. He assembles the Ameli, mounting its large suppressor and a one hundred round belt box. He prepares the light machine gun for firing from its bipod, but leaves the action un-cocked; his target may not appear, despite the schedule Evans and Murphy have established in the months prior, with Seattle SAC Martinelli appearing weekdays at 8:30 a.m. Nasty commute, Doug thinks.

Doug's eyes glaze over periodically as he watches the screen, occasionally performing a radio check with the team. As each moment ticks by, he reminds himself that he must both trust his team's observations and good luck. The stairwell doors are rigged to unlock from the inside only. Doug gets an idea for his escape, remembering a trick Mike discovered in a UW admin building elevator. He walks to the elevator bay and confirms that the same local elevator company services this building; it should work. He eyes the freight elevator, then realizes he has to pee. Too much coffee in the van. Damn. Feeling like an animal, he hoses down the interior of a trash can filled with chunks of drywall on the north side of the floor. Were he not leaving the country today, he'd use a bottle to remove his urine from the scene. Oh, well.

He walks back to the filing cabinet to watch the feed from the camera aimed at Martinelli's temporary office and the meeting room, observing people entering in ones and twos. There she is – Martinelli's secretary – setting up a projector with a male agent's assistance. This must be it. Doug grabs the Ameli, caressing its bolt handle, anxiously watching the screen. FBI Special Agent in Charge Martinelli, looking older and more rumpled than on television or photographs, steps into the meeting room, then back out; this is it. Doug sets the Ameli back on the floor and runs to the elevator bay, selecting DOWN for the freight elevator; he brings an empty trashcan from the mess of the floor and waits anxiously. DING – the doors grind open, and Doug places the trashcan between the doors, which close on it gently, bouncing open. He lays the trash can flat on the floor to prevent the doors from knocking it out of the way and runs back to the desk to check the monitor; the room is filled, the door is closed, and Martinelli sits at the head of the table, passively watching a presentation.

Doug folds the monitor closed and pulls the camera cord hard, dragging the camera across the floor. He unplugs the AC/DC adaptor and stuffs it all into his toolbox. Finally. CLACK-ACK – he pulls the Ameli's bolt handle smoothly to the rear, locking in the open bolt position. Doug stands, placing the light machine gun's bipod on the desk and the butt into the pocket of his shoulder. The short range to the target makes an optic unnecessary – he's running the original iron sights. There they are, a dozen of his hunters less than forty meters from him. Doug keys his mic. "One-one; it's party time." He foregoes radio protocol in his excitement, the adrenaline surging within his body, his head pounding with dazzling energy, the world outside of a narrowing cone of vision fading from view, the sights of his weapon popping sharply before him. He positions the front sight blade in the middle of his father's murderer's chest, just below the sternum, indexing on the shining top button of his suitcoat. Aim small, miss small. Doug takes a deep breath, slowly releases two thirds of the air before holding, then presses the trigger straight back.

BRAAAAAAAAAAAAAAAAAAAAAAAAAAAAAAAAAAAAAAAAA

The smooth, muted clatter of his weapon whines like a table saw splitting resinous pine, amplified within the enclosed space despite the voluminous suppressor on its muzzle. The window explodes outward in crystalline shards as he sends death into the opposite room, the bullets pouring down at a fifteen-degree decline. He gives in to the moment and the weapon's staggeringly high rate of fire, graciously plying his target with fifteen 5.56mm armor piercing projectiles per second, until the Ameli's bolt locks to the rear, its chamber pouring smoke. FBI Special Agent in Charge Antonio Martinelli, or what remains of him, lies shot to mush like roadkill in the middle of a seven foot long bullet-stitched gash in the room, from the middle of the once lovely tropical hardwood meeting room table to the wall behind. Agents, secretaries and functionaries curl up on the floor, alternately cowering or crying in shock.

For months, Doug had envisioned doling out death to a roomful of agents like a generous talk show host. You get bullets! And you get bullets! That had been the plan as of this morning when reviewing with Evans, who longed for revenge against those who had killed his man, Jake Steiner, his respected elder Josef Shea, and rolled up his whole world. But long nights alone had eaten at Doug, thoughts of the wives and children of the men he'd killed on the mountain, they who had to die so that he may live. Blowing away a dozen men and women today, many of them duty-bound patriots, would not leave him freer or bring his old life back. Instead, he paid no attention to any man but the one he had first marked.

Doug sits down on the floor and disassembles the steaming light machine gun, returning the components to his tool box, and slides the short, smoking barrel unit into an asbestos sleeve. Spent casings and disintegrating belt links are strewn across the dusty, foot-printed floor, a forensic play land. Oh, well!

Doug locks his now-lighter toolbox shut and runs to the freight elevator to find the door locked open, pinging angrily. He steps into the elevator and presses P1, holding it and the firefighter call button simultaneously. The door closes obediently, and the car speeds downward without stopping. He steps out of the elevator onto the parking floor to find the blue van pulled up at the door, Evans waiting with the passenger door open. Doug swings his toolbox onto the floorboard and hops into the seat, closing the door while Evans speeds away, and buckles his seatbelt as they transition up the exit ramp. Evans slows the van as they pull onto the surface street, headed south.

Evans mutters into his earpiece, Murphy returning the call, but Doug doesn't understand a word. His ears aren't quite ringing, though his head pulses. He realizes that Evans is talking to him. Doug pulls the radio earbud from his left ear and turns to face him, saying two words: "Mission accomplished."

Stopped at a red light at the end of the block, Evans glances coolly between his side mirrors at the street behind them. He holds out a cellular phone to Doug. "Do you want to do the honors?"

Doug accepts the phone. "Don't mind if I do." He pulls up the preprogrammed numbers and selects the first of three, pressing the telephone handset icon. Seconds later, a muted CRUMP sounds behind them. The street light changes to green; Evans accelerates slowly down the block as Doug calls the other two numbers. Doug finally pulls the battery from the phone and stuffs them both into Evans' small duffle bag. At the junction of Market and South 15th Streets, a Tacoma Police Department patrol car pulls up next to them at the light; within seconds, the driver throws full lights and sirens and peels west at high speed, heading back towards downtown. Doug glances at Evans, who clutches a suppressed Taurus pistol in his right hand, pointed across his lap below the window. Doug nods. "I think we're good. Let's get the fuck out of here."

That afternoon, after another vehicle exchange, clothing swap and a lunch of halibut fish and chips, Evans deposits Doug at a marina in Des Moines, walking him through a sprawling maze of docks to a power sailer. Doug tosses his bag of street clothes onto the deck. They shake hands. "I'm headed to Boeing Field," Evans notes from behind his Ray-Bans, "Hitting the old dusty trail. It wasn't going to end any other way, Doug. So why not burn it all down, and ride into the sunset?"

Doug laughs. "That was some cowboy shit, no lie. Thanks for everything. I owe you, big league."

Evans waves it off. "Nothing I haven't done a thousand times. Go with God. Head on down to the lower cabin, and lock the door. The captain will give you a knock when you're in Canada. And Doug." He removes his sunglasses, squinting from the glare of the summer sun in his face, locking Doug with his dazzling blue eyes. "This time, stick to the plan. We can get Vickers anytime. Once you plug in, we'll touch base and get back to work."

"Where are you headed?" Doug asks.

"Don't ask. Later, Shea." Evans slides his sunglasses back into place, performs an about-face and walks up the dock while Doug watches, disappearing in the maze of shining white masts without glancing back.

Jus Sanguinis

October 2009
Barcelona, Spain

José Rosales, nee Douglas Shea, leans over the intricate white architectural model of a cable suspension bridge with three designers, scribbling notes in the margins of a folded printout. The top of his head is crowned with wavy, jet-black hair perched above the close-cropped sides, and he is slimmer but still athletic, his cheeks less blocky, skin tanned a deep bronze, and dressed in a trim black cable-knit sweater and dark blue denim jeans. Doug sits at a laptop computer on the edge of the polished pine table and pounds out a status report for his firm's executive team, their builder's project manager, and a Scottish municipal review board. He sends his email with a click, then looks to the design team, headed by the sloppy but competent Chilean Joal, who gazes impassively through his thick black plastic-framed problem glasses. Doug clears his throat and wraps up the meeting in polished Castilian Spanish, lispy and upper caste. "Thank you, guys; it is looking good. I have a call with the builders tonight at 2200; we will discuss their feedback in the morning."

Joal stands, moving toward the glass conference room door, but his two junior designers remain standing at the table. Marc, a recent UPC School of Architecture graduate and the younger of the two, asks, "José, are you free to join us for a drink at 1600?" The wiry Catalan is dressed in his futbol club's green tracksuit, pushing the limits of the casual office. "We are going to my uncle's bar. The place with the octopus!"

Doug thinks for a moment, in an expression that Eric mistakes for a scowl, causing him to interject in heavily Catalan-inflected Spanish. "Stupid, you know he has to go all the way to Can Baró."

Doug laughs, waving a hand. "Guys, today is perfect. My wife has a doctor's appointment; she will not be home until 1900. I will be there."

The junior designers perk up, promise to see Doug soon, and disappear out of the room and down the hall, toward their cubicles. Joal slumps by the door, his white and black knit sweater bunched up over his lumpy frame. Doug watches him with a bemused grin. "What is it, Joal?"

Joal grimaces. "Couldn't you tell they were teasing you earlier? You need to improve your Catalan; you're making us Americans look bad."

Doug extends his arms with a laugh. "You'll have to excuse my challenges with understanding their dialect; I didn't get a lot of practice in Canada or Argentina."

Joal flashes a look of concern, switching to lightly accented English. "José, they get *super pissed* when you call Catalan a dialect."

Doug folds his laptop closed and stands, scooping it under his arm. "Thank you for your concern about being bullied by your direct reports, Joal; I'll keep that in mind, and I'll double down on Catalan language practice with Estel."

Joal cringes, deciphering the insult. Doug pats him on the arm. "I'm just messing with you. You'll be there, right? Let me buy you a drink."

Joal walks briskly to follow Doug into the hall and a brightly-lit expanse of low-walled cubicles, continuing the glass-and-bleached-pine design theme. "Only if you buy me something good," Joal says with a laugh.

Doug returns a smile. "Okay; see you in an hour, Joal." He splits off from Joal and turns down another corridor to his desk in the Project Planning cluster. Weaving through the maze in his aisle, Doug stops and looks quizzically at his desk, where a young black-ponytailed woman leans, chatting with his desk neighbors. He slows his pace and approaches carefully, recognizing her profile and the corner of her face as that of an executive assistant attached to his Vice President. With great determination, he manages not to ogle her form-fitting "professional" attire, and fixes his eyes on his desk neighbor, Mike, a 40-something Brit. Mike looks back and forth between the two of them with a smile, signaling Doug's return to the executive assistant with his eyes.

Doug clears his throat as the young woman turns to face him, pivoting back to Castilian Spanish. "Hello, may I help you?"

She forces a smile, though he sees stress behind her bright blue eyes. Slightly excessive makeup mars her youthful beauty. He pins her accent as suburban Madrid. "Ah, Sr. Rosales. Can you come with me to Sr. Vilar's office, please? There is a... matter that needs your attention."

Doug crinkles his face, flashing a confused expression to Mike, who shrugs. He gives in. "*És clar*; lead the way." He falls in beside what's-her-name and heads to the north end of the floor and the executive offices, where no operational worker bee hopes to set foot. Doug feels the familiar tingle of distress go up the back of his neck, a sensation he's not felt, aside from a handful of minor street encounters, for nearly a decade. Immediately his mind flashes to the deniable weapons he has on his person – a stout brass pen, a modified paring knife in his waistband, the small navaja. The hallway seems to elongate and go cavernous for a moment, but he controls his breathing and facial expression, tuning for neutral. There.

The energy changes completely as they cross over the threshold into *Tierra Ejecutiva*. Doug feels every eye on him during the march to Vicepresidente Andreu Vilar's expansive corner office, an increasingly rare indulgence in small- to medium-sized firms embracing the open-format, small-souled bugman aesthetic. As scion of one half of Zamora y Vilar Arquitectes, Andreu Vilar took the company worldwide, focusing his lawyer's mind upon lucrative government and international contracts. Andreu would not involve himself in a day-to-day operations discussion. Regulatory concerns? Failing sub-contractor? Lawsuit?

Ahead, in Vilar's office, Doug sees a clutch of executives and two men in law enforcement dress uniforms. His director, Anaïs, a stern-looking but friendly married woman in her forties, winks at him with a smile. Andreu Vilar steps away from the clutch towards Doug, dressed as usual in his casually aristocratic style, sans jacket, sleeves of his densely-knit off-white shirt rolled up, the matching Cordovan brown leather of his belt and shoes shining deeply. This guy's wardrobe cost more than my monthly salary, Doug thinks for the hundredth time.

"José," Vilar says, extending his hand at the door, taking Doug's proffered hand in both of his, shaking warmly and firmly, his blue eyes gleaming with what appears to be a hint of mischief. "Please come in. *Gràcies*, Marta." He shuts the door behind Doug and whispers quickly into his ear, "Worry not, my friend, this is good news," patting him on the back and chuckling.

Vilar's large office doubles as a casual meeting room when he must hold court, with an expansive sixth-floor view of tree-lined Avinguda Diagonal, where Zamora y Vilar Arquitectes occupies the top two floors of a modern office building. The two uniformed men at the window turn to face inward, hats under their arms, their white shirts distinct, with different colored epaulets, black slacks, black ties, black dress shoes, and dissimilar emblems and shoulder patches. Ah. Doug smiles, recognizing the larger and more muscled of the two officers as his cousin, Marceo, Inspector of the Cuerpo Nacional de Policía, Spain's national civilian police force. The other uniformed man, a Catalan in his forties with wavy, slicked back hair and a thick moustache, looks on impassively.

Vilar releases Doug near the center of the room, those present re-forming into new clusters, Vilar and his counsel standing with the two law enforcement officers, the operational team standing around Doug, a handful of executives on their own. Vilar raises his hand - "Let us begin; Sr. Rosales works long hours, and I do not wish to delay his siesta any further. Inspector Matamoros, please proceed."

Marceo Matamoros takes one step forward, smiling graciously. "*Gràcies*, Sr. Vilar." He still has the bearing of a Marine, and despite his soft tone and slightly deferential word choice, his voice conveys masculine authority. "José, I will skip right to the point. You have been cleared by the government of Spain in a long investigation brought to bear by American law enforcement."

Doug blanches, blinks, looks around the room, and finally asks, "*¿Disculpe?*" Excuse me?

Several attendees chuckle; Anaïs pats him on the back. Doug asks, reflexively in Castilian Spanish, "Marceo, what is happening?"

Andreu Vilar, normally the picture of confidence and stability, betrays the first glimpse of doubt Doug has ever seen cross his face. He asks, "You know one another?"

Marceo nods. "We live in the same neighborhood, and attend the same church. My wife and José's were classmates. I did not conduct the investigation, but was chosen to represent the CNP in this meeting to comfort our new countryman here."

The Catalan officer edges in, speaking in poetic tones, his tongue dancing. "The *Mossos d'Esquadra* handled the local investigation, on behalf of the CNP, though we thank them for including us in investigatory reviews with the FBI. Inspector Matamoros, do you want to explain?"

Marceo nods. "*Gràcies*, Inspector Oliver. The American FBI – their national police – brought this to our attention three months ago. They believed that you were an American national who had committed rather serious crimes in the middle '90s." He pauses, and smiles. "Of course, it was a simple matter of working with the Mossos, and Argentinean officials, to verify your identity. After all, you had just submitted your naturalization request in March, and that went smoothly, considering that two of your grandparents were Spanish citizens, and your marriage to a Spaniard. Nor were you a criminal, here, or in Argentina, or Canada. Yes, we contacted your university in Toronto, as well as the Canadian national police; the Americans had already done so as well. We suspect that the American in question may have borrowed your identity at some point, most likely when you were in Canada. I was aware of the investigation – not participating, mind you, due to perceived conflict of interest – and requested permission to brief you and your employers. To set everyone at ease. I trust that has been accomplished?"

Looking about the room, seeing no concern, Marceo continues. "There is one other detail of which I want you to be aware. The Americans...." He pauses, choosing his words carefully. "They do not respect national borders. Several of their officers have come to Barcelona to investigate, against our instructions, from the States, with support from their Madrid office. This is a very serious diplomatic issue, but keep in mind that they are accusing this American national of terrorism, of murdering a significant number of law enforcement personnel. Given what the

Americans have been doing with other foreign nationals in what they call their War on Terror – there are many *Desaparecidos* – we take this very seriously. The government of Spain has dedicated resources to protect you, José; it may be necessary for you to take a holiday while this is resolved." He directs his attention to the rest of the audience, making eye contact with each of them in passing. "I ask you to please be vigilant, and to put your receptionists on guard for Americans skulking about. If you have any questions, please speak with me or Inspector Oliver. That is all."

Vilar approaches Doug, wrapping his arm around his shoulder – they are the same height – and steers him to the corner, beckoning to Anaïs. He leans down conspiratorially, and speaks in low, measured tones. "José, I do not want you to leave the country for any projects until this matter is settled. And I want you to keep me up to date. Anything I can do to help, please tell me. Anaïs, we may need to arrange a long leave for José. Would that be a problem?"

Anaïs shakes her head. "Señor Vilar, José is queued up for paternal leave; we expect it to begin soon. The timing is perfect. José?"

Doug shrugs. "I can hand off my project at any time. I will do whatever you decide, señor."

Vilar nods, stepping back and donning a formal bearing in keeping with the deference paid to him, emphasizing his words in his casual aristo style. "Very well. José, I will speak with my assistant about providing you with addresses for several of my remote properties. They are excellent places to hide, and will be most comfortable for your wife to recuperate. Are you having a son or a daughter?"

Doug blinks. "I do not know what to say, señor. Thank you. A son, señor; we are naming him for my wife's grandfather, Coronel de la Lanza."

Vilar's eyes flash with recognition; he smiles widely. "Ahhhh... I am pleased to assist a fellow *hijo de la falange*. Congratulations." He pats Doug on the shoulder and steps past him, opens the door, and disappears from view.

Anaïs looks at Doug with a cryptic expression, slightly annoyed yet simultaneously amused. "It will never end, will it? No mind. We have our orders. Take tomorrow off; we will do everything by *fone*. Okay?"

Doug nods. "Okay. Thank you, Anaïs." She reaches up and hugs him.

"Something tells me you will be fine, José. Do not worry." She winks and leaves the room quickly. Zamora y Vilar's junior counsel remains with the two Inspectors, watching Doug, as the room empties. Marceo beckons to Doug casually; he approaches the trio and exhales, exasperated.

"This is very strange, my friend," Doug says, looking from Marceo to Inspector Oliver, who remains impassive, then to the company's junior counsel, a young man who appears to be holding his tongue. "I do not understand, but thank everyone for their kindness."

"It's bullshit, Sr. Rosales. Bullshit." The lawyer's accent, and emphasis on the middle syllable of *mierda*, pins him as certain type of upper middle class Madrileño. Sr. Vilar's "*hijo de la falange*" comment, and guarded whisperings Doug had heard among employees, begin to make sense. "I must tell you also that an American journalist" – he nearly spits the word, *periodista* – "has been inquiring after your Scotland project. I was just explaining this to the Inspectors. They are undoubtedly related."

Doug says, "Yes, a Mr. Harris? I was provided his contact information by a Scottish sub, well," pulling back his sleeve and checking his stainless Tissot watch, "Not thirty minutes ago."

The Inspectors look at each other, the Catalan nodding to Marceo. Marceo clears his throat. "José, undoubtedly he's attempting to contact you, perhaps to perform voice recognition analysis over the *fone*, or to set up a meeting."

"When I spoke with him yesterday, he claimed to be in Madrid, but we should be careful nonetheless," says the young lawyer.

"José, the time to go to ground is now," Marceo says with finality. "The government of Spain provided the Americans with our assessment four hours ago. Let me drive you home; we will collect Estel and keep you safe while this is worked out." He extends his arm and clasps Doug's shoulder in his firm grip.

Doug shakes his head. "Estel has a doctor's appointment. We would have to go there first. In Guinardó. Sr. Vilar has offered the use of his properties. I am to speak with his assistant."

"Better," notes Inspector Oliver, eyeing Marceo carefully. "I will leave it at that."

"No offense," Marceo says. "I agree."

"Then that is it," says the young lawyer, gesturing towards the door. "I will take you to Sr. Vilar's assistant, provide his instructions, and walk away. You will decide what to do. Come with me."

That night, Doug watches the rise and fall of his wife's chest as she sleeps on a smothering pile of pillows atop a luxurious king-sized bed, her swollen belly trussed from below like one of his engineering projects. Her otherwise trim frame nests, after their mutual effort, in a girding of cushion, her only hope for a comfortable half-night's sleep. He glances at the illuminated hands of his watch – just past 0100 – she should awaken in two to three hours due to the baby's acrobatics. He rises from his chair and crosses the tile floor barefoot to double doors leading to the balcony, gently opening one and stepping out, a light breeze coming off the Mediterranean, the dense greenery around the palatial home waving softly. Inhaling deeply, he steps out to the iron railing and leans on it with his forearms, looking out into the darkness of the sea, emptying his mind of anxieties and fears. Some time passes before he hears gentle footsteps on the stone balcony. He rests his hand on the butt of a pistol in his waistband, easing it out and turning slightly towards the sound.

"It is I," Marceo says softly in Castilian Spanish, before stepping around a massive stone column holding up the articulated roof. Doug relaxes and reholsters his pistol. Marceo steps slowly into the dim light radiating from the bedroom windows, two lamps slid to a low setting and pointed at the ceiling. He approaches Doug and leans on the railing next to him. "News from our people."

"*Dime*." Tell me.

Doug listens to Marceo's breath in the near-darkness, his cousin inhaling deeply to prepare for a long exposition. After a moment, he begins. "First. There is an excellent maternity ward at the hospital in Lloret de Mar. Three kilometers from here. I understand that Estel would prefer her OB, but with a good appetite there is no bad bread."

"She will be fine. Second?"

Marceo pauses, exhaling through his nose, then a sharp inhale. "I put some lads on the 'journalist.' He is in Barcelona. Perhaps he actually is a journalist. He has credentials. But we have confirmed through INTERPOL that he had been an FBI agent, stationed in Seattle during your troubles. He officially left the FBI a year ago. That's not all."

"Just tell me, please."

Marceo's voice goes up an octave, a touch of delight buoying his words. "He is staying at the Hilton. Right down Diagonal from your office. He showed up in your office at 1800; of course, almost nobody was there, but he gave the number of a burner phone, which we were able to triangulate to the Hilton. An officer called reception, verified that he was staying there, and demanded payment information for an investigation. You will not believe this."

Doug shakes his head. "Marceo, I am not in the mood for your dramatic tellings. Keep it brief, please."

"Okay, cousin." Marceo straightens, and Doug hears fumbling in the dark, the crinkling of paper, the scrape of card stock, and the metallic snap of a Zippo lighter opening. A flint wheel scrapes and bright, soft flame illuminates Marceo's rugged face, a stubble emerging, one eye closed as he lights a French cigarette with gold band around the base, clacks the lighter closed and re-pockets it. As he drags on the cigarette and the cherry flares and spreads, Doug hears the flame combust the flecks of tobacco. A strong but pleasant smell hits Doug's nose, mitigated by the breeze. "This will take some explaining. Do you remember a Sr. Miller, part of the Brooks organization?"

"I met him," Doug says. "What about him?"

"His real name is Shmuel Baruch; Samuel Miller was a name of war. He worked for the American Department of Justice. A lawyer and a 'fixer.' After you and yours exposed their faction's activities with jihadis, Brooks flipped on him, made him the Judas goat. He disappeared. One of Baruch's operations was exposed in Miami in the late nineties; a major MDMA smuggling ring, production in Israel. Bang!" Marceo claps his hands. "That did it. Tracked to Israel, but there is, of course, no hope of extradition."

"Keep it down, please," Doug says. "If Estel wakes up, she will not be able to get back to sleep."

"Sorry," Marceo mumbles from around his cigarette, taking another draw and lowering his voice again. "INTERPOL has a wealth of information on Shmuel Baruch. We crosschecked the credit card that paid for the room of this journalist 'Brian Harris.' The same card pays for another room in the Hilton, Canadian guest, Samuel Tesoro." Marceo nudges Doug. "The passport photo matches Samuel Miller aka Shmuel Baruch."

Doug laughs, shaking his head in the darkness. "Treasure. Of course."

Marceo turns to face Doug, leaning sideways against the rail, smoking his cigarette throughout his rant. "Now, I can't arrest him; there is no warrant for him relevant to Spain. Even the Americans have dropped it – it figures. But we could have some independents do something. I do not believe that they are here for good reasons, cousin. They may be working with the FBI, but this Miller being here, that is not promising."

Doug ponders this in silence as Marceo smokes, watching individual points of light out in the sea, most likely fishing boats. His gaze follows one craft's bobbing green starboard light around the edge of their bay, disappearing behind the rocky point to the south, headed Barcelona way. "I do not know, Marceo. What do you think our exposure is?"

Marceo shrugs. "Stay low. Let our government deal with the Americans. The FBI agents have left Barcelona. They seem satisfied with our investigation. We will watch Miller and Harris. I reached out to Señor Evans - who sends his regards - to manage outreach to our on-again friend Brooks the younger. So. If we need to move, we will move. It is best for us to keep the circle small. I am not able to cover up any overt actions. This is Spain, not America. We must be very clean. Such as," and he clicks his tongue, pointing out to sea.

"Mmmm. Yes, that is sensible." Doug scratches his head. "How many men are working with you on this?"

Marceo begins to throw his cigarette butt out into the darkness, thinks better of it, and stubs the cherry out on the sole of his shoe, then places the remains on the handrail. "Outside of law enforcement? One. Hugo from the Club. He went to the Hilton tonight to put eyes on Miller and Harris."

"Hugo who worked for Vanguard before we shut it down, yes? The big guy who teaches the hand to hand class."

"Yes," Marceo says. "Now a union rep at the port. Our Club liaison with the nationalist futbol fans. He will handle personnel."

Doug smiles. "One of your Marines. A good man for the job. Okay, Marceo. Do what you think you need to do. Tell me if I can help. In the meantime, I will keep my head down and take care of Estel. Did you get that hardware?"

Marceo flicks open his Zippo and throws another long flame, illuminating his face, a smug grin gripping the cigarette tightly in his lips. "Of course. In two bags in the next room. Does it feel good to be operational again, cousin?"

Doug is glad that the darkness hides his expression. "It is what it is."

The days pass in a blur of excess sleep, anxiety, and comfortable imprisonment in the Vilar family's four hundred year old manor high above a rocky shoreline northeast of Barcelona. The onsite chef keeps Estel happy with a constant flow of comfort food, relieving her of the need to be on her feet much during her thirty-eighth week of pregnancy, and sparing her from Doug's utilitarian cooking "skills." Three days in, they risk an afternoon outing to the white sandy beach in nearby Canyelles, dallying at a beachside restaurant's outdoor terrace, where Estel gags at the thought of any food save their order – bread, grilled Mackerel and olives, which she washes down with half a serving of pistachio ice cream. For the past seven months, they have been slaves to the whims of Estel's digestive and hormonal systems; Doug is happy to oblige. Since their marriage four years ago, he has thought daily of his grandfather remarking wistfully to friends, the trite and true saw, "Happy wife, happy life."

That night, as Estel sleeps in another tangle of pillows, her auburn hair spilling across his shoulder, left hand on his bare chest, Doug sets aside one of Vilar's leather-bound esoteric traditionalist volumes and stares at the bare ceiling, recalling the pivotal moment when honesty became the foundation of their relationship. High above the streets of Buenos Aires' Palermo neighborhood, in a rooftop bar, they plotted the moment when "José" would present himself to Estel's father, bend the knee, and beg for his only daughter's hand in marriage. Drinking wine to fortify himself, but not intoxicated, Doug blurted out to Estel that he had a secret he couldn't bear to hold back from her. The previous week, after a long night at his apartment, Estel had explained – *¡que horror!* – a simple truth she concealed from her prep school and university classmates since arriving in Argentina. She was of a military family, her brother Carlo serving in the Spanish Army as a *Teniente*, her father a young *Comandante* who left the service for overseas private sector opportunities in the nineties. Both her paternal and maternal grandfathers had served with – gasp! – Franco's coalition during and after the Civil War, and were minor nobility from the Carlist camp.

The socialist-educated upper middle class Argentines, with heads full of Che, Peron and Kirshner, would have been scandalized and demanded denunciation. Doug had shrugged, and confessed that his paternal grandparents had been moderate *Republicanos* distressed by the reality of the "pro-government" coalition – anarchists, Bolsheviks, and atheists intent on destroying every vestige of Spanish culture and history. The truth, though more true-lies-of-omission, which nagged at him like a really, really annoying person.

Doug had already decided, well before that hour on the rooftop, that the time for tasteful banter at the wine bar with his girlfriend had ended. While he longed to lay it all on the watermark-stained table, the terrain had not been sufficiently prepped; as a gentleman, he would have to ease into it. Doug started with the facts she knew, addressed the peripheral details gently, and rounded out the picture, leveraging her trust, love and family history as context. He left out a moment in Southern California, in 1997, the most painful ten second conversation of his life; he was not sure why.

The details of his story were verifiable, complete with ugly government and media spin, via online via newspaper archives; he led her to them, using anonymity provided by university computer labs. The official story had evolved, of course, to downplay the effectiveness of one deceased old man and his missing grandson, into a network of phantasmal white supremacist terrorists and bad weather. The Internet had run with the story, focusing on government misbehavior and the CIA-drug trafficking connection. Ruby Ridge. Waco. CIA crack cocaine. Port Townsend.

Did Doug lie? No. Did he spin? Yes. Fortunately for him, in Argentina circa 2004, the people "bombing the world," as Estel put it, burning babies in churches, shooting mothers in the head and crashing economies were not as sympathetic as the handsome, charming, mysterious and virile man who had swept her off her feet and won her father's respect. They confessed a fraction of his story, accordingly, to her family; his family gone, he had left America to seek a more peaceful life, and had found it in Argentina, warts and all. This, finally, was true.

The day of their outing was the bookend of normalcy before an indeterminate blur of several days, all jumbled in Doug's memory, moments conflated with others, fueled by exhaustion, chaos and concern. When was Pablo born? He knows the date well; it is burned into his hardwiring, along with the flash of recognition, the wave of energy that shot through him when he first heard his son's voice, tears of awe on the tips of his eyelashes. A switch had flipped in his head; he was a father, with a duty to this new life, the amalgamation of all who had made him and all who had made his wife, Estel, whose eyes bathed him in the warmest expression he had felt from another in his thirty-four years. This was no mere human glance, but a planar connection to something deeper and seldom glimpsed in a human lifetime. Then, a Day of Rest for the good work performed in the Lloret del Mar hospital, and Marceo was back with orders. Doug obeyed.

Hugo, Marceo's massive dockworker union rep, steers the compact white Fiat panel van down the winding Carrer de Muhlberg into the afternoon sun, goosing the engine in the curves, tossing their bound captives about the cargo area. "Sr. Rosales, do you mind if I play some war music?" he asks in working class tinged Castilian Spanish, holding up a CD in his right hand.

"Yes, but please, two hands on the wheel, Hugo." Doug white-knuckles the oh-shit handle, turned slightly to watch Baruch and Harris, his left hand on the butt of his pistol. "We may need to strap them down better."

"Naw." Hugo feeds the disc into the van's stereo and stops at a wide V intersection, waiting for the signal to change before executing a sharp turn to the left, downhill towards the port. "My boys warmed them up thoroughly back at your lovely home. They are in no condition to do anything but bleed. Do you know this?" he asks, pointing to the stereo. The familiar sound of an old English-dub Japanese samurai movie clip begins, leading into aggressive mid-90s New York hip hop. Doug harkens back to a hand-scrawled mix CD he listened to a thousand times, all over the world, finally throwing it into the Pacific Ocean from a cliff west of Valparaíso, Chile on New Year's Day, 2000, its spell broken.

Doug tunes his expression to avoid confusing, or possibly insulting, his subordinate, as competing visceral reactions war within him. Ultimately, he chooses to smile. "I have lived it. I, as you, chose the sword." He looks into Hugo's mischievous brown eyes, a look of amusement on the Marine's stubbled, wind-burned face.

"And you still live it, sir. It is a sign. Here." Hugo steers onto Carretera del Carmel, holding a finger in the air, waiting for the lyric that Doug knows in advance. "There," pointing at the stereo again, "A sign, is it not?" He waits, watching Doug, holding a knowing smile.

Doug smirks, knowing the line before it hits. A new generation of sons to carry on the fight. "Indeed. It is a good war song."

"Sir," Hugo says formally, as he navigates the winding hillside roads, heading towards the straight, wide avenues leading south, one war song flowing into another. "I want to thank you for the opportunity to assist you. Our Club is of no use if we do not help one another. One question."

"Ask it," Doug responds.

"Do you have more of those?" gesturing to the heavily modified pistol in Doug's waistband. "It looks like a Beretta, but I can tell there is much that is different from mine."

Doug smiles. "This is the realization of my grandfather's last project. A universal insurgency weapon for freedom fighters. In English, 'the Modern Liberator.' The cuts here allow attachment of a folding stock with a two shot burst setting, which only works with the stock extended. The rail in front accepts a folding foregrip with a flashlight. The muzzle, threaded to accept a suppressor. The safety is modified to lock the slide for silent single shots. All of that gear is in my bag here. The next iteration will include a red dot sight. I suspect that, with Madrid, and the influx we are seeing, the Club will need many more of them. I want you in charge of training and dissemination. Once perfected, we'll spread our system to other like-minded groups in Europe that meet our standards."

Hugo, keeping his eyes on the road, nods. "Thank you, sir. In the war, my grandfather preferred the Mauser machine pistol for guerrilla operations. I see the commonality."

"As did mine," Doug says. "As did mine. But our greatest problem is not the enemy. It is the camera and the radio. Hence the suppressor and the option to shoot without dropping brass."

"Mmmmm," Hugo nods appreciatively. They immerse themselves in the drive and the music, their cargo lying still, bound in the back. Southwest of the University and Montjuic they pass under the B-10. "We are almost there, sir." They enter the port via an unguarded gate, where the razor-wire-topped chain link gate rumbles open at the swipe of a keycard. The long sprawl of the Industrial Zona Franca on the other side of a fence to the west, they pass the busy rail transfer area, shipping container yard, and refineries, entering an older, more run-down area of small piers and metal buildings. Hugo steers them to a nondescript white metal building marked only with a meter-tall black "11," puts the van in park and gets out, fiddling with a keychain. He unlocks a door, slides it open, then returns to the van and slowly drives it over the threshold before shutting off the engine. He looks to Doug with a grin. "There is our ride."

Doug gets out and, looking at the opposite end of the building, sees a wide slip, twelve meters across, with a rolling doorway three feet above water level, the slip occupied by a Rubber Inflatable Boat, five meters long, with a hard flat hull, framed with two long bench seats running along the sides. "Ah, Hugo, this is not exactly discreet," Doug says, turning to his host, who closes the garage door behind them then flips on flickering fluorescent overhead lights, casting the room in a sickly yellow pallor.

"Sir, we are waiting until after dark, of course," Hugo says with a wry smile.

"Of course," Doug says. "Of course."

Hugo pats him on the back. "Come on, let's get these faggots out of the van and into place. They want tell you something important."

Sliding open the side cargo door of the van, they find their bagged captives in a heap, one caught halfway beneath the empty shelving unit in the wall. "Come here," Hugo says, grabbing one by the foot, dragging it over to the door. Doug grabs the shoulders as Hugo slides the man out, duck-walking to a large stainless steel workbench against a wall, fortunately empty. Hugo unzips the body bag to reveal the unconscious face of Samuel Miller, aka Samuel Tesoro, aka Shmuel Baruch, bloodied and battered but alive and breathing. Hugo removes the rope gag from Miller's mouth roughly, listens closely to his wheezy respiration, and nods. "A little dull, but no matter." They transfer Harris in his own bag to a long, narrow stainless steel table with raised edges abutting the slip, which Doug assumes is for cleaning fish. Setting Harris down, Hugo zips open his bag to find Harris closing his bruised eyes tightly.

"Do not play dead with me," he says in Castilian Spanish. "Sir, tell him I'm going to remove his rope. If he bites me, I will hurt him."

Doug stands at his side, looking down at Harris, who blinks up at them, moving his mouth behind the rope but not speaking. Doug leans down closely, dropping his guise and speaks in unaccented American English, a slight strain given his years of linguistic retraining. "If you cooperate, this will be easy. He's gonna remove your gag. If you don't cooperate, he will hurt you. Understand?"

Harris nods; Hugo removes the rope from his mouth. Harris gasps, nearly retching; Hugo and Doug turn him on his side roughly to prevent him from vomiting. They release him, leaving him curled on his side in the body bag, his head sticking out of the dull black plastic. Hugo offers him a bottle of water; Harris drinks slowly and carefully, in small sips.

Doug nods, recognizing a man with training. He squats down to bring his face level with Harris' and continues in English. "I don't feel good about this, Harris; you're just a soldier. Like me. But I have to ask you a few questions. Your answers determine how your night goes. This guy?" he says, tilting his head towards Baruch, "He's fucked. His fate is sealed. Yours isn't."

Harris watches silently, blinking, looking from Doug to Hugo, an animal calculation taking place behind his eyes.

"No answer?" Doug looks to Hugo, who slaps Harris' head into the stainless steel table, the thump reverberating in the room.

Harris howls in pain. "Wait, wait. Damn, you did something to my ear." He coughs, disoriented, breathing heavy. "Give me a minute."

Hugo winks to Doug while slowly shadowboxing, warming up his muscles.

"Your minute is up," Doug says. "My man here enjoys this more than I do. Use your head. Time to talk. Who do you really work for? I know you're 'former' FBI," making quotation marks with his fingers, "and I know who paid for your room. From law enforcement to international drug trafficking? Tsk, tsk."

Harris continues breathing heavily. "Okay, okay. Look, journalism is a cover. I'm working for the FBI off the books."

Doug looks to Hugo, speaking in Spanish. "He says that he still works for American law enforcement."

Hugo smirks. "Let me hit him again."

Doug shakes his head. "Not yet." Switching to English, he orders Harris, "Tell me more. Tell me everything. Are you part of the FBI investigation proper out of Madrid, or a side project? I'm aware of that, of course."

Harris nods. "The FBI hit official roadblocks in every nation we tracked you to. Want to know how we found you?"

Doug shrugs. "Sure."

Harris grins. "Vanguard. It took five years, but we cracked the encryption on a Vanguard machine seized in Seattle, which retained a connection log for a government ID system in Ontario. Would you believe that it was easy to tie the timestamp on the handshake to an event in that system? Technology advances, Douglas Shea. If it weren't for that, I wouldn't be here. We lost you completely; we always knew that you killed Vickers with a .41 Magnum in San Francisco in '97 but had no proof. You don't look much like you used to – plastic surgery?"

Doug nods. "Expensive but ubiquitous in South America. Had to soften those cheekbones, tweak the nose to pass as a more phenotypical Hispanio; it also helped me evade facial recognition software at border checkpoints. Dying my hair is a pain in the ass, but I'm used to it. My wife does it for me now, weekly." He scratches the back of his neck, rolling on the balls of his feet to keep his blood flowing, his heart rate elevating. "So why you? Why isn't the bigger FBI operation still here?"

Harris stares at him with cold, dead eyes. "Fucking spics is why. Canada was easy; our governments are very cooperative. Argentina was another story. That place was a mess, even before the financial collapse. We simply couldn't find you. So after a while, we cast our nets elsewhere. Bang, Spain; naturalization paperwork for males around your age. There really aren't that many, Douglas. We gave Spain a list of terrorist suspects, and they investigated independently. Sovereignty." He shakes his head.

Doug nods. "Damned if you do, damned if you don't. That's what I get for moving from a failed state to the first world."

Harris grins. "Don't think you're off the hook, Shea. If Miller and I turn up dead, or go missing, they'll send an off the books team here, snap you up off the street and disappear you, spics be damned. You can run, but will Estel want to follow you, with a newborn?"

Doug looks to Hugo, whose eyes harden upon hearing Estel's name, however mispronounced. Doug shakes his head. "That's not going to happen. You said you were checking out candidates all over Spain. Our friends in the CNP have been monitoring, and will continue to do so. Here's where your story falls apart. Miller. He's blacklisted in the US. You're working with him. Here's what is going to happen."

Doug stands, stretching his legs out. "You're going to watch Shmuel Baruch die a horrible death, and decide for yourself whether or not you want a second chance, or to die similarly. I'm feeling generous, what with being a new father and all. My heart is filled with compassion for all living things." He draws the pistol from his waistband and holds it up. "I'm a pro with zero deaths. As are you. The next few hours determine whether or not you'll keep that streak. Who do you check in with, and how regularly, if you really are working with the FBI? Who do you report pass/fail to? Why is Miller along with you? Is he still working with the FBI?"

Harris laughs. "That's a lot of questions, Doug. You really are in over your head. Can't do it without grandpa?"

Doug looks to Hugo, and says in English. "Hurt him, but not to where he can't talk."

Hugo grabs Harris by the hair. "Wait," Harris says calmly. Doug puts up his hand. Harris continues. "I've been in Spain for three months, verifying each name on the suspect list, because the FBI can't have on the books agents ignoring local governments; the War on Terror alliances are fracturing. Miller is plugged into the Muslim drug gangs, who will do the snatch. Totally deniable. Miller is a dual US-Israeli citizen; Israel will only extradite in the most blatant cases and under staggering pressure. I'm frankly surprised the spics IDed him."

Doug shrugs. "My guess is that INTERPOL tracks guys like Miller, even if they don't move against them, to pick around their edges."

"Ah," Harris murmurs. "Let's make a deal. I'll report that you're a bust, and move on to my next target, a guy in the north. There are three up there, then I'm done. You were the last suspect in this sector. Do what you want with Miller; I'll stay quiet. I suggest that you change names; this one is burned."

Doug nods. "That's a good deal. I will add one painless caveat, which will be completed today, then you're free to go." He slowly turns and looks at Miller, then back to Harris, raising an eyebrow.

Harris swallows. "I think that's fair."

Doug smiles. "Then we're in agreement. Let me confer with my colleague and yours, first." He points to Harris and says to Hugo in Spanish, "We will leave him be. Let us talk to your friend." They step over to Miller, who blinks at them, mumbling from behind his gag. Hugo removes the gag, unleashing a torrent of smug profanity and vicious racial invective. Doug ends it by shoving the muzzle of his pistol into Miller's mouth, chipping two teeth. Miller goes immediately silent.

"That's better," Doug says in English, withdrawing the pistol from Miller's mouth slowly. "You heard all of that, so you know the score. Right now, I'm no longer feeling compassionate, considering who you are, but you have the power to change my mind."

Miller spits in fury. "You filth. Everything I have done is justified. You people; your time is at an end. No matter what you do to me. You're stupid. You're a pawn. As were your father and grandfather."

Doug shakes his head and rubs Miller's with his right hand, almost affectionately. "You should have let it go. I did." He looks up at Hugo, bemused. Hugo flexes his shoulders. Doug smiles and addresses him in Spanish. "He said that our people are at their end, while insulting my dead. This all started when I fought his *Moros* in my homeland; he has brought more here."

Hugo's eyes darken. "*¡Las Puertas de Toledo!*" He slams his sledgehammer-sized fist into Miller's face, shattering his nose; the blood flows freely as Miller cries out in pain. They gag him and zip him back into the body bag, squirming, then lift his struggling form, wrestling him to the slip, and throw him down onto the aluminum floor of the inflatable boat with a resonant bang. The body bag stiffens, squirms slightly, then goes slack.

"Get the toolbag," Doug barks to Hugo, who nods and retrieves it from the van, slinging it over his shoulder. They return to Harris and loom over him.

Doug smiles coldly, transitioning to English. "Exposure suit time. My man is pretty wound up; I'd advise that you cooperate. Can you do that?"

Harris nods, looking between Doug and Hugo. "Of course."

Hugo retrieves three red exposure suits and overboots from the wall while Doug removes Harris from his body bag, first unzipping it, then cutting through the layers of rope and duct tape restraints Hugo diligently applied that afternoon. Unbound, Harris sits on the edge of the stainless table, rubbing his hands, grimacing when touching his face. "This will look suspicious," he says to Doug.

Doug shrugs as he dons his exposure suit. "Moroccan toughs are a problem in Barcelona. Get in your suit."

Thirty minutes after nightfall, Hugo powers up the big outboard on the inflatable, Doug untethering them from the slip while Harris sits in the bow, handcuffed to a drag handle, next to the slowly squirming bag containing Miller. Harris eyes the driftnets heaped in the center of the hull nervously. Hugo eases the boat to the roll-up door now four feet over the water; each man crouches and they slip beneath. Out in the port harbor, traffic is light, with large and medium sized cargo ships moored at the landings to the north, no small craft about save theirs. They make way with their running lights off, Hugo steering them through the darkest shadows of the nearly deserted southern end of the port, heading for a gap in the sea wall for small service craft. Out past the sea wall, the chop of the sea increases to moderates swells. Hugo increases speed as they pass the buoys, aiming due south; at times, the screw of the outboard is the only part of the craft in the water, nose up twenty degrees, flying through the air at forty knots.

The roar of the outboard and rush of wind makes conversation impossible. Doug periodically shines a flashlight on the suppressed pistol in his hand for Harris' benefit; Harris simply nods his assent and passivity. After nearly twenty minutes, Hugo locks on to a blinking red light ahead, maintaining his speed until their destination is close enough to reach out and touch, a vertical steel pole with a light five meters above water level; he lets off the throttle and keeps the engine just above idle. Doug steps to the side of the boat and reaches out toward the post, grabbing it, tying the bowline to a cleat. Hugo kills the engine and they roll in gentle swells, calmer out in open water away from the ship lines.

"*Estamos ahí*," Hugo notes; we're there. Doug and Hugo go to work, setting up a work light aimed to the pintle mount portside and assemble a pneumatically powered hoist, then spread out the nets and weights in the center of the hull. Harris watches in silence, swallowing hard, as the two men drag Miller into the middle of the net, unzipping his body bag and removing the battered and bound man from it, checking his mouth and nose for obstructions. Miller wheezes, clearly injured, most likely broken or bruised ribs; Hugo pronounces him sufficiently healthy. Doug drags a SCUBA tank and respirator from beneath the starboard side bench to the net, unstrapping the harness and reassembling it around Miller. He cinches the harness tightly, opens up the primary air valve, and tests the respirator, adjusting the oxygen flow to his satisfaction. He nods, then removes Miller's gag, unleashing cries of panic and profanity. Hugo grabs Miller by the head and pries his jaw open with his massive hands as Doug shoves the mouthpiece in; they force his jaw shut around the mouthpiece and wrap his head in duct tape, leaving only slits for his eyes.

Harris begins emitting low animal sounds, inching back in the boat away from Doug and Hugo, but there is nowhere to go. The two men strap driftnet weights to Miller's harness, wrapping him in a net, clipping it together with carabiners and wound cable, tugging and testing for a tight fit, then attach the end of the cable to one of the beacon's cleats. Finally, they pull a hook down from the assembled hoist, powering up its motor and pulling Miller up from the floor of the boat. They turn to Harris in the rear of the boat, their eyes like wolves, as Doug unlocks Harris' handcuff while aiming his pistol.

"It's time," says Doug. "You're up."

Harris eventually speaks. "M-me?"

Hugo removes a small digital video camera from their equipment bag, powers it up and looks into the flip-out viewscreen. "*Estamos listos*," he says to Doug.

"You heard the man," says Doug. "We're ready. This is your deal. Get over there. Name, rank and serial number. This is beacon 6 in the Balearic Ridge shallows. This is the traitor Samuel Miller." He adds a rather edgy, proscribed interwar salutation to Harris' assignment. "Say it."

Harris repeats, stumbling over the place name's pronunciation, getting it correctly on the third attempt.

Doug says, "Okay, we're going to videotape now. Say your lines convincingly, push that arm out, then press the red button to let him go. We'll be over here, counterbalancing. And filming. Got it?"

Harris nods, swallowing hard. He narrates as ordered in a steady voice, then stands, pushes Miller out over the side of the boat, sits, flips up a clear plastic cover on the crane release button, then presses it. The hand on the hoist opens and

Miller's bundled body splashes into the water, the boat tilting towards Doug and Hugo, causing them to lean into the center of the hull to balance the craft. Hugo nods, shuts off the camera and returns it to the equipment bag.

Doug knee-walks to Harris and pats him on the back, handcuffing him again. "Well done. Well done. We'll head back to Barcelona now, and you'll check in with your people. Hugo will take you to the airport and will hand you a ticket. You'll fly together to the north."

Harris trembles. "No way. I don't trust you."

Doug shrugs. "Or I could shoot you now. I'd rather not, but it would just be one more. Like I said, you're just a soldier, like me. And we made a deal."

"Isn't he going to die on the way down, from the bends or something?" Harris asks.

Doug laughs while untying the boat's tether from the beacon cleat. "You said it yourself. 'Balearic Ridge shallows.' It's only about thirty feet deep here at low tide. That's why there is this string of beacons. We have video of you dropping your partner to his doom; maintenance crews will find his crab-eaten corpse before long. Our people will release this video to the Israelis if you move on me. My gift to you is a quiet, obscure life that you'd better not fuck up."

Hugo re-engages the outboard and turns the boat around, headed due north, towards the blob of light just over the horizon. Beneath them, in the frigid darkness, Miller convulses, swallowing large gasps of concentrated oxygen, blinking in the alkaline seawater, his mind alive with terror, the weight of the sea pressing down on him, his world shrinking to nothing save his next breath.

Estel Rosales is drawn out of sleep by a flash of late morning sunlight and an insistent tugging at her right nipple, little Hugo clamping on, his eyes closed. She snuggles closer to him, keeping her back bent and her weight angled away from the infant, alert to any potential danger to the child. Squeezing the mass of her right breast, she massages the milk forward, easing the pang of its engorgement. She looks down at her child, brushes his soft brown hair back from his forehead, and smiles.

Her peripheral vision captures motion; she jerks her head to the left then relaxes upon seeing her husband, absent three days, seated in a massive leather armchair, watching her, holding a cell phone to his ear. He nods, smiling. *"Liberarlo."* Doug pockets the phone, stands, and walks across the thick rug to the bed. He sits carefully and slides his hand up the back of Estel's neck, nestling his fingers into the roots of her auburn hair.

"Hello, my love," he says gently in Spanish. "Look at him go. Does it finally hurt less?"

She adjusts her hips in a rustle of sheets, turning slightly towards him, and looks up at him, her bright hazel eyes gleaming. "It is better," she says. "Is everything okay?"

Doug grins, his dewy eyes locked with hers. "It is now. We are safe. We had one little problem, but it is concluded. Everything has been settled."

"We do not have to run?" she asks, her expression hopeful.

"No, I do not believe so," Doug says wistfully. "Time will tell, but I do not believe so. I've spent some time in prayer with Father Manuel. I feel... at peace. Marceo will keep an eye out. As will Sr. Vilar and our other friends. We will spend my leave relaxing and getting to know Pablo. We will go from there." He extends his left hand slowly down to the child's, carefully pressing his index finger into his son's surprisingly powerful grip. "And then it will be your turn, my son."

Printed in Great Britain
by Amazon